THE LAST MARINE

A NOVEL

BOOK 1

THE LAST MARINE SERIES

T.S. RANSDELL

ACKNOWLEDGMENTS

I would like to give a special thanks to author G. Michael Hopf, my friend, brother, and mentor, in making this book a reality. He, literally, spent years encouraging me to make this happen. He has been a big inspiration to me.

I would also like to thank my wife, Shannon, for her love and support through this process. She picked up the slack, when I spent time writing. I'd also like to thank her and my Aunt Christine for their advice and help.

As well, I'd like to thank my friend Kevin for his input and encouragement throughout this process.

Lastly, I would like to thank our Creator for the freedom to pursue my happiness.

"This is my commandment, that you love one another as I have loved you. Greater love has no one than this, that someone lay down his life for his friends."

John 15:12–13 ESV

"People sleep peaceably in their beds at night only because rough men stand ready to do violence on their behalf."

George Orwell (attributed)

T.S. RANSDELL

CHAPTER ONE

Joel hated airports and always had. Today was not an exception; in fact, it was the apotheosis of why he hated airports. It had taken ninety minutes to work through the line of cars backed up because of FedAPS agents searching cars as they entered the new Seattle-Tacoma Federal International Airport.

Since parking was not allowed within a five-mile radius of the airport, travelers were left with the option of hiring a FedAPS-approved car or taking the light rail and then traveling by shuttle to the airport. As a journalist/historian for the *Federal Times of Seattle*, Joel's Federal Government pay was enough to afford the FedAPS hourly rate for the car; or so he thought before the ninety-minute delay.

The line at baggage check-in looked to be as equally miserable, but with just one carry-on bag, Joel skipped that level of hell and went straight to the terminal security checkpoint. Joel was about to embark on his least favorite part of air travel, but he felt a slight sense of emancipation as the escalator rose towards the terminals. This was the last hurdle before he boarded the jetliner that would take him to Washington, DC, for an interview that would, if all went well, escalate him into the ruling class.

After eighty minutes Joel had made his way to the security ropes where the end of the line was intended to be. All sense of emancipation had been replaced by a strong sense of having to urinate. He looked around, trying to take his mind off his full bladder. Keeping it very casual, he did not want to attract unwanted attention from the FedAPS agents by looking anxious. There were no agents within his line of sight, but one always had to assume he was watched. There were cameras and drones throughout the airport.

During the construction of STFI, the *Seattle Federal Times* reported assurances from the Federal Government that its citizens would be more secure than nearly any other place in the Pacific northwest. Indeed, outside of Federal Government office buildings, airports had the most thorough security in the country. Everyone was watched, screened, and profiled for suspicious movements, actions, behavior, and even clothing. Federal practice was that anyone who caught the attention of a FedAPS agent was extracted, detained, and/or questioned to "an extent appropriate for the circumstance." Americans learned the secret to negotiating airport security was to never move too fast, never stand anywhere too long, and never display too much emotion lest you attract attention from FedAPS and be detained for an appropriate extent.

Joel thought the whole security protocol added way too much unnecessary stress to traveling. He understood the purpose of it all; he definitely did not consider himself to be some kind of freedom nut when it came to the public good. He agreed with all the public service announcements posted throughout the airport:

The Price of Security is Convenience.
The Price of Security is Comfort.
The Price of Security is Time.
The Price of Security is Freedom.

As Joel glanced from the FedAPS posters to the extremely large buttocks of an obese white woman in front of him, to the young black mother whose two children were shrieking and giggling as they wiggled across the floor and bumped into people, to the group of brown-skinned men holding cardboard boxes closed with duct tape, to the score of travelers taking off their shoes, belts, and clothes on their way to be questioned, x-rayed, and frisked; he wished the whole process did not have to be so degrading. Did the price of security include dignity as well? His discomfiture was exacerbated all the more by feelings of guilt. Who was he to be angry over safety protocols? Was his dignity worth the loss of even one life? Was he to demand his "constitutional rights," as his grandfather had always done, and put the lives of innocent people at risk?

Joel had very conflicted feelings about his grandfather. He remembered him as a kind, loving old man, always ready to give Joel ice cream. Even in the middle of the afternoon before dinner.

"Abe! You'll ruin his appetite for dinner." Joel's mother used to chastise with a smile.

"You'll clean your plate for Pops. Right?" Abe would smile and wink at his only grandson.

Joel loved his grandfather and, privately, still mourned his death. Joel's father never mentioned him. In fact, Joel's father was embarrassed and ashamed of his own father. Other than to collect a monthly check from a trust fund established by Abe Levine, Joel's father would not even acknowledge the existence of his own father. There were no pictures in the house. No wisdom was passed on from that generation of the Levine family. All that survived were the loving memories in Joel's mind. Yet Joel abhorred everything that his grandfather believed in, everything that his grandfather stood for, everything that his grandfather thought was proper. Abe's entire ideology and philosophy towards life was the complete antithesis of Joel's. To Joel's shame and embarrassment, Abraham Levine had been a vigorous and enthusiastic participant in the American Renaissance.

Most federal historians described the American Renaissance as a period of excessive patriotism, blind xenophobia, and unbridled greed. Joel had learned in school that it was yet another example of sin against humanity and another source of national shame that the American people were so notorious for.

"But we were fighting for our lives, our very own survival!" Abe explained to his grandson. Joel found his memories ironic since his grandfather had not actually served in combat, but served as a Navy doctor. Nonetheless, young Joel was fascinated with his grandfather's stories of the invasion, the war, and Americans pulling together to "do the impossible."

"It was everything that has always made this country great. As a people we looked reality in the face, stepped up, and kicked its ass," Abe would say in a hushed tone, as if sharing a secret. Joel had loved those moments as a small boy. His grandfather would say, "Let's talk man to man." It felt as if his grandfather were sharing a grand wisdom with him and using some grown-up words that his mother would not approve of. He felt loved by the old man. He felt proud to be of that man's family and of that man's nation.

Not without pain and sadness, that pride would dissipate through Joel's education in the Federal School System. For he learned that while President Joseph P. Leakey was a well-intentioned progressive, he was, arguably, not a particularly good president. Of course, some people, like Abe Levine, described Leakey as incompetent at best and a traitor at worst. However, these people had no sense of social justice. They did not understand, or perhaps even disdained, the virtue of equality. Leakey had the courage to make tough decisions, as unpopular as they were. He understood the greater need of the People. He understood that it cost a lot of money to make everyone equal. The American culture of greed was such that many did not want to pay their fair share for the American dream. Their sense of equality and freedom didn't go beyond their own needs and desires. Many Americans could not sense a need for security beyond their own homes and retirement accounts. Leakey understood the needs and dreams of the oppressed underclass. He had campaigned on slogans of *No Sacrifice is too Great for Equality* and *The Needs of the Many over the Greed of a Few.*

Leakey boldly pushed forward his progressive agenda, outflanking resistance in Congress through executive orders. Leakey raised income taxes and initiated a national sales tax, as well as a national communication tax. He nationalized education, retirement, housing, and banking all in one fell swoop. He began the confiscation of privately owned automobiles, recreational vehicles, and firearms. He nationalized agriculture and began to secure the land needed to feed the nation. He ordered the regulation of "destructive" media. He gave legal equality to all "Americans" no matter what their citizenship status was. No debate, no compromise, just action. He masterfully used the taxation and law enforcement agencies at his disposal to enforce social justice for the American people. He fearlessly challenged Congress to impeach him for serving the needs of the suffering.

"What are laws compared to equality?" Leakey responded to a question of the constitutionality of his actions. "If you want an omelet, you got to break a few eggs."

"But he always broke somebody else's eggs," Abe would recall to Joel. However, Joel learned that kind of thinking was shallow and selfish. His teachers had taught him that like many social progressive pioneers from the Gracchi brothers of the Roman Republic to Americans like Senator Robert M. La Follette, Vice President Henry A. Wallace, and Presidents Woodrow Wilson, Franklin D. Roosevelt, and Lyndon B. Johnson, weaker humanity buckled and resisted the change that they needed. While President Joseph P. Leakey had done so many great things for the people, they lacked the courage and the intellect to appreciate his agenda. The fear of national debt, of a regulated economy, and propaganda against fair taxes led to a landslide defeat. Forty-eight states voted against Leakey in his bid for re-election.

Of course, Abe's recollection was that it was a historic night. "He was the greatest president since Abraham Lincoln," he would always say. "Knowing now what was going to happen, it was divine providence that George R. Clark was elected president. He was the right man at the right time." Joel thought if there was a man that embodied the American Renaissance more than his grandfather, it was George Clark. The two men thought exactly alike. Old Abe Levine was indeed right; everyone in the modern world thought the election was historical. It set the world on a path that would forever change it.

Joel had studied the election in detail, not just as an undergrad in his political science course, but as a journalism/history grad student. He'd written three different papers on the event. It was a classic campaign of propaganda and demagoguery. Clark was the face of all that disgusted Joel about the old America. He was tall and muscular. He was white and Christian. He was a veteran of the United States Marine Corps. "He had everything but 'fascist bigot' tattooed on his forehead," one of Joel's professors had joked during his freshman year. The professor had bemoaned Clark's lack of experience. "The man only had a bachelor's degree, and he spent most of his time in college playing football. So he's stupid enough to get his leg blown off in the Islamic Wars and suddenly he's qualified to be president of the American people?!" Actually Clark was not elected to the presidency straight from the Marine Corps, but he was a first-term senator from Arizona.

Joel had written a research paper on the Clark Campaign. He compared America to a child that was too afraid to grow up. Leakey instituted change in America. Change that was needed for social justice, but most did not have the foresight, nor the intelligence, to understand how necessary changes would play out. Just as an older child might become frightened by oncoming adulthood and cling to his teddy bear, so the American people reached out to their past when they elected George R. Clark.

All of Joel's professors chided Clark as a stupid man, but Joel wrote that he thought this assumption was a mistake. He thought that any man that had so successively set back American Progressivism had to have some intelligence. Enough intelligence to manipulate the fear and ignorance of the American people, anyway. As evidence, Joel described the tactics and slogans of the Clark Campaign. Where Leakey had installed change through the efficient means of executive order, Clark would quote the Constitution. Where Leakey cultivated an unofficial alliance with the People's Republic of China to graciously finance change in America, Clark screamed for American independence and self-reliance. Where Leakey's campaign cited Clark's lack of government experience, Clark responded that he had the "American Experience" to guide him. Clark wrapped himself in the Stars and Stripes and claimed that American History and Western Culture was the road map to "Freedom, Strength, & Wealth." Clark claimed that by looking to history, Americans could see for themselves what had worked in the past and what had failed. He often cited stories about the Greeks, Romans, and British as examples of self-government and the rule of law. Conversely, he used examples of the same people to show the pitfalls of centralized authoritarian government. Of course, he threw in examples from the Russians' pioneering of communism and American atrocities in government in order to cover his true racist attacks of Chinese, North Korean, Cuban, and Central Americans' Progressivism and to frighten the voters even more than they were. Joel recognized the cleverness in all this. He had seen his teachers use history the same way for their own progressive purposes. Joel's thesis on that paper was that Clark had perverted history for the purpose of manipulating the fear of the American people and advancing his own agenda. His work had earned him an A+ and the realization that he had a gift for understanding politics and history.

Right or wrong, Joel had conflicted feelings about his work on Clark's election and of Clark's career. His analysis and academic decimation of it had led to his own academic and, so far, professional success. His grandfather, as misguided, bigoted, and nationalistic as he was, still was a loving and kind grandfather. It was his work, his money, that had put Joel through college and graduate school. To have hurt his grandfather so was painful to Joel. Even now, as he waited in line for airport security, Joel could not understand how such an educated and gifted medical doctor, with a passion for helping others, could be so wrong about American history, politics, and ideology. It did not make sense.

"But you weren't there! Good God, we were fighting for our own survival," Joel remembered Abe ranting on more than one occasion, "To hell with the Goddamned Chinese! They hit us first. This is after they had financed and supplied the Jihad against us. This was after they had tried to finance our own destruction through that dumb son of a bitch Leakey, and then those little yellow bastards had the nerve to sucker punch us!"

As a naive boy Joel loved to hear the stories about the war. His grandfather always became so impassioned, it was contagious, it was exciting. As a child, it made him wish he had been there too, so he could have fought the "evil ChiComs" alongside his grandfather.

"Of course now, Joel, it's easy to look back and say it was one of our greatest moments, but at the time we were scared for our lives. Our backs were up against the wall.

"It was on an Easter Sunday of that year. Those lousy, little ChiCom bastards tried to one-up the Japanese Empire, I guess. They hit us at 0500 Pacific Coast Time. It was a multipronged attack. For all their faults, they are a disciplined and precise people. They hit Seattle, Hawaii, and about every major port on the West and Gulf Coast. They hit most of the air bases in California. Hell, they even occupied San Francisco and the surrounding area for a time, from the base that that jackass Leakey leased to them. They attacked our southern border as well from their Mexican bases.

"Had to have been the bombs that woke me up. My eyes popped open that morning and I had a feeling that something was wrong. The rumbling in the distance, you could even feel it, sounded like thunder. There were all kinds of sirens going off. I reached over for my tablet and logged on to the news. Oh, Joel, it was as if the world was coming to an end; and, actually, for many Americans, it really was.

"Around ten or so that morning President Clark addressed the nation. He reported the damage to our country and he told us of the demands made by the People's 'Republic' of China. The ChiComs weren't looking to destroy us. Oh no, that would be like killing the golden goose for them. In exchange for financing all of Leakey's bullshit reforms, that jackass gave them the best that this country could produce. It was like opening the front door of our house and saying, 'Come on in. Take whatever you want.' Leakey called it a 'patriotic' labor tax. The proper term is slavery. They took oil;

they took technology; hell, they even took people! American prisoners were sent off to Chinese labor camps. Leakey gave them land. United States soil! Two military bases in California, all the bases they built in Mexico, plus the jackass let them take full possession of the Panama Canal. American industry was shut down or not allowed to start up, so we had to import Chinese-made goods at high prices. No, the Chinese bastards gave Leakey and his bureaucracy the money, but the American people were paying for it.

"You see, Joel, I know you're tired of hearing me carry on like this all the time, but this is why it is important to remember that we are a republic: a nation ruled by law, but good laws do absolutely no good without good, strong men to enforce them! What Leakey did was illegal! A president does not have that kind of power, but no one stopped him! It was that same kind of altruistic reform bullshit that brought down the Roman Republic; it gave us Mussolini, Hitler, Castro. Sons of bitches all of them. Our Constitution is a beautiful thing; it is government based on the foundation of the importance and liberty of the individual. But it is nothing more than an old piece of paper if we don't stand up for it, enforce it, and defend it with our lives if necessary. That's what Clark ran on. That's what his presidency was about. He put an end to Leakey's policy of tribute to the Chinese, and that's why they hit us. Like a schoolyard bully that roughs you up a bit and says he'll do more if you don't give him your milk money. The ChiComs thought they could scare us back into compliance, but they thought wrong. Clark led us into war!"

His grandfather had always made it sound so romantic. It broke Joel's heart when he learned in school that it was all a lie. Clark had talked about going back to the Constitution, but then broke from precedence and did things without concern for the environment, social justice, or even the collective emotional welfare of the American people. Clark had allowed the states to form their own armies. Businesses were allowed to run without federal oversight. Ironically, through executive orders, Clark did away with federal regulations and oversight on industries that were deemed "vital" to the war effort. He took funding away from bureaus that he thought did not contribute to the war effort, and spent it on the military and war materiel. His grandfather complained about the Labor Tax as slavery, yet millions of Americans were deprived of federal assistance and expected to serve in the armed forces or work in factories that produced war goods. The physical and emotional toll of these policies were something modern academia still studied and debated. Intellectuals were always discovering damage that was done during those years that no one had even realized at the time.

However, despite his sense of national shame, Joel secretly admired his grandfather for his service during the war. While not a young man, thirty-one, when the war started, Abe Levine had joined the Washington State Militia as a doctor. When the People's Liberation Army of China had been defeated in North America, Abe Levine joined the United States Navy to serve overseas. Joel took some solace in that his grandfather had saved lives, but it was shallow. The lives his grandfather saved took the lives of other human beings during the war; so Abe, too, was a guilty participant in the American Renaissance. No, his grandfather was waist deep in national guilt, but he had shown a courage and passion that appealed to Joel on some level; it was his own guilty pleasure.

"Boarding papers! What's wrong with you, moron?" a FedAPS agent barked. "You think I got nothing to do but wait on you all day?"

Snapped out of his reminiscence of his grandfather, Joel handed the agent his boarding pass, driver's license, and federal passport needed for interstate travel.

"So—" the agent glanced through the paperwork "—478F, you like to make me repeat myself, do you?"

"Sorry, I...I'm off to a big interview and just have a lot on my mind." Joel attempted to explain as his voice cracked and stammered.

"I see. You've got all this important stuff to do and us pissants just have to wait on you, huh?"

"No. I'm...I'm sorry. Just a lot is on my mind. I—"

"You seem nervous, 478F," the agent interrupted after he glanced again at Joel's paperwork. "Do you have something you're hiding?" he said with a mischievous grin. The agent keyed his mic. "Section A6, Section A6, internal security, please."

Joel shuffled onto his flight to DC six hours later than he had originally planned. Security delays had caused him to miss his originally scheduled flight. Fortunately, there was a red-eye flight to Washington, DC. It came with a hefty rescheduling/security fee to cover the expense of federal paperwork and protocols. Joel was skeptical of the fee. He thought an additional five hundred dollars to hit a few taps on a keyboard seemed excessive to him.

Never mind that now, he thought, *at least I'll be in DC with eight hours to play with before my interview.*

His rectal pain from the cavity search caused him to slowly ease himself down into his window seat. He was the first one in his aisle and hoped no one else would show. However, this hope was shattered five minutes later when a heavyset man, expelling many grunts and sighs, took the middle seat. The man needed to wear more cologne than he already was and breathed way too loudly. Five minutes after that a very thin, petite woman with long straight brown hair and a pale, frightened look on her face sat down in the aisle seat.

Fucking brilliant, Joel thought, but did not say aloud.

It seemed to him that this whole scenario was just way too clichéd to be coincidence. Could some perverted mind really be pulling some kind of sick joke? Of course, it was a ridiculous thought. Joel recognized that he was tired and irritated and thus prone to a little paranoia. He adjusted in his seat, trying to get comfortable, but he could not. He was too sore. Joel slipped his FedAPS-approved entertainment headphones over his eyes and ears to listen to music, to block out the plane, to block out his pain, and hopefully go to sleep.

The Price of Security is a bleeding pain in the ass! Joel laughed at his own joke, but he would never say it aloud. Never.

National security issues aside, Joel hated airports.

CHAPTER TWO

In the office of the Supreme Commander of the Federal Agency of Public Safety, Nina Maria Perro was ready to have an alcoholic drink and end her day. It had been a long and frustrating week for her. It appeared that several more long days were guaranteed for the immediate future since the Russian Federation publicly threatened a nuclear attack on American soil.

Perro initially scoffed at the audacity of the Russians to demand the return of the American southwest to the United Mexican States, but then the demand was sustained unanimously by the United Nations. President Iguwma Swigolamo, of the UN, said it was a matter of "international integrity." Perro figured everyone in the international community had to have known this was a ruse for Russian imperialism. Mexico was a colony of the Russian Federation in everything but name. Russians were elected to the highest state offices. Russians were the bureaucratic leaders of the United Mexican States. Russians were not only the biggest landowners in Mexico, they were the majority of landowners in Mexico. They owned the resorts, the farms, the ranches, condominiums, the apartments, and the factories. If one went to Mexico, you might hear some Spanish on the streets, but if one did business in Mexico, you would speak Russian. Even Russian organized crime ran the slave and drug trade, along with control of the Mexican-American border.

She glanced over at the bar, eyeing the decanter of vodka. She badly wanted a drink. She wanted to feel the stress of the day, the stress of the week, slip away with that first sip. However, she had one more meeting today with a low-level, nimrod journalist/historian and wanted to have a clear mind.

The journalist, as trivial as a cog in a big machine could be, was still an important part in her scheme. She thought it most important to make just the right first impression; not so much as to successfully enact her plan, but to insure that the journalist would thoroughly be under her control. A well-managed journalist could be a valuable tool indeed. As a leader, Perro understood the value of laws and the power of well-armed federal agents, but to truly control people you had to win their hearts and their minds. Well, at least their hearts, anyway. Perro had made her political career through the emotions she could evoke in others, and when it came to controlling the masses, she found fear to be her most effective weapon. People could never be under your control as much as when they willingly submitted themselves to your authority. General Perro was fully aware that her power, her authority, did not come from the president, not Congress, nor even the archaic Constitution. It came from the mob of American people that demanded security and were willing to sacrifice liberty to get it. Security that she could provide if given enough power, and a well-managed journalist could be very instrumental in persuading the mob to give up that power.

The redheaded receptionist was stunning. She was tall and slender with all the curves men like to see. Joel had noticed that FedAPS uniforms often looked loose and baggy, unless someone was grossly overweight, and at worst, looked unkempt when compared to the memory of how Joel's grandfather had looked in his military uniform. He thought the uniforms were particularly bad on women and gave them something of an androgynous look. This woman, however, filled her uniform perfectly, as if it had been cut to her exact dimensions. Her appearance was very feminine and very professional. Joel found her to be the perfect complement to this most extraordinary facility. From the moment Joel had entered through the security gates into the walled District of Columbia and traveled the streets to the Federal Headquarters building, he had been in awe. Every building, every green space, every statue and monument, and even the streets themselves displayed the most advanced technology, sophistication, efficiency, and dominance.

Nor were they in short supply. There was only one green space in all of Seattle. Joel counted eighteen on the way to his interview. Joel had traveled overseas and to many major cities of North America, but he had never seen any city this powerful. He noticed that even the people were cleaner and displayed a wealth and sophistication not seen anywhere else on the continent. The beautiful redhead embodied everything he had seen in the District of Columbia. It was everything that he wanted.

Joel's guilt failed to quell his yearning for the attractive FedAPS sergeant. It was demeaning and degrading to women for men to think of them as sexually attractive beings, but it was something he could not help. Joel battled his temptation to stare at the attractive sergeant for over nearly forty-five minutes before she finally approached him.

"Sir, if you will come with me, General Perro will see you now."

Joel felt half numb when he looked into her crystal blue eyes, which popped from the contrast of her red hair and navy blouse with the broad collar opened wide and lower than he could remember seeing on any other FedAPS agent. He quickly averted his eyes and took in the name tag that read MacTaggert.

Did she just smile at me? Joel wondered. *Of course, she's a receptionist. She's also a FedAPS agent, they never smile; and there was a certain look in her eyes.*

He watched her hips rhythmically sway back and forth as she walked. Unlike the baggy cargo pants he had seen on most FedAPS personnel, MacTaggert's skirt was slim fitting and complemented her figure. Joel thought the cut of the garment actually accentuated her femininity, as if it were something to be celebrated. Joel gave in and indulged in MacTaggert's figure the short distance to the general's office. His indulgence came to an abrupt end when the sergeant opened the door and introduced him to General Perro.

Joel consciously forced his face to smile. He thought that this might very well be the ugliest woman he had ever seen. Not that she was hideously scarred or anything like that, she was ugly and looked like she was trying to make herself look ugly. If MacTaggert was a celebration of femininity, General Perro was an aspersion to it. The woman had the figure of an avocado. Her platinum-bleached hair was cropped short, in a similar fashion to a man's military haircut, but too long to look that sharp. She wore the formal dress blue uniform of the FedAPS, but it looked like it had been tailored for a short fat man as opposed to a short fat woman. If the cut of the clothing was to disguise the fact that she was a woman, they had failed miserably, yet Joel could not think of what would have helped. Contrary to the masculine character of her clothing and hair, General Perro's face was smeared in makeup. However, instead of complementing the feminine features of her face, the makeup distorted them. It looked as if her eyebrows had been shaved off and drawn back as high arches on her forehead. The rouge on her cheeks and the lipstick she wore were of a bright shade of red that clashed with her olive complexion. Nothing about her appearance seemed graceful or even natural. She had the look of a sadistic clown wearing a military uniform in a child's nightmare, yet this was the most powerful person in the Federal Government.

She was the top commander of all branches of the military, federal law enforcement, and every agency and bureaucracy in the Federal Government. She even controlled the president's own security detail. In fact, many said she was more powerful than the president of the United States.

Joel smiled. His career and his life depended on it.

"Mr. Levine, please come in and sit down. What a pleasure it is to meet you." Perro greeted him with her best fake smile.

"Thank you, Madame General. Truly the honor is all mine." Joel walked a brisk and steady pace and stopped approximately ten feet in front of Perro. With his heels together and a straight back, Joel bowed to a forty-five-degree angle, as was customary when greeting high-ranking government officials, straightened, and only sat down after the general had taken her seat.

"Mr. Levine, can my sergeant bring you in some refreshment? Sergeant! Bring us some coffee," Perro ordered without waiting for a response.

"Yes, Madame General." MacTaggert popped to attention and then crossed the large office to the refreshment bar.

Joel was amazed by the 180-degree view of Washington, DC from the general's corner office. It was the nerve center of the whole country. Where the best and brightest minds collected for the purpose of evolving mankind. Where decisions were made and actions taken that determined the course of the nation and the daily course of American lives. His gazed fixed on a tall white obelisk in the near distance. The Tower of Progress, it was a marvelous symbol for social justice and equality. Joel had a faint memory of watching the rededication of the structure on television as a very small child. Previously it had been named after a past American president. Joel could not remember his name, just that he had owned slaves and was not willing to pay his fair share of taxes. Joel shook off the thought; this was a time for optimism not cynicism. Joel was in the office of the most powerful woman in North America, at her request! His time had come. Indeed, it was his moment to shine, to join the world's leading intelligentsia and make a difference. It was the very opportunity he had been working for since he was a college freshman.

"So, Mr. Levine, may I call you Joel? You're David's son." Perro's plan was to start this conversation by falsely planting the notion in Levine's mind that she had known his father. "I'm a fan of his work on LBJ," she lied again. She was familiar with David Levine's work only because she had been briefed on it two days before. But she was far from a fan of Levine's work or any other academic for that matter. In fact, she really found them quite contemptible. She thought they were such arrogant people. Always thinking that they were making a difference, when in fact, they were pawns of those, like her, in power who really did make a difference. Academics, like journalists, could be more useful than the average fool, but ultimately they were still the "useful idiots" that Vladimir Lenin was so legendary at manipulating. Now that was a man who truly made a difference; that was a man she was truly a fan of. Lenin was an audacious, bold thinker. He was a man of political action. He was the opposite of this modern-day castrato who sat before her today.

Perro's stress of the last few weeks only added to the anger she felt at having to be not just polite, but warm and inviting to Levine. While she felt this kind of behavior was beneath her, she realized that creating an emotional "connection" with him would ultimately make him that much easier to control. At first she had to give him a reason to make him think that she could like him, and then, at some point, she had to give him a reason to fear her. Then she would truly have him. She would be able to control him, use him, and throw him away when he was no longer useful.

"Your piece on how the international community can make Russia feel like 'part of the family' was quite good. Your analogy of Russia as the abused adolescent that needs love, not discipline, was most compelling," Perro said with a well-rehearsed false sincerity.

"Thank you, Madame General," Joel gushed. "I'm really quite flattered. I never dreamed that my work would be appreciated by one as esteemed as yourself."

You got that right, you sniveling little shit, Perro thought. She made a mental note to have Levine red-flagged to FedAPS for an internal security check on his flight home.

MacTaggert arrived at Perro's desk and served coffee to them both. "Cream or sugar, Mr. Levine?" she asked.

"Oh, both, please. Extra sugar, I like it sweet." Joel did not realize his entendre until it was too late. He squirmed and cleared his throat. MacTaggert slightly turned her head to look at him and smiled. Not only was Joel relieved, but his optimism for the day skyrocketed.

I have truly arrived, he thought.

This moment was not missed by Perro. Instantly, she flushed with a controlled anger and jealousy. She had not handpicked MacTaggert from basic training and given her rank, VIP housing, and tailored uniforms so she could be eye candy for the hired help. Well, in fact, actually she was; but she was not supposed to return the sentiment. She reminded herself that when you flaunted something, people would notice; and, after all, wasn't that what she was trying to accomplish? What good was the power to have what you wanted, if no one knew you had it? Besides, Perro had learned how to control her passions a long time ago. Before her momentary jealousy had passed, she was calculating how she could use this to her advantage.

"Thank you, Sergeant. That will be all for now."

"Yes, Madame General." MacTaggert popped to attention and exited the office. Perro watched MacTaggert's slim and femininely muscular figure walk out of the office. MacTaggart was truly a stunning individual, which was exactly why Perro enjoyed controlling her. Perro's attention turned to Joel, who was blowing on the top of his coffee. Even with all the cream, it was still too hot for him.

"Mr. Levine, let me get right to the point. Your work on the Clark presidency was brilliant. Your take on the Russian situation is spot on. Yours is a mind that, I believe, can be of service to the People." Perro broke eye contact, got up from her desk, turned and looked out the massive window that was the wall of her office. She clasped her hands behind her back and let out a deep sigh as a way of expressing the weight and stress of her leadership. It was all for Joel's benefit. She had rehearsed this meeting in her mind while she had sat on the toilet that morning. "Of course, you're familiar with Prime Minister Volkov's demands to the United Nations?"

"It's outrageous, Madame General." Joel set his coffee down on Perro's desk with just enough righteous indignation to spill some over the edge of his cup. He nervously wiped up the spilled coffee with his napkin, quickly stood up, and walked over next to Perro. As soon as he completed the move, it dawned on him that the general might find it too dominating, too masculine a behavior. "For Prime Minister Volkov to claim to be speaking for the Mexican people, especially given your own personal history, is…" He hesitated for a moment. Did he dare go there? Would it be too much? Would it be offensive? Perro's background was internationally known. In fact, her background had been heralded as evidence of America's progress towards racial, economic, and international justice. Two generations earlier, Perro's ancestors had illegally migrated into the United States of America. She was evidence of America's true sense of social justice. Everything had been going his way so far today. Joel decided to risk the statement; perhaps it would really show the general how empathetic he was to her people and their struggles. "Well, it sounds so racist and patronizing. As a Latina woman you are far more qualified to know what the Mexican people really need."

The nod of Perro's concerned-looking face hid the temptation she had to ask him if there was such a thing as a Latina man. She let it go. She wanted a pseudo-intellectual with enough of a guilt complex that she could manipulate.

"Yes, because it is. White men have been doing this sort of thing for millennia, Mr. Levine. Do sit down."

Joel did as he was told. General Perro remained standing. Her grandfather and father had taught her that many Anglos were conditioned to be manipulated through guilt. They often commented on the paradox of the people who had conquered the desert frontier of the American southwest and conquered kings, tyrants, poverty, and disease and could then produce such weak and susceptible descendants.

"Perhaps it is in their nature," Nina recalled her father saying. "Once they conquered nearly all of Mexico, what did the Anglos do? They just gave it back. Who does that? Then they gave away Mexico; now they give away their own country. Nina, if a man is foolish enough to throw away his wealth, you must be wise enough to catch it. It is a 'dog eat dog world.'" He would chuckle over the pun of their family name. "Some species thrive and others die out; it's evolution. We must be the ones that thrive. If these people want to be slaves, then we must be the ones to control them."

Now she did control them, and they had put her in power. As a young woman she was given scholarships. She was given preferential admittance to Federal Agency of Public Safety Academy. Even she was amazed at how easy it was for her to get high marks at the academy, considering how little she understood in her classes. The professors all spoke some kind of pseudo-intellectual psychobabble, and all she had to do was answer in kind and they would all praise her. She had graduated in the top quarter of her class despite her inability to pass the objective portion of the final exam, as well as meet the physical conditioning requirements or pass the firearms training. Once she had accused some of the faculty and students for discriminating against her for being a lesbian Latina, her graduation and commission was assured. Besides, there was more to public safety than being able to shoot guns and jump over walls. Populations had to be managed. Behavior had to be controlled, and this was where Nina's passion lay. This was where her talents excelled.

Many in the FedAPS were happy to place her in positions of prominence as a way of showing their own tolerance and sense of equality. Then they would try to control her. They wanted her to advance their agenda, but they were like pups trying to steal bones from a wolf. They lived in fear of their vices, where she embraced hers as virtues. She could always demand that others were not doing enough to show their tolerance. Accuse them of never doing enough to dispense social justice, and they would cave. Of course, it was always helpful to her cause that she had a talent for collecting information. Perro had a knack for encouraging habits and vices that most did not want to be public knowledge. She read Saul Alinsky, who taught to use people's rules against them. She excelled at holding people to the very standards that they themselves were too weak to adhere to. This guilt allowed her to manipulate many, and what she loved about this tactic was that she was completely immune to it. When she failed to adhere to the high standards that she demanded of others, it was never her fault. She claimed her failings were further evidence of why she needed to be promoted to fight the social injustices that had caused her failure. By this she had risen to the most powerful position in the Government. She commanded the military, she was in command of all federal law enforcement, her department had final authority over all banking and commerce, she even controlled presidential security and thus the behavior, actions, and security of the president of the United States. She was the centralized authority.

For all her authority, Perro still needed more to effect progress. The president, Congress, and the Supreme Court still had ceremonial authority that publicly needed to endorse her. Congress in particular, because of its many members, could be tricky to control. Adding fuel to that fire was that nearly a third of the states were in quasi rebellion. Immigration policies of the several previous decades had done much to erode the American concept of separation of powers and constitutional law. However, there was still a significant number of Americans that clung to these outdated concepts that interfered with institutionalized social injustice. Perro was confident that their time had passed, but they were still offering resistance to the Progressive Movement. This resistance manifested itself in noncompliance with federal mandates and the election of some troublesome congressmen. It was one of these congressmen, on top of the drama with Russia and the UN, that had made the last two weeks so stressful for Perro.

"I assume you are familiar with Senator Ferguson's proposal to recreate a United States Marine Corps and to have it outside the authority of the Federal Agency of Public Safety?"

"Yes, Madame General, I am. Of course..." Joel's voice trailed off. Suddenly he was not confident as to how he should answer the question.

Perro gave him a condescending smile. "I know, Ferguson is just a loon. No one takes him seriously with all his talk of Constitutionalism and American sovereignty. The problem is a fast-growing number of the American public are starting to take him seriously. Russia's demand for the Southwest has only grown his support; and, as one would expect, many congressmen from the region are supporting him. My sources tell me that they are already working on such legislation that would bring the United States Marine Corps back as it was at the time of its dismemberment."

"Oh, Madame General, once the American public is reminded of the Marine Corps's barbarous culture of murder and treason, I think that support will evaporate," Joel righteously replied.

"Those are my thoughts exactly, Mr. Levine." Perro was pleased with how she had conducted this conversation so far. "Who might you recommend to remind the public of this *American* history?" she said *American* with notable disdain.

"Madame General, I would be honored to perform such an assignment. That is, if you deem me worthy," he said with confidence now that he knew where all this was going. He knew more than ever that this was indeed his time.

Perro patronizingly smiled and sauntered over to the desk. "Mr. Levine, you are exactly the kind of *man* I had in mind for the job." She pressed the intercom button on her watch. "Sergeant, bring in Mr. Levine's credentials." Perro picked a piece of lint from the sleeve of her uniform before she turned her attention back to Levine. "You will be given temporary

VIP status for the duration of this project. If you come through, as I believe you will, this will become a full-time status." She paused to let that sink in. VIP status was what everyone dreamed of. It was the goal of every federal employee. It allowed one to live as a human, not as some serf from the Middle Ages. It was something most Americans would never experience. "Unfortunately, we will not be able to give you access to a Federal VIP travel jet on your return trip home. Hopefully you can suffer through one more public transport flight." Perro still wanted to enact her return travel plans for Joel.

MacTaggert walked in with a satchel of electronic ware for Joel. The kit included a laptop computer, a tablet, virtual reality headphones, and a smartphone for his use, as well as FedAPS identification that already had his photo on it.

Perro again noticed the flirtatious look exchanged between the two when she was struck with a sudden burst of tyrannical genius.

"Oh, and one more thing, Sergeant MacTaggert," Perro ordered in a gentle, almost purring voice.

"Yes, Madame General." MacTaggert stood in front of Perro at attention. The general calmly, but firmly turned her around. Perro reached up and placed one hand between MacTaggert's shoulder blades and pushed her over, so she had to brace herself on the edge of the general's desk. Perro bent down and slid her other hand up and under MacTaggert's skirt and began to roughly fondle her genitals. From across the desk, without saying a word, MacTaggert gave Joel a pleading look for help that she did not really expect him to act upon. Joel felt a bit awkward and embarrassed; he became occupied with his new kit and credentials. MacTaggert closed her eyes and clinched the edge of the desk. It was the closest to an escape that she could muster. Perro felt the emotional rush of a successful plan. Joel no longer had the air of confident masculinity about him. He was visibly shaken and submissive in pretending he could not see what was going on in front of him. MacTaggert was submitting without a word of protest, but why would she? Her career, her life would be destroyed if she did.

"Immediately begin researching Marine Corps history, tradition, culture, training, etc. With that equipment you will have full access to all federal websites and files that pertain to the United States Marine Corps. Included is contact information for Sandra LaGard; she is your new agent. Within a few weeks she will start arranging media interviews, where you will describe the findings of your latest research. You have any questions, any concerns, you contact her. You will not contact me. Understood?" Perro looked Joel right in the eye and waited for an answer as she continued to sexually abuse MacTaggert. All pleasantness was gone from her voice.

"Yes, Madame General." Joel complied while looking down at his feet.

"Good. You'll see on your itinerary that next Thursday you will have access to Sean Harris for an exclusive interview. You can have as much access to him as you want. Make him an excellent resource. No one has been allowed to interview him for the last fifty years. You'll have VIP status and access to federal transport. Understood?"

"Yes, Madame General."

"Within two weeks I expect to see the first of a series of articles that will culminate in a book explaining to the American public how a United States Marine Corps would be counter to their happiness and well-being. That the last thing they need, or want, is a bunch of misogynist American men being taught to kill on top of being taught how great they are. Understood?"

"Yes, Madame General."

"Do this right and I will make you big." Perro continued the conversation along with her sexual abuse. "You'll be a contributor to the Progressive Movement. You will be celebrated. Do this wrong and I will personally see to your humiliation and destruction. Understood?"

"Yes, Madame General." Joel was now fighting a wave of nausea. MacTaggert muffled a painful grunt.

"Any questions at all? Please feel free to ask." The pleasantness was back in Perro's voice, only now Joel could hear the perversion in it.

"Yes, Madame General, may I ask," Joel said weakly, "who is Sean Harris?"

Perro laughed at his question. "I expected you to be familiar with Harris from all your research on Clark." Perro thrust her hand harder into MacTaggert. "He's serving a life sentence at Reid. He's the last Marine we got."

CHAPTER THREE

"This is how civilized human beings should live." Joel sank into the plush leather seats of the luxury federal passenger jet reserved for VIPs.

"Sir?" the flight attendant asked.

"Oh, nothing," Joel gushed, knowing he sounded stupid, but not caring. "I'll have a white wine."

"My pleasure, sir," the attendant dutifully responded and was off. Joel enjoyed the view. She was tall, blonde, and looked very much like a woman. She too wore a tighter, formfitting skirt similar to the uniforms he'd seen in the federal buildings in DC.

"One of the 'perks' of VIP status," Joel mumbled jokingly to himself. This kind of luxury still seemed a bit surreal, and he was reveling in it.

The federal jet had tan leather seats that were wide enough to hold him comfortably. These seats could even recline.

"I could sleep in this!" Joel exclaimed. He smiled. Joel thought he might actually begin to enjoy traveling.

"Your wine, sir."

Joel popped up his leather recliner.

"Is there anything else you would like before takeoff?"

Joel thought of several things he would like her to do, but he lacked the audacity to demand them. Yet he could not quite help himself. After all, what was the good of VIP status if one could not truly enjoy it?

"Yes, walk up to the front of the cabin and back. I would like to enjoy the view." He smiled and gave her a wink. It felt a little uncomfortable; this was not his normal behavior. He had been raised to believe that the fact a woman was a woman should not make any difference to him. Although it always had in some way or another, to one extent or another, he had felt a sense of guilt about it. Now after having spent time with federal officers, even the madame general herself, he was beginning to think he should enjoy himself a bit. He'd noticed how they surrounded themselves with attractive young women and men in the same sort of fashion that they surrounded themselves with soft leather chairs, fine art, gourmet food, beautiful vistas, expensive alcohol, and high-quality narcotics. Very little was forbidden to FedAPS officers. The more authority one had, the fewer limitations. Joel loved this new world that he had become a part of, and he planned to stay in it. He would give the history they wanted. By the time American citizens read his book, they'd lose whatever nostalgia was left for the Marine Corps, or the old United States for that matter, and he would gain indulgence.

Joel ordered another white wine from the attendant and got to work; after all, nothing came for free, not even indulgence. He set up his laptop and opened Harris's file. They had their first interview scheduled for tomorrow and Joel wanted to be up on his facts.

He had spent the last three days reading old media about the closing days of the Sino-American War and the return of the US Marines to their native country. Of course, his grandfather was in the back of his mind throughout his research. Abe had served as a Navy doctor during the war. He had always spoken highly of the Marines and of their courage and sacrifice. None of that mattered now. Joel's work would focus on the Marine Corps culture and how their training and the war affected what they had done when they returned from the war. His angle would be to present Marine training, with a bit of Harris's perspective, and how it created a warped, sadistic individual that was not acceptable to the civilized citizen. He would portray the return of the Marines from war as part of the ugliness of the Clark legacy and of the warrior culture he cultivated for the purpose of winning the Sino-American War.

The war itself could be portrayed as unjust and unnecessary. As nothing more than a laboratory of destruction to further cultivate these killing machines. He wanted to show an irony in that the Marine Corps created to protect and propel American greatness would wreak death and destruction on innocent American life, a Frankenstein's monster on a grand scale. Joel loved the idea and thought that other media and academics would eat it up. Harris even looked the part of a monster with a brutal-looking scar running parallel to his cheekbone from his nose to his ear. Joel envisioned himself giving lectures on college campuses and interviews over the Internet. He thought it would get the exact kind of attention and focus that the madame general wanted, and soundly secure his career as a federal historian and his VIP status. Now he just had to find facts that would fit his thesis.

Joel spent a couple of days going through the government file on Harris. He was excited about some of the stereotypes that he hoped to exploit in order to prove his thesis. On the surface Harris was iconic of everything that was villainous of the old America. Born as Sean Daniel Harris, Joel thought the name had kind of an old American-sounding wholesomeness that he could play to the angle he was trying to come from on this. Harris was born and raised in Kansas, of all places. Not the rural heartland, straight off the farm Kansas that everyone thought of, but from the state's capital, Topeka. It was a small city with a diverse population, local university, and crime issues. Joel wanted to present Harris's upbringing as isolated, backward, homogenous, Southern gun-culture. For the purpose of his work, he figured he could get away with presenting it as such. After all, did anyone who really mattered know that much about Kansas? Besides, Kansas was part of an unofficial confederation of central states known for resisting progress and preaching constitutionality. Joel would present Harris as trouble waiting to happen, and he had no doubt that he could use the demonization of Kansas culture to a political advantage in this work.

There was also the victim angle. After all, in the end Harris had surrendered. He, at least to some degree, had cooperated with the authorities. He had confessed to the murder of innocent civilians. There were discrepancies in his account, and his denial of the Coup had caused some controversy during the trial. But there were also discrepancies on the side of the authorities, and a low-ranking Marine would most likely not be privy to the details of an upcoming military coup d'etat. In the end Harris had cooperated rather than face the death penalty. His information had led federal authorities to the bodies of some of his victims and most of his Marine conspirators. All that mattered at the end of the day was the Federal Government had to some degree benefited from Harris's account of events, so his life had been spared. He'd spent the last fifty years in a federal prison. Joel thought that one could argue that Harris was a victim of the old American culture. A boy who believed, who practiced all that his culture taught him was right, and in the end caused pain and misery for himself and brought death to others. What generation would want to reintroduce such an evil back into its society?

Joel salivated at all the potential angles of this story. He believed it could very well make his career. He was pleased with all the potential his life seemed to hold for him. He ordered another white wine from the flight attendant. When she bent over to serve his drink, he reached up and groped her breast. Expressionless, the flight attendant took his empty wineglass and straightened up.

"Will there be anything else, sir?" she asked, still with no expression.

"Not now, but I'll let you know when there will be," Joel said with a wink. He didn't know what would happen next, but he knew it was his choice to make. He loved it. Joel found privilege addictive.

CHAPTER FOUR

Joel got more work done on the flight than he had hoped. The flight attendant had not been as receptive as he would have liked. He chided himself for not being more forceful. He had seen other federal officers simply take the people they wanted, but he was not quite comfortable with that yet. Joel hated the idea that he might be too weak to use people for his benefit. He would have to get tougher if he were to make it as a FedAPS officer. The plus side was he had put his time to good use. He'd studied Harris's life after his conviction and his prison record to look for any signs of rehabilitation. Was Harris a changed man? Was he still the cold-blooded killer that he was fifty years ago?

The record of Harris was paradoxical. After his conviction he was sent to a maximum-security prison near Florence, Colorado. This was standard operating procedure for someone convicted of extremely violent crimes, terrorism, and an overthrow of the Federal Government. Since the United Nations had declared supermax prisons as torture, because of their "reduced environmental stimulation," prisoners were typically kept there for only five years. The prisoners did not interact with other prisoners and only had minimal interaction with prison guards. The prisoners spent twenty-three hours a day in a twelve-by-seven-foot cell containing a bed, sink, toilet, shower, and television screen for educational broadcasts. The thinking was that after the prisoner's spirit had been sufficiently broken down, the prisoner could be introduced to a prison population, typically a federal work camp, where the prisoner could then be re-educated. After five years at ADX Florence, Harris was sent to Guevera Labor & Education Center (LEC) in eastern Oregon. Within six months he killed four other inmates with his bare hands in a chow hall brawl. One of which, he had beaten to death with a serving tray. The only reason Harris's file gave for the altercation was that the other four men "wanted his applesauce."

Harris spent another five years at Florence. He was then sent to the Clinton LEC in southeast Arkansas. Within ten days Harris was the suspect in the fatal beating of another prisoner. A lack of witnesses prevented additional charges being filed against Harris. He spent four weeks in solitary confinement and was released back into the general population. He was incarcerated there for the next twelve years without recorded incident; in fact, some of the staff at Clinton stated they thought he was a model prisoner. Harris was given a degree of independence and trained as a cook. However, he later killed two other inmates; one was choked to death with a pair of cooking tongs in the center's kitchen. Harris's file did not state the reason for this altercation, but did mention that the "prisoner can still become most dangerous when angered."

Harris was sent to the maximum-security wing of the Harry Mason Reid Educational and Rehabilitation Center in southern Nevada. At the time it was a new facility specifically designed for prisoners of a violent and political nature. It was similar to previous secure housing units, but at Reid inmates were given ninety minutes of exercise and up to six hours of education. It was thought of as an ideal facility for prisoners that for physical or ideological reasons did not mix well with others. Inmates could be contained, isolated, and re-educated without violating the United Nations' definition of torture. When rehabilitated, the prisoner could rejoin the general prison workforce and benefit society. It was here that Harris had spent the last twenty-five years. His file showed that he liked the exercise regimen and requested Shakespeare for recreational reading. This threw Joel for a loop; he'd never heard of Shakespeare before. He looked him up on the federal search engine and found out he was an English author from the seventeenth century. Joel made note of the name, wondering what it was about the past author that could shed light onto Harris's violent nature. Sean Harris was now in his seventies and, according to federal records, the last known living veteran of the United States Marine Corps.

Joel was familiar with the security protocols at Reid; they were the same used at the airports. He enjoyed the feeling that his new VIP status precluded him from standard security protocols. He was met by Warden Enrique, a rather unattractive, heavy woman who looked to be about sixty. She wore the pantsuit of the typical middle-management woman who could not advance on her looks. The black color of her hair looked unnatural to Joel, and she spoke with a high-toned squeaky voice that he found grating. She reminded him of an elementary school principal from his childhood.

"What's your impression of Harris?"

"You mean what do I think of him?"

"Yes." Joel wondered what she had not understood about the syntax.

"He's a troublemaker. He won't cooperate with what we're trying to do here." The warden seemed to struggle to keep her breath and pushed her sliding glasses up.

"How so?"

"He won't rehabilitate. Oh, he does all the menial assignments and work. He's shown skill at painting and gardening."

"I read in his file that he's a trained cook."

"Yes, well, that may be, but it serves no societal benefit. What good is his work if he won't believe in why he's doing it?"

"How is that?" Joel again had to consciously slow down to stay with the warden.

She exhaled loudly either from exertion or exacerbation. "Look at his numbers. He has failed every citizen course his entire time here."

"He probably has no intellectual aptitude." Joel interrupted.

"No." The warden seemed unable to catch her breath. "In his last course, the instructor brought to my attention that Harris scored one hundred percent on his pretest. Six weeks later he scored zero on the course posttest. No, he knows the material, he just chooses not to believe. He's been removed from past classes for arguing with the teachers and asking them all kinds of questions."

"You're kidding." Joel was genuinely shocked. In grade school one of the first things Joel learned was not to ask the teacher questions, but to accept the instruction. Even in college it was only considered appropriate to ask questions that enhanced the student's understanding, not to challenge a teacher's instruction.

"Within my first few weeks here," she said with a chuckle, "it came to my attention that some of the prisoners were in possession of Bibles."

"Really?"

"Yes! Obviously a clear violation of their constitutional rights. It never really did become clear how they came into possession of them. Anyway, I ordered all cells to be searched and the Bibles confiscated. Of course, Harris was one of the prisoners in possession of the contraband. He not only demanded an explanation from my officiating administrator, but claimed to have a constitutional right to the contraband."

Joel laughed as if he'd heard the punch line to a joke. "Do you suppose he really thinks that?"

"It doesn't really matter if he believes it or not. He says it out loud so others can hear him. Whether it's in the classroom, the cell block, or the prisoner recreation yard, they hear him. We are trying to re-educate these prisoners to accept federal authority, to accept their place, their function, and to work for the greater good. When he challenges the concepts that the instructors are trying to teach, he interferes with that. I've gotten reports from my assistance administrators that the things he says inspires the other prisoners, and that interferes with their progression."

"What do you do about it?"

"Oh, we isolate him in his cell, suspend his recreational reading, sensory deprivation…"

"How do you do that?"

"Shutter his window. Leave all his lights on, or leave them off, for several days at a time. It shuts him up for a while, but given a few weeks or several months, he's always back at it. Currently I have him barred from any citizen courses, and that seems to have limited the damage he's able to do."

"By the way, I saw in his file that he likes to read this Shakespeare fellow. Can you tell me much about that?"

"Good question. I've had my people look into that. Even our psychologist. No one can make a connection. I've even looked at some of the text myself; none of the dialogue or the plots make any sense. I don't see how he can be getting anything from that. All the same, he's been restricted from reading any of it for the last few years, and it's not had an effect."

"Hmm." Joel decided to drop that line of thought. "What is it like being around him? You said he inspires the other prisoners."

Warden Enrique laughed as they approached the security glass doors. "Oh, I never meet the prisoners. I have assistants for that sort of thing." Squinting her eyes, she looked through the security glass into the prisoner wing. "They tell me that he gives them confidence that they are right. That there is value in what they think, in what they believe, and that is what makes Harris dangerous, in my opinion."

"How so?" Joel was confused how a man in a maximum-security prison could be dangerous to the Federal Government.

"He uses the classroom to speak not of social justice, but of 'moral authority.' He argues for freedom over equality. Freedom of thought of all things! Here! Can you imagine the audacity? We are here to rehabilitate, to re-educate. Harris? He gives them hope in resisting our authority." The matronly warden turned to look at Joel. Her syrupy voice took a chilly edge to it. "I don't believe in the death penalty, Mr. Levine; but if I did, Harris would be the first prisoner I would order killed."

Joel nodded as if he agreed with her assessment. "I see."

"It has been a pleasure meeting you, Mr. Levine. My guard will escort you into the prisoner facility for your interview. Please tell Sandra LaGard if there is anything, anything at all, that she needs only to give me a call. Good luck with your project." The heavy woman turned and slowly waddled back down the hall from which they came. While very pleasant, and somewhat patronizing, Joel found it hard to believe this individual actually was in control of the most dangerous criminals to the Federal Government. Sexist or not, he wondered who really ran the prison.

With a slight humming noise, the security glass doors opened into the prisoner wing.

"Sir, if you will come this way, I will take you to the prisoner for your interview." The guard motioned Joel through the doorway. Joel still thought it seemed odd that this glass door and wall was all that separated the prisoners from the administrative wing of the facility.

"You ever had a prisoner try to break through this glass?" Joel asked.

The guard shook his head and smiled. "No, sir, not while I've been assigned here. I've heard stories from the senior guards about some of the prisoners trying to break through when the place first opened. By now they know it would take a tank to bust through this security glass."

Joel noticed the guard's name tape read REED. What were the odds of that? "And how long have you been working here, Reed?"

"About four years, sir."

"Is this your first job?" The guard didn't look older than twenty-two to Joel. His freckles gave him a boyish look.

"No, sir, it's my second. I was stationed at the Trotsky LEC for three years before this."

"In California?"

"Yes, sir, northeast of Dublin."

"What brought you out here to the Nevada desert?" Joel relished his ability to connect with the lower echelon types. He believed it always helped in getting information out of them.

"Orders, sir. I was reassigned."

"Have you ever met Harris?"

"XPP Harris, yes, sir, I have."

"XPP?"

"Harris is classified as an Extreme Political Prisoner."

"What's your take on him?"

"He's a nice old man. Never gives us guards any trouble. Always polite. Even calls us sir."

"Really!?" Joel was shocked. "So would you say he has become submissive over the years?" Joel found this paradoxical. Harris challenged the teachers, but not the guards.

Was he a coward? A bully? Misogynist? Both? It would certainly fit the profile of Clark's Marine Corps.

"No, sir, it ain't like that. It's more like he likes us."

"Hmm. You think he's just sucking up to you all just to get preferential treatment?"

"No, sir." Reed chuckled. "There's nothing about the man that seems like he's kissing anybody's ass. It's like…" Reed stopped and looked Joel right in the eye. Joel was glad to be making a connection with the guard, but the man's seriousness made Joel slightly uncomfortable. "It's like he respects us or something. I've never seen a prisoner act quite like he does. It's like he enjoys it or something. At Trotsky, where we had mostly straight-out criminal prisoners, they'd cuss at us, spit on us, throw urine, feces, semen, etc. Hell, he's even more polite to me than anybody I come across on the outside in town."

"Maybe he's just trying to get you to be nice to him. Make his time here easier?"

"No, sir, like I said, it ain't like that. He doesn't seem to care about making his time easier. Like he won't stoop to that or something. If anything, he seems to take pride in making his time harder. It's like he takes pride in acting the way he does. Takes pride in speaking what he thinks. As if he's proud of being what he is."

"Huh." Joel was baffled. Could this be the effect of Harris's Marine Corps indoctrination? Marine Corps brainwashing? The two moved on.

"You sound like you kind of have a liking for Harris?"

"No, sir, not at all. As a guard, you have to be vigilant about developing emotions, good or bad, towards the prisoners. I'll tell you though, there is something likable about him. It's hard to explain. He puts out this aura, this positive vibe in the way he acts. Supposedly, my great-great-grandfather, or something, was a Marine in the war against Islam. His dad was supposed to have been a Marine in the war against communism before that. There is something about Harris that makes me hope that they were something like him. That maybe they weren't as bad a people as I've been taught to believe."

"I know what you mean." Immediately Joel thought of his own grandfather. "I think I understand you, anyway." He thought that this was what made Harris dangerous today.

"Remember, sir, good vibes or not, Harris is a trained, cold-blooded killer. The man has brutally murdered innocent people. He has the most violent history of any prisoner in federal incarceration. Never, sir, I repeat, never get too comfortable around him."

"Absolutely." Joel was still drifting back from a flash of memories of his grandfather.

In college Joel had learned of the United States Marine Corps of the Clark era indoctrinating Marines with a large sense of ego. Much of that, however, was based on the dehumanization of others. Everyone else was inferior; thus the Marines were superior. Showing respect and politeness to the prison guards did not fit this model. However, it did fit into the paradox of model prisoner and killer inmate. Most likely, Joel thought, the guard was not smart enough to figure out that he was being manipulated by Harris. But could an old man, after fifty years of prison, be capable of manipulating anybody? Who would he meet, respectful old man or savage killer? Which would best fit Joel's needs?

"Here we are, sir. This is the counseling room. Another guard will bring Harris here shortly. Please feel free to make use of the workstation, armchairs, and coffee maker. You'll notice a big red button located next to all three. Please hit that if you ever get any sense of feeling threatened or frightened. Remember, Harris is a proven savage killer.

"Again, sir, my name is Reed if you need anything."

"Thank you, guard." Joel's attention was divided. Memories of his grandfather were fading, and the realization that Harris was a convicted murderer was starting to sink in. In the excitement over his new status and rise in the federal bureaucracy, it had not occurred to him that he would be spending hours, days, in one-on-one conversation with a savage killer. Joel did not even know anyone who had been in a fistfight, let alone been in one himself. It was scary. He looked at the red buttons. He wondered if he would have what it'd take to hit one of the red buttons if he needed to, or could Harris kill him first?

Joel sat down at the workstation; it was just a table with several outlets next to the red button. He set up his laptop and an audio/video recorder for the interview. He opened Harris's file and immediately his picture popped up. Joel stared at the young man with dark red hair and a fair complexion with close-set, dark eyes that looked narrow above the high cheekbones. The eyes looked intense. The scar looked ragged and savage across the left side of his face. Savage, the same word Reed had used to describe the man. Who would win in a fight, Harris or Perro? Joel felt beyond a doubt that Harris, at least Harris of fifty years ago, would crush Perro without so much as batting an eye. Yet Harris was in prison and Perro was the most powerful person in the Federal Government. At that moment Joel wondered just how that could have happened.

The door opened. Reed and another guard escorted Harris into the room. His ankles were shackled. He had enough chain to walk, but not to run. Did he have a limp, or was his movement inhibited by the chain? His wrists were cuffed to a chain around his waist. Harris was shorter than both the guards, but stood straight. His file stated that he stood seventy-one inches when he was incarcerated. It appeared that he had not become stooped over the years. He appeared to still be in good physical condition for his age, although he looked much thinner than the 195 pounds stated in his file. The guards sat him down at the table and attached the chain that bound his feet to an anchor in the floor. They released his wrists, so he again had movement of his arms. His hair was now all white, but still cropped short.

"Sir, we can stay in the room if you like," Reed offered.

"That will not be necessary, guard." Part of Joel wanted to keep them in the room, but he thought Harris would be more likely to open up if they were alone. He watched the guards leave the room and close the door. Joel turned his gaze to look into the face of the "savage" killer. Perhaps it was the light reflecting off the workstation, but Joel thought Harris's eyes looked more of a dark gray than brown as his file stated. The evil face smiled. His chained hand reached across the table as far as he could reach.

"How do you do? I'm Sean Harris."

CHAPTER FIVE

"So now the Federal Government wants to celebrate my history to, what, mark fifty years since I was convicted of murder and treason?" His tone was sarcastic even when said with a smile.

"The Federal Government wants to honor your service, not your conviction." Ten minutes into this meeting and Joel feared his career was sunk before it could really set sail.

Harris let out a deep laugh. "I thought that's what my conviction was."

"It's—look, we just want to tell your story. We want the people to know what you've done." And in that Joel thought he was telling the truth.

"We? You, sir, Mr. Levine, what do you hope to accomplish from this interview?"

Joel was uncomfortable. He knew the answer, but felt it was taboo to express a desire to do something for his own personal benefit. One was supposed to state desired goals in the context of the common good, not personal achievement.

"If I deliver your story in all its detail, I can get VIP status; it will escalate my career. My lifestyle, my standard of living will improve," Joel said with forced bluntness.

"Well, that makes sense. It's got to be quite a motivation for you."

"It is."

"And, of course, you'll have the satisfaction of allowing millions of Americans to honor my service." The evil face smiled and Joel could not tell what it meant.

"Look, our intention is not to make you look like a bad guy, just to tell the history of the Marine Corps in the Clark era, the Sino-American War, and the attempted coup during the Tang presidency from your perspective. You know, what was the atmosphere like, the people, your influences, that sort of thing. Your story, in your words." Joel felt inspired and thought the last words were rather clever. The tactic had been taught in journalism school. Everyone wanted to have their voice heard. Everyone wanted their moment on center stage, and this desire was easy to manipulate. Harris could have his story told in his words, as long as that was what the madame general wanted.

"My story benefits you; it benefits somebody in the Federal Government for them to have sent you down here." Harris sat up a little straighter. "What's *my* benefit?"

Joel did not know how to respond. This scenario had never played out in his imagination. He was silent.

"Is the Federal Agency of Public Safety going to incarcerate me in a Hawaiian resort? Perhaps the madame general will allow the president to grow a pair of balls and he'll pardon me for my crimes."

Joel was taken aback a bit. He was not used to hearing anyone speak so cynically of their government leaders, outside of his grandfather, especially the madame general and from someone of such a low stature. But then he really only associated with academics and journalists. They at least always qualified their sarcasm. Harris just stared at Joel. What was he to do?

"Is there something you want? I could take your request to the warden."

"You can do more than that! I spent a third of my life here and you're the first journalist to walk into this shit hole. The Federal Government doesn't send us here to 'honor our service' or 'tell our story in our words' kind of horseshit. We're here to be hidden or destroyed. You're here 'cause somebody high up wants to use my story. That means somebody high up is going to have to pay for it."

"What is it you want?" Joel was too taken aback not to ask.

"Well, to start with, I want another Bible, and not one of those government-edited pieces of shit that get floated around every so often. I want an unabridged Old and New Testament—King James, New Revised, English Standard, I don't care, just as long as it hasn't been printed in the last forty years. Then maybe—"

"Wait a minute. There are laws. This is federal property. Even just having religious material here is a violation of your constitutional rights—"

"You ever read the Constitution, Mr. Levine?"

"Well, no, I'm not a lawyer and not trained to understand it. Besides, we have hate speech laws now, and how am I supposed to get an old copy of the Bible?"

"That's for your boss to worry about, not you. Now in addition, if you want me to talk all day long, and I'm betting you do, a little high-quality bourbon would go a long way to loosening my tongue. Oh, and get me outside. I want to see a horizon. Get me outside with a little bourbon, you will not be able to shut my old ass up. Smoking makes me chatty as well, so while you're at it bring some high-quality cigars to go with that bourbon."

"I thought Christians were forbidden to smoke and drink alcohol." Joel seized the opportunity to guilt Harris into submission.

"Are you a Christian?"

"Of course not!" Joel laughingly responded.

"You ever read the New Testament?"

"I don't see what that has to do with—"

"Then you let me worry about my hypocrisy and you tend to your own."

"Harris, this is federal property and that stuff is illegal."

"We both know a lot of 'illegal' things happen on federal property. You talk to your boss." An image of the madame general and Sergeant MacTaggart popped into Joel's head. He resigned to Harris's wishes.

"I'll talk to my boss. Is there anything else you want?"

"Yes, sir, there is, come to think of it. I always want guards around us. As many as you want, but no less than two. You understand me?"

"Yes, but why do you want guards around? I would think you would be less inhibited with them gone."

At this Harris laughed. "Mr. Levine, I'm worried that you might hurt me." The prisoner winked, got up, and with a slight limp walked to the wall and hit the red button. There was a loud buzz, and the guard opened the door.

"Sir, it has been a pleasure meeting you. I sincerely hope to see you again and tell you *my own* story in *my own* words." The sinister-looking face smiled at Joel and then walked out of the room.

Joel did not look forward to the phone call to Sandra LaGard, afraid that she might find him incompetent, but she took all the demands in stride. If she was angry, it was not noticeable on the phone. What surprised Joel even more than her tone was that she told him all the requested items would arrive before 8 a.m. LaGard said she would talk to the warden and arrange for the interviews to take place outside. Her take on the guards was that Harris was trying to put them at ease a bit. He would have known there would be no way to get outside the prison's high walls without an army of guards surrounding him.

True to LaGard's word, when Joel arrived at Reid at 8:30 a.m., there was a large shade tent set up with all the amenities one could possibly want for an outdoor brunch. There was an assortment of fresh fruit, bagels, pastries, juice, and coffee. In addition was a bottle of Federal VIP bourbon. Joel had never tried or even seen it before. He had only heard that it was one of the latest in trendy status symbols that were the benefits of the higher echelon of federal bureaucracy. Joel helped himself to a bagel with cream cheese and a coffee. He was pleasantly surprised that it was better than the stuff at the hotel, and bitterly surprised that the Federal Government would do so much to accommodate a criminal like Harris. The man had committed murder and treason, after all. To Joel's way of thinking, Harris should have been submissive and compliant, hoping to be granted leniency. Instead, he made demands and the government gave in to them. Admittedly, LaGard was doing whatever it took to get the story that the madame general wanted. What really bugged Joel was that Harris seemed to be in more control of the situation than he was.

"Good morning, Mr. Levine. This is a fine day, is it not?" Harris was unchained and he limped his way to the buffet and then sat down with an orange, banana, and a cup of coffee. The old, scarred face stared into the sky and took a deep breath. Harris seemed to relax and to soften a bit. Joel thought he saw an expression of nostalgia in the old man's dark eyes. He immediately felt inspired. Perhaps there was a method to this madness; perhaps he could get this old man to talk, to expose his skeletons, to bare his soul to him.

"Yes, yes, it is," Joel replied as a gratuity. "I thought today we could start off with you telling me about your childhood. Tell me about your hometown, family, childhood friends. You know, that sort of thing, before we get into your time in the Marines."

"Oh, this is fresh. Perfect! Please have a slice." Harris had worked his way through the orange's peel with a chartreuse plastic utensil and now held out a piece to the writer. Joel shook his head and mouthed the word no, as if it were slightly beneath him to go through this ritual. "Sure? It's good stuff." Harris popped a piece into his mouth and grunted with satisfaction.

Joel thought he had never seen anyone enjoy an orange so much. He did not understand just what the big deal was. He liked the taste, but the peel was a hassle to deal with, it made one's hands sticky, and there was all that stringlike stuff. Joel rationalized that Harris was intellectually inferior and, most probably, easily distracted or entertained by things like food and drinks. He was starting to convince himself that LaGard was a genius. He made a mental note to make himself pleasing to her.

"Harris, tell me about your hometown; tell me about your family."

"Well, I'm sure you know that I was born in Topeka, Kansas." Harris spoke between bites of orange. "My dad owned about ten acres just west of town, just south of the Kansas River. Looking back, it was a great place to grow up. We had a pond from a natural spring. There were woods to play in. Railroad tracks and the Kansas River were nearby. It was a great playground."

"Your parents, they just let you run around unsupervised out in the woods?"

"Oh yeah." Harris smiled as the memories flooded his mind. "I remember my dad always telling my mom the woods were safer than the city."

"Really?" Joel was a bit incredulous. He had grown up in urban Seattle. The scarred face smiled like he was in on a secret that Joel was not. Harris straightened up, leaned back in his chair, and stared at the horizon.

"It all seemed so normal then; now it seems like it was paradise. The flowers in spring, shades of green in the summer heat, leaves changing in the fall, the woods glimmering with snow on a full moon." His look went back to Joel. "Hell, I even miss those goddamned chiggers."

"What are chiggers?" Joel asked, hoping it would give him a lead into some kind of racist, white supremacist angle on the story.

"They're a bug, a mite, really. They eat human skin."

"What?" Joel didn't believe him. The scarred face smiled. He enjoyed telling people things that they did not know.

"Tiny little things, bite into your skin and eat for a few days. They leave these little welts. The itching will drive you insane!" Harris leaned back again, looking off into the past. "I can remember waking up from scratching the welts in my sleep. I'd scratch them till they bled," he said, smiling.

Joel's face showed revulsion. "And you miss these things?" Joel's voice was more squeamish than he would have liked.

"Not really." Harris's mind began to drift back to the present. "I miss the summers that I got them."

"You have fond memories of your summer breaks from school?" Joel was pleased with his stealthy segue into Harris's education for just a brief moment; for suddenly the old man's dark eyes narrowed and looked him right in the eye.

"Don't bullshit me, Mr. Levine." The voice sounded much younger and stronger than the man who spoke them looked. "You know goddamn well I was homeschooled."

Joel broke eye contact. It made him too uncomfortable. "Yeah, I know." He began looking around, as if he could find what to say next.

"You think it's part of the reason I did what I did, huh?" Harris's tone had changed to almost sounding sympathetic. "At the time of my trial—" he looked away as was his habit when thinking of the past "—it really angered me that lawyers and journalists argued that my parents, my state, the Marine Corps, my religion were all at fault. I felt as if they were on trial with me, and they were, in a way. That seemed to be the effect anyhow. Now I understand it better." Harris gently laughed. "One of the benefits of time is to think. All of those things did have a role. All of those things made me who I was, who I am today."

"Why did they homeschool you? What did they teach you?" Joel eagerly asked. He wanted to capitalize on Harris's admission. "What kind of influence were your parents?"

***

It was as if the earth had broken open and roared. It was like nothing Sean had ever heard or seen, but it was exactly as he had imagined it would be. That was what had amazed him the most. The gun went off exactly as the six-year-old boy had expected based solely from his experience watching cartoons. He thought the conical flame that had extended from the end of the barrel looked just as it did in the cartoons and comics he was familiar with. The *BANG, BANG* sound effects did not quite capture the experience, however. Even the family's surround sound system had not prepared him for the noise. The gun was a sound that could be felt as much as heard. The smoke drifting from the end of the barrel was also a familiar look from the comics, but the smell was a whole new sensation. The image was fleeting, but it was instantly engraved in the boy's brain. He loved the weapon.

"Now take a look at this," the boy's father said while holstering his Colt Python .357 Magnum. They walked over to the small cedar tree. They grew all over the property. Sean's father hated them, and indeed they did seem to grow on the property like weeds. The base of the tree's trunk was about four to five inches in diameter and had a tiny little hole, less than half an inch wide, in the front.

"See that? That's what the bullet does on the way in. Now look back here." Sean excitedly followed his father to the opposite side of the tree. "See all that splintered wood? The bullet makes a small hole on the way in, but a big one on the way out."

Daniel Harris looked his son in the eye. "You pull that trigger on a man, on your brother, on your sister, your mother or me, you're gonna put a tiny hole in the front and a hole about the size of your fist in the back."

The boy was a bit uncomfortable with the serious tone in his father's voice. It reminded him of getting into trouble, although he knew he was not. He returned his father's gaze right back into his eyes.

"Son, this is not a toy. You play with this and put a bullet through your brother's head, there won't be splintered wood, but shattered skull, blood, and brain matter all over the floor and wall. Your brother will be dead, and you will be your brother's killer. Is that what you want?"

"No." Sean's excitement was still there, but was completely in check.

"Neither do I, son." His father's tone had softened a bit. "A gun is not to be played with. That's what your toy guns are for. I keep grandpa's old gun in my nightstand because if someone breaks into our home to do harm to your mother, sister, brother, or you"—the edge was back in his father's voice—"I will kill the son of a bitch. Do you understand?"

"Yes." The boy looked back into his father's eyes. He so much wanted to join his father in this fight to protect his family. "Daddy, are the men you fought going to come after us?"

Daniel Harris was a veteran of the wars in western and central Asia. He had fought Muslim men who sought the destruction of the United States of America and the Christian faith. Sean had heard his father complain of American leaders that had not done what they could to win those wars, and had even allowed some of those people to migrate into the United States. The same government that sent Daniel Harris to fight Muslim jihadists, but not destroy them, allowed Muslim jihadists to move into the country and set up little colonies throughout the United States. He'd heard his father talk of their predominance around the Great Lakes region.

"I don't know, son." Daniel began to move back to their pickup to retrieve a .22 rifle. "I'd like to tell you no. Thank God the Russians are taking care of those bastards in the Old World, but we're not doing nothing about them here." He opened a box of .22-caliber rounds. "Now watch," Dan said as he opened the tubular magazine of a Colt rifle and began to load it. "Hell, son, the enemies of this country seem to be getting stronger every day. Not just Muslim jihadists either. A lot of native-born Americans are bad guys these days. For whatever reason they hate this country, they hate your God, they hate your freedom, they hate you. They will do whatever they can to make America weak, to make you weak."

"Why?" Sean was truly confused by such self-hating, self-destructive Americans.

"Good question," Dan Harris said with a sad half smile. "Some have been taught to hate themselves and to seek redemption in your destruction. Others are just born hateful people, like it's natural for them to be evil. Others? They hate freedom because they want to control. As if they can make themselves gods if they can just control enough. In the end it don't matter what their reason is. They'll kill you or enslave you if they can." He turned to his son again and smiled. "They'll have to kill me first before I let that happen."

Sean smiled back. "They'll have to kill me too!" Sean felt confident. He thought no one could kill his father. He was too big, too strong, and too smart. Americans were the best people, and his father was the best American. How could they lose if they fought their best?

"That's why today we're teaching you to shoot. In this world, son, a man has got to know how to fight." Daniel stopped and thought for a moment. "A man has got to know how to kill, if he's gonna stay free."

Sean lay in bed, unable to sleep. The clock on his nightstand read 1:49 and changed to 1:50 before his eyes. The realization that nothing could stop the morning hurt; it frightened him. Tears welled up in his eyes and he silently began to cry. Now added was the fear that he would awake his younger brother, who would see him crying and tell their father. He had not always hated school. He had been excited when he had started kindergarten just over a year ago. At the time, he felt like he was starting a great adventure. His mother had bought special school gear for him. He'd gotten new clothes, new shoes, and an official identification badge with his picture on it. His father had complained a bit about the badge, but his mother had chided him to be quiet and not ruin it for the boy.

His father complained that school had changed since he was a boy. Now the school children were required to wear shirts that were blue, white or gray, in addition to a photo ID. Boys were required to wear khaki pants and the girls, skirts. Most parents in the area applauded the new regulations. They expressed pleasure at the new "high standards." Dan Harris had complained. He wanted to see higher standards in reading, writing, and arithmetic.

"Every year kids are learning less and less and the school wants to focus on what clothes the kids are wearing," Sean would hear his father complain. "The kids have a right to be individuals." What had really set his father off was when Sean, on a "student choice day" was not allowed to wear a shirt with an American Revolutionary Minuteman on it, due to the school's no-tolerance policy towards weapons of any sort.

"What kind of horseshit is this?!" Dan Harris exclaimed when he found out.

"Hmmm hmmm!" Sharon Harris warned her husband to watch his language.

"Well, really! How the fu—foxtrot does this prevent crime?" He himself was a law enforcement officer for the Kansas Bureau of Investigation. "It's a bunch of crap. They're not making the kids any safer. If anything, all they're doing, whether they realize it or not, is not letting the kids be Americans or show pride in being American."

Overall, however, Sean liked kindergarten. It was his first-grade year when he really began to hate school.

For the very first art project during the very first week of school, Miss Crane handed out large blue sheets of construction paper.

"Listen, children. Draw a big X on one side of your paper. You will only be allowed to draw on one side of the paper. Okay?" She continued in a slow, saccharine tone, "You will not be allowed to start over. Are you all listening? You all must learn to live with your mistakes. We have to learn to live with our imperfections.

"Very good." Miss Crane walked through the classroom, checking to see that the students followed her instructions.

"Very good. Excellent. Sean?! What is this?!" Sean had drawn a giant X on the back and then four smaller Xs in the four quadrants of the big X. "Did I tell you to draw more than one X? No!" she sternly chastised without giving him a chance to respond. The young teacher picked up his blue construction paper and ripped it in half. "Sean, until you learn to follow instructions, you will not be allowed to participate in art."

His school year went downhill from there. He found the days long and boring. Miss Crane insisted that everyone move at the same slow rate. Sean would often find himself done with an assignment and sitting with nothing to do. He began to hide books in his desk. He read them during his downtime waiting for assignments. At least until he was discovered by Miss Crane. For the next three days he sat in the time-out corner during indoor recess.

Sean found the time of sitting and doing nothing at school painfully boring, but not as painful as the packets of homework that were sent home with him to be completed during the week. He spent at least an hour at home doing schoolwork that was not getting done at school because of Miss Crane's insistence on a slow pace for all students. When Sean complained of this to his parents, he was fluffed off as being lazy. He would then get a speech from one of his parents on the importance of an education.

It was not until one night when his father was home to help him with his homework that Sean felt like his dad could see a bit of his point of view. Dan had become rather flustered with a math assignment that made no sense to him. Not that he wasn't good with numbers. He was a trained pilot and was good at making calculations in his head. He kept referring to the confusing questions as asinine, which would make Sean giggle because it sounded like it might be a bad word. However, it was the social studies work that caused Dan Harris to blow his top. It started out easy enough with a short reading about Rosa Parks, Dr. Martin Luther King Jr., and the Civil Rights Movement of the 1950s and '60s. Then the students were expected to answer hypothetical questions about racist white cops that stole from and murdered black people. As a KBI agent he did not care to see law enforcement represented as organized crime to his six-year-old son, whom he was trying to teach to respect the law and its officers. This led to a discussion between father and son where Mr. Harris learned that Sean had not learned one thing, in school anyway, about George Washington, Thomas Jefferson, or Benjamin Franklin. In addition to finding out how much time Sean spent doing nothing and getting in trouble for reading, it was too much for Dan Harris. The next day he demanded a meeting with the principal and teacher.

Sean was actually a little disappointed that everyone was so nice to each other at the meeting. Secretly he was hoping that his father would tear into Miss Crane. That didn't happen, but it was clear to Sean that between the principal, Miss Crane, and his dad, his dad was the boss. Their behavior was a lot less bossy in front of his father, and they had no good answers when he asked them how they could teach the Civil Rights movement to first graders without putting it in the context of the ideas and values of our Founding Fathers.

As contrite as Miss Crane had been in front of his father, she seemed all the nastier to Sean at school. A couple of weeks after the meeting, the students were working on another art project. The art theme for the project was how people could help others. One girl had drawn a picture of people working in an animal shelter. Another had drawn a picture of someone giving money to a person with a sign on the street corner.

Sean was excited to explain his work before the class. His work, his topic, was a source of pride for him. He'd drawn a picture of his father flying a helicopter, killing bad guys when he was an Army pilot in the Islamic Wars.

"Sean," Miss Crane started in her nasally, self-righteous tone, "how is your father *killing human beings* helping people?"

"Because he's killing the bad guys so they don't kill good guys and before they can come here and kill us," Sean replied with a great deal of pride.

"You know, Sean, over there *they* think *your father* is one of the bad guys."

Sean's six-year-old mind could not figure out how to respond. He was shocked; he was hurt that someone would imply his father could be one of the bad guys.

"That's exactly the kind of work I expect from you, Sean.

"Alexi, tell us about your project..."

Sean sat down, deflated, angered, and humiliated. He didn't want the tears to well up in his eyes, but he couldn't stop them any more than he could stop Miss Crane.

"Sean, are you all right? Are you crying?" the teacher asked before the class to his greater embarrassment.

"No!" Sean answered in a very non-believable voice. He wiped his tears and wished he could disappear.

At times children could be the most vile and cruelest people on earth. Sean got a lesson on that fact during recess that day. Somehow, someway, Jordon Miller had found out that Sean had been crying in class. Jordon Miller was easily the biggest kid in the third grade. In fact, he would have been the biggest kid in the fifth grade had he been two years older. Sean's recess time was for first through third grade, and for thirty minutes twice a day Jordon Miller was the biggest, toughest guy around. For reasons that even Jordon Miller could not have explained, he felt compelled to use his burgeoning size and strength to intimidate and demean others. It was from this that he derived his greatest joy in life. For him to find out that Sean Harris was crying in class about his daddy being a "bad guy" was a gift, a golden opportunity. He could not let it pass.

On the playground he approached the small redheaded boy playing in the sand pit. Plenty of kids were around. He couldn't have picked a better scenario.

"Is this the red-haired pussy crying in class earlier?"

Sean hoped the voice of Jordon Miller was not talking to him, but it was. He tried to ignore it and keep playing in the sand.

"Hey! I'm talking to you!" Miller kicked sand into Sean's face. He spat the sand out of his mouth.

"Stop it." Sean's fear made him sound uncharacteristically submissive.

"Why, crybaby? You gonna call your daddy and have him fly around and kill me? Like he did to other kids during the war? You a big pussy like your *daddy*? Huh, crybaby?" He kicked sand again.

Sean went to stand up, which was exactly what Jordan Miller expected. He'd been through this kind of scene before. Before Sean could completely stand up, Miller nailed him with a right hook, and Sean went down with a bloody nose. He had never been punched before and did not know how to respond. A part of his brain told him not to stand up again lest he get punched again.

"Fucking red-haired pussy!" Miller kicked Sean in the stomach. The air exploded out of him, and he thought he would die for the inability to breathe.

Jordan Miller truly laughed, not one of the fake laughs common with children, and strolled off triumphant and happy.

Shortly thereafter, Miss Crane, who was on recess duty, showed up and asked if Sean was all right.

"You know, you really need to be careful of what you say to others. You make them mad and you'll get this kind of response. Go to the little boys' room and clean the blood off your face."

At that moment Sean's six-year-old brain comprehended that Miss Crane and Jordon Miller were evil. They were the type of people that his father had killed in the war to keep him safe. Yet Sean was defeated by them. He was beaten. He was inferior. He did not know how to respond. He was ashamed. He did not know what to do. His father would know, but Sean was too ashamed to tell him.

Sean's response was to pretend to be sick to avoid school for the next five days. His father was working and it was easy to pull this over on his mother. Then his father came home for the next few days. He was far more skeptical and began to ask questions. Somehow, against Sean's will, he had spilled the beans to his father. He had never seen his father so angry.

"Get your ass out of bed!" Dan Harris shouted the next morning, waking the boy up. Instead of school that day, Dan took his son to a sporting goods store and bought some youth boxing gloves. Before dinner that night, he also had the boy enrolled in a local jiujitsu club. Thus began Sean's training in combat. Dan Harris would not let his son grow up to be a victim.

Sean had jiujitsu class twice a week, sometimes three. When Dan had time off from work, they were down in the basement with the gloves on. Sean loved the jiujitsu classes; he hated boxing with his father. His dad was meaner than Jordan Miller. He'd hit him, call him names; he seemed merciless. When it was all over, Dan would always hug his son and tell him he loved him, but it was hell for Sean until then.

The teasing at school had not ceased. Some days were better; some days were worse. His father told him not to start trouble, but not to run from it. He had been told not to punch another kid unless he was punched. Miller hadn't punched him since their first encounter, but he said things that made Sean feel less than human, made him feel like the lowest life on earth. Sean could never quite think of what to say back, and when he did, Jordon Miller always seem to have a reply that made Sean feel even worse. He hated school. He hated his life. He began to cry in his room in the evenings, thinking about having to go back to school the next day. One night his father saw him crying.

"Sean, what's wrong, buddy?"

"I-I-I don't know," Sean stammered.

"Yeah, you do, little man. Tell me so I can help you with it."

Sean proceeded to tell him all he had gone through at the hands of Jordan Miller over the last few months.

"Son, you mean to tell me you're in here crying cause that big kid is still calling you names or some other silly ass shit?" Dan Harris fought to keep his temper under control.

"I think so."

"Oh, horseshit, son! If you don't know, who the hell does?" Sean stared silently at his father. Hating his father for not understanding. Hating himself for not having done anything about his problem.

"That boy says a goddamn word, he fucking looks at you funny, you break his goddamn nose! You understand me? Kick him in the shin first. Punch him in the sternum, just like we practiced, but you break his fucking nose. Do you understand me?"

"Yes," Sean answered, wide eyed, afraid to say anything else.

"I promise you, son, I catch you crying like this again over some piece of shit like this Jordon Miller and you're doing nothing about it, I will whip your ass with the belt. Do you understand me? I don't care if you win! I don't care if you lose! You come home with your nose on the side of your face, I don't give a damn! You stand up for yourself! You understand? I catch you crying again, I *will* give you something to cry about!

"You're a good boy, Sean." Dan Harris softened his tone. "I love you very much. You are too good of a boy to allow yourself to be bullied by that punk. You, my little man, are worth fighting for, and that is what I expect you to do for yourself."

So young Sean lay in bed, fearful of the next day. Afraid to go to school. Afraid to stay home. Afraid to fight Jordon Miller. Afraid not to.

Jordon Miller was having a particularly bad day. It started when he had complained to his mother about there being no milk in the house for his cereal. She tore into him. Told him he was as worthless as the father he had never met. He was as worthless as the government that could not give them enough money to live on. She made it clear she thought he was worthless, but at school he was a god. Kids listened to him. Teachers coddled him. He was feared; he had power. That made him feel good, and today he needed to feel good.

At recess he saw that little redheaded wimp Harris playing in the sand, building whatever the hell he thought he was building. It was time for Jordon Miller to feel good.

"Well, if it isn't the little red-haired pussy crybaby. You gonna cry for me, redheaded pussy?"

Sean froze in the sand, staring at the "parking garage" he was trying to build. Even at his young age he knew this was the time to confront his fear, to face what he was scared of. His battle had arrived.

Through a sudden inspiration, he stayed on all fours and said nothing. Miller approached. Sean could hear his father's voice in his head, telling him to fight with his mind as well as his fists. Sean figured Miller wanted to get close enough to kick sand in his face again. Sean could use that to his advantage, but he would have to act fast.

"Hey, you little shit, look at me when I talk to you!" Miller shouted, ready to kick his ass.

Sean pretended to ignore him, which he had often done for real in the past. When Miller was within about five feet, Sean jumped up with a hand full of sand and threw it in his face. The tactic was great, but the results would be short lived if Sean did nothing else. While Miller made the mistake of rubbing the sand further into his eyes with his hands, young Sean jumped up and kicked him square in the left shin. The larger boy bent over in pain and howled. His mother had slapped him plenty of times, but this was a new pain to him. Instinctively he bent over. His face was level with Sean's, so Sean did what he had practiced with his father. He threw his hardest right punch into the bigger boy's nose. Followed by the hardest left he had ever thrown. Followed again by an even harder right. Miller went down. Sean wanted to celebrate, but he was too scared to stop fighting. If he stopped, Miller might beat him up. Sean jumped on top of the boy. He kept punching. He aimed for the nose. He could hear the other kids around him yelling, but he did not pay attention. Sean's focus was on Miller's nose. Over and over again he kept punching. Sean felt better with every punch. He felt good. He felt power.

"Stop it! Stop it!" was the hysterical screech of the second-grade teacher on duty. She pulled little Sean Harris off the legendary Jordon Miller, who was sobbing and screaming in pain. Blood was all over Miller's face. Blood was all over

64

Sean's hands. For the first time in his life Sean Harris knew what it was to feel like a man.

"Surely you can understand, Mr. Harris, that we cannot let students just go about taking matters into their own hands."

Dan Harris had not cared for the principal the first time he had met him; now he was really starting to detest him. The man was young and soft. Not really overweight, but just doughy looking with no sign of visible muscle tissue. The guy appeared to be in his early to midthirties, way too young to be that soft and to have the kind of fat that spilled over the edge of his collar. His effeminate softness was accentuated by the fashionable trim cut of the principal's clothes. Dan Harris thought any man over the age of twenty-two that wore those tight, "skinny" pants looked like a queer. Now he had one of these candy-pants-wearing queers sitting in front of him, self-righteously explaining how inappropriate it was for his own son to defend himself from some bully that had spent the previous months earning the ass kicking he got.

The older Harris looked over at his son, who had his head down, staring at his feet as if he'd done something wrong. It broke Dan Harris's heart. It was more than he could stand.

"Listen, boy"—no one as yet realized the reference was to the principal—"just who the hell is my son supposed to depend on to protect him from that dumpy little asshole out there."

Sean looked up, pleasantly surprised. His father only spoke like this when he was angry or with old Army buddies. He wanted so bad to see his father tear into the principal, and maybe Miss Crane while he was at it.

"You've not protected him yet and only been there to chastise him when he takes on a man's right to self-defense." Sean felt proud when he heard his father describe him as a man. He was no longer looking at his feet, but at the doughy principal and his father. He was enjoying this.

"Mr. Harris," the principal interjected, "I don't think you understand. We can't have students defending themselves with acts of violence. It violates district regulations. I understand—"

"Hell, I doubt you even understand how to…" Dan Harris decided not to go there with his six-year-old son in the room. "Understand this, you emasculate little twit, my son is no longer enrolled in your school. I would no more entrust his education to you than the goddamn fire hydrant out front."

Sean loved what he was hearing. He wondered what the principal would do next, but the doughy man sat there red faced, wide eyed, and did not say a word.

"Come on, son. Let's get your stuff and get out of here." They got up and turned to leave.

"Mr. Harris, there are certain procedures—" the principal called out, but Dan Harris shut the door and walked on.

In the parking lot, heading towards Dan Harris's Ford pickup truck, Sean felt on top of the world.

"Don't get too excited, Sean, your mother and I are going to work your young butt off at home. A man's best weapon is his brain, and we're gonna see to it that yours is the sharpest around. You understand me?"

"Yes, sir, and, Daddy?"

"Yes?"

"What does e-mas-cu-late mean?"

CHAPTER SIX

"But you don't think you missed out?" Joel was baffled.

"On what?"

"You know, friends, socializing, parties...your high school prom! for example."

"Ha! I've not missed out on much that this life on earth has had to offer," Harris scoffed as he admired the bourbon in his glass and then took a sip. "I better watch this stuff or your recordings won't make any sense. Is the bourbon not to your liking, Mr. Levine?"

Truth was that it wasn't. Joel knew it was supposed to be the hot drink among the elites, but he didn't care for it. He found the taste, the feel of the alcohol too strong for him. It made his mouth and throat burn. Besides, the little he'd had was already making him feel a little dizzy.

"No, it's fine." Joel did not want to admit his distaste for the latest alcohol fad. "So you have a lot of fond memories from those years?"

"Absolutely. Those homeschooling years before the war are some of my fondest memories of my life. I spent a lot of time playing with friends. I played baseball, and I was on a wrestling team. I spent a lot of time exploring the woods by the river. I learned archery and firearms. Gosh, my exposure to literature and theater was unparalleled among my peers. I'd never gotten that in public school."

"Really?" Joel was somewhat condescending in his tone. He wondered how a mere law enforcement officer and a housewife could possibly give their child a superior education. Harris's eyes locked with Levine's.

"Don't be so cynical or elitist towards my parents, Levine. Old fart or not, I can still kill your candy ass before they can stop me." The scary-looking face smiled. Joel was too frightened by his tone not to believe him. "Both my parents had degrees in English literature. It's how they met in college."

This information was news to Joel. Was Harris lying? If not, why would Harris's file describe his mother as uneducated?

"Time spent with my mother, father, brother and sister," the old man continued, "those memories, those people are so precious to me now. No, Mr. Levine, I didn't miss out on jack shit." The old man's eyes went distant, like he was in another time and place.

"If it was all so precious to you, why end it by going into the Marine Corps?" Joel interrupted.

Harris's eyes darted back and stared with intensity into Joel's. "Because of the war, you goddamn fool." He immediately softened, as if talking to a child. "You talk about the high school prom? Why the fuck would I want to dress up in a monkey suit and go shake my ass on a dance floor when the ChiComs had invaded our land? That's just fucking insane! Our land was invaded. Americans were being killed. We were fighting for our very survival!"

Harris's words reminded Joel of his grandfather.

"Besides," Harris continued, "those sweet days ended as soon as the war started." His voice took on a more melancholy tone. "My father would have been exempt from service. He was already a vet and a KBI agent. He could have legitimately served the war effort in Kansas. But not him." He looked off again. "No, not him. Oh, he loved this country so much. Our culture, our history. He so much wanted to preserve it, to pass it on to us. God, family, country. 'A man is expendable,' he told me shortly before he left. 'A man's duty is to protect the women and children in his life. If possible, give them a better life than he had.' He meant it all right. Not like this American castrati, who say one thing and do another. He lived by it and he died by it."

Joel's memory involuntarily went back to his own grandfather. With effort he focused on the history he needed to write, trying to capitalize on the reminiscence at hand. "Tell me about the day you learned of your father's death."

"I was fourteen years old. It was November 10, the Marine Corps's birthday, although I didn't know that at the time. I was at wrestling practice at Prairie View High School. Even though I didn't go to school there, I was still allowed to participate on the team."

"Really?" Joel asked, again with his condescending tone that was starting to really irritate Harris. "Does that seem fair, you don't go to class, but you can benefit from their sports program?"

"Yeah, really, you dumb ass! They were lucky to have me. I was the best goddamn wrestler they had!"

"I'm sorry. I didn't mean to be disrespectful." Which was true, even though Joel had felt disrespectful.

"The coach got my attention and asked me to follow him out of the gym. When we got out into the hall and I saw one of my dad's KBI buddies and our pastor from church, I knew what was up. After nearly three years of war, I wasn't the first boy to lose his father. I saw them, and I wanted to run away so bad. Even then in death, my dad was there. He's the one who made me man up and confront the situation. They told me my father had been shot down over southern Mexico. He was dead. I'll tell you, it was easy to hear them say it compared to telling my mother. They took me to our house. My mom had noticed the car pull into the drive. She'd seen us all walking up. She too had been through enough war to know what was going on; we didn't have to say a word. She opened the door and I saw the pain in her eyes. That was when I lost it. I was trying to be a man at that age, but I was still such a boy. I bawled in her arms. She was such a strong woman." Harris looked up at the sky and was silent for a minute.

Joel watched the eyes of that evil face tear up from the recollection of his father's death. He was conditioned to think this Harris despicable, yet he was tempted to feel sympathy for him.

"Within the year, we'd won the Mexico Campaign," Harris concluded.

"Did you blame the country? Did you blame the Government? Was that the motivation for your treason?" Levine tried to empathize.

"Treason?" Harris let out a sarcastic laugh. "Did I commit treason against the Government? Or did the Government commit treason against me?"

"How can the Government commit treason? Against you?"

"Can no one in government do wrong? Can no one in government be corrupt?" Harris threw back at him.

Of course Levine knew many government workers were imperfect, but he also knew that was nothing to be discussed publicly. He wanted to redirect the interview. "Did you blame the Chinese? Did you want revenge? Is that why you joined the Marine Corps?"

"You bet your goddamn ass I wanted revenge. I wanted to kill all the bastards that had any role in the death of my father. You know, under Clark, for the war effort you could enlist at the age of sixteen if you could pass a graduation exam and had parental consent. That was my new goal in life. I finished the high school curriculum by fifteen. The South China Sea Campaign had gotten under full swing. We needed available men in the war effort. I worked at the scrap yard, collecting metal to recycle into war material. Hell, anybody that was worth anything did something for the war in those days. I couldn't wait to turn sixteen."

"How'd your mother feel about you enlisting in the Marine Corps of all things?"

"Well, in those days I had my sights set on the US Army, like my dad had done in the Islamic Wars. But my mom would have no part of it. I told her I would enlist when I turned eighteen anyway, why not let me sign on now? She told me she could wait for me to turn eighteen. I can see her point now. To have lost a husband, and then to send a son off to war. Of course, at the time I was pissed. There was a major offensive to destroy Chinese Communists. The military needed men. It seems laughable now, but at the time I was afraid it would all end before I could turn eighteen. I was still such a boy, so anxious to become a man.

"But then, at least it seemed that way to me, a miracle happened. Congress passed and President Clark signed a wartime law lowering the legal age of enlistment, without parental consent, to seventeen. On my seventeenth birthday, I was up and out of the house before sunrise. Truth be told, I wanted to get out of the house before my mother woke up. I got to the military recruiting complex at the mall about an hour before it opened. I sat out front, eating a chocolate-frosted donut and a milk I bought at a convenience store on the way into town…"

***

"You looking to become a Marine, young man?" The gunnery sergeant stood in the doorway of his office, holding a giant coffee mug with an Eagle, Globe, and Anchor on it. Young Sean Harris was impressed by the four solid rows of ribbons that stood out on his khaki shirt in combination with the blue pants with the red stripe down the side. The veteran Marine's patch over his right eye seemed to speak to Sean of a life of action and adventure that had been lived.

"Uh, well...I don't know. I was kinda thinking of the Army, maybe." Sean had actually been set on the Army, but the Marine recruiter looked impressive and Sean was suddenly hesitant to close that possibility. There had been much news about the Marine Corps's victories in the Philippines. Like most Americans, Sean was intrigued. There was a mystique that had developed around the United States Marine Corps after President Clark had removed federal training regulations. Sean had liked the statements "Marines know best how to make Marines" and "We're using the best of our American past to *WIN* our American future." News reports harped that Clark was "taking the leash off the Devil Dogs" and letting them train and fight the way Marine Corps generals wanted to train and fight. To Sean the Marine Corps seemed iconic with what Clark called the American Renaissance.

Sean had observed that two different media campaigns had evolved during this war. One side decried President Clark and his war effort and especially the changes in the United States Marine Corps. Clark was undoing the *progress* made under the Leakey administration to the great peril of the United States. Americans needed to accept a less dominant, more collusive role in the governing of the world. Removing United Nation Humanitarian regulations and inspectors from the American military process was to invite distrust and disaster. Far from winning the war, Clark was making the United States a pariah in the international community.

The other side of this media war argued that there was no progress, only decline, under Leakey. That there was a reason the United States was no longer the great nation of the past: Americans had rejected the cultural values that had made

America great. The nation needed a rebirth of Americanism. This side constantly gave historical examples of American greatness: the American Revolution, American Capitalism and Innovation, the Civil War, the Economic Boom of the 1920s, the American War Effort of the World Wars. Clark insisted that Americans were a great people from a great culture: "If we embrace Americanism, China doesn't have a snowball's chance in Hell!"

Because of a Supreme Court decision, that this latter side claimed unconstitutional, Clark's reforms had been limited. Thus the formation of state militias for the war. The only branch free from international regulation was the United States Marine Corps. Over the last few years Sean found himself aligning with the American Renaissance movement; and if the Philippines and South China Sea Campaigns were any indication, he'd chosen the winning side.

"Well, the Army's got some respectable units. No doubt about that." The gunny sipped his coffee, turned and began to walk back into his office. "Army recruiter isn't here yet. You can have a seat in here until he arrives. Or you can stand out in the hall until he arrives, if you want."

"My dad was in the Army when he served in the Islamic Wars." Sean followed the Marine recruiter, curious to see inside the office. He recognized some of the posters on the wall from around town, and slogans he had heard on the Internet: "First to Fight," "Always Faithful," "If you WANT to fight, Join the MARINES." On the wall was a picture of a statue of a group of past Marines raising the Stars and Stripes. Sean knew it was from some past battle, and he agreed with so many that had stated how symbolic it was of their current struggle.

"Do you know who your dad served with in the Army? Help yourself to some coffee if you like." Sean didn't drink coffee.

"He flew helicopters. He flew a gunship in the Islamic Wars. He did med evac in the Kansas Militia in Mexico. We were told he was shot down while trying to evacuate the wounded from battle."

"I'm sorry for your loss. It's a shame to lose so many good men." The gunny began to sit down. "Please have a seat. And now you honor your father by serving your people. I respect that."

Sean felt flushed with pride to receive such a compliment from a man like this.

"So tell me, you gonna do your mom a favor and sign up for something safe?"

"I ain't doing her or my family a favor if we lose this war and our country." Sean's voice had cracked a bit from the adrenaline he was feeling. The recruiter didn't seem to notice or care.

"I agree with you there. Well, your endeavor speaks well of your father and your mother. So what is it you want to do in the Army?"

"Part of me would like to fly." Sean sat back in his chair, feeling less intimidated than before. "Part of me wants to be in the infantry."

The recruiter's ears perked up. "Infantry?! Now what motivates you for the infantry?"

Sean thought he could see just ever so slight a smile on the recruiter's face. Sean was feeling rather emboldened. "I want to look those ChiCom bastards in the face when I kill them." Sean's voice was not that of a braggart, but of an earnest young man.

The recruiter stared at the young man for a moment. "I volunteered for the infantry as a recruit. I'd still be there if I hadn't lost my eye and my leg." The gunny knocked on his right knee. "I'll tell you though, infantry is an easier choice than a decision. Most men don't even have the desire to try. Those that do, we lose about forty percent of them through the training. They just don't have the mental, emotional, or physical stamina to succeed. Those that do stand a better than average chance of getting themselves killed or maimed on the battlefield. Those that survive..." The gunny paused a bit in order to let the gravity of his words sink in. He wanted to be understood. "Those that do will never be the same. In the Marine Corps we will break you, bleed you, and then send you into battle. We will find your inner killer and turn you into a warrior. You will hate it. You will love it. For better or for worse you will be forever changed. That poster"—the recruiter pointed to the wall—"ain't no bullshit. Once a Marine, son, always a Marine. There ain't no going back." The salty warrior saw that he had struck a chord with the kid.

"Look, the Corps, the military in general, needs a lot of people in this war. Most of them are not in combat arms, let alone the infantry. Check out what the Army can do for you. The Navy, Air Force. They'll give more money for school and shit like that. They got better bonuses for enlisting and that sort of thing. Do your research and sleep on it before you make a decision."

"How come the Marines don't give better bonuses than the Army?" Sean was curious why a prideful, elite force would not try to be more competitive.

"Because the Marines ain't promising you a chance to go to school or get technical training. We're not trying to better prepare you for the civilian world. We're trying to win a war. We want, we need men who have the heart to kill our enemies and probably get themselves killed in the process. Once that's done, we'll worry about civilian life." The gunnery sergeant fished out a pack of cigarettes and lit one up without offering Sean one or even asking if he minded him smoking. He didn't care if Sean minded or not.

"I want to sign up. I want to kill the ChiComs, the Muslims, whoever. I want to win this war. I want my family to live in peace. I want to be a Marine." Sean had never been more serious in his life. The gunny looked the boy in the eye for several moments. He exhaled all the smoke from his lungs and without a word began the paperwork to give Sean Harris the opportunity to become a United States Marine.

***

"All that was easy compared to telling my mother."

"Was she angry?" Joel was surprised to hear Harris say that. He had this notion of the Harris family as being somewhat blind in their patriotism.

"Oh, you're goddamn right she was." Harris slightly slurred from the effects of the bourbon. "She didn't say a word though. She just stared at me with those dark brown eyes of hers." Harris's demeanor became very solemn. Joel even wondered if the old butcher would even begin to tear up again, and if so, how he could spin it for maximum literary effect. "I get it now. I didn't then. She didn't want me to join. Specifically, she didn't want me to go to war. At the time I thought maybe she thought I wasn't good enough, I wasn't man enough. But that wasn't it. Every male relative she had, had been in war. Her granddad fought the Nazis. Her father was in Vietnam. She lost a brother in the Islamic Wars. She lost her husband in the Sino-American War. And was about to lose her firstborn son to the same war. Fuck yeah, she was mad. Not 'cause I wanted to fight. She was a strong woman born of strong men and was married to a strong man. She wasn't mad that I wanted to fight. She was mad that I had to." Harris's tone became more resentful. "She was mad at bullshit politicians who are so fucking slow to want to stop evil, then are so fucking quick to want to go to war against it, just to be so fucking hesitant to destroy it."

CHAPTER SEVEN

Harris stood up and limped over to get himself another drink and fill up another plate of food.

"This is some goddamn good cheese. You should try some of this, Mr. Levine. Better than the prison's chow, that's for sure. You keep up with the food and booze, you'll keep me talking all day." The evil old man smiled from his scarred face and sat back down.

"How soon after you enlisted did you ship off to your training?" Levine wanted to pass off the comment about the good food as if it was routine for him, but it was not. His pride compelled him on this matter, but it did burn him that the government that he had tried to serve so faithfully would cater to this murderer for information. However, he needed this man to talk as much as the government was wanting him to talk, so Joel smiled and nodded his head in response to the comment.

"It was only three days. I couldn't wait to get the hell out in those days. How I miss it now, though."

"Was that the last time you saw your mother?"

"No, I had five days leave after I graduated boot camp, and we'd video chat now and then when I was overseas. After my visit home, I didn't see her again in person until my trial."

Joel had never been to Kansas. No one he knew had anything good to say about Kansas. He had no idea how anyone could miss it, but given the region's recent resistance to federal authority, it really didn't surprise him that Harris felt that way.

"So you left for boot camp?" Joel said, not certain he had the syntax right, but he was wanting to get on with the history.

"Yeah. She drove me to the recruiter's office. The recruiter drove me to the bus station. From there I was taken to Kansas City and put up in a hotel for the night. They fed me breakfast the next day and then sent me to the airport. From there I flew to San Diego.

"At the airport I reported to a liaison office. It was where other recruits like me waited for the bus that would take us to MCRD."

"MCRD?"

"Marine Corps Recruit Depot. San Diego's where I went. They had another recruit depot on Parris Island in South Carolina back then. If you were from west of the Mississippi, you went to San Diego."

"Were these other recruits, guys you would serve with?"

"Honestly I don't even remember. We were ordered to sit on the floor. No talking. No looking around. I really didn't notice anyone who was there. I was gung ho, and I wanted to do everything right from the very start. So I didn't say a word. I didn't look around. I didn't pay attention to anyone else. I sat there, cross-legged, until the bus came to pick us up.

"It was nighttime. Hell, for as long as a bus ride it was, you'd have thought MCRD was in Arizona." Harris's jest seemed cut short a bit as his mind seemed to wander.

"What? What did you just remember about Arizona?" Joel inquired.

"That's where it all ended. The end of my war. The end of my great adventure." Harris waved his hand around at nothing in particular. "But that's the end. Let's go back to the beginning…"

***

Sean tried to see San Diego from the bus window. Nighttime was hurting his efforts. His father had told him San Diego was a beautiful part of the country, just too many people ruined it. He'd never been there himself. A family trip to Orlando, Florida, once, was as far as he had ever been from home. He had no idea what time it was, just that the bus ride from the airport to MCRD seemed to take a long time.

When the bus pulled through the security gate, Sean's excitement and apprehension soared to a new height. He was no longer a child on the sidelines of life, watching and listening to what men were doing or had done. He was in the arena now. He would face the challenges and risk his life for the sake of others, just as his father and Harris men of past generations had done for him. Intellectually, he knew there'd be pain. He knew he could die. Emotionally, Sean Harris thought he was invincible. He would face and defeat the demons that had caused so much pain for him and his family.

The bus stopped in front of a pale yellow warehouse. A very tall, muscular drill instructor stepped on the bus. He succinctly stated in a loud, clear, gravelly voice that the first and last word out of their miserable mouths from this time on was to be *sir* and to be stated with as much volume as their miserable little lungs could muster. He continued with instructions to move as fast as their miserable little fucking legs would carry them off the bus and onto yellow footprints outside. Once the order was given, all hell broke loose.

The base's streetlamps glowed gold against a purple sky heavy with moisture. There was an odor in the air that was foreign to Sean, but pleasant. He relished the moment.

"Sound off when I call out your name," the muscular drill instructor commanded. "Ackerman."

80

"Here."

"What's your malfunction, shit for brains?!" another drill instructor emerged from the dark and screamed into recruit Ackerman's face. "What's the first fucking word out of that miserable suck hole of yours?!"

"Sir! Here, sir!"

"No fucking shit there, Einstein," another gravelly drill instructor voice called out.

"What the fuck are those asshole recruiters giving us to work with?" yet another gravelly voice commented.

And so it went for the next seventy-three names.

"Listen up, douche bags. When I call out the first row, you will in a fast and orderly fashion line up through those doors and stand asshole to belly button. Do any of you sorry-ass shit stains not understand me?" Sean didn't know what "asshole to belly button" meant, but seeing how he was in the middle of the formation, he thought he could watch the others and figure it out. He knew for sure he did not want to ask what it meant. He was glad to move. His legs and feet were starting to hurt.

Sean learned that asshole to belly button was as bad as it sounded. They stood in line so close to each other that the phrase was nearly literal. Sean was not used to standing this close to other men and he did not like it. Feeling the body heat of other men grossed him out. Staring at the sweaty neck in front of his face quickly became psychologically painful, but he wasn't going to say a word.

Sean had never considered himself pampered, but the brutality of the haircuts was shocking to him. Gone were the capes and tissue around the neck. Recruits were yelled at to quickly sit down in the barber chair. Clippers were recklessly combed over their scalps. No sooner was their hair gone than the recruits were yelled at to get out of the barber chair and stand asshole to belly button in the hallway. More psychologically painful minutes were spent staring at a sweaty neck covered in hair and streaked with blood from the nicks on the recruit's scalp.

From the next line Sean entered a warehouse, where he was thrown a seabag to place all the gear that was thrown at him after that. Once all the gear was issued to the recruits, they stood in formation and undressed and redressed "by the numbers" as per the order of a drill instructor in government-issued boots and utilities. The last of Sean Harris's civilian persona was boxed up, labeled, and shipped back to Kansas. He was now one of seventy-five hairless recruits dressed in camouflage. Life as he had known it, ended that night.

The next twenty-four hours was disorienting. Lines, formations, yelling, paperwork, testing—all was at a hell-bent-for-leather pace. Harris was so exhausted he actually was dozing off while slumped in the only chair he was allowed to sit in during an aptitude test. Only his falling head would wake him up.

For what he hoped to be the last time, Harris humped his seabag across the hot asphalt of the MCRD's parade deck. The remnants of his haircut dug into his neck and shoulders. The cool breeze was incapable of penetrating the new, stiff cammies now stained with sweat and reeking of body odor. Another training platoon marched by in shorts and T-shirts, PT gear; Harris felt envy. Not only did he want out of the sweaty cammies, the recruits looked so organized, in control and confident. Nothing like his platoon.

The gaggle of new recruits were called to a halt before a dull, rectangular barracks. To Harris's surprise they were being turned over to another group of four drill instructors that would see them through basic training. The shortest of the drill instructors stepped forward.

"I am Junior Drill Instructor Sergeant Jameson. When I call out your name, move your nasty ass through that ground-floor hatch. You will stand at attention in front of the first available rack until further orders. Do you understand me?"

"Sir, yes, sir, Junior Drill Instructor Sergeant Jameson, sir!" Harris was impressed that they seemed to get it right the first time around; however, Junior Drill Instructor Sergeant Jameson was not. He made them repeat it three more times at maximum volume before he proceeded with calling out names.

"Ackerman, Liam T."

"Sir, here sir!"

"Fucking move, maggot! Fucking now! Go!" Again outflanked by another yelling drill instructor, Ackerman spastically ran towards the barracks, the yelling drill instructor on his heels the whole way. In his awkward attempt to run fast, Ackerman fell and skidded to a stop on the asphalt. Harris's chest hurt just watching it. The drill instructor pulled Ackerman up by the collar of his shirt and kicked him right square in the backside to get him moving again, yelling at him the whole way in.

Drill Instructor Sergeant Jameson glared at the remaining recruits from under his "Smokey Bear" cover. His disgust was blatant.

"Atchison, Connor J." Atchison was quick to beat feet into the barracks without incident.

"Holy fucking shit! Fat body, are you that goddamn stupid? Get your ass down here!" boomed the voice of the other drill instructor from the open squad bay windows. Harris fought the notion that he might have made a mistake. Perhaps something just wasn't right. How was he going to survive this for the next three months? How was he going to survive this until evening chow?

Once all the recruits were lined up in the barracks, they learned to make their racks the Marine Corps way. After which all the recruits were ordered into the "classroom," which was the front of the squad bay by the drill instructor's office known as the duty hut. Once they were all sitting on the floor cross-legged, left over right, the tallest of the drill instructors came out of the office. He was dressed like the drill instructors except he wore a thick black leather gun belt instead of the green gun belts worn by the junior drill instructors.

"I am Senior Drill Instructor Staff Sergeant MacAlister. Over the next three months I will turn you all into the greatest of all warriors, United States Marines, or I will kill you in the process. YOU do not join the Marine Corps, the Marine Corps accepts you, but only after you prove yourself to me. Before your time is done here, you will all hate me. I don't give a fuck. My job is to turn you into the toughest, meanest motherfuckers on the whole goddamn planet; or I will not let your sorry asses into my Marine Corps. Being a US Marine is a privilege, not a goddamn right. You recruits will have to earn the title US Marine.

"When you earn that privilege, your job will be to defend the Constitution of the United States and the American people so that the freedom and the natural law of our Creator will prevail upon this planet. You will be sent to kill the people of those that oppose our freedom and oppose our Creator.

"The United States Marine Corps is an all-volunteer force. If at any time during your training you decide you do not want to be a Marine, report to Junior Drill Instructors Sergeant Jameson, Sergeant Jennings, or Sergeant Finch. You will not be accommodated here. You will meet the Marine Corps's requirements or you will get the fuck out." The senior drill instructor's dark blue eyes glared from between his Smokey Bear cover, his high cheekbones, and black shadow of a beard. Harris thought the look of his face alone might be enough to kill a man. If that was not enough, Senior Drill Instructor Staff Sergeant MacAlister had the largest fists and forearms he had seen. He truly looked like he could easily beat a man to death with his bare hands. His demeanor left no room for doubt in the recruits' minds that he probably had, multiple times.

"Now, are there any questions?" MacAlister asked in conclusion of his pep talk.

Harris actually had a lot, but was too afraid to ask. Perhaps they all were, for they sat in silence for an awkward few seconds.

"Answer your senior drill instructor, you fucking maggots!" Jameson shouted.

"Sir, yes, sir!" they answered in a discombobulated fashion.

"Bullshit! Sound off like you got a pair!"

"SIR, YES, SIR!" the recruits screamed in a quasi-hysterical manner.

"Fucking pathetic," Jameson spat out with contempt.

MacAlister turned to the junior drill instructor and told him to carry on.

"Aye, aye, Senior Drill Instructor. Now listen up, you maggot-invested piles of horse shit. Due to our blessed country's candy-ass public school system"—Jameson's tone was casual and very matter-of-fact—"most of you have been raised to be a bunch of effeminate pussies. Most of you have no idea how to take a punch let alone handle yourself in a fistfight. Within a year some of you will be on a battlefield against men who have been beaten into compliance and training to kill since they were six-year-old boys, yet still they cannot compete with the deadly skills of a United States

Marine. The path from schoolboy pussy to deadly US Marine, while shorter than the ChiComs', is a whole fucking lot more intense. Instead of teaching you to be strong young men, your teachers over your school years have taught you to be whining victims. Therefore many of you will want to quit and will not have the balls to say so. You will want to pass on the responsibility of your failure to the United States Marine Corps and to your fellow Americans. Many of you will attempt some chickenshit form of suicide in order to get out of training and make others feel sorry for you. In order to expose your cowardice or to assist you to die if you find that preferable to becoming a US Marine, your first lesson will be how to effectively and efficiently kill your nasty self."

While the subject matter caught Harris completely by surprise, he did find himself fascinated by the lesson. Jameson showed them where vital arteries were in the neck, groin, underarms, forearms, and thighs. He was amazed at the speed with which a man would die if a blade were inserted under his sternum or behind his clavicles. Contrary to what he had always believed about people killing themselves by slitting their wrists, Jameson taught them it was far more effective to slice one's self deeply under the armpit. Another deadly place to slice one's self open was the groin. While Harris could not imagine slicing his own groin open, or even killing himself for that matter, he could envision using this knowledge against the enemy of his people. Using this knowledge to kill those that had killed his father. He was fascinated. He wanted the information seared into his brain.

After the lesson, and much yelling, the recruits formed up and marched to evening chow. The food was all right. Harris savored the air-conditioning in the chow hall. He would have liked more food and more time to sit down in a chair and not be yelled at, but that was not to happen in boot camp.

On the march back to the squad bay, somebody made some kind of mistake and the whole platoon was introduced to the sand pit. They were also introduced to a new exercise: the bend and thrust. It required one to drop to the ground and kick one's legs out to full extension, bring them back in and stand up again. Harris hated having the sand kicked in his face; however, he did find it preferable to being kicked in the hands and face by his fellow recruits. To add to the misery even more, some sadistic individual had planted cockleburs in the sand pit. Even with the thirty minutes allotted to "shit, shower, and shave" at the end of the day; there was no way to get the thorns out of his palms.

After the yelling and cursing involved in teaching the recruits the protocol of a health and hygiene inspection, the recruits shouted with as much synchronization as possible, "I'm up. He sees me. I'm down," as they hit the rack. The lights were off at 2200 hours sharp. Harris's easiest day of Marine Corps training came to an end.

CHAPTER EIGHT

Harris had no idea what time it was, but he relished the quiet. As tired as he had been at lights out, he had still woken up to use the head at some time during the night. Now he lay in his rack, enjoying the peace. He had no idea what time it was, nor how much longer the peace would last. No sooner did he have this thought than the peace was ended. The lights flipped on. A metal trash can was kicked down the squad bay.

"ON YOUR FUCKING FEET, RECRUITS!" Jameson's voice boomed. Day two picked up where day one left off. "Ackerman, unfuck yourself and stand at attention."

Harris jumped off the top rack he was assigned to. No sooner done than Junior Drill Instructor Sergeant Jennings was in his ear.

"Stand at attention, asshole!"

Harris popped to.

The first lesson of the day was how to get dressed by the numbers, which they had started to learn the day before. Or was it the day before that? Either way, it didn't matter to Harris. He found it an indignity, especially when Jameson began to skip numbers. What was the point of not giving them the time they needed to dress properly and then scream at them for not dressing properly? Harris was not at a point where he wanted to voice his complaints, and besides, there wasn't much time to think about it anyway. As soon as Jameson was done counting, they were to stop at whatever state of dress they were in and wait for orders to start on the next article of clothing.

At the end of it, no one was properly dressed. The next order was that one side of the squad bay had thirty seconds to make a head call while the other side made their racks. Then the sides would switch duties. From there they would go to morning chow and come back to clean the squad bay.

"How am I going to do this for three months?" Harris unconsciously mumbled to himself while making his rack before his chance to use the head.

"You're not one of those pussies looking to kill himself already to get out of boot camp, are you?" his rack mate mumbled back as he ducked while he stood up to help Harris straighten and smooth out his government-issued wool blanket. Hastings, William C., had an inoffensive smirk on his face, one that made Harris instantly decide not to be angry about the comment. In fact, he instantly found Hastings likable. Whether it was his rosy cheeks that made him look way younger than seventeen or the mischievous twinkle in his dark brown eyes, Hastings had a look that conveyed that nothing in life should be taken too seriously. Harris couldn't take offense.

"Fuck you," was the cleverest reply Harris could come up with at the time, but it was said with the same kind of smart-ass grin, and no offense was taken. The bonding was cut short when the recruits were called to attention so they could reverse assignments.

In time Harris would learn that thirty-five men running in half-laced boots to use a head that had six toilets, three urinals, and six sinks was just a typical recruit gaggle, but at this time in his life it seemed like madness. He could not understand why the DIs would put them into situations where it was impossible to get done what they were told to get done. It seemed crazy, but then his father had told him that war could seem crazy. "There's a method to the madness," his father always said, and for now that faith kept him going. But still, this just seemed plain nuts to him.

The recruits made it to morning chow with no major incidents. On the way back to the squad bay, however, something happened. Harris didn't see it. They formed up by height and at five foot eleven he was in the middle of the formation. He heard the DI yelling at Ackerman for being a spaz. Ackerman was first among the recruits alphabetically, and at six foot three he was the tallest. Despite his height, he was skinny. Harris thought he had a birdlike appearance. For a reason not known to Harris, the recruits found themselves back in the sand pit.

The morning cleanup was another cluster with a lot of yelling, push-ups, and leg lifts. Despite all that, what Harris hated the most about the morning was that he'd not had a chance to brush his teeth. This, of course, was to have been done during his thirty-second head call earlier in the morning. Once the DIs were ready to move beyond the morning cleanup, they were instructed to grab their "knowledge," notebooks full of Marine Corps wisdom, and form up on the parade deck. This turned into another gaggle and the recruits found themselves doing bend and thrusts. To make up for the delay, the drill instructors had the recruits double time to their first class of the day.

When Harris joined the Marine Corps, he had not envisioned classrooms and book work as part of his warrior training. But after the morning he'd had, he was thankful to be sitting in a chair in an air-conditioned room.

"Listen up, shitheads," Junior Drill Instructor Sergeant Jameson commanded. "You're about to be instructed by one of the greatest living legends in the United States Marine Corps, Major General Edgar T. Ragnarsson, commander of the First Marine Division. If I catch any single one of you dick-skinning faggots with your eyes closed or otherwise not paying attention, every single fucking one of you will wish your fucking bitch of a mother had gotten a goddamn abortion instead of wasting life on your sorry motherfucking ass. Do I make myself clear?"

"SIR, YES, SIR!" a platoon of hoarse recruits screamed back. Enthusiastic, but still out of sync.

"Good God, give me strength to deal with these pathetic piles of shit you have given me to work with. Now listen up, you will be called to attention when the general walks into the room, and you all had better fucking pop to. Do you understand?"

"SIR, YES, SIR."

"Fuck's sake." Jameson shook his head in disgust as he slowly walked over to converse with another drill instructor.

Other training platoons filed into the auditorium until it was filled to capacity. Occasionally a drill instructor would bark out at a recruit for talking or looking around. Harris found it surreal to be in a room with so many people and to have so little noise. He moved as little as possible and didn't say a word. Though mentally painful, he was glad to be sitting in a chair instead of cross-legged on the deck. Not being able to keep track of the time, the wait seemed long and tedious.

Harris's boredom was broken by a drill instructor with a sleeve full of stripes walking out to center stage. He looked older than the other drill instructors, but just as intimidating, and had rows of ribbons on the left side of his chest. Harris waited for him to speak, but he just stood there, silent and still. He aggressively stared at the recruits as if he were challenging them not to pay attention to him so he could seek retribution.

"Recruits! Atten-hut!"

Everyone popped up like they had a spring under their ass. Harris could see nothing, but he could hear boot steps coming down the aisle. It was not until Ragnarsson stepped onto the stage that Harris could get a clear look at him. He was taller than the drill instructor and had as many, if not more, ribbons. He was broad at the shoulders and narrow at the hip. His forearms looked huge under the short sleeves of the khaki shirt. His white hair was cut to a short flattop and looked natural to his bright blue eye and fair skin, which only made the black eye patch stand out all the more. The drill instructor saluted, did an about-face, and walked off the stage. The general was centered on the stage, flanked by Old Glory and the Marine Corps flag. Behind him hung a giant Eagle, Globe, & Anchor: the emblem of the United States Marine Corps.

"At ease, recruits. Be seated." Harris had just started to wonder how many Marines actually ended up losing an eye in combat, when the general let them sit down. Ragnarsson's tone was much more relaxed yet still just as commanding as the drill instructors'.

"The very fact you are here speaks well for each and every one of you. Most American men never attempt to become a United States Marine. Even fewer have the physical and mental capacity to acquire that honor. Approximately one-third of you are going to fail to complete your quest. Your drill instructors will find your limits of endurance. It will be up to you to push beyond that. If you do, you'll find your drill instructors again finding the limit of your resolve and, again, you have to decide to push through or fail.

"If you graduate from recruit to United States Marine, you will have graduated to among the most elite warriors in all of world history. But you will find that you will have only started your hardship. Being a warrior, being a US Marine, is not an accomplishment, it is a way of life. If you make it to the Fleet, your platoon sergeants and squad leaders will run you, work you, and bleed you until you die or become the meanest, toughest, most resilient sons of bitches on the entire planet. Then you will have the skills, the stamina, and mind-set to go into battle against the heathen Chinese Communists and slaughter the little bastards.

"Along the way to this objective, many of you will question your choice. All of you at one time or another will want to quit. All of you will question whether it is preferable to die than go on. Many of you will question if all this is worth it. You will wonder if our fight is just, if your sacrifice is worthwhile. First Marines suffered nearly forty percent casualties in the South China Sea Campaign. Indeed, as free American men, you should ask these questions. As free American men volunteering to go to war, you should have those questions answered. That is why I am here today to tell you why your sacrifice is worthwhile, why our fight is superior to that of the communists.

"Since the dawn of mankind ours has been a struggle for survival. Our ancient ancestors learned the strength of numbers and the power of teamwork. From this realization governments were born. Before recorded history, there existed government; and thus a new struggle was added to the struggle of survival: Freedom. History is of those who have struggled to be free and those who have struggled to control them. From the ancient Hebrews that sought to be governed by God's law, not man's, to the ancient Greeks who gave us democracy—the power of a political voice—and fought to the death to defend it from the Persian emperors. To the Romans who overthrew their Etruscan kings and gave us republicanism: government by law and a culture that values the potential of the individual human. Much of history is made up of how these people would defend and ultimately lose the freedom their people cherished.

"And finally, our own American Founding Fathers, who upheld the Anglo-Saxon concept that a king serves his people and to do otherwise is to exceed his authority: a government of limited power. Our history and legends abound of those who have fought to be free against those that would enslave them. For nearly three hundred years there has been no more essential participant in this struggle than the United States Marine Corps. Since our birth at Tun Tavern in 1775, US Marines have defended America, and even the world, from tyrannical kings, emperors, dictators, Islamic jihadists, and other deadly ideologies.

"Now, many of you have heard some journalists and politicians claim we can't defeat communism. That even the Marines were not able to defeat the communists in Korea and Vietnam in the last century. We can't win, why even try? Their premise is as wrong as their facts. American warriors devastated their communist foes of the twentieth century, none more so than the Marine Corps. It has been our Commander-in-Chief, the US President, that has always lacked the heart to complete the victory our people have sacrificed themselves for. For the first time in our war against communism, American warriors have a Declaration of War from Congress and a mission from the president to destroy or obtain the unconditional surrender of the People's Republic of China, along with all her allies. Just as the Marine Corps had been America's preeminent force in the destruction of the Chinese Red Army in our borders, the US Marine Corps will be the preeminent force in the destruction of the Chinese Red Army in THEIR borders! By the time we're done, there will not be one Marxist, Communist Manifesto-thumpin' son of a bitch left in all of Asia!

"The same castrati who whine that America can't win, also bitch that the United States has no right to invade the People's Republic of China and impose our will on them. HORSESHIT! It is they who invaded our home, killed our fathers and sons, and raped our mothers and daughters to impose their will on us! Don't you ever forget that!

"You men have been blessed by our Creator to be born into a land where the government exists to serve your Natural rights to life, liberty, and property, be that the fruits of your labor or the thoughts of your mind. The ChiCom is born into a world of shit. He has no right to property. He has only what his communist rulers allow him to have. Where we have the liberty of capitalism, he has the slavery of work camps. Where we have the right to life, he has government-enforced abortions.

"Communism is evil. It demands that mankind serves government. There cannot be freedom, there cannot be peace as long as it is tolerated.

"If you men agree that this is worth fighting for, then you can EARN the privilege to be a United States Marine. If you don't think that is worth fighting for, then get the fuck out of my Marine Corps."

Harris sat in awe. Everything about the general reeked of confidence and strength. He was a man of sound mind and body. A man who knew the difference between right and wrong, with the courage to state it. A man who found fulfillment and righteousness in all that he loved. A man like his father. The kind of man Harris wanted to be. The consummate warrior.

Harris never enlisted with the idea of quitting, but found his determination invigorated. He would become a US Marine or die trying. Even if it was the last thing he'd ever do.

CHAPTER NINE

Ragnarsson was right. Every day of boot camp Harris found himself wanting to quit or at least take a break from it. Everywhere the recruits went, they ran. Everything the recruits said, they screamed. The mind games where the worst for Harris. He was tired of everything not being good enough. Everything having to be redone to a level of perfection that didn't even seem achievable. The new vocabulary was a pain. Learning new terms like bulkhead instead of wall, head instead of bathroom, deck instead of floor was awkward for him. No longer using *a.m.* or *p.m.* for time was a hassle, but Harris was starting to get used to it. Not being allowed to use pronouns was what tripped him up the most and had gotten him thrashed on several occasions. He found all the attention to detail a hassle. More often than not, he could not make sense of all of it. None of it, though, was enough to make him quit, and he felt guilty whenever the temptation crossed his mind. Over the weeks he'd learned about far greater hardships endured by Marines in past wars and battles. They never succumbed. They always overcame. Could he? With all the odds against him, could he adapt, improvise, and overcome?

For the first time in boot camp Harris did not wake up before reveille. He was dead asleep when Hastings slapped him on the chest.

"Get your ass up!" Hastings's voice was muffled, but stern. He was sympathetic to Harris's cold, but he didn't want him or his friend thrashed for not jumping out of the rack soon enough. Harris jumped out of his rack, stepped into and tied his boots. He pulled up his trousers, the legs of which had been slipped over his boots the night before. He merely had to step into them and pull them up. He put on his blouse that hung on the end of his rack. Within thirty seconds the entire platoon was completely dressed, standing at attention and waiting for permission to make a head call. Harris had the routine down and could do it half asleep, which he had nearly done this morning. A cold was working its way through the platoon; as of late it was Harris's turn.

What he needed was extra rest, but that wasn't going to happen. The platoon was in the first week of training on the rifle range. Reveille was now at 0300 not 0530. The lack of sleep in addition to the extra rigor was taking its toll on Harris.

The morning was spent snapping in. Recruits dry fired their weapons from the prone, kneeling, and standing positions. Harris had been shooting firearms since his childhood and found dry firing exceptionally boring. He found several minutes in the kneeling position exceptionally painful, torturous in fact. While at the range, another recruit found kneeling too painful to endure. He jumped up crying and limping. The drill instructors hovered around him, ordering him to resume the kneeling position and resume training. He refused. He was quickly ushered away, never to be seen by another recruit again.

Good riddance, Harris thought simultaneously with wondering, *Will I break like that?*

The platoon of seventy-five was now down to fifty-five. After the platoon survivors did a series of bend and thrusts, push-ups, and leg lifts for their "buddy's" performance, they got back to snapping in.

Noon chow was a blessing for Harris. He needed to sit and rest. Other than religious services on Sunday, chow was the only time he could sit in a chair. It felt so comfortable that Harris swore to himself he would never take another chair for granted. He was too congested to taste the food, but he didn't care. His body craved calories.

After chow the platoon formed up outside the chow hall and read their books of knowledge, waiting for orders from the drill instructors. Then they double-timed back to the squad bay. They were allowed a thirty-second head call. Then Harris sat cross-legged, left over right, on the classroom floor at the front of the squad bay. There he listened to a lecture on target, front sight, and rear sight alignment. His eyelids grew heavy. Harris shifted his weight around, straightened his back, and took a drink of water from his canteen. Soon again, however, his eyelids grew heavy. He fought the urge to close his eyes and thought he was winning until he noticed the primary marksmanship instructor's finger in his face.

"You, over there." The PMI pointed to the door of the drill instructor's office, known as the duty hut. A recruit had a status just below that of an old pile of dog manure. Therefore a recruit didn't argue, disagree, nor negotiate with a Marine. Harris walked over to the duty hut and stood by the hatch at attention. He waited for the inevitable "world of shit" that was coming his way.

Of course, it has to be Jameson, Harris thought as the short drill instructor stormed out of the duty hut. Jameson stopped suddenly with a surprised look.

"What the fuck you doing next to my hatch, Recruit Harris?"

"Sir, this recruit fell asleep during rifle class, sir!" Harris shouted, still standing at attention.

"What the fuck, Harris!" Jameson stepped in closer to Harris. The recruit could feel the warmth of the drill instructor's breath as spittle hit his face. The young recruit thought he might vomit for a second. "You are that fucking worthless that your lazy ass can't even learn how to shoot for the sake of your piece of shit buddies"—Jameson pointed to the other recruits without looking—"or your fellow Marines?!"

Harris didn't know for sure if it was a question or a statement, but bellowed out, "Sir, no, sir!"

"Bullshit! I don't believe you, Recruit Harris! Haul your ass to the back of the squad bay!"

"Sir, aye, aye, sir!"

Harris ran to the back of the squad bay, knowing he was screwed. At least outside or in a group, there were witnesses; but this was an indoor one-on-one thrashing. This was how many recruits were broken.

"Push-ups, Harris." Jameson stood solid with his hands on his hips. Harris cranked them out as fast as he could. He began to slow down around eighty and began to grunt around ninety.

"So you want to sleep during weapons training, Harris?"

"Sir, no, sir," Harris grunted under the exertion.

"Bullshit. Leg lifts," Jameson said in a matter-of-fact voice.

Harris immediately rolled over with his hands under the small of his back and lifted his heels six inches off the ground before lowering his feet and doing it again. Over the next several minutes his thighs, lower back, and stomach began to burn.

"Push-ups," Jameson ordered. "See that tile under your nasty face, Harris?"

"Sir, yes, sir." Harris struggled.

"Your nasty ass is going to do push-ups until that tile square is covered in your nasty sweat."

"Sir, aye, aye, sir!" Harris managed. Harris was in the habit of doing as many push-ups as he could as fast as he could so as not to show a lack of enthusiasm; however, his stamina was starting to fail him. His hips were starting to sag. He was grunting, groaning, and breathing heavily. Harris dreaded the types of comments this always elicited from the drill instructors.

"You trying to fuck my squad bay, Harris?"

"Sir, no, sir!" The mental picture was repulsive to the young man.

"Leg lifts. Now. Move," the drill instructor ordered.

"Sir, yes, sir." The change of exertion was a relief, but a short-lived one. Soon he found his aching body failing him in his physical endeavors.

"Push-ups, now move."

All of Harris's energy went into push-ups, and he forgot to acknowledge the order. Junior Drill Instructor Sergeant Jameson expected this; in fact, he was glad to see it. He knew Harris was reaching his limit.

"What the fuck, Harris? Your nasty, low-ball ass don't acknowledge orders no more?"

"Sir"—Harris's voice strained—"this recruit doesn't know, sir." His voice was starting to fail him, so was his mind. He knew it was a bad answer, but his brain could not offer anything better.

"Leg lifts, now. Move."

Again, Harris's brain failed to verbally respond. All his energy went into moving.

"Oh—" Jameson dragged out "—you want to move so slow. I guess you still want to do push-ups. Now move."

Harris went back to the push-up position.

"Too fucking slow. Leg lifts, now. Move!"

Harris barely got rolled over.

"Push-ups, now. Move."

Harris's arms and torso were weak. He could barely lift himself at this point. He looked out the barracks' window at the blue sky. This time of year the sky was cloudy and gray in

Kansas. He could see a bit of a palm tree. He told himself how pleasant and mild the weather was in Southern California this time of year. The thought gave him little comfort, but he was desperate. He had to find solace, he had to find comfort somehow; but he could not. Harris saw blackness form in the middle of the blue sky and spread across his vision. His arms numbed and he dropped to the floor. He could feel the impact, but not its pain. Harris lay on the ground without the strength or the will to move.

"That's it, Harris. You just lay there and sweat a while. When you're done, you start doing more push-ups."

The smugness, the arrogance, the contempt in Jameson's voice made Harris's body and mind writhe.

What the fuck is this?! Harris's inner voice was indignant. *This is not how life works. People get sick. People need sleep. This is stupid! I don't have to put up with this shit!*

Harris jumped up with a newfound vigor. "Fuck you! I quit! I don't need this shit!" he screamed hysterically. No sooner said, fear ran through his body and struck his mind. What had he done? Had he forsaken his God, his family, his country in a time of war? Had he just betrayed all he valued, all he loved, all he believed in a moment of fear and anger? His father had never quit, Ragnarsson never quit, nor John Basilone, nor Dan Daly. Had he?

The realization that he had been somewhat delusional was a relief to him. He was still on the tile floor, sweating. He hadn't quit. He wouldn't quit. Jameson couldn't make him quit. *I'll do more push-ups, pass out again, get up and do more push-ups all day long. Fuck Jameson. Fuck the Corps, if that's what it takes. Fuck the ChiComs. They can't make me quit. If they don't want me to be a US Marine, they'll have to kill me. I WILL NOT QUIT!*

He lifted himself up and began to do more push-ups. Jameson was not impressed with Harris's resolve, not that

Harris cared. As far as Harris was concerned, Jameson would rather see him dead than let him become a Marine, but Harris no longer cared what Jameson wanted or thought. Harris knew he would sooner die than ever surrender.

Eventually the thrashing ended. Harris didn't die. He even found the strength to run and catch up with his platoon as they marched to evening chow. He had lived to endure another day.

CHAPTER TEN

Harris stared directly at the head in front of him, just as he had been trained. The awkwardness was gone. It was natural now for them to move in synchronization with Senior Drill Instructor Staff Sergeant McAlister's cadence. It was second nature to march in unison in time with the music. The young Marines' arms and legs moved; their heads remained steady and level. All were focused. All were determined. They moved as one body.

It was graduation day for the forty-nine recruits left in Platoon 3103, India Company. The day that had seemed so far away, so incomprehensibly distant, was finally here. Harris was under no illusion that the journey was over. He knew the hard work was just beginning, but he had completed the first step. Today he was a US Marine.

It was a beautiful San Diego day in May. Part of him wanted to enjoy the moment, the people, the ceremony, but his brain kept drifting to the five days of leave he had coming. Five days of sleeping in, Mom's cooking, and a private bathroom. The weather would be nice in Kansas this time of year. Five days, he could worry about the rest later; for now five days seemed like a lifetime.

Harris was lost in his thoughts and completely unaware they had been dismissed. His fellow Marines breaking formation and heading to family members in the stands of MCRD's parade deck clued him in that boot camp was finally done. He stood there visually taking in the whole scene. He had no family there. Harris had wanted to spare his mother the expense of flying his brother, sister, and herself to San Diego. Besides, as much as he wanted to see the city, he wanted to see home more. He would meet his family that night at the Kansas City airport. Still, he stood there and looked around and found Hastings.

"Congratulations, Devil Dog!" Harris stepped up with his hand out. Hastings, somewhat surprised, wide eyed, and grinning, turned and lunged at Harris. He wrapped him up in a big bear hug.

"Semper Fi, brother! Is the world ready for the two most badass Marines that ever set foot on the planet?"

"We'll find out." Harris thought his response lacked gusto, but he was happy enough not to have been knocked over by Hastings's enthusiastic hug.

The two of them walked over to where their platoon had staged their seabags. They debated whether to go to the base e-club and get something to eat and drink. Both agreed they'd rather do that at the airport. They'd both had enough of MCRD for the time being. They headed over to wait for the bus to take them to the airport.

Harris and Hastings were flying on the same airline, but had different destinations. Hastings had a flight to Omaha, Nebraska. They checked in their bags and got their boarding passes. Both expressed their gratitude for President Clark's easing of security checks on military personnel, as they were able to avoid a long line getting to their terminal.

Feeling on top of the world, they straddled up to the nearest bar and sat down. A young woman was working, but to their disappointment a middle-aged man walked over to serve them.

"What can I get you gentlemen?" The bartender smiled.

"A glass of your finest bourbon, good sir! For me and my friend," Hastings ordered with his typical gusto.

After the briefest of hesitations, the bartender replied with a smile, "I'm afraid I'm going to have to see some ID first, gentlemen."

"You know"—Hastings lightly slapped the bar quickly three times—"we both have a long afternoon ahead of us. Better make it two Cokes instead."

"I'll have a double cheeseburger as well. With fries," Harris chimed in.

"Same for me, good sir, same for me," Hastings concluded.

"Sure thing, gentlemen. Coming right up."

"What's with all this 'good sir' stuff? You trying to sound like you're from Old England or something?"

"What's wrong, Harris? How can you not be in a good mood? I'm just trying to be polite."

"Polite is one thing. You're just acting goofy," Harris said with a smile.

The bartender brought over their sodas, and they both turned around to watch the crowd walk through the airport. Both agreed it was good to be back in a world that had women in it. They didn't need to say much. Both enjoyed watching the view.

When their cheeseburgers arrived, that got their full attention. Both took pains not to get a mess on their uniforms. They ordered another round of sodas and the bartender brought them over.

"Dang! He put whiskey in here!" Hastings said in an usually hushed tone.

"What?" Harris quickly took a drink. It did taste a little funny. "Are you sure?"

"Hell yeah! Don't you know what whiskey tastes like?"

"Well, I've never had whiskey before," Harris admitted. In fact, he'd never had alcohol before.

"Cheers, Devil Dog!" Hastings held up his glass.

"Semper Fi," Harris responded as the two toasted. They enjoyed their drinks and then asked for the bill.

"This one is on me, gentlemen," the bartender replied. "Thank you for your service, and you men be careful out there. We want you boys home again alive and in one piece."

"Thank you, sir," both Marines said in unison, still fresh from boot camp.

The two walked down the terminal together. They agreed to meet at the same bar in five days when they returned from leave. They'd report to Camp Pendleton together. They said good-bye and went to go spend time with their families.

***

"So how were your five days at home?" Joel sensed that this was a good place to conclude for the day. It was late afternoon. He wanted to head out for a happy hour somewhere and catch a dinner.

"It was all I could have hoped it to be," Harris's tone was distant, as if he were still in the past. "It's one of my most cherished memories now."

"Was there anyone special you saw while you were back?" Joel's tone implied he meant more than just the Harris family.

"What? You mean like a special girl?"

"Well, you know, whoever." Joel tried to imply that the sex didn't matter.

"This fucking world." Harris sighed and looked down at his glass of bourbon. "I didn't have a girlfriend back home. No, the only special people I saw were my mother, brother, sister, my dog, and some friends. It'd be the last time I ever spent with them." Harris looked up from his glass, over Levine's head and into the setting sun. "No, the next time I saw my mother in person was at the trial. They wouldn't let her speak to me. She'd just sit there in the courtroom and look sad, occasionally tearing up and dabbing her eyes with a tissue. Sometimes I wondered if she believed any of the things they said about me.

"That's my biggest regret of all this—putting her through it. She'd been through enough; she didn't need all that. To hear all that. To be asked all the questions by reporters. They should have just come after me and left her alone."

"That's your biggest regret?" Joel was somewhat shocked. He couldn't imagine there wouldn't be more to regret than his mother's hurt feelings. "What about your betrayal of the Government? What about all the people you killed?" Joel asked with more righteous indignation than he had intended.

Harris had a hard expression on his face when he looked Joel Levine in the eye.

"Fuck them."

CHAPTER ELEVEN

The bacon was the best Joel Levine had ever eaten, but it was a guilty pleasure. He believed eating meat was bad for the planet, as well as being unfair to those in underdeveloped economies, but it smelled so good he had to try it. The hotel wasn't serving food of this quality, so why not take advantage of the accommodations being made for Harris? After all, LaGard had been very pleased. She thought that Harris's notions of Americanism's supremacy over communism, America's righteousness in the Sino-American War, and especially his lack of remorse in the murder of American civilians upon his return was perfect for their purposes. She told him he was doing an excellent job and to keep it up. So why not indulge a bit himself? Was he not moving into an elite status in his own career?

"If the elite cannot enjoy life, who can?" Joel quietly mumbled and smiled to no one but himself as he got up for seconds on the bacon.

"Good morning, Mr. Levine. I hope you had a good night's sleep." Harris wore a big smile and spoke in such a congenial tone. Gone was his harsh manner and ice-cold stare that had concluded their interview the day before.

"I did." Joel went to take another bite of food, but then thought better of it. "And you, how did you sleep?"

"Oh, I slept like a baby. My room has a great bed, but the view leaves something to be desired." Harris chuckled at his joke and sat down with his breakfast.

Levine didn't get Harris's sense of humor about living in a prison cell, but dismissed it to enjoy his bacon.

The two ate in silence for several minutes. Joel noticed that Harris had already finished when the old man limped over to get a refill of coffee from the buffet.

"So you and Hastings met up at the airport when you got back from your five days of vacation?" Levine kicked off the day's interview.

"Leave. In the military it's called leave, not vacation."

"Yes, yes, of course it is." Levine chafed at being corrected over such a trivial matter. He would have thought Harris would let something like that slide given his circumstances. Who was the old man to correct him?

"Yeah, Hastings was always a man of his word." Levine thought his tone became despondent at the sudden recollection. "When I got back to the San Diego airport, I went back to that bar and found him there waiting for me." Harris sadly smiled and leaned back in his chair. "In fact, the same bartender was working there again. He served us a couple of bourbon and Cokes on the down low. We then had to head out to catch a bus that'd take us to Camp Pendleton. We had to report to the School of Infantry, at San Onofre, by 1800 or something like that. After the years some details are fuzzy."

"Harris, is everything all right? You don't quite seem yourself today?" Levine conjured his most sympathetic tone.

"How the hell would you KNOW what my self is?"

"Now 1800, that's eight p.m., right?" Levine's career focus was all that kept him from saying screw you, old man! That and the fact that he was just a bit afraid of Harris despite his age.

"No, no. You've got to add twelve. 1800 is six p.m." Harris's congenial tone had returned. "Those five days of leave. Those three days at home. That was the last time I spent with my mother, my brother, and my sister. I would never have a face-to-face conversation with any of them again. In retrospect, when I went back to Camp Pendleton, it was kind of as if they died from my life. It would never be the same again. But then at that point, whether any of us realized it or not, the whole country would never be the same again."

Levine felt a sudden wave of nostalgia for his grandfather. He pushed it to the back of his mind and got back to his task at hand.

"I see, so tell me about the School of Infantry." Levine turned on his recorder and set his fingers on the keyboard, ready to type.

"Well, hold on there, Skippy. I'm going to fix myself a drink first."

"Drink...drink?!" Levine was baffled by the new nickname as well as Harris's call for an early happy hour.

"Ain't like I got to drive anywhere. Don't worry, if my narration gets too incoherent, you can cut me off." Even though Harris was an old man, Levine wondered if he, personally, could prevent him from doing anything he really wanted to do. He felt preposterous for the thought, but there was something about Harris's attitude that made him think it.

"So School of Infantry?" Levine tried to get back on track.

"Yeah, SOI." Harris sat back down with a bourbon. "In those days it was an eight-week course. The old salts used to tell us we had it easy. You see, at the start of the war they only had four weeks. They had to learn on the job. Do or die, as they say. They lengthened the course when the mission shifted from liberation to invasion.

"The Marine Corps's philosophy, at the time, was that every Marine is a rifleman. So every Marine had to prove himself proficient with a rifle to graduate boot camp. If you were an infantryman, which many Marines were at that time, you were proficient with all infantry weapons. We did some

110

work with the M5, our basic rifle. It was a 5.56 mm. It was based off the M4, but had a piston system. We even got to shoot the M458, like an M5 but fired a .458 caliber.

"What's wrong?" Harris asked, interrupting his own narration.

"Oh, nothing, really," Levine stammered a bit, "the numbers get a bit confusing for me."

"Yeah, well," Harris continued, "let's just suffice it to say we were exposed to nearly every weapon system. Light and heavy machine guns, mortars, antitank. The Army always got the new stuff. Many of the weapon systems we used were thirty or forty years old and the Corps would just dress them up with new electronics, optics, and such. Hell, we were still using the M2, that's a big machine gun, and that's been around since the Second World War. Damn good gun though.

"Live fire training was minimal. Saving the rounds up for the invasion, most likely. We did a lot of electronic training. Computer simulation and that sort of thing. I imagine what changed the most with the extra time was that we just did a lot more running. They ran us everywhere, every way. Uphill. Downhill. With packs, without packs. Anyway…" Harris broke from his ramblings.

"We learned to love those big-caliber weapons. They really did a number on that Prick body armor. If it didn't kill 'em, it'd really fuck 'em up."

"Prick?" Levine's sense of moral superiority slipped through.

"Yeah, acronym for People's Republic of China: PRiCk." Levine knew what the acronym was, as well as the derogative connotation that was applied to it. Even in grade school, Joel had learned the hurtful effect it had had upon the People's Republic.

"Even at the time didn't it strike you as demeaning, as a *dehumanizing* way to speak of these people?" Joel was attempting to get Harris to open up about racist indoctrination in his Marine Corps training. He thought a self-righteous tone might guilt Harris into a sort of confession.

"They invaded our land, raped and killed our people, and tried to enslave us. We were preparing to invade their land and kill them, and you want to get worked up over our nomenclature?"

"No. See…I…what…" Joel stammered, trying to figure out an excuse that wouldn't anger Harris.

"Nomenclature means names for things, used by particular groups or in particular fields."

"I-I *know* what *nomenclature* means." Joel felt his face getting hot. "I simply—"

"Anyway," Harris firmly continued as Levine stewed over his lack of control of the situation, "it was a grueling eight weeks, although combat would be a hell of a lot worse. However, at that time, we couldn't imagine that. All of us complained about how we couldn't wait to get to the Fleet, a deployable unit."

"How were you trained to think of the Chinese?" Levine wanted to steer the conversation back towards indoctrination. "You said earlier you called them Pricks, why not PLA? Why not call them by their name, the People's Liberation Army?" Levine was much more pleased with his own tone this time around. He thought it was more reasonable. More intellectual.

"You really care about names? Seriously? We were trained to kill people and break things. To kill the people who had been killing us, in OUR land. Hell, Pricks was one of the nicer things we called them."

"Did the Marine Corps teach you to hate Asian people? Particularly the Chinese?" Levine sensed a slant that he could use. "How were Chinese-American recruits treated?"

"Well"—Harris was a little taken aback by the break from his narrative—"anyone that looked too Asian or Chinese wasn't really used in the infantry. Things were already confusing enough at times."

"Don't you think they could have contributed to the war effort?" Levine was feeling good about where the conversation was going.

"Are you fucking kidding me?" It was Harris's turn to be incredulous. "Are you trying to play some kind of racial discrimination angle on me? Are you familiar at all with the strategy behind Operation Mandate of Heaven?"

"Of course," Levine somewhat lied.

Joel's grandfather had bragged to him that it was one of the greatest covert agent operations in all of world history. Hundreds, perhaps thousands, of Chinese-American and Taiwan operators infiltrated China to begin a propaganda campaign to undermine the Chinese faith in their communist government and nationalism based on the ancient belief that the gods mandate who is emperor of China. When an emperor became corrupt, he lost that mandate and thus a revolution, resulting in a new emperor. Operatives would build up the Chinese fear, corruption and dissatisfaction with the communist government while emphasizing that Chinese industrialization and modernization was a better fit with a democratic style of government. Joel's grandfather had been adamant about the heroism of these brave operatives, many of whom were imprisoned and executed by the People's Republic.

In high school and college, Joel's teachers discredited Abe Levine's memory of events as just another racist, American lie. Operation Mandate of Heaven, according to academia, was more about American self-righteousness. Intellectually speaking, it was descended from the concept of Manifest Destiny and American Revolutionary ideas of divine providence. They taught that the overwhelming majority of Chinese were happy with communism. They had all the necessities of life. Housing, healthcare, and education. How could they possibly be dissatisfied with communism? No, it was all a lie from the Clark administration to cover up the destruction, murder, and rape American servicemen imposed upon the Chinese people.

Joel had sadly concluded that it was just another lie his grandfather had told him to try to make him proud to be an American. President Clark had had a brilliant propaganda machine, as evil as it was. Joel had learned in school that Operation Mandate of Heaven was nothing more than an American justification for the overthrow of the People's Republic of China and the slaughter of their people.

But did Harris truly believe it? Or was he just putting a righteous veneer over his past crimes. If the man was truly good and trying to help, to "liberate" others, why come back to America and slaughter Americans?

Levine decided to try another angle. "Well, tell me, what else do you remember of—" Levine checked his notes "—SOI?"

"I was assigned to Hotel Company. Units were assigned by alphabetical order. I think…" Harris stopped to remember. "I think F through K. It doesn't really matter now anyway.

"Boot camp was tough. SOI was tougher, at least physically anyway. But by then we were used to that type of training. I mean, there were still some of the silly boot camp mind games; it just didn't have the same kind of impact it had had in boot camp.

"For me the worst part about it was the last week. The last two weeks, we participated in a big war game that we needed to pass in order to graduate. Well, that last week I came down with pneumonia. There was no way I could go to sick bay without being dropped from the course. If I was dropped from the course, I would have to start again and have to do the whole thing all over. I decided there was no way in hell I was going to do SOI again if I could help it, so I just sucked it up. Oh, but I was so miserable."

"How did you know you had pneumonia?" Joel was incredulous. Who could really not be bedridden from pneumonia?

"I went to sick bay the day after I graduated from the course and was diagnosed with pneumonia. I was given a shot of penicillin and a day of bed rest. After what I'd been through, it felt like a vacation. I was supposed to go back to sick bay the next day, but I skipped it."

"Why do that?" Joel was even more skeptical.

"We were getting shipped out to our units that day. I didn't want to miss out and get separated from my buddies."

"Couldn't you have just stayed in sick bay until you were better and catch up to them?"

"Maybe. Once I got out of sick bay, who knew where or when I'd be assigned to a unit. I didn't want to take that chance."

"It was that important to you?" Joel had not lost any of his skepticism.

"Yeah. It was." Harris left no room for doubt.

"Tell me"—Levine thought his timing was perfect to get Harris to reveal genuine thought and not a rehearsed memory—"what lesson do you remember the most from SOI? What knowledge or wisdom did you acquire that you think served you best in life?" Levine was rather pleased with his question. He expected a long and thoughtful response, perhaps even provoking an epiphany of the pain and destruction Harris's education had caused him and others.

"When in doubt, shoot," Harris immediately responded without batting an eye.

Levine found Harris's confidence and certainty unsettling. Levine doubted he would ever be able to truly understand what motivated people like Harris, and what made them think the way they did. Fortunately for him, as a journalist and historian, he didn't have to. He just had to convince people what the government did and said was right.

CHAPTER TWELVE

Harris fought the idea that he might throw up. *Mind over matter.*
If you don't mind, it don't matter. He wished he had a dollar for
every time he'd been told that since he'd entered the Marine
Corps. It was not the time or place. He had to compose
himself. He didn't know if the nausea was from the air
turbulence or his nerves. This was not the first time he'd
ridden in an MV-22 Osprey. It was the second, but this ride
was nothing like the first. This time he was amongst a fleet of
MV-22s flying into combat, and his nerves were in high gear.
The fact that the aircraft felt more like a roller coaster to him
only added to his stress. Everyone was strapped in or had to
hold on to something tight in order not to be thrown around
the aircraft. Harris couldn't tell for sure, but he thought he
could hear explosions. The ship's guns weren't firing. Were
they being shot at, or was it all part of the distraction? Perhaps
it was his imagination. Harris had come to terms with the fact
that he might well die fighting for his country. Key to that was
he would die fighting. To him the notion of being shot out of
the air without having even yet seen a Prick terrified him more
than death itself.

He wanted to ask Edwards about the noise, but doubted
Edwards would hear him. If he did, he could imagine Edwards
telling him he had other things to worry about. That was
Edwards's style.

The crew chief motioned they should get ready to land.
Harris turned on his night-vision goggles. He turned the
ignition of the LSV, light strike vehicle, outfitted with a TOW
(antitank) package. Edwards was already positioned behind the
gun. That was Edwards's style.

117

The crew chief motioned that it was time to disembark. Harris drove the LSV straight off the MV-22, and they cut a hard left. Just as he had practiced at Camp Daily in the Philippines. The Ospreys took off. No one was shooting at them yet, but there were definitely explosions. From this distance it sounded like thunder. Jets roared over their position. They were headed west. Most likely they were American. If they were Prick, at least they hadn't shot them. Perhaps this wouldn't be so bad.

Harris had envisioned his first moments of combat to be more violent than this. He was partially relieved and disappointed at the same time.

"Move up another thirty meters," Edwards commanded right after he kicked the driver's seat. Harris did as ordered and then could see Blue Four Alpha about fifty meters to his right.

"Blue Four Alpha, Blue Four Bravo in position. Over," Edwards communicated over his microphone.

"Blue Four Bravo, Blue Four Alpha, roger. Over and out," Harris heard through his earpiece. Harris wanted to ask what was next, mostly out of nervousness, but he knew what was next. Stay in position, shoot anything that was moving east. After two hours, move east and shoot anything that did not look American. Harris was nervous. At this moment he wanted nothing more than a cigarette. It dawned on him just how hooked he'd gotten on those things in the Philippines. Oh, and how safe, secure, and homelike the Philippines seemed right now.

Harris scanned the horizon through his night vision, positioned behind the SAW, squad automatic weapon, mounted on a swivel on the side of the LSV. The weapon was a belt-fed light machine gun that fired a caseless 5.56 mm cartridge. It could be mounted on either side of the LSV, as well as on top of the vehicle. In the Philippines they had been issued improved ceramic-lined barrels with built-in suppressors. The SAW gunner could now fire longer without changing barrels and was less likely to be spotted by the enemy.

So far, despite his nervousness, he was finding the war boring. Harris thought it wise not to share this with Edwards. That said, he was on edge. It was a quiet night. The LSV's engine was off. Edwards was running the TOW system in silent mode. A lithium-ion battery would give them about nine hours' energy before they'd have to recharge it with the LSV's engine. Despite the quiet, Harris couldn't understand how the Chinese could not know where they were with all the Ospreys landing and the humming of the LSVs as they drove into position. He strained his ears to filter out the crickets, cicadas, and listen for unnatural noises that could be Pricks. He scanned the sky and listened for any possible drones. So far nothing, or was he just missing it? He fought back the fear that was telling him it was too overwhelming. He had to; this was not a good time to knock off and try another day.

"Harris, you best be on my nine and keep your shit together," Edwards quietly ordered. Harris heard the pop, but no "fire in the hole" this time. Harris jumped when the missile went off. He was surprised at being surprised by the noise. He'd heard the TOW missile fired before, but this seemed so much louder. He realized that he didn't have earplugs in this time. His ears rang. Instinctively he'd closed his eyes to not lose his night vision from the back blast. A short eternity had passed before the missile hit its target.

"Blue Four Alpha, Prick tanks at our eleven—" Another TOW fired before Edwards could finish. Two more quickly followed. The other squads had joined in the killing. Edwards discarded the empty missile casing. Harris was already handing up a new missile to reload.

"Echo Three Echo, nice confirmation." Sergeant Bohanan's voice came across the speaker.

"Roger that, Echo Five Bravo," Edwards replied.

Bohanan had told them to confirm with him before they fired. Edwards took his own initiative to fire the first shot from Task Force Grant in the campaign for Shanghai. That was Edwards's style.

After the School of Infantry Privates Sean Harris and William Hastings had both been assigned to Weapons Company, First Battalion, First Marine Regiment, First Marine Division. Many from their SOI class went to 1/1, as First Battalion, First Marines was known. Harris and Hastings, along with Samuel Grey and Steven Jones, had been made TOW gunners and assigned to Weapons Company. They were shipped out of Camp Pendleton to Camp Daily, Philippines, where 1/1 was stationed.

His first impression of the Philippine Islands was that it looked like some of the movies he'd seen about the Vietnam War. He'd watched several when he was growing up and watched those several times at that. His grandfather had served in the Ninth Infantry Division during that war, so he was fascinated by it. He'd been fascinated with the Islamic wars as well, but his father told him Hollywood couldn't bother to make a movie worth watching about that. It was always said with an edge of bitterness that Sean didn't fully understand. His father loved the United States and American culture. Not showing proper respect for the Stars and Stripes, the Constitution, or any of the Founding Fathers earned you the belt or a quick smack upside the head. His father fought in America's wars overseas. He fought crime in the country and returned to war when needed. Yet he was always angry at the country's leaders.

"Never trust those goddamn bastards, ever!" he'd often say after a drink or two. "For anything you take from the government they'll want your soul in return."

Still, he was excited to be in the Philippines. He'd been told that his great-grandfather had fought in the Pacific and served in the US Navy in World War II. He'd served on the USS *Yorktown* when it went down at the Battle of Midway. The story was that his great-grandfather had won big stakes in a poker game a few days before the battle. When the order came to abandon ship, he ran down to his berthing area to retrieve his winnings. Ships sink fast; his great-grandfather claimed to have barely made it out alive and that going back for the money was the dumbest thing he'd ever done.

As well, he had an ancestor that fought in the Spanish-American and Filipino War. That ancestor had been a career soldier. Twenty years in the US Army. Story was that he'd lied about his age; he was seventeen when you had to be twenty-one to enlist in the Army. He'd fought in the Philippines. Supposedly he had once retreated with his unit into Subic Bay, neck deep into water, to wait for reinforcements. The Moro Indians were too short to go out that far. Family legend had it that the former Harris had brought back a .455-caliber Webley pistol he'd taken from a Moro Indian he'd found hiding up a tree.

"I'll give you my pistol if you don't kill me," the Moro had offered.

"Well, what did you do?" everyone would ask.

"I got his pistol, don't I?" was all the further detail the old man would give.

Harris had never been to the Philippines before, but he thought it felt right to be there. He might have been the only Marine in his family, but he felt like part of his family's tradition of American warriors. Being where he was, fulfilling his role in the war, made him feel worthy of his family, his nation, his culture. This was the best he'd ever felt about himself in his short life.

Harris couldn't wait to set foot on the ground. He'd like to have seen Subic Bay, but the carrier didn't pull in for whatever reason Harris wasn't privy to. Instead, they were flown into the interior of Luzon to Marine base Camp Daly. It was named for Marine Corps legend Sergeant Major Dan Daly. It was here that Harris and the other replacements would hook up with First Marines, be assimilated, and trained for their next mission.

"I lose six good Marines, and this is the shit I get?" was the greeting Harris and the others got from Staff Sergeant Callahan, the platoon sergeant for TOW Platoon, of Heavy Weapons Company. The man had a strong Texan accent, and acted like a stereotypical drill instructor. Harris was uncertain what he thought of the man. Time would tell.

The boots, as the replacements were called, were all split up. TOW platoons were split into three sections, four squads per section. Five Marines per squad. Ideally, that was. Heavy Weapons, as the rest of 1/1, was in the process of getting back to full speed. Grey was assigned to Section One; Harris and Hastings to Section Two. Jones went to Third. Hastings went on to First Squad; Harris to Fourth.

His squad leader, Sergeant Bohanan, seemed to be a short man with a big attitude, from Oklahoma. Short could be misleading. Harris could imagine his father saying the man was built like a shit brick house. At five feet eight inches, Bohanan was not tall, but the man had massive shoulders and thick muscles. Bohanan assigned Harris as a driver for Lance Corporal Edwards, the senior gunner of Fourth Squad.

In many ways, Harris thought Edwards seemed like the ideal Marine on a recruiting poster. The man stood six feet one inch. Broad shoulders, big arms, and narrow hips. He kept his dark blond hair buzzed short. He had steel blue eyes that always appeared confident. There were times Harris thought Edwards's confidence was perhaps arrogance, but then Harris never really thought he could tell exactly what Edwards was thinking. Unlike Callahan and Bohanan, Edwards spoke in a calm voice. He never seemed angry. He always seemed serious.

With a new missile in the snout, they were moving towards the enemy. Since Edwards had fired, all hell had broken loose. They pulled into a new firing position. Harris thought he could hear a slight buzz.

"Harris, watch for drones," Edwards ordered. Harris was angry at himself for being told what to do before he had taken the initiative to do so. By the time he'd pulled the 12 gauge from the bracket, he'd definitely IDed the buzzing, sighted the observation drone in his night vision, and downed it with the 12 gauge on the first shot.

While training in the Philippines with his new unit, he had excelled at drone target practice. He began to swell with a bit of pride over his first kill.

"Let's fucking move in case they got a bead on us." Edwards didn't take time to congratulate Harris on his marksmanship. They hadn't gone fifty meters when a rocket exploded near their previous location.

"Hold up at that knoll at your two o'clock," Edwards ordered, indicating a spot for good cover. Harris could see tracer rounds, but in the dark, he couldn't place the distance. Judging by the sound, it was several hundred meters. It was quickly drowned out by the explosion of more missiles. Harris stood watch, looking and listening for more drones or PLA infantry heading their way. From what Harris could tell, it seemed they had caught a Prick column by surprise. This was a

123

source of amazement to Harris after all the noise of buzzing Ospreys and LSVs. But then they were dealing with an enemy thousands, even tens of thousands, of meters away.

Harris blasted another drone. Time to move again. Another hundred meters, Edwards nailed an armored car. Time to move again.

"Hold up. Where we at? Where's everyone else?" Harris checked his GPS screen.

"We're about three hundred meters ahead of Blue Leader, about one hundred meters ahead of Bohanan," Harris answered.

"Blue Four Alpha, Blue Four Bravo, we're ahead at about your eleven. Over."

"Copy Blue Four Bravo. Got a visual on you. Stay if you can. Over. Out."

"Roger."

Harris almost stated how much he wanted a cigarette, but decided not to engage in small talk. Most likely Edwards wouldn't answer, and they all had more important things to do anyway.

As if out of nowhere jets screamed overhead. The sound was earsplitting. Within a few seconds there was a huge fireball in the air to the east of them.

"Looks like Prick air finally showed…bastards!"

"What?!"

"Check this out." Edwards jumped down. Harris jumped up to look through the TOW gun's night sight. About one kilometer away he saw a burning LSV. In the driver's seat was a body completely engulfed in flames.

"Do you know who got hit?"

"We'll find out soon enough. Get down. Nothing we can do about it now anyway. Just focus on killing as many of these bastards as possible."

124

"All Blue Four units, move northeast. Copy?" Every Blue vehicle answered in the affirmative. Harris looked to the northeast. Rockets, flames, explosions, and tracers filled the sky. It looked like Hell. If the sky had parted and the Four Horsemen had ridden onto the field, Harris would not have found it shocking. There was nothing about the environment that was inviting to him. It was literally, at that moment, the last place he wanted to go.

Harris scanned the land in front of him, looking for a route, looking for drones, looking for anything that could kill him or anything that he could kill. He was no longer finding the war a bit boring. A voice inside his head told him to go the other way. Another voice was telling him he needed a cigarette. Another voice told him that he was a United States Marine and Marines go into war.

Harris started the LSV and moved northeast into the fighting.

CHAPTER THIRTEEN

There had been much concern as to the reaction of the locals. One theory was that the Chinese were fanatical communists who would fight to the last man. Another was that they could be converted or at least compromised. Many of China's cities had become very industrialized and very Westernized. There was no shortage of political dissidents. Some American political and military leaders, not the least among this group was President Clark, saw this as a weakness for the communist regime to be exploited. Hong Kong was thought of as a potential member of the coalition Clark had built with the United Kingdom, Canada, and Australia. With the South China Sea Campaign, Taiwan, Japan, South Korea, and Philippines were part of the Allied effort. On the sidelines in the South China Sea was Vietnam, and to the north Russia. Both were willing to accept a weakened, or destroyed, People's Republic of China, for a price. For now they were happy to accept some territorial "table scraps," and Clark was happy to let them have it. Clark ordered Operation Mandate of Heaven.

Asian and American intelligence operatives began to lay the groundwork for a democratic rebellion and, ideally, reestablishment of the Republic of China with the help of the United States military. An American force in the south, Task Force Grant, would "liberate" the Westernized industrial cities with the promise of greater profits and freedoms. Those that didn't join would be destroyed. One way or another depriving the PRC of much of its industry and resources.

The American strategy in the north was less complex. Task Force Sherman would decimate all resources for war and living, causing Beijing to be flooded with refugees at a time when they were least able to take care of them. This was to cause an even greater loss of faith in the PRC. All this was to culminate in the collapse of the communist government in China.

Zhang Min was going on three days with no sleep. He really hadn't felt like he needed it either. His country was under attack by the very barbarians he had sought to conquer. All too late he was realizing his mistake. After decades of weakness and compliance, even downright submission under Leakey, he could not have possibly imagined the American people could have so much fight left in them. Now he was struggling for his political, and literal, life. In the last seventy-two hours he had ordered the executions of four members of the National People's Congress (NPC) and three generals. Not that they bore any responsibility for the invasion, Zhang knew that was on him, but he was not going to admit that, and the invasion was an excellent opportunity for him to cleanse the party of some of his opponents and possible political threats. His hope was that war with the United States, and new territory in North America, would be enough to manipulate the NPC into his third term as president, general secretary of the Communist Party, and chairman of the Central Military Commission. In short, the most powerful man in the history of Communist China and the Middle Kingdom. So far, nearly nothing had gone according to his plan.

Zhang Min thought Taiwan would capitulate after the United States was neutralized. Neither of which had happened. China's limited excursion into North America was a complete disaster resulting in the surrender of nearly two hundred thousand troops and approximately one hundred fifty thousand dead. The People's Republic was badly hurt. Now President Clark and the American people wanted more blood.

Nor had China's invasion of the Philippine Islands gone as planned by the communist commissars. The Filipino guerrillas only got harder to handle, no matter how many cities were bombed or villages were burned. When the PLA Navy was ambushed by the US Navy at the Battle of Luzon, the biggest naval battle since World War II, the Chinese lost all their aircraft carriers. The Philippines were no longer considered attainable. The PLA's new goal was to slow the loss of the Philippines, not prevent it. Now reports were coming in that the remaining PLA troops in the Philippines were surrendering in droves to the Allied forces.

The Philippines Campaign had been a loss of face. Zhang executed two generals. Not because of their military decisions, but they were wrong politically.

Zhang would not be careless. He had worked too hard and come too far. He believed he had earned the right to rule China. He knew of his power to persuade the people with his words; he was also aware of his greater talent to intimidate people. He would survive this. He would recover. His career would thrive once more.

He gave speeches on CCTV about the greatness of the Chinese people. He ranted about the evil and corruption of the West and especially of the American people: the greatest barbarians on earth. He activated reserve forces, and Chinese men and women were drafted into the PLA; but still, Zhang and none of the communist leaders, that would admit to it anyway, thought the American people had the courage to attack the mainland. Zhang thought he was dealing with an enemy that lacked courage and intelligence. His only anchor now was to believe that their courage, without the balance of judgement, would be the Americans' undoing. He worried if he was accurate. He pushed the thought from his mind. It was against his nature to doubt himself. Problems and mistakes were always the fault of others, not him. Zhang Min was of a superior mind, a superior will that all others bent to. But he knew now he had misjudged this. He had estimated the absolutely worst-case scenario to be the loss of recently acquired territory in the South and East China Seas. Now the barbarians were in the homeland. How?

Simultaneous invasions in the south, from Taiwan, and the north from Korea. How could North Korea fall so quickly? The Chinese ambassador Li Cong was raising hell at the United Nations and charging that the United States attacked Pyongyang with UN-banned nuclear weapons, in the hope of cementing an international alliance against the Americans. The problem was the Russians, who had privately given China support in their war against the US, now seemed too complacent about the American invasion. The Russians were no help in the UN.

In fact, the Russian ambassador had even volunteered Russian troops to restore order, keep peace, and distribute food to North Koreans, or at least to some of them along the coast, anyway. Zhang always knew not to trust the Russians, but he never thought they would get into bed with the Americans.

Of course, their women get into bed with anybody, why not their men? He chuckled at his own joke, as he was prone to doing. He poured himself another shot of baijiu, "Chinese vodka," and thought of his next move. One way or another, he would survive this invasion.

Wang Fai had hidden in his factory dorm room with seven other workers for the last two and a half days. Life was becoming desperate. He had not eaten for thirty-six hours. The residents had drunk the toilet dry twelve hours ago. His room was cramped. The humidity was stifling. Jet planes were screaming overhead. Every so often the building shook from an explosion. For a while he had watched from the rooftop. It was exciting at first. The mayor had advised all residents to stay in their buildings and promised the People's Liberation Army would repel the ugly American invaders. That was the last public announcement. He'd seen PLA fighter jets crash into the city's buildings. He'd heard distant small-arms fire grow louder as it got closer. Now he was hearing statements broadcast from the streets in Chinese: "China, yes! Communism, no!" "Democracy now! Freedom now!" "China unite for Mandate from Heaven!"

Wang Fai had moved from his small rural village of his birth to work in a textile factory on the outskirts of Fuzhou. The government needed workers. The pay was better than farming. His family suffered from lack of food and healthcare. The increase in pay would go a long way to improving his family's lot. Wang Fai received the government approval to move and went to work in the big city.

Disappointment was immediate. Wang learned he would be starting at half the promised wage. However, with overtime he could come close to what he'd been promised. He shared a small room with seven other workers. He worked one hundred hours a week. He ate a steady diet of minced pork meat with rice. He used a common restroom. The showers did not drain properly, so he showered ankle deep in waste water. The toilet stalls did not drain properly, so he often squatted over a twelve- to eighteen-inch pile of feces when he had a bowel movement. He was not allowed to date. He was not allowed to have sexual intercourse. He was not allowed to be a man, because it did not fit the priorities of the People's Republic of China. He was a slave to governmental overlords. His obedience was motivated solely by the belief in the superiority of his race and his nation. Now that was falling apart before his very eyes. Not only had the barbarians arrived, they were winning. Why couldn't the PLA stop them?

Wang stood on the rooftop of his building. The explosions had stopped. Small-arms fire could still be heard, but it was minimal and fading. Now he could see and hear Chinese marching down the streets, calling for peace, calling for unity, calling for freedom and democracy. It was everything the People's Republic of China had promised, but never delivered. Would this new movement work? Were the gods dispensing of the old corrupt government and bringing in a new? He did not admit to being a religious man, it was discouraged by the PRC, but he'd been taught the old beliefs. Was this truly a Mandate from Heaven?

Wang knew communism had not worked to his benefit. He was miserable. He was a slave. The promise of something better was too seductive. Why not take a chance on it? Could his life get much worse? Would he be more miserable if he was dead? Wang Fai walked down eight flights of stairs and threw his arms in the air. He gave himself to these other Chinese soldiers who promised a better life and a new beginning. Wang figured whether he survived or died, he would take an active role in his future. He would try for something better than what he had. Would he be better off? Would he survive? Were the gods about to bring change? He didn't know for sure, but he knew he'd been miserable and that he was willing to risk his life for a better future. What did he have to lose?

Harris was going on three days without sleep. He really hadn't felt like he needed it either. About twenty-four hours earlier he did try to take a nap during a lull in the action, but it didn't take.

First Battalion had been fighting and moving in an easterly direction. Their job, as Harris had understood it, was to counterattack the PLA's counterattack. They had stayed on the move and successfully driven the Chinese forces north. They had gotten word that a beachhead was established. They could now head to the rear and be resupplied.

Harris drove the LSV. Edwards was behind the TOW gun. They followed Blue Four Alpha, the other gun team in their squad. TOW squads were made up of five Marines: squad leader, junior gunner and senior driver, senior gunner and junior driver. The squad leader often rode with the junior gunner, so that team would be alpha. The TOW platoon was made up of three sections, four squads per section. Harris was in Section Two, thus the blue designation on their call sign.

In SOI Harris had found the TOW gun's destructive powers intriguing. He thought it a fascinating weapon. The gun actually shot a missile guided by a radio frequency with a range of approximately two miles. As long as the gunner could keep the crosshairs of the scope on the target, moving or not, the missile would hit. It was an awesome weapon. Harris was glad to be assigned to it. Especially since it was too big to be practically carried, Harris would be "mounted infantry." That meant less hiking, but he was also a bigger target on the battlefield.

"There they are, over by the big antenna," Edwards pointed out. His voice betrayed some excitement. Harris too was glad to be meeting up with the rest of the platoon, although he hardly knew anyone outside of his own section. As they pulled up, Sergeant Bohanan jumped out of the LSV to guide Harris into a parking spot.

"I know how to park, nimrod," Harris said within the confines of his own mind. Harris found this much direction, this much control, to be condescending and irritating; but it was something he was learning to deal with in the Marine Corps.

"I see your boot driver ain't got you killed yet," Cortes shouted across the makeshift parking lot. Harris chafed at the comment. Cortes was a good buddy of Edwards, and thus Harris had gotten to know him a bit. Harris had not expected this kind of greeting, and it pissed him off some. Before he could get angrier, Cortes shook his hand.

"Good to see you, Harris." Cortes offered the junior Marine a cigarette. Harris's hurt pride was suddenly mended.

"Thanks."

"Hey, don't fuck with my driver there, Hank. He did good. Damn good." Harris took pride from the comment. It was the first indication from Edwards that he'd done a good job in combat.

"Thanks," Harris responded with genuine gratitude.

"Don't thank me," Edwards said while jumping down from the LSV. "You get me killed, I'm going to fuck you up." Edwards always spoke in a dry and even tone. Harris never had any idea if Edwards was joking around, serious, or what. Edwards took a cigarette from Cortes, who lit it for him from his own cigarette.

"Hoorah, Devil Dog," Edwards said with what might have been a bit of sarcasm as he exhaled smoke. "Did we lose anybody?"

"Freedman and Marks." Cortes's demeanor went from jovial to stone in a heartbeat. Harris knew who they were, but hadn't really known them.

"Fuck." Edwards spit and kicked dirt. "Ain't bad for flying in like we did. That's it?"

"I heard Henry and his boot driver, in First Section, got it. Ain't heard how."

"Fucking boots. Probably fucked up and got Henry killed." Edwards spat. Cortes said nothing, but did look at

Harris. Again, Harris had no idea exactly how to interpret Edwards.

"Was it Jones?" Harris asked Cortes.

"Sorry, I really don't know."

"I went to SOI with Jones in First Section," Harris offered while looking at the ground.

"Every Marine here went to SOI with some other Marine here," Edwards stated, adding more awkwardness to the awkwardness.

What seemed like out of nowhere, Harris got slapped on the back.

"Good to see you, buddy!" It was Hastings, alive and well. "And I've got gifts." He handed Harris two cartons of cigarettes.

"Man! Where'd you come up with these?" Harris was genuinely impressed. Most of what he'd seen other than the PLA were shacks and pigs. How'd Hastings end up with smokes? Harris had only brought one carton with him and was down to only three more packs.

"I got a little shopping done while I was getting the LSV washed and waxed," Hastings joked with a cigarette dangling from the corner of his mouth.

Edwards and Cortes appeared apathetic, but stared at the cartons.

"No, I'll tell you," Hastings continued. "Sellers may be a bigheaded bastard, but the man knows how to scavenge." Harris thought Hastings was the pot calling the kettle black, but he laughed all the same. "We drove by a half-demolished shop about ten miles from here. Sellers wants to stop and check it out. We got a bunch of smokes, some dried seaweed shit we tossed out, and some Oreos!"

"What the fuck, man! You holding out on the Oreos?" Cortes chimed in.

"Hey, you got to talk to Sellers about that." Hastings dodged the responsibility of sharing.

"You watch yourself, Hastings," Edwards sternly interjected, breaking the celebratory conversation. "Some Prick motherfucker booby-traps that shit, and you'll be lucky just to get your fucking arms blown off."

"Got it." Hastings stared back at Edwards and then shifted his gaze down. At times Edwards could be just too intense.

"Fall in, TOW Platoon," Staff Sergeant Anderson, Second Section leader, called out.

"Formation! Fall in, Fourth Squad," Sergeant Bohanan quickly reiterated. The Marines broke up their conversation to find out what the Marine Corps had in store for them.

CHAPTER FOURTEEN

Harris found it ironic that his ass hurt so much. Throughout most of his training it was his feet that were his source of pain. But then he was running or hiking everywhere; now he was sitting behind a steering wheel.

He was driving in a column, headed north. TOW platoon had not lingered at their last rendezvous. They were there long enough to get resupplied with food, ammo, and water. Thanks to Hastings, Harris and Edwards were now well stocked on smokes.

Harris was glad to be following somebody because he had no idea where he was. They were to head north, following along the route of a highway, G25. The PLA was disorganized and on the run. The Marines were in hot pursuit to chew their ass.

That was what they were told, anyway. Harris hadn't told anyone except Hastings, but he had expected more resistance from the PLA. Over the last few years he had heard news stories of nasty fights with the PLA in Mexico and the Philippines. The last naval battle had been of epic proportions; some reports claimed it was the biggest naval engagement in world history. So far, Harris hadn't considered anything he'd been involved in epic by any means. He had found moments to be terrifyingly intense; others were insanely boring. All his gunfights lasted several minutes at the most and then broke off. The PLA was falling back; some said it was a full-scale retreat. The "salty" Marines kept talking about how easy this was compared to past battles. Some said it was too easy and that the PLA was setting them up for a trap. Others swore that the PLA was broken and the war would be over within the year.

"I swear I'll punch the next Jarhead that tells me 'this ain't shit! The real fight was in Luzon'!" Hastings had threatened to Harris, but Hastings was just blowing off steam.

However, Bohanan, Edwards, and Schmitt, the other gunner in Fourth Squad, agreed that if the Pricks were falling back now, it was probably to hit back all the harder later. They all hoped that the high command didn't back off and let the PLA regroup. Bohanan and Edwards had been in this war since Mexico. They wanted it done, but done right. They wanted this war won, not postponed for another generation. It was what Harris wanted. It was what his father had wanted.

Their objective in this campaign was the Shanghai Pudong International Airport. So they headed north, taking little comfort from the PLA's retreat. Ultimately, their objective would be the destruction of the People's Republic of China; there was still too much war left to fight.

General Jack McCullough, Allied general-in-chief, also found PLA's lack of fight worrisome. So far, everything seemed to be going according to plan. A best-case scenario, and this was his source of stress. Four years at the Virginia Military Institute and thirty years in the United States Army in four theaters of war, McCullough knew of no campaign where everything went according to plan.

Still, he figured if success was a problem, it was the best problem to have. The Republic of China's (Taiwan) forces and operatives had been great. Many Chinese noncombatants seemed comfortable with being liberated by the Republic of China. Many of the industrialized cities of China's east coast seemed happy, and some eager, to abandon the communist state if it meant they could keep what they had and gain the freedom to acquire more.

The Australian and Canadian forces were perfectly fulfilling their role as an occupation force, freeing up American troops to fight. The Philippines and Japan were hitting a home run with logistics.

He thought it was ironic, under the circumstances, that the only weak link he could think of at the moment was General Mythers, chairman of the Joint Chiefs of Staff's concern that things were moving too quickly. McCullough looked back at his last correspondence with Mythers, questioning whether or not it would be prudent to slow down a bit to allow for better organization and coordination.

"For who? Us or the fucking Pricks?" McCullough said to no one but himself as he puffed on his evening cigar. Jack chuckled. He got a kick out of the troops using the term Prick for the ChiComs. Of course, he didn't use the term in public, but he loved it all the same.

"Slow down?" McCullough again talked to himself, then laughed. He imagined what it would be like to tell his old classmate and friend Edgar "Fast Eddie" Ragnarsson to slow down the First Marine Division. The man was like a bull terrier once he sank his teeth into something. Once he started fighting, only death or victory would stop him. Ragnarsson was a good leader, and his mind-set permeated throughout his command.

No, he was counting on the fact that nothing would slow Ragnarsson down. Still, though, McCullough had a premonition that something bad was about to happen. He poured himself two fingers of bourbon, puffed on his cigar, and stared at his giant map of Eastern China.

"What would I do if I were a Prick general?" he said to himself.

"If I were a slimy, communist bastard, what the hell would I do?" McCullough continued talking to himself.

President Zhang Min entered the conference room. He was wearing a military uniform and carried a holstered pistol on his belt. He wanted to emphasize to his audience that he was the supreme commander. He knew his position was tenuous at the moment. He had another pistol concealed under his military blouse, because a dictator could never be too complacent. He had already chosen his target. He'd rehearsed how he wanted events to unfold for maximum effect with his generals and other political leaders.

General Ding Yong had served thirty-five years in the People's Liberation Army. It was in his blood; he was third generation PLA. His paternal grandfather had even survived the Long March and was a fervent Maoist. Ding considered himself a patriotic son of the People's Republic. He had had a central role in the takeover of the South China Sea, Luzon, and the North American invasion. While he had not always agreed with Zhang's agenda, he felt it was his duty to serve the PRC to the utmost of his ability. He had managed a long career by keeping his mouth shut, or at least being discreet in voicing his disagreement with political leadership. Yet he had been overheard stating to his junior officers that the PRC was in the predicament it was in because of its lack of allies: a political comment. Thus Zhang had targeted him for execution.

"Why, after three months, is our army still in disorganization and *laowai* still in our homeland?" Zhang paused and looked around the conference table. "Why are our people choosing corrupt democracy over communist virtue? Why is our brave People's Liberation Army either in retreat or surrendering to the American barbarians?"

"General Secretary—" General Fu Gang began to answer.

"Could it be that some in here would prefer to serve the capitalist bastards than the People's government?" Zhang was not interested in explanations. He had already decided what had gone wrong. He understood that most Chinese, given a choice of freedom or repression, would choose freedom. Zhang's first priority was not the people of China, but his political career. His first priority was the feeling of power that he had craved his entire life. Today's show wasn't about the *laowai* invaders, it was about him maintaining control of the People's Republic of China, no matter how diminished it was.

Zhang walked around the conference table as he spoke. He preferred to look down on people when speaking to them. When he came to General Ding Yong, he swiftly, but calmly, pulled his nine-millimeter pistol from its holster and shot Ding in the back of his head. Zhang could not have asked for a better reaction from the others. Everyone visibly jumped in their seats. The sound of trickling fluid told Zhang that someone had urinated himself. Zhang thought his performance was perfect. Most likely, he thought, they expected someone to be arrested and executed at a later date. Zhang, however, wanted to do the unexpected and make the biggest political impact among China's elite that he could.

He read once of the American gangster Al Capone, who actually smashed the skull of an underling to scare others into compliance. Zhang had loved that kind of execution of power and control. Ding had displayed what could potentially be seen as political dissent. That was enough to get Ding killed. He thought this provided the perfect opportunity to exercise such a show of strength. So far, he was thrilled with his performance, but he had one more card to play.

"Given the danger of these times, comrades, I took the liberty of ordering the families of all key political and military leaders to be gathered into a secure location. As we are speaking, your wives, children, and, for some, your grandchildren are being escorted to a bunker at an undisclosed location. This is where they will be safe"—Zhang looked around at his commissars and generals—"under my supervision and care. It is up to all of us to protect them, to protect our China. My countrymen, will you fail them?" Zhang asked as blood flowed from Ding's shattered skull over the elaborate wood of the now ruined table that was worth about seven years of wages to the average Chinese worker.

"President Zhang, if I may speak, sir?" Zhang was satisfied with General Wang Tao's timidity.

"Please, General."

"General Secretary, General Ding, myself, and some others have devised a plan to defeat the *laowai* invaders. It may be a good one, sir. If I may explain it."

Curse Ding, Zhang thought, *for not telling me about this before I killed him. And this Wang has to bring that part of it up!* Zhang decided who would be his next example.

"Please, General Wang, enlighten me. Enlighten all of us, and perhaps save the People's Republic of China," and by that he meant his political career.

"Bullshit, Arty!" Lieutenant Colonel William "Bulldog" McGregor expressed his exacerbation to his superior, Colonel Arthur "Lucky" Liddell, commander of First Marines. McGregor only exercised this privilege in private. He was only allowed to do that because he and Liddell were in the same NROTC company at Texas A&M. They were also cousins.

"Settle down, Billy." Liddell was a bit patronizing, McGregor hadn't gone by "Billy" since grade school.

"Taking Shanghai is arguably the biggest campaign of the war. It'll be second only to the fall of Beijing, and we're stuck in goddamn reserve! What the hell is Ragnarsson doing?"

"Your daddy would whip your butt with a belt for swearing like that." Liddell was a bit patronizing, and he was enjoying tweaking his cousin. The men shared a grandfather, who had been a Southern Baptist preacher. Generally speaking, swearing wasn't tolerated in the family, especially on the McGregor side. Ironically, as men, it was William who was foulmouthed and Arthur who had a disdain for cussing.

"Come on, Arty." McGregor wasn't feeling the humor. "You got 1/1 way out on the left flank and rear. We're the reserve of the reserve. What are we going to be doing? Filling sandbags?"

"If that's all you got your Marines doing, I'll fire your butt and you'll be commanding animal control back at Camp Pendleton." Liddell's tone had gotten serious. "Ragnarsson is not a detrimentally cautious man. You know that. If he thinks we're the best to watch the division's rear, we do that. I think you're the best to watch the regiment's rear, you will do that.

"If Shanghai falls like the rest of the coast, 1/1 is going to see plenty of action between here and Beijing. If Shanghai turns into an urban dogfight, we're going to need 1/1, First Marines, and a whole lot more. In the meantime, Lieutenant Colonel, you best be focused on who and what might just slip up our left flank and our rear."

"Aye, aye, sir." McGregor would carry out his orders or die trying.

CHAPTER FIFTEEN

"Take a turn behind the gun. I want to take a piss and have a smoke," Edwards ordered. Harris was always anxious to get behind the gun. While both positions were essential to a TOW gun team, Harris liked the idea of being a gunner better. Besides, both wanted a change in the action. They'd watched American bomber groups flying north and back all day. While not engaged in combat, they were close enough to hear the bombing. It sounded like the low rumble of distant thunder. From their position they'd seen some ROC (Republic of China) patrols and convoys, but nothing else. They weren't in the action and they knew it.

Most of Second Section had had a sense that they were on a back burner for Shanghai. For some this was a good thing; they'd had enough of war. However, for most of the section, it was a blow to their morale and collective ego. Those who wanted to avoid action typically did not volunteer to be infantrymen in the United States Marine Corps. It was harder for a unit to stay sharp and focused when the members thought they'd been given a nonessential assignment. This was where Second Section found itself. Harris and Edwards were no exception.

Edwards lit a cigarette with a match and inhaled deeply. He liked the way the sulfur from the match tasted on that first inhale. He slowly let the smoke out of his lungs and scanned the sky.

"Not a goddamn drone in sight. Unless the Pricks finally came up with the mosquito-sized drones we keep hearing so much about."

Harris had been working with Edwards for almost a year and had never seen him act so agitated.

"So fucking Sellers thinks we'll be home by Christmas or some such shit?"

"That's what I heard. Second hand," Harris answered while scanning the terrain through the TOW's sight.

"The fucker's been smoking crack. Ain't gonna happen that soon. I've been fighting these Pricks for nearly four years. In this big-ass country I don't see the ChiComs going down by Christmas. Hell, we'd be lucky to have it won by the following Christmas. They're a tenacious people. Some are flat-out fanatics. We'll have to kill a shitload of these communist bastards to break their will to fight."

"But we will," Harris added from behind the gun.

"Goddamn straight on that." Edwards smiled a bit. "You might just evolve into a hard-charger yet with that kind of attitude. Provided you don't get your fucking ass killed, anyway."

"Hey, one way or another, as long as I take two Pricks out with me, it'll be worth it."

"You need to get more than two, Harris."

"I figure one for me, one for my dad."

"China's got about one and a half billion people. We can't win trading them one for one."

"That's a fact, but I at least want two."

"You want revenge, or do you want victory?"

"Victory is the best revenge."

Edwards laughed as he exhaled smoke. "I like your attitude, Harris."

Harris wanted to cry out, but he restrained himself. He wanted to be sure. After all the tank ID he'd done in SOI, it was still difficult to tell from a long distance. All those little details of a tank didn't show up at three thousand meters.

Basically you had to recognize the shape of your tanks and the shape of Prick tanks.

They were not ROC, not from that direction, and they sure as hell weren't American. Harris was hit with the sudden realization of how essential this was. His adrenaline surged.

"I think we got Pricks. At ten o'clock. Headed east from west."

Edwards threw his cigarette down. "You think, or you know?" Edwards's awkward attempt to make conversation was done. He grabbed binocular range finders from the LSV and scanned the landscape. "Yeah, they're T99s." Both watched their enemy in silence for several seconds.

"That looks like armored cars and infantry too." Harris's adrenaline was making him chatty.

"That's 'cause it is, Harris. Rear, my ass. Welcome to the goddamn front!" Edwards was ready for battle.

They were already positioned well on the high ground to see the valley and the draws for several miles out, but not so high as to skyline themselves. The PLA columns were emerging from a draw into the valley and moving into battle formations and, unbeknownst to them, had hit the extreme left flank of the First Marine Division.

"Blue Four Alpha, this is Bravo." Edwards was on the mic. Harris stayed behind the gun.

"Go, Bravo."

"Party crashers, ten o'clock."

"Can't get a visual," Bohanan responded after what had been a painful sixty-second wait. "We got your position. We'll come to you."

Up to this point Harris had been wanting more than the small skirmishes he'd been involved in. Now, as the last gun team on the left flank, he had what looked like half the PLA in front of him. He felt cold. He felt fear. He felt ready for this.

"Harris, looks like you kill your first tank today." Edwards seemed more relaxed with the impending battle than he had making small talk fifteen minutes earlier.

Adams drove up with Bohanan and Schmitt. Without prompting, Schmitt began scoping out their ten. Bohanan had the range finders out. Adams manned the SAW.

"Fuck yeah," Bohanan exclaimed with extra Oklahoma twang. "Blue Leader, Blue Leader, this is Four. Over." Harris hadn't seen Bohanan that jazzed up since he'd won a big poker hand two weeks earlier.

"Go, Four."

"Thermopylae. Say again Thermopylae. Over." That was their code word for finding themselves deep in shit.

"Roger. Be there ASAP. Over. Out."

"Saddle up, Marines! We got a fight on our hands. Adams, Schmitt, move down about twenty meters. If you do not have a visual, move your ass till you do." Bohanan would have liked less foliage. They couldn't advance far without losing a visual on the PLA. He would have liked more of a plain, but Marines worked with what they had, not with what they wanted. "Make these first missiles count, Marines. We ain't gonna be able to move around much once they know where we're at."

Staff Sergeant Anderson arrived and got a visual on the PLA. He immediately gave orders for Second Section to redeploy, and notified the commanding officer of Charlie Company.

Harris had had a bead for some time, but was told to wait for orders. Anderson wanted the first volley to be as damaging as possible. Once the Pricks knew where they were, all hell would break loose, and they would not be able to maneuver without disengaging from the enemy and potentially losing a visual on them. That would not do. Their assignment was to protect the left flank of the First Marine Division and that took priority over their own safety.

Within fifteen minutes all of Second Section had repositioned themselves. All gunners had a designated target. No need to waste two missiles on the same tank. Anderson gave the order to fire. It only took twenty-five seconds for the PLA to discover their surprise flank attack was no longer a surprise.

Harris was stoked that Edwards let him stay behind the gun. It was the moment he'd spent the last eleven months of his life preparing for. He told himself that this first shot was for his dad. This one would even the score, but he was lying to himself. Harris's first shot was for himself. Deep down inside, it was for himself that he wanted to kill one of those Prick bastards. It was for his sense of pride for his family, for his country, for his father that he wanted to kill the enemy that would destroy all that. When he got the order to fire, there was no way in hell he was going to let the crosshairs of his sight leave his target. He nailed the bastard right where the turret sat on the body. The turret flipped into the air as the tank exploded. Harris turned from the gun to see Edwards handing him another missile. He immediately reloaded the gun. Now that the PLA knew where they were, all hell would break loose. Within forty-five seconds he'd killed his second tank.

The PLA tanks were spreading out and firing in the direction of the TOW section. Explosions became a part of both battle lines. Artillery had been called in on the PLA. Soon after, PLA air support showed up. The jets screamed in low and dropped their payloads. The hillside the TOWs were on lit up.

Harris felt the earth shake and roar. He stayed focused on reloading and acquiring another target. The tanks, the armored cars, everything seemed to be headed their way. For his third shot he chose an armored vehicle, hoping it was loaded with infantry and would kill more ChiComs. No sooner had it hit than he had the spent missile casing out of the gun tube and Edwards was handing him another missile to reload.

TOWs from First and Third Section were starting to show up and deploy. Within seconds TOW missiles were screaming across the valley, destroying Prick tanks. American air support showed up. First jets hammered the Prick line, followed shortly by attack helicopters chewing up the advancing ground forces. Then PLA attack helicopters showed up, and a dogfight erupted in the air over the dog fight on the ground.

Harris had no idea how normal this was or how it compared to other battles. At the moment he didn't care. There was a malfunction on his fourth missile and it had spiraled out of control. He only hoped it had taken some Pricks out wherever it landed.

More PLA were pouring out of the draw and headed towards the hill on which the TOWs deployed. Harris had one more missile, then two. Somehow, someway, Bohanan had brought over another missile. Harris made them both count. More Prick jets screamed by, firing missiles. Harris felt the explosions, but he was still alive. Somebody was screaming, someone had been hit, but it wasn't him. He had to keep fighting. Anderson's driver stopped by; he had a trailer of TOW missiles. He resupplied Harris and Edwards and headed back to where he came from. Before he made it one hundred meters, he was nailed by a Prick missile.

The heavy machine guns, .50-caliber M2s, and 40 mm Mk 19s had shown up, and not too soon. Prick infantry was starting to work its way up the hill and through the foliage. Harris could now hear small-arms fire around him. He fought the urge to shoot at the first thing he saw through his scope.

He tried to look for vehicles with antennas, knowing they would be set up for communication and thus critical. With explosions all around him, this was hard. One was so close, that against his will, he dropped to the floor of the LSV. He felt the air around him move. His ears rang loud; he couldn't really hear. Edwards was yelling at him. He could not understand specific words, but figured out he was to get his ass up and start shooting again. As he was getting up, Bohanan hauled another missile over to him, slapped him on the back and said something about kicking ass. Harris reloaded and looked for another target.

He felt the explosion before he heard it. Even at the time it seemed very surreal for Harris; he was flying through the air before he heard the explosion that had caused it. He knew he had no control, he didn't know how far he'd fly or how he would fall, but he told himself as soon as he hit he had to get up and keep fighting. Something deep inside told him he'd die if he didn't.

The rim of his helmet hit first. His own momentum pulled his helmet down and smashed it into his nose. As well, his left shoulder took the brunt of the impact. His body skidded; his skin burned as he slid to a stop. Harris tried to jump up, but he fell down right away. His mind screamed get up, but at the time he couldn't figure out which way was up. Harris felt like his head was going to spin off his shoulders. His ears rang; he could hear nothing else. He got up to his hands and knees, but then fell down face-first. Edwards pulled him up, yelling something that didn't register with Harris. He looked to the LSV. Bohanan was dismantling the gun from the LSV's gun mount. This was no easy task since the LSV was on its side.

Edwards began to assist Bohanan. Harris saw Schmitt struggling to remount his own TOW gun, his vehicle having been destroyed. He ran towards Schmitt with his head still spinning. Harris stopped short of an arm he noticed right in front of him. Through the blood and dirt he could see a tattoo of a black rose intertwined with a banner that read Death Before Dishonor. The right forearm belonged to Adams. Suddenly Bohanan was in his face.

"Go to your gun." He pointed to Edwards. "Kill fucking Pricks!" Bohanan slapped him on the helmet and ran off to assist Schmitt. Harris ran back to Edwards and helped him ground mount and load the TOW gun. More jets were screaming overhead, but Harris was too busy to pay attention to them. They were no longer crucial to what he had to do. His head buzzed, he could see blood on his hands, but he didn't feel any pain.

Edwards fired another missile. Despite checking his back-blast area, someone had run into it by the time the missile fired. Harris heard the scream over the missile and saw the burned body writhing on the ground. Harris ran over to apply first aid, but when he saw the charred body, he didn't know what to do. The wounds were way beyond a bandage. Edwards caught up with him.

"Hey, dumb shit!" Edwards pointed back at their gun. He said more, but Harris didn't hear him. He didn't need to. His job now was to kill; all else was a distraction.

Small-arms fire broke up the conversation as both men hit the ground. A Prick attack helicopter buzzed over them, firing at the Marines. Another TOW gunner took the PLA attack helicopter down. Both men ran back to their TOW gun. They reloaded the gun and Edwards fired. Harris helped him reload. The valley in front of him was filled with smoke and fire. Their line was receiving small-arms fire. The PLA was advancing towards them. The .50 cals and Mk 19s poured rounds into the trees in front of them.

"Our other gun is toast. Harris, cover us with the SAW." Bohanan was back. He and Edwards manned the TOW gun. Harris glanced over and saw Schmitt, now about ten meters away, on the other SAW. Harris dismounted the SAW from the wrecked LSV, checked the ammo belt, and flipped down the weapon's bipod. Through his scope he could see PLA infantry was starting to make its way through the brush and up the hill. They were closing in.

Everything seemed to be exploding. Harris could feel them more than hear them at this point. PLA mortar men had zeroed in on the Marine position. Harris heard aircraft; not knowing if it was PLA or American, he paid it no mind. He fired five- to six-round bursts on anything he saw moving in front of him. In the chaos and the fear, his training kept him grounded. He briefly considered finding a better spot to shoot from, and just as quickly dismissed it. With everything getting shot up, he figured one spot was as good as another at this point. At that moment his priority was to kill, and let his death come as it may.

Harris loaded his fourth of five drums of belt ammo for the SAW. Fear started to creep into his mind. How much longer could he keep this up? Harris shoved the fear out; it was worthless right now. A series of eruptions tore through the brush that was concealing the PLA. Marine artillery had zeroed in on the Pricks, and now they were paying for it. Harris found it a beautiful sight; it gave him hope. He picked his targets. He wanted no refuge for his enemy. He wanted to kill them all while the killing was good.

Just as he was loading his last drum, Edwards fell in next to him with more ammo. Harris figured he'd run out of missiles. It wasn't the time to ask about it. The artillery had stopped and a minute later Marine attack helicopters flew in and lit up the ChiComs.

We got air superiority, Harris thought. *We got to have a chance here*. Harris could see rounds coming into the PLA from the east. He scanned his scope in that direction. First Tank Battalion had arrived. It was also around that time he noticed more Marines on the ground. He didn't know what company they were from, but was glad to have them.

The ChiComs were not advancing, nor were they retreating. The artillery fire was devastating the Pricks, but they were gutting it out. This was the most resilience Harris had seen from the PLA up to this point in the war, but now they were getting hammered. Everybody had a breaking point. Harris figured the PLA had to be coming up on theirs.

Let them stay. Better to kill them than let them live to fight another day. Harris was so preoccupied with the PLA troops in front of him, he jumped and nearly screamed when a light armored vehicle began firing its twenty-five-millimeter cannon ten feet to his right.

Light Armored Reconnaissance had shown up. This seemed to give the outnumbered Marines a bit of an edge. Many Pricks began to fall back. Those that didn't were killed. The Marines began to advance.

Second Section was ordered to rally around the blue smoke. Edwards and Harris worked their way back. They ran into Bohanan and Schmitt, glad they were still alive. As they approached the blue smoke signal, Harris was happy to see Hastings.

"Hey, buddy." Harris smiled. Hastings didn't smile back. Harris reached into his pocket to get a pack of smokes for himself and Hastings. He found that his hands were shaking so bad that they hardly functioned for him. However, he managed to get two cigarettes lit and gave one to Hastings.

"I'm the only one left from First Squad," Hastings responded in a flat quiet voice. Harris fought the temptation to ask "what?" in case he'd heard wrong. He knew he hadn't. Second Section had been hit hard. There were a lot of deaths that day.

By the time Staff Sergeant Anderson roll-called the twenty-two Marines in Second Section, TOW Platoon, eight had been killed. Another three were wounded and were med-evaced out. Hastings's squad had been hit the hardest. Sergeant Jackson, Sellers, Grey, and Forest were all killed. He was transferred to Sergeant Washington's second squad. It was just a three-man TOW squad now, with Tooley and Reno as two of the wounded. Sergeant Crespo's third squad was down to two men, MacIver and Reese. Dennison was among the wounded. Gomez and Saxton were among the dead.

The section was left with two working LSVs at the moment, not counting Anderson's. These were assigned to the reconfigured Second and Third Squads. Fourth was gonna have to hump it for the time being. They headed out with the rest of Charlie Company to the northwest. That was the direction the PLA was falling back. That was where the enemy was.

CHAPTER SIXTEEN

"Liddell, you lucky bastard, you did it!" Ragnarsson exclaimed, looking at his battle map and absorbing the report. As good, as relieved, as he felt, he regretted saying it out loud in front of his staff. It wasn't just luck that carried the day. "I'll take First Marines and Divine Providence any day against those communist sons of bitches!"

It was moments like these that made Ragnarsson proud to be a Marine. Shanghai had fallen. More like they had surrendered. Similar to their experience along the coast with many of the industrialized and Westernized cities of eastern China, Shanghai was happy to become part of the ROC as long as business, more or less, could continue as usual. Turning the east coast of China into a giant "Hong Kong" of the old days was a tempting prospect to many commissars who saw the potential for greater autonomy, profits, and personal power.

To add to the success of the Shanghai Campaign, First Marines had annihilated a PLA force about twice its size. His report was that First Battalion had spotted the PLA force emerging out of a mountain pass that would have attacked First Marines' rear had they not intervened. The regiment then proceeded to repel the attack and then pursue them as they attempted to retreat through the pass. Air and artillery proceeded to turn it into a slaughter.

What bothered Ragnarsson the most in the report was that few of the PLA forces surrendered, even when facing annihilation. To him this fact confirmed what he had always suspected and, in fact, had counted on for the Shanghai Campaign: that the industrialized east would quickly capitulate.

However, he thought the farther north and west the Allies advanced they would encounter a more fanatical enemy.

Chairman Mao Zedong had commented on his losses and his desertions during the Long March, when the Red Army was nearly destroyed by the Nationalists and on the run in 1934–1935, as shaking the gold from the dust. Ragnarsson had studied Zhang Min. He figured Zhang to be a clever, ruthless old bastard that would tap into that history. The Allies had chosen East China for the very reason of its vulnerability of the local leaders' loyalty to their personal power and wealth over the People's Republic of China. Ragnarsson's gut told him the character of this invasion was in the process of changing. That the hardest fighting was yet to come.

Once again General Secretary Zhang Min met with his generals, minus General Wang Tao. Zhang was irritable. He had not been sleeping well. He longed for good news; he longed for success. Yet success avoided him, and he had not had any really good news for the last five years. His Sino-American War had been a disaster. Far from his promise of a dominant China controlling Asia and the Pacific, the People's Republic was invaded and the PLA was in retreat. Even now he was fighting for the survival of his political career.

The United States Navy now dominated the Pacific Ocean. The United States Army and Marine Corps were laying a path of devastation from North Korea, through Manchuria, and heading towards Beijing. Hundreds of thousands of Chinese citizens were pouring into Beijing, looking for relief that was increasingly becoming harder to give. Of course, the PRC would not let these people go to waste. Many were being relocated to rural districts to assist in food production, or sent to factories to build war materiel. So far, however, the American military had shown they could destroy much faster than the People's Republic of China could produce. The loss of East China only added to that loss of production.

Zhang was worried. He was very worried. He knew he needed a new plan, he knew he needed to turn things around, but he did not know how to do it. All the past communist tricks and propaganda used against the Americans for decades no longer seemed to work. President Clark was not trying to win hearts and minds, he was not trying to build a "legacy." He was genuinely interested in destroying the PRC and using all the power and the resources of the American people. Zhang was at a loss as to how to defeat such a man, such a people, as the Americans when they were unleashed.

The only positive that Zhang could see coming from these past events was the loss of dead weight from the PRC. All the desertions and betrayals that he had suffered left him with the strong and dedicated with which to fight now. Slowly but surely, he was winnowing out the disloyal and incompetent from among his leaders. The PRC was growing smaller, but he saw it growing stronger!

"Why, Chairman Mao finished the Long March with only six thousand soldiers and with that he conquered China!" he reminded his subordinates and the Chinese people. They would get stronger. Zhang believed in himself. He believed in his leadership. The PRC would not quit. The PRC would not surrender. Zhang might not be the man that conquered the Pacific, but he would be the man that would save the PRC from its greatest threat since the Sino-Japanese War.

"Good day, gentlemen." Zhang started the meeting as soon as he walked into the room. "We will not be joined by General Wang Tao today. I regret to inform you all that he has betrayed and undermined our heroic efforts to save our people from the American barbarians. I put the responsibility of this on myself." Zhang lied. He thought a show of humility would increase loyalty. "Had my intelligence officers discovered Wang's betrayal to our People's Republic earlier, perhaps we could have saved Shanghai." This caught the attention of General Fu Gang of Intelligence. "Trust me, comrades, when I tell you that he and his family have died deaths worthy of those that betray the People.

"More pressing, however, is the American defeat and our ultimate victory. General Li Xia, brief us on our propaganda campaign."

"President Zhang, news reports have been sent to all the major news outlets that we control. We emphasize the deaths of noncombatants, famine caused by American troops, as well as war crimes and atrocities of American and ROC troops." The general hoped her answer would suffice, but she did not think it would.

"What do our informants tell us of the American reaction?"

"Not much is new, President Zhang. The usual factions and Clark's political enemies are protesting and making a fuss, but as yet it is not lessening the American war effort." She refrained from telling him that polls showed that the American people sensed victory, and the majority was more determined than ever to win the war effort.

"Our people have still found nothing we can use against Clark?"

"No, Comrade President, but we are still searching." General Li hated that she did not have a better answer for Zhang.

"Keep digging, General Li. If we cannot weaken Clark's resolve, then we must weaken the Americans' faith in him." Zhang didn't state the frustration of owning American media outlets, funding charities, funding politicians, and still not being able to influence American politics. He knew of the polls

Li didn't mention. He did not want to frighten the others and thus weaken their resolve to fight for him. He did so yearn for the days before Clark, when American politicians and presidents had been so easy to control and manipulate.

"Meanwhile we must deal with the American invaders. The more of their soldiers we send back in body bags, the weaker the Americans' resolve will be to win this war."

Zhang loved to play general. He thought of himself as something of a Chinese Napoleon, although his racist opinion of Caucasians and his socialist sense of nationalism nearly prevented him from admitting this to himself, let alone others. Some of his earlier conquests in the South China Sea, Indonesia, and East China Sea had affirmed this belief. The defeats of the Sino-American War might have weakened his faith in the Chinese people, but had done nothing to weaken Zhang's faith in Zhang. He thought himself cursed with incompetent subordinates.

"Comrades, our homeland is very big. The more the *laowai* try to hold, the weaker they become. We will destroy our own railroads and highways, cutting the southeast from us like a cancer and slowing the American advance." No one brought up that the American force had done much of that for them already.

"We"—at that cue Zhang's orderly turned on a projector filling a big screen with a map of China—"will use our homeland itself against the Americans here"—Zhang pointed to the mountains to the northeast of Beijing—"and here"—he pointed to the Yellow River about two hundred miles south of Beijing in the North China Plain. He would keep the plan for his own personal evacuation from Beijing to himself.

McCullough had had nothing but good news; however, his mind was not at ease. The Allied Shanghai Campaign had worked out, for all intents and purposes, as a best-case scenario. American casualties had been substantial, but were not for nothing. Southeast China had fallen ahead of schedule. The Northern Campaign was progressing as well and flooding Beijing with refugees. McCullough knew eventually the PRC had to reach a breaking point. The PRC didn't take very good care of the majority of its people before the invasion, it would only be able to do less so now. With each day, with each American victory, tens of thousands of Chinese were abandoning their faith in communism.

Taiwan, the Philippines, and Australia had come through for the Allied cause in the south as an occupational force. Japan, Canada, and South Korea were essential to success in the north. As the PRC grew weaker with every American victory, the Allies grew stronger.

McCullough's greatest source for concern was not from China, but from Washington, DC. Mythers was still running his mouth more than ever to the president about negotiating with the People's Republic of China. Clark had showed tremendous resolve so far. To McCullough's relief, Clark acted more like a former Marine than a current politician. Clark understood enough history to appreciate Hard War.

War required sacrifice. A nation, a people must practice discipline and self-denial. To those living under a centralized despotism, this was how one lived in peace as well as war. It was enforced on them. For a free people accustomed to pursuing their own interests and destinies, it required self-discipline and self-sacrifice. No ruler told them to do it, they told themselves to do it. Why? So they could remain free to pursue their own interests and self-chosen destinies and not be enslaved to the interests and desires of a totalitarian elite.

History provided many examples of free people who temporarily denied their happiness and freedoms to fight in order to secure those freedoms and opportunities of prosperity for their children, for the next generation. The Greeks against the Persians. The Romans against the Carthaginians. The United States against Nazi Germany and Imperial Japan. Even when Americans fought Americans in the Civil War, President Lincoln sought a complete and utter defeat of his enemy, desiring to return to self-government and the people's freedom to pursue their own self-interest as soon as possible. Indeed, time was of the essence. History had shown that these very same cultures had lost their desire to win when wars were long and indecisive. Over time victory began to seem unattainable and lost freedoms seemed like a past age.

McCullough and Clark understood this lesson from history. General Mythers, for all his military training, did not. McCullough found Mythers to be more politician than soldier. The man was great at organizing garrison life, but McCullough thought Mythers would be a disaster if given too much say in the Allied war strategy.

He was also getting word from a contact in Central Intelligence that Vice President Harmon and Secretary of State Weeseman had, within inner circles, stated agreement with Mythers. McCullough hated the idea of getting this far to back off now.

McCullough remembered a time when he was about twelve years old at baseball practice. He'd gotten into a fight with a kid that was not on the team, but would show up to harass the players during batting practice. For whatever reason the coaches never did anything about it. One day Jack had had enough. As soon as he finished batting, he walked over to the kid and kicked him. The kid deflected the kick and jumped up. Young Jack followed up with a few punches, and the kid screamed that he'd had enough. No sooner had Jack stopped throwing punches than the kid threw a hard right and nailed

Jack right in the nose. Ultimately the punch left him with two black eyes. Jack threw more punches before the coaches finally broke it up, but he never regained the momentum in the fight. When John Sr. found out about the fight and how it went down, little Jack got his butt chewed out.

"Never, ever, ever quit a fight until the other guy is beat. That means he is on the ground, bleeding and not capable of defending himself, or else he's run away. You deserved to get your nose busted for being so stupid. Do that again, and I'll punch you in the nose myself!" Jack would never again do that in a fistfight, and if he could help it, he would not do it in this war. The blood of lost Americans demanded complete and total victory over the People's Republic of China.

If Zhang were to actually try now to make a stand on the Yangtze River, McCullough would love to nuke the main body of the PLA. It would save American lives, but the Republic of China's desire to retake Nanjing, UN disapproval, the American lack of nuclear arms made it highly unlikely. The question was would Nanjing give up like Shanghai? It had been the old capital of the ROC, but that was nearly a century ago. A city of nine million would be a nightmare to take street by street. Screw that. McCullough would rather bomb it back into the Stone Age before he ordered that.

However, force the PLA to fall back, and the city would be far more likely to capitulate. Once in the North China Plain, there would be no great geographic obstacles until the Yellow River. At that point then…maybe?

"Four aces, dude!" Schmitt chuckled.

"Mother…shit!" Hastings threw down his cards in disgust. Harris enjoyed watching the other two play more than playing himself. He hated to lose money gambling, especially since they had only recently come into possession of cash.

Initially, they were given what they needed from supply and received debit cards with a limited amount of money on them. However, some of the more enterprising locals really wanted to do business with the American GIs. So in the name of collaboration with the newly expanded Republic of China, the soldiers and Marines began being paid some amounts of cash when possible.

As if on cue, Harris and Reese pulled out cigarettes and lit them up. They were soon followed by Hastings and Schmitt. The four had become rather cliquish after Shanghai. They were also friends with Edwards and Cortes, but to a lesser extent. They'd both been promoted to corporal and made squad leaders when Second Section was rebuilt. Bohanan was their section leader now. Anderson had been taken out by a sniper. He'd been standing on top of an LSV, looking through his binoculars when he bought it. Head shot. He was dead before he hit the ground. It was a hit-and-run affair. The sniper only fired once.

The PLA had been on the run again. However, resistance was stiffening. More guerrilla, hit-and-run type of strikes, like the one that took Anderson out. Scuttlebutt was that Nanjing would be the next big target. Of course, the source for that rumor was probably because Nanjing was the biggest Prick city in the region. Word was if they took Nanjing, they'd get the Yangtze with it. That might be true, but the Pricks weren't going to give it away. If the Marine Corps wanted it, they'd have to earn it in blood.

Harris was confident of victory. He didn't know if he'd live to see it on this earth, but he knew the United States would win. Harris had become rather theological about death. Some elements about dying still frightened him, but he had no fear of being dead. He believed in Christ; he believed in an afterlife. No matter his outcome, he would either see his mother, brother, and sister again in this life; or he would see his father again in the next. God's will be done. A story by Lieutenant Colonel McGregor had helped to give him this sense of peace.

"Marines, I'll tell you what my granddaddy, who was a Southern Baptist preacher, told me the first time I went to war. He said, 'Billy, when God wants to call you home, there ain't nothing you can do to stop him. But remember, there ain't nobody that can rush him either.' Fight with heart, Marines! Your lives, your souls are in God's hands, and I have it on good authority that He loves a bold Marine. Have faith in that love. Those communist sons of bitches ain't got that going for them. If they win, all they get is more of the same ol' bullshit tyranny they've always had. You? You've got the love of our Holy Father. You've got the freedom of our Republic. Let that give you strength in battle!" Harris had come away from meeting McGregor feeling more motivated than at any other time while he'd been in the Marine Corps, except perhaps when he'd heard General Ragnarsson speak to him in boot camp.

They all liked McGregor, even Edwards, who tended to be a little too cynical for Harris's tastes. It was hard not to be a fan of the battalion commander after he had come to meet them. The lieutenant colonel had said he wanted to shake their hands and personally honor them for spotting the Pricks and standing their ground until the rest of the battalion and eventually the regiment had shown up. He personally pinned corporal stripes on Edwards and Cortes. He'd called Harris "Hard Charger." Then he found out that Hastings had been given the nickname Bulldog from Sergeant Anderson because of the tenacity he'd shown in battle.

"What the hell, Marine, you stealing my nickname?" McGregor had jovially charged.

Hastings was taken aback for just a moment. "No, sir! I earned the motherfucker!" Hastings answered with a smart-ass grin in typical Hastings style. McGregor had loved it.

"Hoorah, Devil Dog!" McGregor vigorously slapped Hastings on the shoulder, who didn't move an inch. "I wouldn't give two shakes of piss for those limp-dick Pricks against you hard-chargin' Leathernecks! Keep it up, Marines!" Cheers of hoorah erupted from the Marines.

Much to the chagrin of First and Third Sections, McGregor had called Second Section the Death Squad. He said he would use them to kick the ever-living hell out of the ChiCom bastards. The section loved it.

When they were issued new armor for their LSVs, they all painted a skull and crossbones as their section's emblem. When the replacements for Second Section showed up, they were told they could not say the words *Death Squad* until they'd proved themselves. Bohanan did not want them to get bigheaded. Nor did he want them to get their asses kicked for bragging about something they'd not earned.

Now they sat playing poker and smoking cigarettes to kill time until they found out their next assignment.

"Here it comes, Death Squad." Harris had spotted Bohanan and the Second Section squad leaders returning from a meeting. The only Marine who enjoyed the section's nickname more than Harris was Hastings.

"Third Squad, get your drivers," Edwards ordered, "and fall in." The card players grabbed their weapons and moved out for formation.

"Listen up, Marines." Bohanan had Second Section form a semicircle around him, resembling a football huddle. "We're crossing the Yangtze here, about one hundred miles south of Nanjing. Give or take a bit, that kind of detail don't mean too fucking much to y'all anyway. It is expected that Nanjing will be one fortified motherfucker. So thank the good Lord above you ain't been assigned to take that city. Our job is to cross the Yangtze just south of Tongling, here." Bohanan was drawing a map in the dirt that added very little clarity to his description. "We get across here, we cut off the Prick troops holding Nanjing, and that means more dead Prick bastards. Now, in case some of you are prone to acting like self-pitying, whiny-ass types, Fifth and Sixth Marine Divisions are going to be landing here." Bohanan indicated the coastline north of Shanghai. "Second Marine Division is to the north, and we got half of the United States fucking Army to our left. There is no excuse for failure. Marines—" Bohanan took the time to look every one of them in the eye "—we smash them here, they got nowhere to hide until they hit the Yellow River, and if we fight in traditional Marine Corps fashion, we will have this war won before that can happen. Any questions?"

"Sergeant Bohanan, how are we going to get across the Yangtze?" Private First Class Hawke, Harris's new driver, asked.

"We will give cover and support Charlie Company as they take a bridge here. If the Pricks blow it, and they're too goddamn smart not to, combat engineers will build us a pontoon bridge. Short of that, we will swim our asses across the Yangtze River, Marines. Failure to cross that river is unacceptable. One way or another we will move north, or we will die trying. Am I understood?"

"Aye, aye, Sergeant," nearly every Marine answered.

Liu Zhiqiang had slowly filtered into Beijing. The highways were packed with refugees moving south. He had merely followed the crowd, but it had been more difficult than that sounds. He was from an agricultural village about six hundred miles northeast of Beijing. He had no idea why the Americans would have attacked a village that primarily produced potatoes and apples, but they had.

Before the attack, pamphlets had dropped into the village, telling people they should go to Beijing, where they would be safe. The local commissar told them not to worry about being attacked. Their village was of no concern to the Americans. After all, all they did was produce food; they were not a military target. They should not worry. But even the commissars could not comprehend the barbarity of the American invaders. As far as Zhiqiang knew, he was the only one from his family to survive. His village had been completely destroyed. First, bombs were dropped and everything exploded. Then the drones came in, followed by helicopters and then the Marines. They killed anyone that offered resistance. They burned any building still standing after the bombs. They killed any animal that had not yet died. They drove the Chinese from their land. Zhiqiang could see no explanation for why they would kill other than their natural thirst for blood.

Before the attack they had been warned by political officers not to trust the Americans and their overtures offering food and protection. United States Marines were taken from the American penitentiaries. They had to have been convicted of murder, rape, or arson to even be considered for service. Zhiqiang had seen the American pamphlets warning people to leave, but he and his family had followed the PRC's advice to ignore them.

When the Americans did show up, Zhiqiang was the only one able to escape. His grandparents and parents were too old and too slow. His cousin was killed in the bombing. He'd hoped that he would run into other survivors from his village, but he did not. Instead, he ran into three men, also refugees, who raped him. They had promised him protection, but then that night he awoke when one man was climbing on him. He screamed for help from the others; instead they held him down. One of the rapists, a man with a hideous mole on his chin and missing a front tooth, shoved the tip of a knife into Zhiqiang's face, cutting his cheek. The vile man yelled at Zhiqiang to stop making it so difficult for himself, but he would not stop fighting his attackers. They beat him unconscious.

Zhiqiang came to sometime the next morning. He had hoped in his semiconsciousness that this had all been a bad dream. As he fully woke up, he painfully realized it had not been a bad dream. The cut on his cheek was deep, so he tore a sleeve off his shirt to use as a bandage.

Two days later, Zhiqiang was following a mob of refugees on the way to Beijing. A man squatting behind a broken-down car in the middle of a bowel movement caught his attention. He thought the man looked familiar. As he got closer, he recognized the ugly mole and the lack of a front tooth. The man had not noticed him. Zhiqiang walked by as if it were any other man taking a crap at the side of the road. Once past, he doubled back. He scanned the ground and found a stone the size of a grapefruit. That would work. He crept up behind the squatting man, who was too involved in his business to notice until Zhiqiang had walked right up behind him, but it was too late. Zhiqiang brought the stone down with all his might on the back of the man's head. However, his swing was awkward, and it was not a fatal blow, but the rapist had his pants around his ankles, what could he do? He stumbled and screamed in fear and pain. Zhiqiang followed in quickly for another blow. The rapist screamed for help, but none came. Zhiqiang moved with the speed and ferocity of a wild animal in the eyes of some of the onlookers. Zhiqiang pulled his third blow, inspired by a sudden thought. He brought the stone down on the side of the rapist's jaw, shattering bone and teeth. Now the rapist's screams were muted and blood poured from his mouth.

"Quit fighting and making it so difficult for yourself," Zhiqiang mocked the rapist as he grabbed him by the back of his shirt. He dragged the rapist over to his own pile of feces and shoved him in face-first. Zhiqiang brought the stone down again and again until the rapist's skull had been shattered and his brains scattered among the human waste. Zhiqiang looked up at the refugees who had stopped and watched. He was surprised and relieved that they looked at him with fear and scurried away as if he might hurt them next.

Zhiqiang felt exonerated. He had righted a wrong. Even more, through violence he had risen to dominance. He was not a boy to be taken advantage of, but a man to be feared. Zhiqiang felt the kind of satisfaction that comes when one thinks he has discovered his calling and the secret to his success.

He went through the dead rapist's bag and clothing. He took food, money, and the man's extra shirt. He left the shirt that was on the rapist's corpse. Despite his new sense of empowerment, Zhiqiang was robbed while he slept at night and lost all his food.

By the time he'd made it to the outskirts of Beijing, Zhiqiang had not eaten for three days, and the wound on his face was festering. When asked by administrators what he could do for the People's Republic, he answered that he could kill the invaders. The administrators seemed to appreciate his spunk. He was given medical treatment for the wound on his face, and at the age of fourteen he was enlisted into the People's Liberation Army. He began training to defend his homeland and to avenge his village.

Ten months later Private Liu was stationed to defend Nanjing, and his wound had healed into an ugly V-shaped scar. His training had taught him many ways to kill and had only encouraged his desire to do so. He had also learned of how the Americans had tyrannized China for centuries. They were beasts, who would only be satisfied when they had enslaved all the Chinese. He was surprised to learn that the Americans had invaded his homeland many times during the eighteenth and nineteenth centuries. However, the Chinese had always prevailed and defeated them. Even now, when the Americans were using military technology they had stolen from the People, they still needed the help of Chinese traitors in order to have had the success they had up to this point.

But that was all on the verge of changing. The People would no longer be naive, and traitors to the State would no longer be tolerated. They would learn there was a consequence to their betrayal of China. Zhiqiang was trained how to identify and deal with those that put their own interests before that of the State, before that of the People.

They were told that the fate of the People's Republic rested on their generation's ability to hold Nanjing. If it fell, so did the Yangtze and perhaps all of China. Liu swore he'd die before he let that happen. He was taught how to kill these people, as well as the American barbarians, in such a way as to have a maximum psychological impact. The Chinese would be too frightened to put their interests before that of the People's Republic. The Americans would become too afraid to continue their unjust war against the People.

In the People's Liberation Army, Liu Zhiqiang felt that he had found his true calling. He no longer missed his family, nor his village. In fact, he found himself at times happy that it had been destroyed by the Americans and had thus brought all this about. He loved the People's Liberation Army for the skills they had taught him. He loved the People's Republic of China for the power and authority they had given him. He gleefully swore to defend his homeland and kill all the people that needed to be killed to protect the State.

Lieutenant Kai Yong, of the Republic of China, could not sleep. Staring at the night sky, he came to the conclusion that honor came with stress. More than stress, it came with fear. The taking of Nanjing was going to cost a lot of lives on both sides. Intellectually Kai had accepted that his life and the lives of his men were in God's hands. Right now he wasn't feeling his faith. At first he thought he was just anxious; Nanjing was where his ancestors had lived. They had been minor figures in the nationalist government. With the rise of Mao's Red Army and the fall of the nationalist, his family had escaped to Taiwan. Generations later he was here to rid his ancestral homeland of the communist cancer that controlled it. For Kai Yong it was more than a duty, it was an honor to be involved in this assault. He still felt that way, but forty-eight hours out from launching their assault, the euphoric excitement had been replaced by fear. Now he could not sleep. He kept telling himself he needed the rest, for tomorrow night there would be none. This only made it harder for him to relax. He prayed for peace of mind, but it did not come. Finally, he got up. He figured if God wanted him awake, there had to be something for him to work on.

Ragnarsson stared at his battle map. Something just wasn't sitting right with him. Why would the PRC try to hold Nanjing? It was on the wrong side of the Yangtze to work to their advantage. Even if they held the city, Allied forces would cross farther west. Intel claimed Army Special Forces were already well north of the river, and he knew Force Recon and

SEAL units had already crossed. Any PLA unit south of the Yangtze would eventually be annihilated. Could it be a delay tactic? It would not be the first time the PLA had sacrificed troops. Was it just a dumb move, or was he missing something? Perhaps it would be clear within the next forty-eight hours. Ragnarsson just hoped the lesson wasn't too brutal.

"Thanks, man." Harris took the smoke offered by Hastings and rolled his eyes. "I need a break." Hawke and Littlejohn, the new drivers of the new Third Squad, were going on about some kind of shooter video game, and the topic bored him. Harris's parents had never been big on letting him play video games. His mother would make him read instead. Sometimes, as part of his homeschooling, she'd make him and his siblings watch Shakespeare plays on DVD. Harris usually found them painfully long and hard to understand. He didn't understand them the way his mother did. The memory of her talking about Shakespeare flowed through his mind, and he found himself missing those plays. By the time he had exhaled his first drag on his cigarette, he was feeling homesick. He shook it off; bigger stakes would soon be at play.

"Oh yeah, I remember the days when I thought video games were a big deal," Hastings casually spoke as he exhaled. "Perhaps they will be again someday."

"I'm ready to get this show on the road," Harris confessed to Hastings.

"I hear you. This waiting-around shit gets old fast. But it'll happen when it happens." Hastings looked around. Everything and everyone was darkened to blend into the night. The base, however, was loud with the buzzing of the generators that powered their lights. "Hey, how about we get in a game of chess?"

171

"Sure." Harris had hesitated in answering. He was lousy at chess and really didn't care for the game. However, Hastings loved it and had picked up a small portable set he kept stashed in his LSV. He'd promised to teach Harris the game. His teaching of Harris included whipping him every time they played.

No sooner had they started heading towards Hastings's LSV than they saw Edwards walking straight towards them.

"Third Squad, mount up!" Edwards ordered when he saw them.

"Hastings!" Cortes yelled. Harris slapped his friend on the back of his body armor and stuck out his hand.

"Good luck, Bulldog!" His stress vanished. Harris was feeling the adrenaline for the fight.

"Good luck." Hastings smiled, feeling the same buzz. The two Marines ran to their vehicles and headed out to battle.

CHAPTER SEVENTEEN

Harris laughed from behind the gun when word came across on the radio that the bridge at Tongling was out. Hawke had been very concerned as to how vulnerable they'd be crossing a bridge. Edwards told him not to worry about it.

"If we've not blown the fucker up, you can damn well bet the Pricks will." That had not settled Hawke's mind a bit. The boot was nervous going into his first battle. They all were; some just hid it better.

Edwards didn't mention, and Harris didn't remind him, that one way or another they had to cross that river. With or without a bridge. No one expected this to be easy. Edwards had told him privately that he thought it was hard to see even a good best-case scenario on this one. Harris kept telling himself, *It will be what it will be.* All he could do was his best. Along the way, he prayed to be an effective killer.

The ride was slow and boring. Harris would have fallen asleep if not for the tension of the impending battle. Word came on the radio that First Platoon Charlie Company was engaged and needed heavy weapons. Hawke stepped on the gas and Harris found himself bouncing around behind the weapon system. He held on so as not to smash his nose into the TOW gun. Under the circumstances he wasn't going to tell him to slow down; he'd leave that up to Edwards. Within fifteen minutes they could hear the *pop, pop, pop* of small-arms fire, then a roar. They had found the battle.

They could hear the tanks. Problem was it was too wooded to see the tanks let alone get a shot at them. They followed a road into a clearing looking more like some kind of dirt parking lot. They'd come across some kind of complex. In the dark, Harris couldn't tell for sure what it was. It reminded him of the quarries along the Kansas River. Harris scanned the horizon through his night sight and could not find a target. By the sounds of it, a firefight was taking place in the woods south of them.

"Look across the river, and watch for helos," Edwards ordered Harris and Schmitt over the radio. Harris could see movement, but no tanks, armored cars, nothing—until a round was fired.

"These bastards upgraded their thermal camouflage," Harris yelled.

"Say again?" Edwards responded. Harris ignored the question and checked his back blast area. It was clear.

"Fire in the hole," Harris said just loud enough for his gun team to hear, and fired. The TOW sight read that his target was 1285 meters out. Harris's missile hit the tank, disabling one of its tracks. Edwards was out to help reload. Hawke was on the SAW. The potential for PLA riflemen popping out of the woods was a real threat. Schmitt, about fifty meters to their right, fired a missile that went straight to the turret, but the missile was blown up by an antimissile weapon. By the time Harris was reloaded and had crosshairs back on the target, he could see the tank turret turning in their direction.

"Fuck! Tell Schmitt to move it!" Harris yelled right before he fired. Shortly after Harris hit the trigger, he was blinded through his thermal sight from the missile's back blast.

Private Zhiqiang Liu watched Sergeant Zhang Jing set the final wires. The man seemed to move with such grace. He exhibited such passion while he would scout and plan where to plant his bombs. Liu was fascinated with his sergeant's thought process in killing the maximum number of people while creating the greatest amount of chaos. Liu was anxious for the attack so he could witness the effects of his work.

"Now all we do is go back and wait for orders," Zhang told his protégé. He loved the boy's enthusiasm. At a time of so many desertions and uncertainties, Liu gave him some hope for the next generation.

"When do you think it will start?" Liu's excitement could barely be contained.

"Who knows? My guess is it won't be much longer. They'll move out before daylight most likely. They'll start bombing us before that. If the captain is right, they'll avoid bombing the city, which is why we're planting these bombs.

"Come on, let's head back. As I was saying, they'll look to strike our defenses south of Nanjing. Perhaps to the north as well. Just remember, our mission is not to fight the Americans or ROC. Our mission is in the city. When that is done, no matter what happens, get yourself north of the Yangtze by any means necessary." Zhang spoke with almost a fatherly affection for the young soldier of the PLA.

"Yes, Sergeant. I will stay focused. I look forward to the mission with enthusiasm and the opportunity to serve the People," Liu said with complete honesty.

The attack was launched. Lieutenant Kai buzzed with adrenaline. The PLA was falling back. Everyone was concerned about greater resistance, but the ROC forces were advancing. They had coordinated an assault from the south at the moment the ROC marines had launched an attacked from the north via the river. The only things slowing his troops down were the compliant civilians looking for protection and PLA trying to surrender. As had been the case in Southeast China, many of the civilians were not interested in resisting. In fact, many seemed eager to comply with the ROC and US forces. In Nanjing's suburbs many people had hung white sheets, pillowcases, shirts, etc. to show their compliance. Those who had electricity had kept houses and streets lit for the Allied forces. Despite the air pamphlets' instructions to the contrary, many civilians were flooding the streets, looking for refuge. This had started to become a problem.

Kai's rifle platoon would disarm the surrendering PLA and hold them until military police showed up. Kai was worried that they could be attacked by hostile PLA while occupied with enemy prisoners of war, EPWs.

Suddenly his worries became reality when his platoon received fire from their left flank. He saw some of his men go down along with the EPWs that they were patting down for weapons. Naturally, his men began to return fire, but at what? Kai saw more EPWs and civilians being shot. By his men or the PLA? People scattered and took cover. Kai looked for incoming tracers, but couldn't see any. His mind was screaming to figure out where the enemy fire was coming from, but he couldn't make an assessment. Were the EPWs just a cover for the assault? Were the civilians? Meanwhile civilians were dying; his soldiers were being killed. Shots were definitely coming from the west. He ordered an airstrike on the area he thought the attack was coming from, and prayed the helos would take them out. Meanwhile he directed his platoon's fire in that direction. Kai hated to see that his troops had killed the EPWs that hadn't already run away. But his mind processed that this was war and men got killed. He focused on his enemy.

The attack helicopters quickly arrived and devastated an entire block of the Nanjing suburb in less time than it took them to arrive. Enemy fire had ceased. Lieutenant Kai and his platoon moved on.

Liu had never been happier in his entire fifteen years of life when the word came that the PLA was falling back to the river. He was on the Allied side of the battlefield. He and the others of his squad changed into ROC uniforms. Sergeant Zhang did a quick weapons and uniform inspection; then the band went out into the Nanjing suburbs to wage violence against the enemies of the People's Republic.

Li Wei had hung a white sheet out the window of his two-bedroom apartment, where he lived with his wife, teenage daughter, and his in-laws. He was scared, but his fear was overridden by the hope of a better future. He had spent the last twenty-five years working as an instructor at the local teachers' college. His career had consisted of teaching to indoctrinate the younger generation. That was not how he had seen his career at first. He'd felt enthusiastic in the early years. The People's Republic had seemed on the rise. Their economy had exploded thanks to the high price of labor in the West. Factories had opened. New buildings and new technologies were created, but not new freedoms. The promised acquisition of a better life turned out to be as empty as many of the new buildings the government constructed. They looked good from the street for all the Western tourists and TV cameras, but there was no one inside to enjoy them.

Over the years Li had seen many benefit and prosper from political connections, not from merit. He had worked to build a better Republic for the next generation. However, to his dismay, many of his peers killed scores of that generation when they aborted their babies for being female. The legacy of the People's one-child policy was a severe shortage of women. He'd raised his own daughter with the fear of her being kidnapped and then forced into a marriage.

As his career progressed, he was ordered to report students for having the wrong ideas, opinions, and reactions to the material he was told to teach. He was even ordered to report the names of students he thought were romantically involved with one another. And for what purpose? Was this not natural? Could a mind grow if it did not question? Could mankind exist without attraction to the opposite sex? For years Li could not understand, nor could he talk about, why the People's Republic of China always insisted that the people deny themselves as people. Yet that was the system they lived in. From what he'd seen over the decades of his life, it only benefitted those that ran the system. No more. He would not tolerate any more now that someone was standing up to it. He and his family would embrace the new China. As he saw it, they had nothing to lose.

When he heard gunfire erupt nearby and then attack helicopters shooting up the street, Li decided it was a good idea to move his family. The last thing he wanted was to be in the middle of a gunfight.

When his family exited the building, Li became desperately afraid. Why was his the only family leaving? Had others already left? Was he too late? Should he take his family back inside? He audibly exhaled with relief when he saw the ROC patches worn by the group of soldiers approaching him.

"Excuse me, sirs, please, can you help us?" Li called out to the soldiers.

"Yes, sir, of course," what looked like the senior man yelled back. The soldiers approached, smiling. Their guns were pointed at Li and his family, but they were smiling. Li thought that had to be normal; they were an invading force, after all. He would be very polite and show them he was on their side. They'd have no reason to hurt him or his family.

"Sir, where can we go where it is safe?"

178

"Papers, do you have papers?" the senior man asked. This baffled Li. What PRC papers could he possibly have that would satisfy the ROC? The hairs on his neck stood. He realized too late he'd made a mistake.

"Keep your hands up where we can see them!" another soldier barked.

The Li family complied. They were shoved over to the nearest wall. The soldiers began to pat them down. They took their identification and any money they had. One of the younger soldiers, he looked barely more than a boy, kicked the leg out from under Li's elderly father-in-law. The old man cried out in fear and pain. Li saw a smile on the young soldier's face.

"Please, my father-in-law has weak legs. He needs his cane," Li pleaded, to no avail. He, his wife, and daughter were being frisked when he heard a loud ripping noise. His wife's blouse had been torn by a soldier, who proceeded to molest his wife. Li protested, but found himself forced to the ground. The air kicked out of his lungs. He fought to breathe again. His mother-in-law began yelling and chastising the soldiers. Li saw her abruptly and harshly silenced by the young soldier's rifle butt. He watched as the young soldier brought the butt of his rifle down over and over until the old woman's body was silent and lay twitching. The other soldiers laughed and began to molest his daughter as well as his wife.

"Please! No! Please! We are on your side! Please!" was all Li could say to defend the people he loved. He watched in horror as his wife and daughter were raped, and the young soldier went on to beat his father-in-law to death. Then the others invited the young soldier to rape his wife. They cheered and laughed as he awkwardly assaulted his wife. Li sobbed; he was heartbroken to be so weak and impotent in protecting his family. They had had so much to lose after all.

179

As a cruel reminder that things could always get worse, once the young soldier was done, he stood, looking proud of himself. He even smiled at Li as he sobbed on the ground like his wife and daughter.

"No! No! Please don't!" was the only defiance Li could offer at that point after a life of communist indoctrination and compliance. The young soldier tilted his head a bit, but his smiling expression didn't change. With a choreographed-like elegance, the young soldier pulled out his knife, reached down, and slit the woman's throat from ear to ear. The woman Li had built a life with for the last thirty years convulsed and bled to death. The young soldier straightened, still smiling. The other soldiers were silent and seemed, ironically, in shock given the violence they had instigated. Li's cries were only outdone by his daughter, who had watched the whole thing, to her terror. Before a word was said, the young soldier slit the throat of the young girl. Li had lost everything. His only solace was that his own death would end his pain.

"Enough! Stand down!" the senior soldier ordered. "We are not to kill everyone."

"Kill me, kill me, you fucking bastard!" Li screamed when he thought he was about to be denied that as well.

"Go on, get out of here!" the senior soldier ordered as the others lifted Li up and kicked him on his way. The young soldier just stood there smiling. The soldier's gall, Li's loss—it was too much. Li didn't care anymore. He'd spent an entire life being compliant, being careful, never offending anyone; and all it had gotten him was misery. All he had ever gained was pain. He screamed and charged the smiling soldier. Come what may, he would not tolerate any more.

With cold and swift precision, Private Liu raised his rifle and shot the screaming man running at him. It felt good. The power over life. The power of death. Liu loved it. The sight of the man's shattered skull was a beautiful thing to him. Within the course of fifteen minutes he had exercised the power of death over five people. Liu had truly discovered his passion. He knew at that moment this was what he wanted to do with the rest of his life.

"Liu! Don't be foolish! We're to leave survivors to blame the ROC. Dead people don't talk!" Sergeant Zhang worried that his rebuke might have been too strong. He liked Liu and saw potential in the boy. "Don't let your passions get the best of you." His toned softened as he placed his hand on the boy's shoulder. "The People's Republic of China needs your talents."

Lieutenant Kai looked at his watch. Almost zero five hundred. It would be twilight soon. He desperately awaited daylight. Perhaps that would make things easier. Perhaps. This battle had not gone the way he'd envisioned it. For the first time in his short military career, he thought he might not make a good general. He had no idea if what he'd done today had been the right thing or not. All he knew for sure was that he'd lost four men. His platoon had come across bodies of butchered civilians, yet he'd not seen any PLA who were not surrendering. He had not seen one PLA plane or helicopter, yet he'd seen buildings explode and collapse. He understood more fighting was in the north of the city towards the river, but there was death all around in the south. None of it matched up. The fear and paranoia had led to him and his men shooting surrendering PLA. They weren't taking prisoners. Was it murder? Was it survival? It was more than his brain wanted to comprehend. He shoved the thoughts from his mind; he needed to keep it clear. He was responsible for the lives left in his platoon. He would focus on that for now. Any price he had to pay, he'd pay later. If he was still alive.

Harris had always preferred the cover of night during this war. Now he prayed for daylight. He didn't know if it would make the fighting any easier, but at least he could have a cigarette. He thought he'd experienced chaos earlier in the war, but he was wrong. He'd given up trying to follow what was going on in the big picture. He'd leave that to Edwards, although he was probably just as confused and just trying to make it through the night like he was.

They'd gone to secure the bridge outside of Tongling, and the GPS told them they were in the right area. Of course the bridge was gone, like Edwards had said it would be. Then all hell broke out. There were trees every place they didn't need them. There was some kind of quarry or factory where they were. Harris didn't really care what it was, it just seemed to get in the way of killing Pricks.

The commie bastards had tanks and artillery across the river and infantry on this side of the river. The tanks across the river had been hard as hell to see, and every time he got a good bead on one, Prick infantry would pop out of the woods. The Pricks coming out of the woods reminded him of those old zombie shows he used to watch with his dad. He'd spent more time with the SAW than the TOW.

Harris thought, so far, that Hawke had really proved himself. Earlier in the night Harris had lost track of a tank in his thermal sight right as he'd fired. It was too early to have been from the back blast, and he wondered if it was some type of new thermal camouflage the Pricks were employing. He'd held the gun steady to ride out the blindness, but to no avail. Prick riflemen had popped out of the woods. Rounds ricocheted off the LSV's armor. Harris was lucky not to be dead. Hawke had floored the LSV and took out three of the bastards, stopping only when he'd smashed a small tree that was no match for the LSV's grill guard. Edwards got some others with the SAW. Harris told himself if they survived this, he wanted to see Edwards demonstrate how to shoot out the passenger window. He had been deadly that night.

There never was what seemed like a coordinated assault, just small groups coming at them here and there. Or somebody taking potshots at them. Then throw in Prick artillery and jets. They'd call in airstrikes on the Pricks, and the Pricks called them in on them, as well.

Bombs, rockets, mortars, and small-arms fire had been going on around them all night. It was hard, if not impossible, to tell whose was what. They had been in contact with others in the section throughout the night, but had yet to get a visual on any of them. They felt isolated and vulnerable, but not helpless. They'd killed a lot of Prick infantry, and Harris had managed to take out a PLA attack helicopter.

Schmitt and Littlejohn were a whole other matter. Harris thought the tank he was shooting at was shooting at them. That was when they were attacked by Pricks creeping out of the woods. They'd not seen or heard from Blue Three Bravo since then. Perhaps the daylight would bring answers. Perhaps not.

By dawn the north bank of the river looked clear. Prick artillery was still dropping in batches of two or three rounds every so often. Harris wanted to see Americans on the other side of the Yangtze, but as yet had not. They had decent cover from a berm the Pricks had constructed along the road. Harris had an all right visual of the Yangtze's north bank across the quarry. Bohanan wanted them to hold up until he could catch up with them. His GPS was damaged and he was trying to track everyone down. Edwards had also complained that theirs was not working efficiently as well. Schmitt and Littlejohn were not showing up on it, nor could they reach them on the radio. Was their equipment not working? Were they on the wrong frequency? Had they been killed?

Three Marine riflemen emerged from the quarry compound. Hawke had a bead on them with the rifle, and Edwards had the twelve gauge on them until Harris visually confirmed they weren't Asian through the TOW gun's day sight.

"Where can a Jarhead get a goddamn hotdog around here?" one of them asked as they approached.

"Same place you get peanuts," Edwards responded with agitation. He knew these guys weren't PLA and found the passwords redundant.

"I'm Corporal Jacobs, Third Platoon, Charlie," the leader of the approaching gun team introduced himself.

"Corporal Edwards. What can we do for you?" Edwards offered the other corporal a cigarette.

"Thanks." The three riflemen looked black from all the mud, face paint, and whatever else they had been crawling through during the night. Harris lit up a smoke, as did the other riflemen, who took it as a cue that the smoking lamp was lit. However, all three kept looking around, watching the woods, watching the skyline, watching everything.

"You TOWs are missing an LSV." The entire TOW squad noticed that Corporal Jacobs was not asking a question.

"The gun team?" Edwards spoke. The other corporal shook his head no, but said nothing.

"Don't know how it happened. We found them last night. Thought they were dead PLA. Wasn't until dawn we got a visual on the Death Squad logo y'all use. I'd have brought you their dog tags, but the fucking Pricks took them."

"Fuckin' Pricks took the dog tags," Edwards repeated. Harris noticed a change in Edwards's tone, unlike what he'd heard before. Edwards always struck Harris as a man under control. Never too relaxed. Never too angry. Edwards's voice had an emotional edge to it that Harris had not heard from him before. It made the hairs stand up on the back of his neck. "Show us the LSV," Edwards demanded. "You want a ride?"

"No, thanks, we'll walk." The riflemen turned around and spread out and led the way. Harris didn't blame them for not riding in the LSV. At that moment it was the biggest target around.

Harris thought it was a cruel twist of irony that Schmitt and Littlejohn had not been that far away from where they just were. They'd had no way of knowing where they were when they were killed. The armored LSV had not been a match for the Prick 12.7 mm machine gun that had ripped up the front end. By the look of it, Littlejohn had taken a shot in the head while in the driver's seat. Schmitt had not been that lucky.

"This is how we found them," Jacobs informed Edwards as they passed into the rifle squad's perimeter. Another Marine pulled back the poncho they'd covered him with.

Schmitt's left leg had been torn off below the knee. The PLA soldiers had put a tourniquet on, but not to save his life. Schmitt's clothes had been stripped off. His eyes had been gouged out, his body mutilated, his skin sliced to ribbons, his genitals removed and placed into his mouth. Harris had seen plenty of dead and torn bodies, of friends and enemies, since he'd been in China. This was of a grotesqueness and horror that he had not yet seen. Hawke immediately walked back to their LSV. A Marine from the rifle platoon re-covered Schmitt's body with a poncho.

"We checked the LSV for any of their personal effects. Couldn't find any."

"Fucking Pricks took 'em. They pulled this shit in Mexico and Luzon. That way we can't send personal items home to their families." Edwards stared at the poncho covering his friend. Jacobs put a consoling hand on his shoulder and then stepped back.

The solemn moment was interrupted by Hawke vomiting next to the LSV. The Marines looked away and ignored it, to let Hawke have his privacy and maintain some dignity. Edwards turned and walked over to Hawke. Harris had an uneasy feeling about Edwards; he didn't tolerate displays of weakness easily from his squad members. Hawke wiped his mouth with his sleeve and straightened himself. He looked as white as a ghost and embarrassed.

"Hang in there, Devil Dog," Edwards said in a quiet, but strong voice as he patted him on the back. Then he sat down in the front passenger seat. "Blue Leader, Blue Leader. Blue Three. Over."

"Go, Blue Three," cracked over the speaker.

"We found Blue Three Bravo. What's left of them anyway. Over."

"Are you at a new location, Blue Three?"

"We're in the quarry." Edwards unkeyed the mic. "What's our location?" Edwards asked Jacobs.

"It'd be easier to bring him in. We can watch your buddy for you," Corporal Jacobs offered.

"Blue Leader, we'll meet you at original location and bring you in. Over."

"Roger, Blue Three. Be there in about five mikes. Over. Out."

As they left the quarry compound to go back to the road, Harris saw six bodies walking along the road about two hundred yards off.

"Bodies ten o'clock," Harris shouted. He had the SAW trained on them as they approached. All six men threw their hands up. All waved some kind of makeshift white flag.

"Stop the vehicle," Edwards ordered when they got within fifty yards of the enemy prisoners of war. Edwards opened the door, but stood behind it with the twelve gauge pointed at the surrendering ChiCom soldiers. "Halt. *Ting zhi, ting zhi!*"

The EPWs stopped. Edwards knew Bohanan should be there in a few minutes, but that could be an eternity in combat. The ChiCom soldiers began to mumble among themselves.

Shit! What's the word for quiet? Edwards tried to recall. One of the Pricks pointed his finger towards the LSV. *Is that a fucking smile on his face? What the…*

Edwards jumped a bit when the gunfire started. He saw Hawke do the same. He went prone under the LSV door until the shooting stopped. All the EPWs were down. Edwards got up and scanned the tree line. Nothing. None of the downed ChiComs moved. Hawke was out with the rifle and had them covered.

"Stupid Prick bastards don't know when to shut the hell up," Edwards heard Harris from over his shoulder. He turned around to looked up to see Harris, who had just lit a cigarette and was leaning forward into the SAW. "Wouldn't you agree, Corporal Edwards?"

Sergeant Bohanan didn't know whether to believe his Third Squad or not, nor was it his priority. He had lost two gun teams during the night. Equipment failure had made it difficult for him to keep track of his section, on top of a less than ideal environment for TOWs to have been deployed.

"The brilliant planning of Lieutenant Charles Foxtrot," he'd privately vented to Edwards in reference to their new platoon leader. Edwards found humor in the remark, but was in no mood to laugh. "We've also lost Ingraham and Jones.

For now I'll keep your and Crespo's squads as one-gun team squads."

"Roger." Edwards glanced over at Hawke, who was patting down the dead Pricks. "So now what?"

"We got Marines north of the Yangtze now, so keep an eye out for them. We don't want any more friendly fire bullshit. Engineers are to come to this area and build a temporary bridge; Second Section will rendezvous here, and later with the rest of TOW Platoon. Then it's on to Beijing to win this goddamn war."

It was one week to the day since Lieutenant Kai had entered the Nanjing metropolitan area. He was told by a senior officer that it was a short time to take a city of eight million people. It did not feel short to Kai, but he also felt satisfaction in liberating the land of his ancestors from the communist regime that had ruled for nearly the last century. The mayor had surrendered when the PLA had pulled out of the city. Like in the south and east, most citizens were happy, or at least didn't seem to care, to have the PRC out of power. It had not been as smooth an operation as the cities along the coast, however. There were disturbing reports of ROC troops raping and even killing some of the noncombatants. None of the ROC officers had witnessed any of this, but civilians were reporting it. Another mystery was the destruction of several civilian apartment buildings. There had been reports that the Allies had destroyed the river tunnel and bridge while civilians were trying to escape the battle. High command was upset that civilian casualties were unnecessarily high. This was not how the Republic of China had wanted to retake its former capital city. The People's Republic was already screaming to the United Nations about war crimes, and some media were running stories of another "Rape of Nanking." Kai figured all that would wash out once they had full control of the city and could rebuild it to its former glory. When the Chinese people were free and prosperous, how could they talk of atrocities?

His platoon had pushed through to the river. Some, presumably PLA, were jumping in and trying to swim across the river to escape. Kai thought it suicidal. The Yangtze was supposed to be about two miles wide; all but the best swimmers would drown. He raised his rifle and zeroed in on the back of a head of a man stripping his clothes to swim across. When he straightened up, he turned around to face all the soldiers shooting in his direction. Kai thought the man crazy, or perhaps he was choosing to die from a gun rather than the river. He placed the crosshairs on the man's face only to see he was little more than a boy. Even with what looked to be a bad scar on his face, he looked so young. At less than two hundred meters, Kai was confident he could not miss, but he lowered his rifle. Besides, the boy didn't stand much of a chance with all the incoming rounds and the last of the PLA fleeing. If the guns didn't kill him, the river would. After a few seconds the boy dove into the river to swim for his life.

"Good luck, my friend, good luck." Kai spoke out loud to the boy, who couldn't hear him. Those that could have heard him were not paying attention. Kai was suddenly filled with the warm sentiment of him and the boy someday living in a united China and being united in a common goal of freedom and prosperity for their people. He thought perhaps then he could look back at this past week and think it was all worth it.

For all the power Private Liu had felt during the past week, he now felt so helpless. He regretted staying in the city as long as he had, but how could he walk away from an opportunity to kill those not loyal to the People? If they did not deserve to die, who did? He'd stayed to do his duty. He'd stayed to serve the People's Republic.

Now, however, no matter how righteous his actions might have been, he was truly frightened that he would die for it. Exits to the city were cut off, ironically he had played a big role in that, but now he could not get out of the city. Some said they could swim across the river. It had sounded simple enough, but now that he saw it, he wondered how he could. He knew how to swim, but he had only done so in ponds and pools. This river was so wide. As he stripped down, he thought he'd rather be shot than drown. He stood exposed, facing the enemy fire. He even thought he saw a man pointing a rifle right at him. He waited for a quick end, but nothing happened. Bullets flew all around him, but none struck. Perhaps he had been right all along. He was the master of death. He had power over life. It was by his will, and not that of others, that he stayed alive. He bellowed a crazy laugh and dove for the water. How could he possibly drown? He was the master of death.

CHAPTER EIGHTEEN

"It would line up perfectly," General McCullough mumbled as he stared at all the maps and screens in front of him.

"Sir?" his aide, Lieutenant Colonel Fraser, responded.

"Oh, nothing, Lieutenant Colonel, I'm just thinking out loud."

"Yes, sir." Fraser moved off to another part of the warehouse that was currently being used as a command center.

Fraser was a good man, but McCullough's thoughts at that moment were highly classified. As far as he knew, outside of those involved in the project, only he and General Mythers were privy to President Clark's thoughts on this contingency. McCullough didn't even know if the resources were available for this option, or if Clark would even go through with it. At the start of the Invasion of China, just over two years ago, McCullough wasn't even certain he would be in favor of such an option. Any doubts had long since been swept from his conscience.

The PRC defense of Nanjing had been to delay the Allies. He could see it now, but at the time he'd thought they'd use that natural barrier for defense. Since the crossing, the PLA would fight and fall back, fight and fall back, destroying anything in their path. The damn PLA had gone scorched-earth policy on them north of the Yangtze River. To the general's chagrin, the little commie bastards would then whine about the destruction of their land, cities, people, etc. to the Western press. The plan was ludicrous and audacious, but not without its merits. Whether most of the Western media actually believed the charges was questionable, but it did not matter.

They reported it. They obsessed over it. It had been the major news cycle for going on ten months.

In the United States, Clark's political opponents made hay out of it. If national polls were accurate, it had not affected the American public's resolve to win the war. It had, however, weakened the resolve of many of those in Clark's party who were more in touch with media elites than their own constituents. Of course, there was that fringe element in the American population that would protest, rant, and rave in order to subvert the American war effort. McCullough generally had ignored domestic matters during the war; he had other obligations and responsibilities to those actually fighting the war. However, he had begun to pay more attention. He thought reporting had gone from politically biased to being more subversive of late, and it sent off all kinds of alarms in his military thinking.

After twenty plus years in politics, McCullough thought Clark was still more Marine than politician. To Clark's credit, his resolve had remained strong. He had promised to use all the nations resources to drive the PLA from its shores and leave the homeland safe. He had been reelected on the promise to destroy the regime that had tried to destroy the United States of America. He had won reelection in a landslide. Politicians were fickle, however, and the bad press, or rather communist propaganda, had many focused on political careers instead of national service.

Still, when Clark had brought this option up to him two years ago, the whole topic was hypothetical. It might still be, but the president had told him if he ever thought the perfect moment presented itself, to communicate that to him personally. McCullough now thought that moment had arrived. He was obliged to follow that order.

President George Rogers Clark sat alone, contemplating his decision. He stared at a photograph of President Abraham Lincoln. Clark didn't know when exactly the photo was taken. He presumed it was sometime during the Civil War. The old photograph had fascinated him for some time. Lincoln, with no smile nor posturing, just stared into the camera. He thought it was such a blunt picture of Lincoln, especially when compared to the crafted photos of modern politicians. Clark thought Lincoln had such a hard look on his face, such a hard look in his eyes. He saw a strength and a hardness in Lincoln's face that he wanted to exercise as president.

Lincoln had led the country in a time of Civil War. He had made decisions based not on what would preserve his political career, but on what he thought would make a stronger United States of America. At a time when many had questioned the war as it became more destructive, Lincoln stated publicly that victory was owed to those that had sacrificed all. He'd seen it as a duty to win the war as quickly as possible, despite the immediate pain, so the healing could start as soon as possible. He'd won America's most difficult war in four years.

President Franklin D. Roosevelt found himself leading a nation caught in a two-front war against the greatest military powers in world history. Like Lincoln, he had also used the nation's resources and had used all his resolve to win that war as soon as possible. Although Roosevelt would die before the end of that war, President Truman would see that vision to its conclusion.

Clark thought it ironic that had Truman shown that same kind of resolve to win the Korean War, perhaps this current war would never have taken place. But he didn't, and now Clark found himself making the same choice that Truman did in the summer of 1945, and later in the Korean War with a different conclusion. However, there was a big difference between Clark's and Truman's decisions: in World War II the United States was the only one with nukes. Now many nations had them to one extent or another. His decision would not be isolated and could kick off a destructive chain of events. Another big difference between World War II and the Sino-American War: Truman could act on his own decision. Clark had to get "permission" from Russia. The United States' world dominance had declined so much since 1945 that Clark needed the Russian Federation's approval to prevent United Nations' support for the People's Republic of China.

Ten minutes earlier he had gotten that approval, on the condition that the United States looked the other way as Russia used nuclear weapons in their war against the jihadist forces in the Middle East. As well, the Russians were looking to expand their sphere of influence in parts of Eastern Europe and Central Asia. Clark had no problem with the former. The Russians were dealing with a problem that American political leaders had walked away from a generation ago. Clark had been a young Marine in those wars. He'd lost friends. He, as did the American nation, had dealt with the wounds of unhonored sacrifice as politicians crafted careers and political factions tore the country down.

Clark had sworn he would not allow the same thing to happen to the men, women, and families that were fighting this war. Not on his watch. He had publicly vowed to do everything within the power of the United States to defeat the People's Republic of China before the end of his presidency. Would he walk away from that vow now? This decision could have political repercussions. Members of the opposition party would cry for impeachment. Even the moderate members of his own party would love to see his political power and agenda diminished a bit. He hated the thought of his political enemies leading the United States back into descent.

He stared at Lincoln. His hard eyes stared back at Clark from the photograph. Clark had thought and prayed over how to win this war for nearly six years.

"You know what the right answer is." Clark spoke out loud to himself. "Fear is the only thing slowing you down now."

He reached for his phone.

"Get ahold of General Mythers and Secretary of State Weeseman. Tell them to be here in thirty minutes."

Alexandra Harmon would not have admitted it to anyone in the world, but she was excited. When the phone had woken her up two hours before, her first thought was has something happened to the president? That idea dissipated as she realized she was being called on her unofficial, and untraceable, cell phone. Still, something was up for Mythers to have called her and want to meet. She loved the intrigue. Without it, the last six years as vice president of the United States would have been like a prison sentence, which was more or less what it had felt like anyway.

Harmon had never cared for Clark. She thought his political style to be too blunt and unsophisticated. She believed he never would have made it in national politics if it had not been for the progressive extremism of Leakey. She thought Clark had a gift for quoting the Constitution in such a way that she thought made him sound smarter than he really was. After all, the man had never even attended law school. No doubt his Marine Corps war record had been well received by flyover country, but what did that really mean? She had done enough campaigning and politicking to know shooting a gun did not make you good at governing. And quite frankly, something else she would never admit to anyone in the world, she was sick and tired of war veterans always getting a free pass when it came to politics. As a philosophy major in college, she had come to the conclusion that some were born thinkers, some were born laborers, and some were born fighters. Being good at one did not make you good at another.

In her mind Clark was not a thinker, or at least not a good one. His directness, the way he wore his patriotism on his sleeve, his righteous approach to decision making. As if all decisions could be based on a matter of right and wrong. She found his thinking naive and not what America needed to move forward. But he had won the primary, much to the chagrin of her party's elite. However, another four years of Leakey would have been dangerous. The country appeared to be dying right before everyone's eyes. The party had had to unite and defeat Leakey. Clark had asked Harmon to be his vice president as a way to unite that party. She'd accepted, not because she completely supported his agenda, and she definitely didn't like his style, but to promote her career. After all, Clark was very popular with many Americans. Besides, if he was a failure, she would claim she always tried to temper his extremism, even if he would never listen to her. If he was successful, then she would ride his coat tails into the White House.

Like most Americans, she was happy to have a fighter in the White House when they were attacked by the People's Republic of China. Her political path had seemed very clear to her at the time. Harmon was not surprised that Clark was reelected, but to be reelected on the promise of destroying the communist government of China had flummoxed her. She thought it too aggressive and provocative. She thought it could create an international backlash and go very badly for the United States. She had wanted an international coalition, headed by herself, to negotiate terms by which the United States and the People's Republic could coexist. After all, she had built and maintained a political career on her ability to build consensuses. Why not use it for the war effort?

In usual Clark style, he had wanted to go for victory, not consensus. Harmon had begun a subtle campaign to distance herself from Clark. The fact that the United States was winning with the use of a total war strategy, she saw as her bad luck. But then the war was not over, and she had her own cadre of secret Clark dissenters. Not the least among that group was the chairman of the Joint Chiefs of Staff and Secretary of State Weeseman, the two that had requested this early morning meeting.

Sitting in the Morning Star Café at two hours before it opened to the public, waiting to have a secret meeting with two of the highest members of the president's cabinet made her feel important.

Harmon's nephew, for whom she had procured this choice establishment, always allowed her to unofficially meet with people when she needed to during off hours. She sat there in the middle of the shop with a cup of her favorite dark roast and a plate of pastries, wondering what could be so important that Mythers and Weeseman would have requested this meeting at four o'clock in the morning.

Weeseman walked in, looking paranoid and disoriented, although he'd been secretly meeting Harmon at this location for over two years.

"Where's Mythers?" Weeseman sounded short of breath.

"Did you run here? Why are you so short of breath?"

"I went around the block and ran through the back alley. I wanted to make sure I wasn't being followed." It was an extreme effort for the short heavyset man, and now he could barely talk.

"Seth, you're going to give yourself a heart attack. What is going on?" Harmon had gone from feeling important to feeling concerned for her career, but had no sooner asked than Mythers walked in, looking far more relaxed.

"Sorry for all the cloak-and-dagger drama, but then I guess that's exactly what it is." Mythers had a smile on his face. His demeanor could not be any more different than Weeseman's.

"What are you two up to?" Harmon's voice betrayed more concern than she would have liked it to.

"He hasn't told you?" Mythers nodded towards Weeseman.

"I just got here myself." Weeseman was still trying to catch his breath.

"Hell, Weeseman, what'd you do, rappel through the ceiling? What took you so long?"

"So what's this all about?" Harmon was feeling impatient. Weeseman looked at Mythers, which Mythers noticed, then turned to Harmon.

"Are we alone?"

"Yes. My nephew won't be back until 4:30 a.m. He opens at 5 a.m."

"Cowboy Clark"—Mythers's favorite nickname for the president—"wants to nuke the PLA."

"What?! How? Leakey dismantled our arsenal." Harmon sounded more outraged than surprised.

"He's been secretly building our arsenal. It's been his top secret pet project," Mythers stated with casual contempt.

"How come you've never mentioned this to me before?!" Harmon was genuinely pissed off.

"I didn't know until tonight," Weeseman pleaded.

"How could you not know of this until now?" Harmon's question was pointed at Mythers.

"He brought it up as a hypothetical before we started the invasion. Of course, I advised against it at the time. We didn't have the weapons anyway. He never brought it up to me again until tonight. He didn't ask my opinion. He gave me an order. He wants this planned out and done within the next forty-eight hours."

"The Russians will freak out over this. Have you talked to them?" Harmon's question was to Weeseman.

"No. When I asked him what we will do about the Russian Federation, he told me to worry about our interest, not theirs."

"Typical. It's always 'America First' with that man." Harmon was exasperated. "At a time when we need an international consensus to win this war, Clark wants to act like America is the only country that matters."

"It such a Jarhead thing. Ragnarsson is the same way. His first response is to kick ass or 'kill them all, let God sort them out.'" Mythers waved his hands and rolled his eyes. Then his tone went from mocking to serious. "The last major battle we had to fight was Nanjing. The PLA has since been beating a path all the way to the Yellow River. They're beat, and that's all we need to negotiate our victory. Clark, McCullough, Ragnarsson—they're all kill happy. We should be at the conference table now, not the battlefield; and we sure as hell shouldn't be talking about nukes and total victory, not with China we shouldn't."

"Oh God." Harmon leaned back, crossing her arms and exhaling loudly. "How do we impeach a president in a time of war?"

Weeseman didn't say a word, just sipped his coffee.

"With all due respect, Madame President—" Mythers chuckled a bit "—excuse me, Madame Vice President, but we're well past impeachment at this point."

All of Harmon's political instincts and acumen kicked in. She could ask him what he meant, but she knew. Besides, Mythers wouldn't appreciate the show of naiveté. Her mind raced, calculating how possible this could be, also the fact that if it happened, she could serve for nearly ten years as president of the United States. She would have time to do great things. She could leave her mark on history.

"Don't tell me how, but you can make that happen?"

"Yes." Mythers didn't need time to contemplate. Weeseman was content to sip his coffee and see how this played out.

"There will be an investigation…" Harmon didn't finish the thought.

"There won't be an investigation. Not if you're president. There would be no need for one. In this time of national crisis, there are more important things to worry about." Harmon didn't care for the way Mythers smiled as he said this, but what was she to do about it at this point?

"Why would you arrange this?"

"I'm a patriot and this is a time of war. I don't want to see American men and women die to win a war, or Chinese for that matter, when we can negotiate a peace. And besides, Madame President"—this time Mythers did not correct himself—"I know you can do great things that would benefit this country, that would make us safer."

Harmon smiled. She thought Mythers was cynical, but she did like his thinking.

"I presume, General, that you'll be at the vanguard of a new administration?" She wasn't quite ready to say "my administration" yet.

"Madame Vice President, as a public servant I am here to do my part for the country." Weeseman had finally found the nerve to say something.

"War is hell and sacrifices have to be made." Mythers sounded more sarcastic than patriotic. "You can bet your career I do expect to do great things for this country, Madame Vice President."

Harmon decided at that moment she was in. She told herself that duty was calling; she must respond. Her mind was racing as to how Mythers could pull this off. She decided it was probably best not to ask and to give herself some deniability if things went sideways.

"Of course, remember, we serve at the pleasure of the president. Our duty is to see to it that the needs of this country are taken care of." Harmon felt more alive than she had in decades. She felt in control. "Gentlemen"—she stood up to leave the room—"I think this has been a productive meeting. We'll meet again when we have something new to talk about."

With that, the vice president walked out of the Morning Star Café and got into her limousine. She ordered the driver to take her to her office. She had a lot of work ahead of her; she needed to get started.

CHAPTER NINETEEN

"Yes, sir, heart failure is all it says." Lieutenant Colonel Fraser couldn't even believe his own words, how could the others? General McCullough's staff stood in stunned silence for several seconds.

"God help us." Major Jardin's voice cracked as she walked out to compose herself.

McCullough hated the news. More than that, he hated the feeling in his gut that an opportunity was lost and would never come back. He pushed the thought from his mind. Now was not a time to be ruled by fear. Without a nuclear option at this point, the war still had a lot of fighting left to be done and a lot of lives to be lost before the People's Republic of China would fall.

His mind immediately went back to thinking of how to win this war. Task Force Sherman was tediously working its way through the north. Task Force Grant had to get across the Yellow River. Zhang had completed a command center west of Beijing to fall back to. McCullough figured that Mythers would lobby President Harmon to negotiate. He didn't know exactly how much pull Mythers had with the new president, but he feared it'd be substantial. He'd heard from contacts in DC that they were of a similar mind-set, as a reaction to the negative press about the war over the past year.

His mind wrestled with the dilemma now before him. Should he move forward at full speed to destroy the PRC and achieve complete victory? Or should he hold back to see what new priorities the new president would have? Should he risk the lives of troops whose sacrifice would potentially be wasted in a political negotiation? But to hold back now could cost them momentum against their enemy that might never again be regained. It was against his nature not to fight to win. He would not go against his instincts now.

"Listen up, soldiers," McCullough bellowed, "we all mourn the loss of President Clark. He was a great leader at a time when our country needed great leadership the most. However, he's not the only casualty of this war. We can only honor him and our fallen countrymen through complete victory: the unconditional surrender of the People's Republic of China. Initiate the final phase of Operation Mandate of Heaven."

McCullough prayed it would not be in vain.

Zhang was overjoyed. He thought his speech on China Central Television could not have gone better. He'd told the people that destiny was on the side of the People's Republic. The death of Clark was evidence that the People's Republic would emerge from this time of trial and the youth would be remembered as the greatest generation in the history of the PRC.

The death of Clark was just icing on the cake for Zhang. His guerrilla campaign against noncombatants and collaborators was paying dividends. The Western media was more than eager to present the PRC perspective that these deaths were caused by the corrupt ROC and American troops. Every time he turned on an American or European news broadcast, it was all they were talking about, outside of the philanthropy of Hollywood actors.

He would have thanked the gods, if he believed in any. Instead, the course of events had only worked to affirm his belief in himself. He would not be denied his place in history. So he would be remembered as a great defender instead of a great conqueror. He was already envisioning how the former could lead back to the latter. He'd watched and studied the use of grievance politics the Left used in the West. He had played that card well with American and European media. That sort of thing had never worked on Clark, who'd seemed stubbornly stuck to doing what he thought was right. Now he had the opportunity to play it on the new American president, whose reputation for compromise and resolution was well known. Zhang was more optimistic than he'd been for the last six years. He relished this new opportunity.

Harris scanned the burned-out village for any sign of danger. He hunkered down a little lower behind the TOW weapon system as the LSV creeped along. He wanted to make himself as small a target as possible for any potential Prick snipers. Second Section had been told that Bravo Company had already secured the area, but it paid not to take anything for granted. A sniper had taken out Sergeant Washington last week in another village that was supposedly "secured."

It'd been like that for the last several months. The PLA would put up a small fight and fall back. Destroy villages and farms. The cities were generally left alone until the ROC showed up. Then buildings were destroyed and small numbers of people turned up dead. Harris's mother had told him that more and more the news talked about Allied atrocities and crimes. She didn't believe any of it, but was tired of hearing it on the news every night. Even when she had stopped watching the news, she heard people talking about it at work. It was driving her insane.

Harris and the other Marines thought it was the Pricks employing some kind of propaganda strategy against them. As long as they kept moving north, they would win the war. When the war was won, the truth would become known.

"Over there," Harris heard Edwards order Hawke to pull over to the fuel truck. Crespo's First Squad had already arrived, as had Sergeant Bohanan and his driver, Hart. After Sergeant Washington's death, Sergeant Crespo had taken over First Squad. His only surviving gun team, Reese and Sheridan, were moved to Edward's squad. Cortes's squad was the only one still intact.

Harris was relieved to see Cortes's squad roll in. It was a chance to catch up with Hastings. While their drivers filled up the LSVs, they walked a few yards away and had a cigarette.

"Man, they fucked this little place up," Hastings said as he shook his head and exhaled.

"Yeah, there's a lot of that lately," was all Harris could think of to reply. He enjoyed his conversations with Hastings, but he was tired and really didn't feel like trying to talk.

"I suppose some faggot-ass professor in Lincoln will blame this on us also." Hastings's sister attended the University of Nebraska and would fill him in on the insane things going on with the fringe element of the student population and the faculty. He and Harris always found it good for a laugh, and Hastings had asked his sister to keep him posted on that stuff. Lately, the two had found it less funny as their vitriol increased.

"Hell, joke 'em if they can't take a fuck," Harris said with a smile. Hastings appreciated the humor. There had not been much to laugh about lately.

"Second Section." Bohanan whistled loudly and waved his hand in circles above his head, indicating he wanted everyone to gather around. "Listen up, Marines." His demeanor got very serious. It gave Harris that bad feeling in his gut that he got with bad premonitions. "It has been confirmed to me by Captain Richards that as of yesterday evening President Clark has died, and Vice President Harmon is now president.

Secretary of State Weeseman is now her vice president. I have no word yet as to who the new Secretary of State is."

The six full seconds of silence seemed like an eternity.

"How'd he die?" Cortes spoke up first.

"As of now, heart failure is the official cause of death."

"Well, no shit," Edwards hostilely spat out, as if he knew he was being lied to. "We all die of fucking heart failure sooner or later."

"Compose yourself, Corporal Edwards." Sergeant Bohanan's rebuke was quick, but he was a bit uncomfortable with it. He'd known Edwards for several years and liked the man. He also knew Edwards to be very cynical and didn't want that spreading to the other Marines in the section. "Look, I, as I imagine most of you, admired President Clark. He was a Jarhead like us. He fought this war with a warrior's mind-set"—Bohanan made eye contact with Edwards—"not a politician's. He will be missed. But he's not the only casualty of this war. Like you, I signed up for the duration of the war; and I signed up to win, not for college money or technical training. We volunteered for the Marine Corps; we volunteered for the infantry because we wanted to fight this war. We wanted to defeat the motherfuckers who invaded our land, raped our women, and slaughtered our children. We do that with or without President Clark. We fight for our country. We fight for the Constitution. We will continue that fight. We will continue to kick the ever-living hell out of the Prick bastards, or we will die trying! Do you understand me, Marines?"

"Aye, aye, Sergeant! All the way to fucking Beijing," Harris shouted, uncharacteristically verbalizing his emotions. It went over well. The survivors of the Death Squad yelled a hoorah. Even Edwards displayed emotion.

"You a fucking cheerleader now, Harris?" Edwards said with a smile and slapped him on the back.

Liu Zhiqiang had heard the news about President Clark, and it had bothered him. He worried that the Americans might quit the war without their leader. Would he be allowed to continue killing? His sergeant had told him not to worry; there were plenty of ROC and traitors to the state.

"When does the killing ever stop? The People's Republic will always have a place for its loyal party members." Sergeant Wen tried to put the boy at ease, although Liu no longer looked like a skinny, boney fourteen-year-old. Physically he had responded well to the physical rigors of military training. He was sixteen now and bigger than most men, especially those from the south. His training, improved diet, and natural growth spurt had turned him into a physically formidable young man.

Liu had made a mental note to become a party member. His current life was the best he'd ever had. If the Communist Party of China could ensure that it would continue, then he must have an active role in it. First, however, he had a mission to accomplish. One that he was particularly well suited for and could carry out alone. Sergeant Wen appreciated Liu's talents, and knowing this was exactly what the People's Republic had in mind with this type of unit, he trusted Liu to conduct these missions with minimal assistance. Besides, he made Liu go in civilian clothes and sterile, no military ID. If he were ever caught, the People's Republic and the People's Liberation Army would claim him to be an American agent. Western media would love a story like that.

Just south of the American forces, outside the city of Xuchang, Liu walked the streets. He combed a local street market, looking for his next target. Soon he found her. By all appearances she was a helpful young girl. Her mother was selling vegetables, and she was running from stall to stall, communicating and delivering items for her mother. The young girl's constant traversing was what made her such an ideal target.

Liu felt the rush from the power over life. It was intoxicating, and why shouldn't it be? If one controlled life, if one had power over death, then what could not be controlled? He took the time to position the little corpse just right; he truly believed it was an artistic talent of his to create a scene that would shock and disgust lesser human beings. Just before he left, he placed an American dog tag in the little corpse's hand and closed it tight. He emerged from the alleyway, made eye contact with Sergeant Li, and nodded. Li moved in to "discover" the body and the dog tag that "obviously" belong to the assailant. He would get word of it to international media to see to it that justice was done. The name on the dog tag: Derrick Thomas Schmitt, USMC.

Major General Edgar "Fast Eddie" Ragnarsson did not want to waste any time. He was absolutely in favor of moving ahead with Operation Mandate of Heaven. He knew of Harmon's and Mythers's reputations. He had been a strong supporter of Clark when he ran in the primary over six years ago, but he had been disappointed in his selection of a vice presidential candidate. Ragnarsson had just chalked it up to politics. For as much as there shouldn't be, there was a lot of that in his business. Ragnarsson thought of himself as a warrior and a student of history. Schmoozing and kissing ass just wasn't his thing. That meant for as good as a combat leader that he was, he had political enemies in and out of the Marine Corps. He didn't know how the change in Commander-in-Chief would affect his career, but more importantly to him he did not know how it would affect the war effort. But he based his decision on two facts: politicians always wanted to take credit for success, and it was better to ask forgiveness than permission. His goal was to get the First Marine Division across the Yellow River as soon as possible. He knew Major General Jackson of the Second Marine Division and General McCullough were of the same mind. The more success they had, the harder it would be for the politicians to pull out. The faster they moved north, the less of a target they were for the PLA guerrillas and the leftist media. If they were going to win this war, they were going to have to do it fast before the president could change her mind.

Lieutenant Colonel William "Bulldog" McGregor was relieved when he received orders from his commander, and cousin, Colonel Arthur "Lucky" Liddell to move north. He was preparing to move his battalion forward; the orders only reaffirmed what he had started. He had prayed the new president would let Clark's strategy play out. He knew of her reputation and figured she'd be happy to accept credit for any success, but would be too timid to take any serious risk. He had also heard rumors of Mythers's desire to negotiate a victory. That had not been Clark's style, but it sounded like Harmon's. They had come so far, with better than imagined success; he didn't want to stop now. The United States now had the advantage of air superiority. The loss of industry was hurting the PLA. They were using less technology on the battlefield. They were resorting to guerrilla tactics that, while they did kill some American troops, were ineffective at stopping the American advance. They were really good at ginning up pro-communist propaganda with some of the Leftwing media in the United States and Europe. None of that would matter if the US won the war. Until now it had not been enough to weaken the resolve of the American people or

President Clark. He prayed that would not change with the new president. So with even more vigor than at any point in the war, McGregor planned how to get his battalion across the Yellow River.

CHAPTER TWENTY

Harris had the T-99 in his sights. From the distance he thought it looked well armored. He had worked it out with Reese to fire at it two seconds after he did. Better to kill it with two missiles than not to with only one. Besides there were not many Prick tanks nor armored cars within sight north of the Yellow River. He'd heard rumors that the PRC was starting to run out of armor and fuel for vehicles. Harris had written most of the talk off as wishful thinking. However, he'd also heard that they were running out of jets and helicopters, and today seemed to bear truth to that. He'd only seen two Prick jets, and both had been shot down. He'd yet to see one helicopter today, and the biggest sign to him that the Pricks were slipping was that they had not even blown the bridge. For all the talk that the People's Republic was teetering on the edge of collapse, there was an equal amount that said the toughest of the fight was yet to come; street fighting in Beijing would be a nightmare. On the other side, there was talk of being home for Christmas. To Harris it was just talk. He'd learned from his father's experience that you were not home until you were home. Until then it was just a wish. As a lot of the Marines were fond of saying, you can wish in one hand and shit in the other. Harris had to deal with what things were, not what he wanted them to be.

Harris was somewhere northeast of the city of Zhengzhou. The ROC had moved into the city of about ten million without a fight. The death of President Clark had not strengthened the resolve of the city commissars to die for the Communist Party of China.

211

Harris and Reese took out one of the two tanks in their field of fire; otherwise there was nothing else to shoot at that moment. Crazily enough, there appeared to be a small number of civilians trying to get across the bridge in a middle of a firefight. Prick riflemen were still trying to hold the bridge, or at least delay its loss. It was a weak attempt to hold the bridge. Harris saw more than half the Pricks turn and run. He scanned the area, looking for another target; he couldn't see one.

The thought crossed his mind: What if the Prick bastards had planted explosives on the bridge and were only waiting until the bulk of Marines were crossing to blow it? Or perhaps get a bunch of civilians on the bridge, blow it, and then whine to the leftist media that the Marines did it.

Harris was antsy. He hated just watching a firefight take place and to be little more than a spectator. He soon heard the noise of choppers—Pricks. Three attack helicopters. It looked like such a pathetic attempt to hold the bridge compared to what he'd seen from the Pricks until now. All three helos fired rockets. Harris got his crosshairs on one and fired on his own initiative. The helicopter cut away shortly before impact, and Harris had not been able to cut with it. A second missile took the chopper out.

"Glad to help you out, Harris," Reese cracked over Harris's earpiece.

"Yeah, me too, you foxtrottin' bastard," Harris replied.

"Someone tell me how a whole goddamn US Marine division crosses a river and nobody sees it?!" Zhang shouted at his staff in his fortified command post that he'd nicknamed the Dragon's Lair. He immediately regretted the display of emotion, but his anger had gotten the best of him. This was not supposed to happen. General Fu Gang was in command there. Had he gone over to the ROC, or was he just incompetent? Zhang had thought he'd found a party member he could count on, but then who could be counted on in times like these? He began making a mental list of who else would need to be purged from the People's Republic.

General Fu Gang didn't need to talk with General Secretary Zhang Min to know he was in hot water. Fu had spent enough time in the Communist Party of China to know he might very well be a dead man walking. His wife and grandchildren were under the "protection" of Zhang. His sons served in the People's Liberation Army. They were under his command. If he didn't stop the American forces from crossing the Yellow River, they would all be killed. They might all be killed anyway, but the only chance they had was for him to stop the American advance. Within a matter of seconds of receiving the news that the First Marine Division was crossing the Yellow River, General Fu Gang decided to go all in. He had nothing to lose. He would use every military resource available to him to stop the American advance. He might lose tens of thousands of troops, he might even lose his own life, but he thought it worth it if it might protect his grandchildren from President Zhang.

Liu packed the rifle with the scope first into his duffle bag. He had just gotten it, and he loved it. He'd wanted it so badly and was honored that Sergeant Wen had thought he was worthy of it. He packed his PLA uniform on the bottom. He would be traveling in civilian clothes, hoping that if he were seen, he wouldn't be checked by American soldiers or Marines. He slipped in a bag of rice and an extra shirt, trying to hide the shape of the rifle. He found an old rations box and crammed it in there; that did the trick. He had a knife and a nine-millimeter pistol secured in the front of his waistband.

Sergeant Wen had told them to act like civilians trying to evacuate north of the river. On an emotional level the plan made no sense to Liu. How could projecting weakness as helpless civilians be a sound tactic? However, in nearly two years of war with the Americans, he had become familiar with their weakness of concern for innocent life. They did not like to kill people they did not have to. Older veterans had told him this weakness was easier to exploit before Clark, and were hopeful they could again with this new President Harmon. None of that mattered to Liu at the moment; he wanted to get across the river. He thought it ironic he that had been concerned about the Americans losing heart with the death of their leader; instead they had attacked. Perhaps the veterans had lied about the softness of Americans. At least Liu could still have the opportunity to kill, but first he had to get away from the Zhengzhou metropolitan area and cross the bridge to get north of the Yellow River.

They'd crossed the bridge shortly after First Tank Battalion had crossed and set up a perimeter. The bridge had not been blown. Harris thought perhaps the end was in sight for the PRC. They moved up onto the side of a large hill on the right flank of First Battalion and Third Light Armored Infantry. Harris scanned the horizon twice and didn't see anything. He backed away from the scope to relieve his eye and scanned the skyline. He saw what looked almost like a flock of birds coming towards them.

"We got drones, eleven o'clock," he shouted down to Edwards. No sooner said, they heard Cortes over the radio, stating the same thing. Harris went back to his day scope. Where there were drones, Pricks were sure to follow.

In some ways Lieutenant Kai was relieved when he got the news. He'd feared that President Harmon would be less aggressive in fighting the PRC than Clark had been. At the same time there was the tension of a sudden and unexpected engagement. His unit was on standby. His orders were to inspect his platoon and make sure they were ready if needed. He prayed the PRC would not launch guerrilla attacks on the civilians and that the ROC army would indeed be ready.

"Prick bastards," Harris complained. "The drones got high explosives on them. They're exploding them overhead!" Harris informed Edwards as he watched Prick drones rain shrapnel down on the Marines in the river valley.

The scream of jets surprised Harris and he involuntarily ducked down behind his gun. Of course, by the time he heard the jets, they were already overhead and flying north. Harris got back to the day sight. They might have been caught flat-footed, but all indications were that they were responding big.

"Hawke, drive north about five hundred meters or so. Stay off the skyline. Pricks are coming. I want Harris to reach out and touch them. Copy, Harris?" Edwards ordered.

The fact that Liu had made it across the bridge had only confirmed, once more, in his mind, his own invulnerability. His platoon had split up into their four-man teams, thinking it would be easier to get through the American line in small numbers and less likely to attract attention. Once in the safety of some woods on a hilltop overlooking the valley, his team leader, Li, gave the order to put on their uniforms and ditch the civilian clothing. Liu had his scoped rifle out. Yang had the binoculars. They scanned the valley and watched as US Marines moved north. Wang worked the radio with Li to establish contact and communicate intelligence.

Liu's bloodlust was provoked by the exploding drones killing American Marines. He found himself yearning to kill.

"Liu, nine o'clock, about three hundred meters," Yang instructed. Liu turned and eventually saw an American LSV stopping on the side of a hill. Obviously they were trying not to skyline themselves and to remain unseen.

"No hiding from the master of death," Liu mumbled softly.

"What?" Yang whispered loudly, thinking there was a good reason for it.

"I got the target," Liu segued. "TOW gun. They got the skull and crossbones we've seen." Liu salivated. He particularly enjoyed killing those he thought were powerful. He'd convinced himself that he added their power to his own when he did so. Marines were his favorite targets, especially when they were powerless over him. He'd heard of these Marines with the skull and crossbones on their LSVs. They were supposed to be very good or very lucky.

He attempted to put his crosshairs on the gunner. He wanted the gunner, but the Marine was hunkered down close to the weapon's scope and he could not get a clear shot. Liu tried to acquire the neck or someplace not protected by body armor. Suddenly the Marine straightened. Liu had his shot, but he held back. The Marine had taken his helmet off, and Liu could see that he had red hair. He'd been told the Brits referred to redheads as gingers. Liu didn't understand the association. Ginger was not red. Not that it mattered now; he had never seen a person in real life with red hair. Now he would kill one. Liu began to squeeze the trigger. He was just to the point where the trigger stopped and the slightest amount of added pressure would discharge the weapon. Suddenly the Marine dropped down out of sight.

"Dammit," Liu whispered in anger.

"Discipline!" Yang quietly rebuked. The Marine popped back up through the turret and hunkered down behind the weapon's scope. Liu patiently waited for the Marine to straighten up once more. He would not let another opportunity pass him by.

Harris studied the skyline. It was only a matter of time until tanks and armored cars would try to intercept the Marines. He could hear the thunder in the distance as US jets dropped bombs on the Pricks. How much longer would it take for Prick artillery to respond on their position? Battle was imminent and Harris realized he had a full bladder.

"Hawke, I got to piss. You want the gun for a while?"

"Hell yeah." The boot had been itching to get behind the gun and kill his first tank.

"Dang!" Harris shot up straight and took his helmet off. He'd felt a sharp pain in his scalp, as if something had bitten him hard. He felt his head, checked his helmet, nothing.

"You letting me up or what?" Hawke badgered.

"Yeah, I'm coming down." Harris slipped down through the turret and out of the LSV to go relieve himself.

"See anything?" Harris inquired after a couple of minutes.

"Not yet." Hawke sounded optimistic that he would sooner or later.

Edwards looked at Harris and nodded towards the SAW.

"I'll take the SAW for a while, Hawke," Harris complied.

"Hawke, you shoot anything with a red star on it, now. You got me?" Edwards threw in.

"Aye, aye, Corporal," Hawke enthusiastically responded, not seeming to notice Edwards's sarcasm. It was his moment. He wanted to do it right.

Harris got behind the SAW and lit up a cigarette. The smoke kept getting into his eyes and was a bit irritating, but the cigarette helped his nerves. He scanned the tree line. He saw nothing.

"I wish I could get paid for all the minutes I've spent watching a skyline for something to shoot," Harris jokingly complained to alleviate tension.

"You're alive, ain't you," Edwards cynically responded. "That's pay enough. Keep watching. You've been around long enough to know there's always something out there."

"Yeah, well—" Harris was cut off by Hawke dropping down like a sack of potatoes.

"Harris, drive!" was all the orders Edwards gave. Harris didn't need to be told twice. He'd put it all together very fast. Edwards climbed into the back with Hawke. "Backwards, go backwards!" Harris figured Hawke must have been shot from the front. Harris put the LSV in reverse and stepped on the gas. He backed over something hard, but the LSV kept running and Harris wasn't going to stop. He needed to get somewhere safe. He slammed on the brakes, cut the wheel hard to the left, and shifted into drive, turning the LSV around and headed to turn up into some trees for more cover.

"You can stop," Edwards ordered. Harris braked the vehicle to a halt. He turned around. Edwards had blood on the front of him, but he wasn't hurt. Hawke had been shot just under the bridge of his nose. The ChiCom 5.8 mm had traveled through his skull. Blood and brain matter were all over the back of the LSV. Harris was not new to death on the battlefield, but this still made him feel sick. Mind over matter, he didn't have time to be sick.

"Hand me the mic," Edwards commanded. He then proceeded to call in an airstrike and then artillery on that goddamned hill in front of their previous position.

"I'll take the gun." Edwards stood up in the turret. Harris looked back at Hawke's lifeless body. It was such a hollow reminder of the life that had been there minutes before.

"That should have been me," Harris mumbled to himself. Intellectually, he knew this was not his fault, but it did not make him feel any better. He couldn't have felt more guilt if he'd pulled the trigger himself.

Harris and Edwards weren't surprised that Prick tanks showed up in large numbers, just that it had taken as long as it did. Initially, it was the Prick armor fighting vehicles, AFVs, that Edwards spotted about two miles out on their right flank, but the tanks weren't far behind. Soon there were several TOW missiles launched. All found their targets. Within twenty minutes Edwards took out a T-99 and three AFVs. Then they drove back to the convoy to restock more missiles. They were going to need them.

Ragnarsson was pleased, but he was tense. His Marines had moved fast and hard. Now they had started slugging it out with the PLA. As of yet he didn't know what units he was up against, but from reports, it was a significant force. His intel reported Prick units moving south and east toward First Marines. A move like this was likely to bring more PLA into action. First Marines had drawn first blood on this one; Fifth Marines had crossed and was approaching from the east. The last of Seventh and Fourth Marines were crossing the Yellow River and heading into the battle. If the Pricks wanted to try to end it here, it was as good a place as any.

Liu had been part of a team of four killers. Now he was a team of one. The joy of his killing one of the "Death" Marines with the skull and crossbones was short lived. Artillery rounds began to pulverize the hill soon after. Liu and his team ran to the north, but Wen, Li, and Yang all died. Liu wasn't surprised. The hill had turned into hell. He probably would've died too had it not been for his power over life and death.

He ran as fast as he could. Within several minutes he came across the People's Army. A sergeant told him to find a Lieutenant Hueng. Liu moved along the troops, calling for the lieutenant, but to no avail. Eventually, another sergeant told him to fall in with his riflemen or he'd shoot him for cowardice. Liu's first impulse was to put a bullet between the sergeant's eyes, but the PLA had given him greater discipline than that. Besides, they were headed south towards the Marines. There was going to be plenty of time for death.

McCullough had not slept for forty-eight hours. He really hadn't missed it until about two hours earlier. As he had done many times throughout this war, he reflected back to his days as a young infantry officer at the start of his career. The chaos and fatigue of his command center was nothing compared to what his men on the frontline had experienced for the last forty-eight hours straight. He had looked for a quick resolution, and the PLA obliged. General Fu had gone all in. McCullough figured Fu must have been up for execution if he lost this one, so he'd given it all he had. Perhaps Fu was already shot, in which case his successor would want to give it all he had to avoid the same fate. Currently, he had First and Second Marine Divisions and First and Ninth Infantry Divisions of the US Army engaged. Fifth and Sixth Marine Divisions were meeting light resistance to the east. McCullough could envision a scenario where if enough units moved west fast enough, they could potentially surround the much larger PLA south of Beijing. Could this be another Cannae? Payback for the Chosen Reservoir? Could this be the fall of the People's

Republic of China? McCullough didn't expect the PLA to ever completely quit until they'd killed the last communist. However, if they could be relegated to an insignificant force in West China that the ROC could handle with minimal US support, it would be a victory. After six years of war, McCullough could finally see daylight at the end of the tunnel. Problem was, there was still a whole lot of tunnel.

When Mythers was informed of the engagement, he had been furious. He figured McCullough was just trying to make himself look good. The bastard would use it to try to steal his job. Of course, Mythers knew he was considerably more intelligent than McCullough and had, in fact, a plan to prevent something like that from ever happening. Mythers wasn't going to let his job go to anyone. In fact, he envisioned taking over the jobs of others. He had ambitions to become the most powerful man in the United States, perhaps with the exception of the president of the United States.

Who, by the way, is no longer a man.

The idea made him laugh. He needed the comfort of humor at a time such as this, when a battle, which appeared to be evolving into one of the war's biggest, had thrown a major speed bump into his agenda.

He'd not had much sleep over the last forty-eight hours. His mind festered over all possible outcomes and how he could play it out to his advantage. He'd come too far to let his career stall now. Whether this battle ended in victory or defeat, he intended to benefit from the outcome. After two days of intense thought and stress, General Mythers thought he had the foundation for a plan that would fulfill his ambition and desire for power.

Harris was back behind the gun. He was in a rhythm. He felt a lust that needed to be satisfied. His parents had raised him to believe in the sanctity of life, yet now all he wanted to do was kill Pricks. There was a voice in his head that told him he shouldn't want to kill as much as he did at the moment, but it was too quiet and shouted down by the voice that screamed to kill them all, even if it meant the loss of his life. Counter to natural instinct, Harris had not thought about his own safety for three days since this battle had started. Christ, his ancestors, his father, and even Hawke had been willing to die for his family. Was he too good to do anything less? He remembered Drill Instructor Sergeant Jameson saying wars were won by making some poor, dumb bastard die for his country. Now Harris would kill all the poor, dumb, communist bastards that he could. If he died in order to win this war, so be it.

Lieutenant Kai was itching for action, and it perplexed him. His family was Christian. He was raised to believe that life was given by God. Now he found himself wanting to take human life, yet it was the lives of those that empowered tyrants that destroyed life, that destroyed truth, that destroyed all that was natural as God had intended it. Could that be such an evil act? Kai knew many Americans had died for the freedom of his people. He was touched by that. His parents had taught him that Americans were unique; they fought to liberate people, not enslave them, so they could fulfill the destiny God had created them for. As appreciative as he was of the American effort to liberate China, Kai had a strong desire to free his own people. He felt a strong desire to directly participate and to share the risks of liberation. He knew for China to be free, the Chinese must be willing and capable of fighting for that freedom. He wanted more than a supporting role.

His platoon was ready. All he needed was his orders. He was willing, at the risk of his own life, to build a free China, where his people could choose to accept the destiny their Creator intended for them, or not.

Liu woke up with a start. He hadn't thought he'd actually fall asleep with a battle going on. After three days, however, he was overcome by his exhaustion. Private Sun was keeping watch in their foxhole. He was not firing, but artillery was exploding everywhere. Small-arms fire was nonstop. Yet in all the noise, fear, and death, Liu had been able to sleep. But why not? He was the master of death. It would not touch him, but he'd seen it touch his comrades. Many had died over the last three days. Many had talked of surrender or running away. Many had disappeared. Liu was confused as to why he could control life and death, but his army could not. Perhaps the People's Republic was not as powerful as he. Perhaps he was just superior? Would he be better on his own?

However, it was the People's Republic that had made him strong. It had trained him, fed him, given him medicine when he needed it. All it demanded was all he could give. From each according to his own ability, to each according to his own need. He had needed, the People had given. No, he owed a debt, and he would pay it. Besides, it was not as if he did not enjoy the work. However, this battle was different. He did not have the same sense of control and the same sense of satisfaction he had had behind the lines. He preferred the special missions, not this direct style of combat. Things didn't go according to plans. There were too many individuals that knew what was going on. How could he advance the cause?

On top of the frustration of being less efficient in this environment, Liu had to put up with the fears and concerns of common PLA soldiers who were afraid to die. They feared the

Americans at this point; many talked about it being a lost cause. Liu didn't understand how. It was easy behind the lines. Liu was coming to the conclusion that most of his comrades were inferior, and if so, why should he be subject to them? Watching Sun chew his lip and tentatively point his gun to no effect infuriated Liu. He quietly pulled out his knife, slipped up behind Sun, and slit his throat from ear to ear. If nothing else, he would at least be done with this inferior. His next task was to come up with a way to advance his status. A man of his power deserved more than being a private. How could one who controlled life and death rise up through the ranks? Liu decided to attack, but not in the silly-ass way the officers had told them to. Jumping up and running into the American bullets was stupid. No, Liu would use his intuition and skills that served him so well to kill the enemy. Through killing he had found power. Why let that end because of the incompetence of others?

President Harmon was on pins and needles. She had just started her presidency and a major battle had broken out. She had not started the war; she had not controlled America's participation in the war. Yet now she might very well be held accountable for the outcome of this battle.

"This is so unfair," she kept saying out loud to herself and her staff.

It was something way beyond her control, at the moment anyway, and she did not like it. These military officers had just acted on their own, with no consideration for her agenda. Perhaps not even for the lives of their soldiers, for that matter. Now the first part of her presidency would be something that she had no control over. She had less than one year to make her mark as president of the United States before she would have to focus on her election campaign. It wasn't that much time. This was not how she had wanted to start her presidency, and it infuriated her to no end. The way she saw it, she had no choice but to wait and see how it would play out. She had to think of every possibility, every contingency, in order to plan out the proper response to this engagement. Her career depended on it.

One thing was sure in her mind, if the early days of her presidency were turned into a failure because of some glory-hungry general, there would be hell to pay. She would make certain that that man's career, his reputation, and his life would be ruined.

Liu was able to understand the panic to a certain extent. After all, he had turned and run with everyone else. They would fall back and live to fight another day. The political officer told them to stay brave and continue the fight like President Zhang, who would never surrender. They would retreat west to the mountains and valleys. From there the fight for their liberation, for their revolution would continue. He said that the Americans might have more tanks and jets, but China had more people. China had five thousand years of civilization and a tradition of sacrifice and revolution. The setbacks of the last two years were small in the big picture. As the strong survived, the People's Republic would only become more difficult to defeat.

The desertions were beyond Liu's comprehension. How could they not believe in the People's Republic of China? Had they no faith in the Communist Party that had given them everything? The party had given him a place. The party had trained him to do what he loved, and in return he would do what he loved for the party.

So many others were weak; it wasn't just the Westernized cities of South China. When the Marines arrived from the east, orders were given to retreat before they were surrounded. Many soldiers, even some officers, were saying the war was lost. It was time to surrender or take off the uniform and act like a civilian. Rumors were that the Americans were good to those who stopped fighting. But if one quit fighting, how could one keep killing?

After seven bloody days, the PLA line had broken. It pained him that the American force had not been able to encircle the PLA and destroy it. The silver lining, in his opinion, was that the PLA troops had broken. It was now a disorganized rout. Certainly, their officers had tried to make it an orderly retreat, but McCullough had intel that it was chaos. The roads to Beijing were quickly becoming jammed with ChiCom soldiers. He saw such a golden opportunity here. Just a few well-placed nukes could end this war within the week. Short of that, saturation bombing could potentially end it in several weeks.

McCullough figured, short of nukes, Zhang would be protected in this Dragon's Lair he was held up in. But could he maintain control of the government? Would he be assassinated? Could the PLA, at least, be relegated as an outlaw force in China's western frontier?

McCullough put in a call to Joint Chief of Staff Mythers and President Harmon, and prayed they would see things the way Clark did.

CHAPTER TWENTY-ONE

"Madame President," McCullough strained every ounce of personal discipline not to lose his cool at this moment, "with all due respect, I don't see this as a priority at the moment."

"Well, I do, General, and I am the Commander-in-Chief." Harmon found herself enjoying the moment a little more than she actually thought she would. She had even dreaded this conversation earlier in the day, but now she felt like she was emerging as a leader. "We need to show the international community, as well as the PRC, that we are willing to hold ourselves to the same standard of civility and due process that we demand from others."

"Madame President, please let me state again that I believe we have an opportunity to win this war with a strategic nuclear strike. The war could be over within a month. Hell, maybe within a week!"

"No, General, we will not violate international law. How would the United States look as an international leader of the Free World if I order a violation of international laws agreed to in the United Nations, on top of ignoring charges of war crimes among our own military personnel? The media would have a field day with that! And while you're off playing 'army,' General Mythers, as acting Secretary of State, will be dealing with a diplomatic nightmare."

"Madame President"—McCullough attempted another pitch—"the Russians have already set a precedence here. There has been no international backlash of any consequence. Who is it going to come from at this point? Even the whining leftist media has reported that Russia has effectively pushed the jihadist caliphate out of western Asia. No one has the moral authority to stop us. There is no political downside right now. More importantly, it will save American lives; that alone will be a political win for your administration."

"General Mythers." Harmon cued her general and acting Secretary of State.

"Listen, Jack"—Mythers wanted to tweak McCullough a bit by using his first name—"the president and I are ready to implement a diplomatic strategy that will effectively end this war. We can use your recent victory as well as pressure from the international community to contain the PRC to their western provinces, which you yourself agreed could be an acceptable definition of victory when we started this invasion. In addition, we can isolate them economically with UN sanctions. We'll have them on a tight leash. They'll have to do anything we want, and no more American troops have to get killed."

General McCullough felt sick to his stomach. He could envision six years of war that had cost the lives of nearly six hundred thousand dead Americans now being lost when it was on the verge of being won.

"General McCullough, John...Jack, if I may." Harmon was now trying to soften him up a bit. She believed it was one of her tactics that made her so successful in consensus building. When McCullough had failed to verbally concede to being called Jack by the president, she continued. "We're not asking you to give anything up, just don't advance. Let's let everyone catch their breath for a moment. In the meantime, I want your people looking into this matter of the Marine that allegedly killed this girl, and any other allegations of Allied war crimes."

"Madame President, it has already been made public that the Marine in question was killed in action months before the allegation was ever made by the press. I really believe the war effort would be better served by defeating the enemy."

"Jack, I get it, but you need to understand the enemy is virtually defeated. There's not much else they can do to hurt us. It's in the PRC's best interest to now do what we want; it's in our best interest to show the Chinese people they have a better advocate for their needs than the PRC." Mythers asserted himself on this point.

"So that's it, huh? We're back to winning hearts and minds again." McCullough had more he would like to say about all the times that strategy had failed throughout American history, but he'd made it a habit throughout his career not to let politicians know everything he was thinking. Besides, he'd been around long enough to know at this point that people like Harmon and Mythers were too arrogant to learn from history.

"Jack, you've been a vital part of our nation's war effort." President Harmon now felt it was her turn to step up and say something that sounded conciliatory. "History will show that. Our nation is eternally grateful for what you have done."

At that point in the conversation, McCullough knew his military career was coming to an end, although he didn't think either one of them would have the integrity to tell him to his face.

After the conference call had come to an end and the satellite link was broken, Mythers began to nervously shuffle papers and shake his head in disappointment. It was all theater on his part; the call, the recent chain of events were all going exactly as he would like them to.

"By the end of the week, General, I want McCullough's resignation one way or another. Sophia"—Harmon turned to her Chief-of-Staff—"before then I want him thoroughly, and I do mean thoroughly, discredited. If I'm going to accept the resignation of the Allied commander, I want the American people to think that it's a good thing. If McCullough decides to voice his professional disagreements with us, I don't want anyone to pay attention."

"Yes, Madame President," Sophia Porter said, knowing how much Harmon liked to hear it. "I think the media obsession over the war-crimes angle gives us a perfect opportunity for this."

"Yes!" Harmon liked her thinking. "What was that Marine's name? The one the PRC blamed for that girl's death."

"Schmitt, Madame President." Mythers almost reminded her that the Marine's death had been confirmed long before the PRC had made the allegation to the press, but decided it was trivial at this point.

"Mythers, you work with Sophia to leak more stories to the press. Leak stories of possible lack of discipline, lack of control from the 'General-in-Chief' or whatever the hell Clark called him. I want the people to know things have gotten out of hand, but now I'm reining it all in."

"Yes, Madame President." Porter and Mythers looked at each other and smiled about the fact they had responded in unison. Harmon was loving it. She felt like things were coming together and a sense of cohesion was setting in with her team.

"General Mythers, who do you have in mind to replace McCullough?"

"I have a few options for you, Madame President." Mythers pulled out a new folder. At this point, he and the president were doing everything on paper to avoid creating an electronic trail of their agenda. "And, by the way, I've got a couple of other ideas that I think you will be interested in."

CHAPTER TWENTY-TWO

"This is it? Looks pretty fucking lame if you ask me," Hastings complained.

"This is it." Harris confirmed the address on the business card.

"No one's asking you anyhow, Husker boy." Reese's jest was good-natured.

"Blow it out your mouth there whatever the fuck you all call yourselves in Montana," was the best Hastings could come up with.

The three of them, along with Sheridan, headed toward the front door of the Sea Dragon Hotel. The door was opened for them by a smiling Chinese man, and no sooner were they in the lobby than two boys ran up to take their bags up to the front desk.

"Hold on there, Rocky," Harris ordered the boys. They seemed confused. Harris didn't know if it was from their lack of English or if they weren't familiar with the Marines' term for anyone from the ROC. The older door man walked over, smiling, to see what the hesitation was about.

"We need to confirm we're in the right place. We're meeting other Marines here." Hastings's speech was slow. He hoped it would make it easier for the doorman to understand him.

"Yes, yes, Marines." The doorman politely and graciously led them over to the hotel bar with a big smile on his face. Harris wondered how much the doorman had actually understood, or if the old man just thought Marines would want to go to the bar. Either way it was the right call. Edwards and Cortes were there and already having a drink.

"There they are! Get over here, Harris, all of you. I'm buying you a round!" Edwards bellowed across the bar. Harris had never seen Edwards act so jovial and carefree.

"I bet they're drunk already," Harris mumbled to Hastings.

"Well, let's join them, buddy! What are we waiting for?" Hastings answered, louder than Harris would have liked, but nobody cared.

This was new for Harris. He'd known Edwards for over two years, but had never seen him drunk. Nor had he ever seen Edwards wear anything that wasn't camouflaged. They were all wearing "Charlies," Marine Corps-issued short-sleeve khaki shirts and green trousers.

"*Garçon!*" Edwards snapped his fingers as he commanded the boys to take the bags of the new arrivals. "What are you Devil Dogs drinking?"

"Whiskey. Bourbon." Hastings was quick to speak for all of them.

"I like your style, Hastings." The slightly intoxicated Edwards slapped Hastings on the back a little too hard, but with no malice. "Bartender! Four bourbons for these men!" Edwards was still snapping his fingers.

Harris figured either the employees really liked Edwards or were intimidated by him. From what he'd seen so far, Edwards was easily the largest man in the bar, or the hotel for that matter.

The smiling bartender set up four glasses and poured an ounce and a half in each.

"Cheers, Devil Dogs!" Cortes, who'd been quiet up to that point, loudly toasted.

The sweet, burning whiskey hit Harris's throat and he felt it go all the way down to his stomach. The booze hadn't had time to take effect, but it felt good. For the first time in over two years Second Section, TOW Platoon, Heavy Weapons Company, First Battalion, First Marines had seven days of liberty in Shanghai.

It had been ten weeks since they had defeated the Pricks at the Yellow River. The relief that was so desperately needed after such an intense battle had been slow to arrive. At first they were baffled by the lack of pursuit when they had the PLA on the run. It was so unlike what they had come to expect in the aggressive strategy of the war.

Despite the Allies' overwhelming victory at the Yellow River, morale had become precariously low. Word came that General John McCullough had died of a heart attack. Though a soldier, not a Marine, he was highly respected by Marine Corps infantrymen for his leadership during the Sino-American War. Most of the Marine Corps grunts were leery of General Jordan Hinneman and his strategy of negotiation.

Scuttlebutt on Hinneman was that he was just a mouthpiece for General Mythers, and that he and President Harmon were more interested in peace talks than battlefield victories. Not that their victories were noticed anymore. The American media had become obsessed with possible Allied war crimes and lamenting the death of the last great communist empire. Finally, when the news came that their brother-in-arms Schmitt had become some kind of media poster boy for American war crimes, it had been particularly devastating to their morale. Edwards had been especially outraged.

"Next reporter I see, I'll kill the motherfucker," Edwards had privately confided to Harris. But there had been no opportunity. 1/1 had been moved to the rear. They spent two weeks positioned just south of the Yellow River. Then sent farther south to Camp Puller, where they were reinforced, then assigned to working parties and fire watch. When not folding general-purpose tents, burning human waste from the latrine, or doing some other task too menial for anyone not in the infantry, Harris spent his days cleaning weapons, exercising, or reading any book he could find.

One highlight to Camp Puller was access to the Internet, and this allowed him to talk with and see his family through video chat. Another plus was the opportunity to get some new cammies and boots. His, like many in his platoon, were falling apart. Torn cammies and boots with holes were not a problem for those in the rear. Everybody had new and pristine gear.

For two months they had languished in boredom and poor morale. Then Sergeant Bohanan had brought word that they were being given seven days' liberty in Shanghai. They were taken to Camp Wronski just outside of Shanghai. It was the first time Harris had been quartered inside a building since he had arrived in China. It was also his first hot shower in two years. Before they were allowed to go into town, they had two days' worth of classes on Chinese culture and how they should conduct themselves now that they were no longer in a combat zone. The classes had given them useful information about not urinating in public and that not all Chinese were members of the PLA and thus should not be killed on sight. As well, they were versed on appropriate behavior around women and given reminders not to fart out loud, or to force their sexual desires upon those of the opposite sex, and definitely not to masturbate in front of Chinese civilians. Most had had a good laugh about the classes. Edwards observed that whoever had created this curriculum must have had a lot of contempt for Marines. Harris had not found the classes quite as funny after that. But still he found it a small price to pay for a week in a city, and a week around women.

The officers had made certain that all enlisted personnel were showered, shaved, and dressed in a newly issued Class C uniform. After inspection, they were formed up, given a half dozen condoms each, and marched onto buses. As they were on separate buses, Edwards had given Harris a business card of a hotel he had been informed of by a naval recreation officer, with plans to meet up.

After two rounds of bourbon, Edwards insisted they slow down with a beer.

"Harris, I ain't gonna carry your baby-faced ass over half of Shanghai, so you better keep yourself halfway sober."

Harris thought he might be feeling some effect of the booze, so he decided to follow Edwards's lead. At the age of nineteen, Harris had never been out for a full night of drinking with a group of men. He did not want to be too drunk to enjoy it. Besides, he'd heard stories of what Marines did to other Marines that ended up too drunk.

"So now what?" Hastings blurted out as the Marines sipped on their first beer and stared at a muted TV that was showing President Harmon talking before members of her press corps.

"The doorman says the Greased Monkey is a happening spot. We'll check that out next," Cortes answered.

"I want to get a tattoo." Sheridan finally spoke up.

"What, only one?" Edwards laughed.

"Ethan, if the man wants a tattoo"—Cortes spoke directly to Edwards—"let's get him tattooed." Both NCOs laughed at their inside joke.

"What's so funny?" Reese asked what the rest were wondering.

"Back at Luzon," Edwards, enjoying the moment, began to explain, "we knew this boot Boddington; he wanted a tattoo. Well, we got three days libo in Olongapo City, and Boddington wanted a tattoo really bad. So anyhow, we all went out, and he just got completely shit-faced."

"Fuck yeah, drinking that Mojo shit they got over there," Cortes threw in.

"What is it?" Hastings's interest was piqued by the exotic drink.

"Ah fuck." Cortes sighed. "Who knows. It's always different. Dr. Pepper is the only ingredient I can remember."

"Yeah, so Boddington," Edwards continued, "and us, we go to—"

"Rock'n'Roll Tattoo," Cortes finished.

"Oh fuck, Rock'n'Roll Tattoo." Edwards smiled, enjoying the nostalgia. "Anyway, man, Boddington gets fucked three sheets to the fuckin' wind and we all go out to get a tattoo. Now being the hard-chargin' Devil Dog that he was, Boddington wanted an Eagle, Globe, and Anchor tat on the left side of his chest, and he gets it. But while in the chair, the drunk bastard passes out." Edwards and Cortes both began to laugh uncontrollably for several seconds.

"So we pay the tattoo guy extra to tattoo a fucking unicorn flying over a rainbow on Boddington's stomach," Cortes continued.

"I thought for sure the fucker would wake up before that little tattoo guy finished. But he had no fucking clue. When it was done, we hauled his ass up and dragged him back to base." Edwards could barely speak from his laughing.

"The next morning when he saw it, he was so pissed off." Cortes picked up the story again. "The real fucking kicker is he blamed me, when it was Edwards's idea. The bastard clocked me right in the mouth." Cortes rubbed his jaw like it still hurt.

"Hey, let's not play it like you're innocent here." Edwards could hardly defend himself for his laughing so hard.

"Fuck you, hillbilly," Cortes attacked good-naturedly, and Edwards took it as such. Shortly thereafter the laughter stopped.

They were all combat veterans. Nobody asked "whatever happened to Boddington?"

"Well, any of you bastards tattoo a unicorn on my ass, I'll kill ya." Sheridan broke the melancholic moment.

"Hey, fuck that unicorn bullshit, check this out." Hastings reached into his pocket and pulled out a folded piece of paper. "This is what me and Harris are getting tattooed."

"Yeah, check this out. It's pretty badass," Harris added while Hastings was getting his drawing unfolded.

"That is pretty fucking badass." Edwards was back to serious.

"You bet, I told you Hastings is a good fucking artist," Cortes added. "He did the whole skull and crossbones thing in the first place."

Hastings had drawn the Eagle, Globe, and Anchor insignia of the United States Marine Corps; however, in the globe he'd replaced North and South America with a skull and crossed bones like the ones he'd designed for their LSVs. Underneath the design read "Semper Fi," from the Marine Corps motto Semper Fidelis: Always Faithful.

"Fuck yeah, man! That's like our emblem." Reese approved.

"Dude, you mind if I get that tattooed also?" Sheridan asked.

"Fuck no, man! Fucking go for it! You all can feel free to use it." Hastings loved the praise and it made him generous. "Bartender! More whiskey for my buddies!"

The pain began to wake Harris up as his consciousness emerged from the fog in his head. His brain immediately began trying to process what had really happened and what had not. This was not easy. The thumping in his head made thinking hurt. He looked down at his left forearm. Tattoo was there, so that had happened. He didn't remember going to sleep on the floor, but apparently he had. Reese was also on the floor, with a pillow thrown over his face to shield it from the sunlight coming in through the opened balcony door. A fresh tattoo was on his forearm as well. Sheridan was facedown on one of the beds. He too had the Eagle, Anchor, Skull and Crossbones on his forearm. In addition, he had an elaborate unicorn leaping over a rainbow tattooed on his back that had left some ink stains on the sheets. Hastings was in the other bed, with his newly tattooed forearm draped over his eyes. Harris walked out to the balcony to take in the sun and the smell of car exhaust from the street. Cortes was already out there smoking a cigarette. He sported the Eagle, Anchor, Skull and Crossbones tattoo as well. It was only then that Harris clearly remembered that they had all gotten one.

"Morning," Harris grumbled and lit himself a smoke. Cortes reached down into a bucket of ice, pulled out a bottle of beer, and handed it to Harris.

"Morning."

"Edwards still asleep?"

"No. Went down to the lobby to get some smokes and some orange juice."

"Why didn't he just call room service?"

"I think it was an excuse to get out of the room." Cortes spit some tobacco from his tongue.

"Man, I'm going to hate giving up this hotel suite and going back to living out of an LSV." Harris was already contemplating the end of their liberty.

"Don't complain too much. Hell, in a few weeks living in an LSV may seem like a goddamn luxury."

"Hey." Edwards walked into the room, carrying two buckets of beer and a bottle of orange juice under his arm. "Told the front desk to send up some chicken fried rice."

"Good man!" Cortes got up. "I got to go take a shit."

"Thanks for sharing, Hank." Edwards was back to his usual sarcastic self. Cortes only grumbled in reply.

"Fuck! I need the hair of the dog." Reese shuffled out onto the balcony, and Edwards handed him a beer. "Thanks. Man, I don't remember Sheridan's unicorn tattoo looking that big last night."

"That's 'cause you were passed out, getting one tattooed on your ass," Edwards said with a smile, but Harris noticed Reese checking his backside to his relief. "He'll have something to remember Shanghai by."

"We all will." Harris held up his arm.

"Were you serious last night when you said you're gonna get a new tat every night we're here?" Reese asked.

"Might as well," Edwards responded. "What the hell else we got to spend our money on? Besides, we should be lucky enough to live to regret our tattoos." It was the usual Edwards.

A feminine voice emanated from the bedroom. It was only then that Harris remembered that Hastings had brought an Asian girl back to the room the previous night. Shortly after that Hastings joined them on the balcony.

"Morning, Devil Dogs!"

"Well, ain't you chipper," Harris chided.

"I got every reason to be." Hastings smiled as he lit his first cigarette of the day. "Goddamn, look at that beauty. Money well spent." Hastings was proud of his new tattoo of his design, with the words *Semper Fi* tattooed on his forearm. "I can't decide what I like better. This or my bulldog tat?"

"What about your Lil' Red tattoo?" Edwards threw in and handed Hastings a beer.

"Thanks. What Lil'…oh, fuck you!" Hastings picked up on the joke. "I ask you, how can one man have so many good tattoos and on such a good-looking body!" Hastings bragged.

Edwards and Harris looked at each other and shook their heads. Reese managed to fart really loud.

"Damn, Reese, you better go check yourself," Hastings fired back.

"Let's figure out what we're going to do today." Harris felt the sudden urge to be productive.

"I want to see some of the city. Believe me, there ain't a city like this in Montana," Reese put in.

"No more fucking Grease Monkey for me. I just want to get some good street food and find a cool place to drink beer. None of that disco bullshit," Edwards said as he stared down at the street, more as if he were talking to himself. "We only got six more days. I don't want to waste them."

The last three months had been very good for Liu Zhiqiang. His motivation was the highest it had ever been. Despite the American victories, the PLA had stopped them just as his commanders had said they would. The media had blamed the Americans for the civilian deaths, just as his commanders had said they would. Now, the American command was caught up in investigating themselves instead of fighting. They had a new general that wanted to talk instead of fight. President Zhang of the People's Republic of China was more adamant than ever that the People would be victorious. On top of all that, Liu had been promoted to sergeant when his regimental commander became aware of his actions.

The promotion was quite a turn of events. He had followed the mass of troops during the retreat from the Yellow River. For a reason that he was never made aware of, a colonel had ordered the group of soldiers arrested for treason. Initially, an officer had taken Liu's name and seemed unfamiliar with Zhang's Gansidui (Death Squad) Units that he was assigned to. Liu had spent three days in a PLA prison camp. Finally, he was

240

released to a Captain Chang, a political officer, and taken to another camp. While it was not called a prison, and he was not called a prisoner, the conditions were the same as in the previous camp. He was interrogated for another three days by Captain Chang before he was promoted to sergeant and released.

Liu was promoted to a squad leader in a Gansiduì platoon that was to go behind enemy lines, south of the Yellow River. Their mission was to kill American soldiers and Chinese traitors in such a way that Western media would blame Allied forces. The "war crime" propaganda was working, and President Zhang didn't want to back away from it now. Not only was Liu still doing what he loved, but he had more authority and he had more confidence in his cause. President Zhang and the PLA appeared to have regained the same control over death, real and political, in this war that Liu had over in his life. He admired President Zhang; he loved the PLA; he believed victory would be theirs.

Liu had inspected his troops before they had deployed, but he looked over them again for anything he might have missed. They looked like perfect soldiers of the Republic of China. They had set up a roadblock on a semi-busy road. They didn't want to deal with too much traffic, just enough, ideally, to find a very likable Chinese family driving home to Zhengzhou after a weekend outing.

Tan Li was tired, but not asleep like his wife, son, and daughter. They had had a great day. Tan already thought that this would be a day he'd remember for the rest of his life. When his wife and he were old and their children grown, he'd be able to remember this day and see his wife young and beautiful, his children small and innocent. After more than two years of war in their homeland, the fighting had stopped. Peace

241

talks were under way. The ROC and the United States were promising greater freedom and opportunity. Tan thought his future, his family's future, looked promising. With the security of the peace talks, it seemed like a good time to take his family out to celebrate their survival, their fortune, and their family.

They had gone on a day trip to Mount Song, just east of Zhengzhou. The spring weather had been perfect. They had toured the Shaolin Temple, the Pogada Forest, and found a shaded spot to picnic. Later the Tans played in a field with their six-year-old son and four-year-old daughter. It had felt good to be in the sun, to run, to be in a wide-open space with no borders, no confinement. His wife had enjoyed the day as well, and it gave him pleasure to see her happy.

His brother-in-law had been killed fighting for the PLA a year and a half earlier, and they had not been able to communicate with her parents, members in good standing with the Chinese Communist Party, for the last six months. New ROC officials had tried to be helpful, but to no avail. Tan understood; their world had changed so much, it was hard for anyone to keep up. But today his wife had been happy. She'd even mentioned the ROC was encouraging larger families, and perhaps they should have another child. Tan loved his family, and the idea of making it bigger only gave him joy.

"Tan Li," the man said to himself, "this will be a day to remember." He thought the day might very well have been the best of his life.

The sun had just set, it was dusk, so it was hard for him to see the soldiers in the road. Tan braked just inches short of the sergeant. Tan was relieved, hitting a ROC soldier no doubt would have ruined what had been a perfect day. Tan could see that the sergeant was irritated by his late stop, but then Tan thought one shouldn't stand in the road at dusk if you didn't want to get hit by a car.

"Identification," the sergeant ordered. Tan complied. The sergeant's demeanor reminded him more of the PRC than the ROC. Still, he obeyed. Tan had been raised to comply with authority and did as he was told, no matter the manner in which it was done.

"What is it?" Tan's wife was waking up. The children were still asleep.

"Nothing, dear, go back to sleep," Tan tried to reassure her, but failed. He saw the look of fear on her face.

"Out of the car," the sergeant ordered. Armed soldiers had surrounded the car. Only when Tan had stepped out did he notice the ugly, V-shaped scar on the sergeant's face. Tan felt embarrassed when the sergeant caught him staring at it.

Tan Li had always been compliant, as he was raised to be by his parents, to the Communist Party. Secretly, he had never liked communism. It delivered nothing of what they promised. Prosperity and justice in the PRC depended on who you knew, what family you were in, and/or your political authority. Throughout his life he'd seen the People's Republic of China take from the Chinese people and take from neighboring nations. Yet still, the communist government always wanted more. The PRC always justified this in the name of past injustices done to them. Tan had always wondered how people who had done nothing but take from others could be a victim. However, in the People's government it was illegal to express that thought. Doing so could get him arrested, perhaps killed, and what good would that have done? Instead he had kept his eyes down, his mouth shut, and complied with the People's government. He didn't know if the Republic of China would prove to be any better or not, but the promise of a free democracy had appealed to Tan; so he worked to become a citizen in good standing with the Republic of China.

When Tan stepped out of the car, another soldier nudged him over to the side of the road. Another soldier got behind the wheel and drove the car over behind a large military truck.

"Sir, where are they going?" Tan spoke up out of concern.

The man with the V-shaped scar responded by striking Tan across the face with a metal baton and knocking him to the ground. Before he could even fully comprehend the pain and what was happening to him, Tan was kicked repeatedly in the ribs. His instinct was to curl up into a fetal position. The blows kept coming. Tan's mind raced to think of what he could have done to warrant this, until the screams of his wife reached his ears. He realized too late that he'd done nothing to warrant this, other than encounter evil. Tan rolled onto his knees and tried to brace himself up with his arms. A boot came down on Tan's left elbow, snapping the joint. Tan cried out with pain, but still tried to raise himself. Then a boot connected with his chin, shattering several teeth and jamming his lower jaw back towards his ears. Completely unconscious, Tan fell forward and landed on his nose and right cheekbone. Both broke from the impact.

"He's done." Liu stopped Private Chen from kicking the unconscious man. They could now hear the children scream, along with the mother, and the laughter of their comrades. They left the traitor of the People on the side of the road to see what their colleagues had accomplished.

The woman was pleading for mercy as the soldiers ravaged her body. The children cried and screamed as they watched from the car. The woman's pleas infuriated Liu. Who was she to plead for mercy? Here she was with her nice clothes, her car, her family, all acquired while others suffered. Here they were out as a family, enjoying time together during a time of war. North of the Yellow River, people sacrificed and suffered. Not only had this couple done nothing for the People, they had betrayed the People by living for themselves.

"Enough!" Liu shouted. His size and his presence made him seem much older than his seventeen years. The soldiers of his squad froze, waiting for his next command.

Liu walked over and grabbed the woman by the hair. She still attempted to maintain what was left of her modesty in the presence of her children. The feeble attempt only angered Liu all the more. In front of the children he slit the woman's throat. He let her body fall to the ground as it went through its final death convulsions. He ordered the children to be put in the front cab of the truck with him and the other soldiers in the back. They had done what they needed to do; now it was time to leave before the situation got more complicated.

"Children"—Liu attempted to soothe the crying children—"this is your lucky day. For today you have been rescued by the People's Liberation Army. We will take you away from this place and these people who would corrupt you, and take you back to your people where you belong. Don't cry for those villains back there. The People are your parents now. They will tell you what you need to know. They will give you what you need. They will train you how to serve. Don't cry, good fortune has found you at last."

CHAPTER TWENTY-THREE

Harris was in direct sunlight. He was uncomfortably hot. The new body armor was supposed to be more effective and more breathable. Harris thought the breathability was doubtful; he'd have to get shot before he'd know how effective it was.

"Only if you're lucky," he mumbled.

"What's that?" Edwards barked. He was on edge, and for good reason. Lately, they had come to expect the occasional sniper or improvised explosive device on what had become known as "meals on wheels" missions.

"Just mumbling to myself."

"Stay sharp, Harris."

"Roger that." Harris said it, he knew it, but he didn't feel it. Harris was suffering from low morale. It had been just over a year since First Marines had pushed across the Yellow River. The battle front had not moved an inch north since then. For the last several weeks Harris had woken up wishing he was out of the Marine Corps and could go home to his family. He hated the thoughts. He knew he'd done the right thing. He knew the fight he'd joined, the fight his father and friends had died in, was righteous. He'd signed on to fight for the duration, because he wanted to see this fight through to the end. In boot camp, General Ragnarsson had stated the objective of defeating the People's Republic of China. Now the president was trying to negotiate with them. Harris could grasp the destruction of a tyrannical government, but he could not grasp the objective now. Nor could anyone else. Even the officers had to give long, obtuse answers when asked what the purpose of a mission was. Everyone caught certain buzzwords or phrases, like: "building cultural bridges," "create foundations of understanding," or "benevolence tactics." Harris had yet to hear anyone of a higher rank be able to specify exactly what those were, or how they would win the war. If the president did not want to win the war, why was it being fought?

General Hinneman was more interested in talking than fighting. President Harmon seemed more interested in investigating potential war crimes than defeating the PRC. Over the course of the last year, Harris had come to the conclusion that this war would not be won. He didn't like it. He didn't want it, but there was no indication from the current leadership that there was a strategy for victory. Harris struggled to push these thoughts from his mind. They could come to no good. He could not afford to have low morale; his life, his buddies' lives, depended on it.

A year ago the PLA had been on the run north of the Yellow River. Now, patrolling north of the Yellow River was something to be dreaded. The Allied forces, as per the agreement in the peace talks, were not camped north of the Yellow River. However, Allied forces were allowed to deliver food and medical supplies to towns and villages south of Beijing. For the last six months these missions had become increasingly dangerous. His TOW platoon had lost five Marines in the last six months to snipers. Two of them, Gordon and Wilson, were from Second Section. TOW platoon had lost three gun teams due to IEDs, two from First Section and one from Third. Harris didn't see the point of driving in to deliver food or medicine to some village every so often, and lose Marines in the process. Why not destroy the enemy and let the killing come to an end? After that they could give away food and medicine to the people that needed it. At least until a new group of bad guys brought it to an end.

On these missions he felt like they were sent out as target practice for the PLA, not that the PRC ever took responsibility. The ChiComs claimed it was local militias just trying to defend their homeland. This line had played well with the American media and was now the daily mantra on TV news and the Internet.

A year earlier Harris would have thought the American people would reject that sort of thinking, for they had up to that point. Now, even his own mother had asked him what exactly was going on over there when they last talked. She seemed very concerned that he would get caught up in some sort of violence against noncombatants and perhaps get into some kind of trouble. Indeed, she had updated him on the very public court-martial going on stateside of a Marine infantryman who had shot and killed a Prick, witnessed by an American reporter, who had claimed it was unnecessary. All Harris could do was tell her not to worry and not to believe anything she heard on the news.

There had been a lot of scuttlebutt that those that had signed up for the duration would be allowed to terminate their enlistments, but as of yet it had just been rumors. Edwards said it wouldn't happen.

"If the president won't kill the enemy, then she's got to scare them into quitting. How's she going to do that if she lets damn near the whole Marine Corps go home?" Edwards had argued. Harris thought he had a point. President Harmon seemed to be trying to win a war by showing their enemy how likable Americans were, while threatening to attack them if they didn't comply with her. Harris didn't like it. Marines were still dying, but instead of moving north towards Beijing, they moved east and west along the Yellow River.

Lieutenant Kai was glad to be out in the field again, although he wondered how effective distributing food and medicine to villages was to the war effort. His view, and that of several of his fellow officers, was that this was something to do after they had defeated the PRC, not something to do in order to defeat the PRC. However, his duty was to implement orders given, not create strategy, so he strived to keep a positive attitude. So far American leadership had been brilliant, why would the new American president turn away from that?

Kai had recently returned from one week of leave visiting his family in Taiwan. The attitude there was not as positive. Many, including Kai's father, now saw the United States as hampering the war effort. Others were afraid that if the PRC were not destroyed, it would come back to destroy the ROC.

Kai understood those fears, but could not actually envision that happening. The PLA could not compete with the Allied forces. He, personally, had seen many Chinese happy to be liberated from the control of communism and excited to participate in democracy. How could this lead to a defeat? Even now as he oversaw his men distributing food to these villagers who had been ravaged by war, he could see their smiles. He had experienced their appreciation; why would they reject democracy now?

Even if the Allies were not advancing north, Kai thought some of the work they were doing was good. The people in this village were in need of food. He saw their smiles and he heard their appreciation. The old and the young would find it difficult enough to survive in the summer. Winter could be impossible.

Kai heard an ear-piercing scream. He spun around, his hand reaching for his pistol, but saw it was just several small children kicking a soccer ball around, playing. Kai smiled; the scene of carefree joy did his heart good. Turning back to the line for food, a young man caught Kai's attention. He appeared to be in his early twenties, a rarity in this region where young men were either fighting for the PLA or the ROC. There was

249

little room for neutrality along the Yellow River. Kai noticed the young man had a severe limp and a nasty V-shaped scar on his cheek. Kai thought perhaps the man might be a wounded veteran, but for what side?

"Hello. Good morning." Kai walked by to engage the young man. He thought he could perhaps judge the man's standing by his reaction. Instead, the young man blankly stared at him with his mouth open. Kai thought the young man must be severely retarded, and his mental slowness had gotten him injured in the course of his agricultural labor. Kai thought the man too stupid to survive combat.

Harris used his TOW sight to look for potential threats to Charlie Company's heavy machine gunners surrounding the small village below. In turn, the machine gunners were covering ROC troops that were distributing food to the villagers. Even in the heat of the direct sun, Harris found himself craving a cigarette. He sat back from the TOW gun and efficiently dug out a cigarette and matches. Within seconds he had it lit and was enjoying the first inhale with the taste of sulfur from the match. He was about to put his eye back to the day sight when he noticed the black spot in the sky.

"Shotgun!" Harris demanded.

"Where?"

"Two o'clock. Scott, drive slow, drive casual. I want to get in range." If Pricks were watching, Harris didn't want to tip them off that he'd seen their "eye in the sky." He slipped on amber-colored glasses to cut down on the sun's glare.

"Blue Leader, Blue Leader," Edwards called on the radio, but before there could be any reply, they all jumped from an unexpected explosion. Harris aggressively searched for the site of the explosion, but could see nothing. He heard nothing other than the chatter on the radio, but he let Edwards worry about that.

"What do you see?" Edwards demanded.

"Nothing," Harris replied. Scott kept driving in the same direction. Another explosion. This time Harris instantly picked up that it came from the village. They all heard machine-gun fire and soon saw smoke, but still no visual on an enemy. A bit prematurely, Harris fired the twelve gauge at the PLA drone. It flew away, but began to sink. Harris hoped he had damaged it. He fired again and nailed it. As if the shot was a cue, there was another explosion. It came from the hills to his right. Jefferson's and Cortes's squads were in that area. Harris saw smoke, but that was it. While looking around, he saw a flash, heard a bang, and another explosion in the village. An antitank rocket was fired into the village. He heard the explosion, but did not know if it hit its target.

"Stop!" Harris ordered and kicked the back of Scott's seat in case he hadn't heard him. Harris scanned the area where he'd seen the flash. He spotted Pricks reloading an HJ-12 antitank missile. Without word, without warning, Harris fired his TOW and took them out before they could get another shot off.

Machine-gun fire erupted from the village, but Edwards ordered Scott to cut a hard right and gun it. Harris had missed what was said on the radio. He ditched the empty tube and slid down from the gun to get another missile. It was a difficult process in a fast-moving LSV crossing rough terrain.

"Fuck that, use the SAW," Edwards ordered. "Cortes's LSV is hit."

Harris spotted the dead vehicle. It was getting blasted. He spotted tracers coming out of the foliage. He began laying down fire in that direction. Scott pulled right next to the LSV. Small-arms fire rained in on them. Harris hunkered down as much as possible behind the turret's armor and laid into the woods with the SAW. The drum ran out and Harris scrambled to reload. Scott fired the M5 rifle from the driver's seat. Edwards jumped out, firing the twelve gauge, and ran to the downed LSV. He dragged back a bloodied Metzer and threw him in the back. Harris hated being this exposed in one spot for this long, but knew they weren't leaving until they got all their guys. A high-explosive TOW missile struck into the tree line with devastating effect, but small-arms fire from both sides kept up. Edwards had dragged Braddock back to the LSV. Harris realized none of them were moving under their own power, and Edwards went back for Cortes. Harris cursed when he realized he had to replace another two-hundred-round drum. His five- to six-round bursts were becoming indistinguishable. Edwards flung Cortes from over his shoulder into the backseat of the LSV.

"Go! Go! Go!" Edwards screamed, although Scott did not have to be told. He had already hit the gas.

The windshield was cracked from small-arms fire. Scott was nearly driving blind, but even if he couldn't see well, it did not slow him down. However, the flat tires did. The LSV's tires were designed to run when flat, but it did inhibit performance. Even at that, Harris could tell the LSV was working too hard to be going that slow. The engine had to have been damaged. Harris prayed that the engine would at least get them out of range of enemy fire.

"Come on, hang in there!" Scott yelled as if he could will the engine to perform better.

Harris jumped back into the turret to fire the SAW.

As the LSV slowed down, forty-millimeter grenades dropped into the Prick riflemen. They were getting backup from a Mk 19 gunner. Another high-explosive TOW missile was fired into the Prick line. As long as the LSV's engine kept running, they could limp out of there. Harris noticed another TOW gun team about two hundred meters to his left, firing their SAW. Harris ducked down into the LSV to get another drum. Their mortality crossed his mind. It angered him that they could all get killed today on some meals on wheels mission. Not winning the war, not saving American lives, but delivering food into enemy territory.

Harris didn't notice the American attack helicopters until after he had reloaded another two-hundred-round drum and began firing again. It was not a moment too soon. The LSV managed to limp away, but would not make it back to base. Hastings and Riccardi's vehicle pulled up next to them. Hastings and Harris laid down cover fire from their SAWs as Edwards, Scott, and Riccardi began to move the wounded into Hastings's vehicle. Renoir and Jacobs pulled up and covered them as well. The helicopters were a Godsend; they were more than the Pricks could handle.

Edwards motioned Harris into Renoir's vehicle. With their own vehicle empty of personnel and essential gear, Edwards placed a white phosphorus "Willie Pete" grenade on top of the weapon system to destroy it. Then he jumped into Renoir's vehicle with Harris. Jacobs punched the accelerator.

Edwards turned around to face Harris from the front seat.

"Cortes is dead," was all he said, and then he turned back around.

At first Lieutenant Kai could not figure out what was happening. After the last of the food had been dropped off, he watched as his troops loaded up into the trucks. He was the last man to get in and rode in the last vehicle headed out of the village. Before the noise had a chance to register in his brain, he felt the back end of the truck lifting up, flipping over the front. As the vehicle flew upside down, the truth occurred to

Kai; they'd been hit by a rocket. His brain told him to prepare for impact, to prepare for pain, and to prepare to get out as fast as he could. The latter part turned out to be very difficult. Kai couldn't figure out why, but not all his body parts were working. The top of the vehicle had collapsed most of the way, so there was less than a foot of window for him to crawl out of. His entire right side was numb. The rest of his body was racked with pain. He fought to stay conscious. He fought to stay focused. He had men to lead. As the ringing in his ears faded, he noticed there was a lot of screaming and small-arms fire.

Through the smoke and dust he saw the young, retarded man with the ugly scar running up to him. Kai tried to ask for help, but found even words were escaping him at the moment. He was relieved that the young man smiled and pulled him from the wreckage. His relief turned to horror as the man used a knife to gouge out his eyes. Kai tried with all his might to scream for help, but as if in a nightmare, his voice just would not manifest more than a hoarse groan. As if his feeble cry was offensive, Kai soon found his mouth pried open and his tongue was pulled out and severed. As his mouth filled up with blood, Kai feared that it would choke him, but as his mutilation continued, he welcomed his death.

CHAPTER TWENTY-FOUR

President Harmon leaned back and kicked her feet onto the ottoman. She was tired after a long hard day following weeks and months of long hard days. She was tired of being harassed by reporters. She was tired of being questioned by members of her own political party, not to mention by the opposition. The primary campaign had been rough and was leaving her feeling frazzled. She hoped things would slow down, and she would get the chance to recover a bit. She'd need it, the general election was less than five months away.

She had not expected to have an opponent in the primary. She was even more shocked that he would gain enough traction to win the Iowa Caucus. Senator Robert H. Gall, of Wyoming, had been brazen enough to challenge a sitting president; and he'd done it advocating Clark's hard war strategy. The last five months had been a debate as to who had the best strategy to win the war. Gall had won the support of their party's base, but Harmon had been able to survive the primary challenge with the support of her donors and the political and media connections she had established over her twenty plus years in Congress. She now feared that she was too weak, politically, to win the general election.

Negotiations with the People's Republic failed to bring transition. President Zhang was tough, resilient, and tone-deaf to the international community. To add to her woes, no matter how much she went after military personnel over alleged war crimes, the media still painted her as a bad wartime president. That had been a problem for her. The only advantage she had with the media was that they liked her better than Gall. She feared that would change in the general election. At a minimum, she had to make it look like progress was being made by November. The "Partisan Resistance," as the media called it, and possible US war crimes had to be knocked out of the news cycle. She could only court-martial so many soldiers before it would hurt her even more with her own base. If Zhang did not abdicate from UN pressure, she was going to have to make it look like military gains were being made. Thus leading her to a late night meeting with General Mythers.

"Madame President, General Mythers is here to see you." Sophia Porter popped her head through the door of the hotel's presidential suite to notify her boss.

"Thank you, Sophia. Give me ten more minutes and show him in, would you?"

"Yes, Madame President." Miss Porter curtly bowed her head and backed out of the room.

Harmon downed the last of her white zinfandel. She was surprised to find more in her glass than she had counted on. Still, she decided to have another. She figured Mythers would like a drink as well, so why not?

I deserve a little treat after all I've been through lately, she told herself.

"Good evening, Madame President." Mythers walked into the room, wearing casual civilian attire so as to attract less attention from the press watching at this hour of the night.

"Good evening, Peter. Please have a seat."

"Thank you, Madame President," Mythers said with his compliant smile.

"Can we get you anything, Peter? It's been a long day. Have a drink with me. Sophia, get the general whatever he wants."

"Oh, Madame President, I don't—"

"Nonsense, Peter. You at least deserve a drink for all you do for this country."

"Oh, all right. Any scotch?"

"Of course, Peter. Sophia, get the general a scotch—"

"Neat, please," the general finished.

"Yes, Madame President." Porter smiled and did an excellent job of looking happy to do a task she thought was completely beneath her.

"Peter, we've got to win this election, and I can't get beat over the head for Clark's war or I, we, will lose."

"I know, Madame President. Thank you, Miss Porter." Mythers got a lot of inside scoop from Porter and wanted to stay on her good side. "And I hate to tell you, but it's worse than just China. We have cartel activity in Occupied Mexico. They're coming into conflict with the state militia units guarding our border.

"On top of that, since the Russians have taken out the caliphate in the Middle East, my intel tells me we've got jihadist cells in the Great Lakes, looking to become the new epicenter of Islam. These fires are on the brink of becoming infernos if we don't get a hold on them now."

Mythers had the president's attention. She knew of these problems, but hoped to deal with them through money. Start programs and funding that would benefit the groups that represented those interests. It was a time-honored practice to use taxpayer money to buy the compliance, if not the loyalty, of groups opposed to American interests.

"What do you propose, General?"

The use of his rank was not lost on Mythers. He knew he had tapped into issues she was insecure about. He resisted the urge to smile, when he really wanted to laugh. He thought of politicians as predictable and easy to manipulate.

"First, Madame President, dealing with enemy insurgency within the United States is beyond the ability of the local law enforcement agencies of the Great Lakes region. Even with the help of the FBI, these people cannot be handled by law enforcement because they are not a law enforcement problem."

"What do you mean by that, General?"

"They are a national threat. They are an enemy to the State. With all due respect, Madame President, they are a threat to your authority and the voice of the American people. They're no less of an enemy than the PLA or the cartels on the border. You wouldn't send local police or state troopers to deal with either of those. Is it fair to expect them to handle jihadists?"

"Cut the crap, Peter. You know damn well that is exactly what we've been doing. What is your point?"

The general noticed the switch back to his first name. He also noticed a change in her tone he'd not heard before. Was the wine getting to her? Or was his presentation that good? He suspected the former.

"Madame President, volunteer state militia is not trained to deal with violent, sophisticated, organized crime. You need to get them out of Occupied Mexico."

"General"—Harmon sounded incredulous—"you know I never supported Clark's militias, but they are a fact now. If I pull them off the borders, I anger millions of Americans who want the border protected. There is no other alternative until after the election."

"Madame President, as well you know, our negotiations have stalled. Zhang doesn't have a chance, but he's daring us to come after him. He's exploiting your desire to save human life and the media's bias against you for his political gain, or really just his political survival at this point."

"General"—Harmon sounded like she was losing the good feeling the wine had given her—"you've told me nothing I don't already know."

"Madame President, what if I told you I had a plan that could deal with all three national security issues. Dodge legal jurisdictions and limitations in the Great Lakes, 'deactivate'"— Mythers did the quotation symbols with his fingers—"the militias, give Zhang the motivation he needs to step down, and make yourself look like the biggest national security hawk in our nation's history. Would you be open?"

"Peter"—Mythers inwardly cringed at the sound of slurred impatience in the president's voice—"don't waste time with foolish questions."

"I propose we combine the State Department, military, intelligence, and all national law enforcement under one command. Instead of several independent entities trying to do the same thing, combine our resources and combine our funding for the same goals. We can replace, or co-op rather, all three organizations under one command. We'll save money. We'll be more efficient. We'll be more effective."

"I don't know." The president began to nervously tap her pen against the sofa's armrest. "I'm not certain how voters will react to this. Our government was formed on the concept of the separation of powers, after all, and I've got to try to appease all those Constitution fanatics in the party."

"Madame President, practically speaking, what separation is there now? As it stands, you've got multiple people and multiple organizations with the stated mission of the public safety. If just one of those law enforcement officers, militia commanders, or military generals fails, it is you who is held responsible. It is you who is held accountable. If you are going to be held responsible, why not take control of the responsibility? Put one person in command, who you have authority over and is accountable only to you, to deal with all national issues of public safety. Why not have one person, who you can directly control, to implement your agenda and see to it that your will is done for the sake of public safety?"

"An agency for public safety," Harmon thought out loud and stared beyond Mythers, thinking of the possibilities this new control could give her. "Yes, we consolidate for the sake of national security, for the sake of the people."

"Precisely, Madame President."

Harmon's eyes darted back to Mythers's. "And just to whom should I entrust all of national security and safety? Do you have anyone in mind?"

"Of course I do, Madame President." With that, Mythers took his first drink of scotch. *Enjoy it. You've worked hard. You deserve it*, he told himself.

Zhang smiled. The first true smile of happiness he'd felt in the last four years.

"General Huang, please tell me again. I want to be sure I understand what I believe to be the genius of your plan."

"My pleasure, President Zhang." And Huang Jianguo meant it. He thought his plan to be absolutely brilliant and sensed that Zhang did as well. Fully aware of his president's intolerance for failure, he was relieved to see a smile on the face of the People's leader.

"I assert that we use the Americans' tactics to our advantage. Over the last three months we've seen a significant increase in the deployment of ground troops. I believe this increased activity on the American line is not a military strategy as much as it is political. In other words, I think the Americans put more 'boots on the ground' to gain a factor of intimidation in our negotiations, and/or convince the American populace that President Harmon is serious about winning the war. This is not for the sake of defeating our People's Liberation Army, or even to conquer more territory for the criminal Republic of

China, but rather to ensure President Harmon's election this November, just over three months from now.

"On the other hand, President Harmon does not want to seem like she is escalating the war or provoking us to respond. Thus General Hinneman has dotted the Northern China Plain with all these military outposts." Huang again pointed out several of these bases north of the Yellow River to Zhang. "But many of these, particularly in the west, have very little support beyond artillery. These I think are particularly vulnerable to being cut off, surrounded, and destroyed.

"Therefore I put to you that we launch a coordinated assault against all American military outposts north of the Yellow River. The majority of what is left of our tanks, armored cars, and jets will attack in the east. In the west, we will overwhelm the American bases with our superior numbers of people. For more than a year, we've built a vast partisan network among the farmers and rural villages. There we have millions of armed peasants and soldiers that can overwhelm the American camps with their sheer numbers alone."

"Yes, we have the numerical advantage, but the Americans have the technological advantage with tanks and air superiority at this point. If they respond to defend the bases in the west, the assault will fail." Zhang had liked Huang's answer to this the first time and hoped it would sound even better a second.

"Yes, President Zhang, but if they respond with their jets to the western assault, they will not be able to answer our thrust in the east, nor the center of their front. However, I think they will meet our tanks and jets with theirs, leaving their western outpost with little to no air support. General Secretary, we do not need tactical success to achieve a strategic victory.

"Remember, our goal is not to repel the American forces. We overrun just one American base, even if our troops cannot hold our gains and fall back, the American media will report the defeat of US troops nonstop. The propaganda will be invaluable."

"And if no bases are overrun?"

"Our objective is political, not military. Even a massive assault against US troops will be reported as a failure of President Harmon's by their media. They obviously favor her rival candidate in the presidential election, Senator Tang from California.

"Worst-case scenario, as I see it, President Zhang, is that even if we fail to overrun one military base, the American media will be so anxious to report their own military failure in order to promote their preferred candidate, they will grossly exaggerate any success we have, great or small.

"They will declare failure. They will declare defeat. They will blame Harmon. Even if media exaggerations are eventually discovered, it will be too late. Damage will have been done. As the Americans say: it will be an 'October Surprise.' Tang will be elected. The United States will have a weaker leader and thus will be easier to defeat."

Easier to defeat? Most likely Tang would happily pull US troops out and even pay for damages, Zhang thought. He relished the idea of a "President Tang." No doubt he preferred Harmon to Clark, but Tang could be like having his own man in the White House.

Benedict Xavier Tang, in fact, had had much of his previous political career nurtured by the People's Republic of China. He was a native Californian that claimed some descent from Chinese immigrants of the nineteenth century. He had gotten his start in politics when he was a student at Berkley. He was a champion of progressive causes and advocated many Marxist ideals. As the People's Republic of China looked to make connections and inroads into the United States government, Tang had caught their attention when he first ran for the House of Representatives. The man did not look Chinese to Zhang, but that was of no matter as long as he was of use to the PRC. Their investment had paid off. Tang had always fought for China's interests in the United States, going back even before the Leakey administration. He had happily accepted many gifts and campaign donations for his loyalty. As a senator, Tang had been one of Clark's most outspoken critics. Now he ran as an antiwar candidate for the presidency of the United States. Tang's promises to withdraw from the war would not only reverse the PRC's losses over the last seven and a half years, the political vacuum could allow the People's Republic of China to achieve even greater glory.

"General Huang, can you execute your plan in three months?"

"Yes, sir. Much of our foundational work has already been done by our Gansiduì units."

"A President Tang would be a great asset to the People." Zhang looked up from his cup of tea. "I approve your plan. If you are successful, General, you will be one of China's greatest heroes."

Zhang had every intention to be China's greatest hero, and he could deal with Huang when he was no longer useful.

THE LAST MARINE

CHAPTER TWENTY-FIVE

Harris was glad to have the summer heat broken. He would drink hot coffee in the heat, but found it more enjoyable in the cool mornings. He'd gotten the process down to something of an art. One heat tablet would boil his canteen cup of water. He then added the instant coffee, hot cocoa, cream, and sugar packets from his MRE (Meals Ready to Eat) packet. His morning coffee and cigarette while playing a game of chess with Hastings were the highlight of his day. After that, it was all downhill until the next morning.

Life for Harris had been duller recently, which did have certain advantages over the terror of combat. However, this kind of boredom was not what Harris had had in mind when he had joined the Marines.

His TOW section had just started their month-long rotation at what the Marines affectionately called Camp Michael Foxtrot. It was a small camp positioned on some high ground that over looked the headquarters for 1/1, known as Camp Charles Foxtrot.

"Hey, would you rather be at Camp Alpha Foxtrot?" Hastings liked to joke.

The only reason anyone could think of for the existence of Camp Michael Foxtrot, was to deny the Pricks high ground over Charles. No one seemed to know, or admit to anyway, the exact purpose for Camp Charles Foxtrot.

Lately, the Allied plan seemed to be to set up fortified field camps north of the Yellow River. Perhaps to scare the PLA from heading south. Most of the Marines were skeptical, but that said, they had not been attacked by Pricks for several weeks. On the other hand, they weren't attacking the Pricks either. The meals on wheels missions were reduced, and they stayed closer to camps for support.

There was no longer a clear sense of mission or objective among the Marines. They holed up in camps, not winning nor going home.

While scenic and at times tranquil, Camp Michael Foxtrot was not a favorite duty for the Marines. On top of being boring, it was small. Many compared it to ship duty, because of its confining nature on the hilltop. Only one company occupied the camp at any one time. They would rotate through on a monthly basis. While only twenty kilometers from Camp Charles Foxtrot, one did get the sense of isolation out there. The conscious knowledge of artillery and air support was too abstract, at this point, to be of much comfort. Month-long duty at the camp circulated around watch, exercise, and weapons maintenance. The camp was too small for LSVs, so the heavy weapons attached to Charlie Company manned ground-mounted weapons.

Harris had hit his sweet spot where his coffee was at the perfect temperature to drink while he smoked. He was losing the chess game to Hastings, but the game wasn't the high priority. Right now he was comfortable and enjoying the time with his friend.

"Company formation ASAP," Reese announced to the half dozen TOW gunners in the general-purpose tent that housed the TOW section.

"Figures," Harris spat in disgust at having to sacrifice a perfect cup of joe. "This better be something important."

"Come on, Harris! Since when have you been in the Corps and had to fall out for a completely worthless formation?" Hastings replied with his usual smart-ass sarcasm.

All the Marines grabbed their weapons and covers and headed for the camp's parade deck.

As they headed towards the area where Heavy Weapons Platoon formed up they saw Newton and Tanzer, both machine gunners, talking intensely.

"Hey, man, either of you got a cigarette I can bum? I got a pack back at my tent. Promise I'll pay you back." Newton, who was always bumming cigarettes, asked. However, Harris had always found Newton good on paying him back, so he offered his pack to him.

"Light?" Newton pressed. Harris extended his lit cigarette to him.

"Thanks, Red." Newton handed the pack back.

Harris had managed to go most of his Marine Corps career without a nickname. He was called "Hard Charger" by McGregor, and that had stuck for a while. But much of Second Section had died off since then. Hastings was the only one who called him Hard Charger these days. After playing baseball and having a barbecue during "Beach Day" at Camp Charles Foxtrot one afternoon, it was painfully obvious at the end of the day that Harris was badly sunburned. With red hair and red skin, from that day on he'd become known as "Red" Harris by the machine gunners.

"Dudes, listen." Tanzer leaned in and lowered his voice. "I got word from Henschel minutes ago that the Pricks are on the move. Big offensive."

"Come on, Tanzer! The war's won. I read it myself on the Internet. The Pricks just want to drink tea and peacefully oppress their fellow man. You need to read the news more." Hastings facetiously shook his head and inhaled on his cigarette.

The Marines fell into formation and were called to attention by the company gunny, who then turned them over to Captain Shelby, the commander of Charlie Company.

266

"At ease, Marines," Shelby ordered. He was a tall and confident man, with a loud and commanding voice. "Last night the PLA launched a major offensive between Dongying and Jinan. As of now Zhang is claiming it's led by a renegade general who has aligned himself with partisans. The official word is that we are to presume the peace talks are still a go. As you know, however, the peace talks have not been peaceful for over this last year. Until further notice we will be on fifty percent alert. There is never a time to be complacent in a war zone. We will not start now. Marines, this war is NOT over."

"Sergeant Liu, you have done fine work. You have served the People well," Lieutenant Xi Tian rui complimented his platoon sergeant.

"Yes, sir. I live to serve the People and to kill our enemies." It was the proudest moment of Liu Zhiqiang's life.

He had not known until this day what his work of the previous three months had been geared towards. When orders had come down to stop killing, Liu had felt heartbroken, almost betrayed. However, Zhiqiang had kept his faith in his government, kind of. He had managed to kill two people over the last three months. This he had done on his own and with great caution not to be caught. In fact, he'd felt the experience had made him a better soldier of the Gansiduì. Having to avoid his own authorities, as well as his enemies, had pushed him to a higher level of creativity and ingenuity that he thought would make him better in the field. Meanwhile he had focused the rest of his energy into recruiting partisans and transporting weapons into the villages and suburbs north of the Yellow River. He had been under the belief that his mission was of a defensive nature. Now that he knew that his platoon had been part of the crucial groundwork to prepare for an assault on two US Marine bases, with the objective of annihilating an entire battalion, he swelled with pride. This would be his greatest killing yet.

Harris hated going through the night without a cigarette. He always found it tempting to hunker down behind the sandbags and sneak in a quick smoke break. Under the circumstances he settled for a packet of instant coffee chased down by a swig of canteen water.

Scott was taking a turn at the thermal night scope, scanning for any signs of enemy activity, any signs of movement.

"Harris!" Scott's voice was hushed, but his tone was urgent.

"Yeah?" Harris moved in behind the SAW, concentrating on the dark terrain in front of him for movement.

"Aw, fuck me! It's just another rat." Scott leaned back, stretched, and exhaled in relief.

"Be fucking positive before you go taking a nap, you slack bastard." Part of Harris regretted sounding so harsh with Scott. The kid was running a fever and looked like hell, but hadn't complained once pulling his duty. The other part of Harris knew the Pricks didn't give you a pass because you weren't feeling well. Everyone got sick. Everyone got tired. Everyone got hurt. Everyone had to suck it up in war, or get killed. Even if you did suck it up, you could still get killed.

"I'm sure." Scott let his irritation be heard. He wasn't a slack bastard and didn't like being called one. He admired and respected Harris. He didn't want to fight with him, but Scott wasn't going to take a lot of crap from him either. "It's been five days. You think the offensive really is contained in the east?"

"Who knows. Doubt it. What reason have we got to trust the Pricks?" Harris still had some attitude towards Scott.

"What's your fucking deal? You pissed about something?" Scott demanded.

"Yeah. I'm pissed that Pricks attacked my country, killed my dad and my friends, and I'm pissed that we have to sit here and wait and see if they fucking attack us." Harris realized he was just being an ass because he was on edge and stressed from the lack of sleep, and that was as close as he'd come to expressing that to Scott.

"Other than that, what's your problem?" Scott tried to lighten the mood. Harris appreciated the attempt.

"This war's my problem. The communists have a history of deceit and dishonor, but they're clever motherfuckers. Maybe it's contained in the east. Maybe they want us to think it's contained in the east. I don't know. Just be ready for anything."

"What's going on?" Edwards said quietly, but from enough distance so as not to startle them. He wasn't looking to be a casualty of friendly fire if he could avoid it. "You ladies keeping watch or trying to build a rapport with each other?"

"Nothing but rats." Harris's mood was instantly improved by Edwards's joke.

"Just wondering if the offensive is contained in the east." Scott continued his question.

"For now, you just assume it ain't. You got me?"

"Roger that, Corporal Edwards." And with that Scott went back to the scope.

"Both y'all listen up. The president may have quit fighting this war, but we ain't. Not until we're victorious or we're dead." Edwards attempted to inspire them.

"I'll hold off on my two weeks' notice, then," Harris shot back. Edwards liked his humor and laughed a bit.

"Fuck that quitting shit," Scott replied, feeling motivated by Edwards's attitude.

"What makes you think President Harmon's quit?" Harris caught that his question sounded more like an accusation. He'd not meant it that way, but he wanted to know Edwards's thinking. The sentiment was similar to his own.

"Well, what are we doing to win it? Other than deliver food and medicine, we've just sat on our asses for over a year now. You know your history. That ain't how wars are won, that's how they're lost."

"You think we're losing?" Scott sounded about as surprised as he did concerned.

"In war, if you ain't winning, you're losing." Edwards grinned slightly. "But if you're still alive, you ain't lost yet. Never quit."

Private Chen shivered in the cold. So much was at play: the weather, his nerves, his excitement as he lay in the wet grass, waiting for the order to advance. He was honored to be part of a generation that would fight one of China's greatest battles in one of China's greatest wars. He was thrilled to find out the work he had done as a Gansiduì, under Sergeant Liu, had been to make this historical moment possible. Private Chen Gang was from a farming village so small it was not on any map of China. No one in his family history had ever moved beyond the status of a poor farmer. But Chen Gang already had. He had become a member of an elite military unit of the People's Liberation Army. He defended the People from the barbarian invaders and the traitors that conspired with them. Yet even that would pale in comparison with tonight. Tonight would be the start of one of the greatest moments in all of history, in all of China. The People's Liberation Army would surround and destroy an entire battalion of United States Marines.

"Stay sharp, Devil Dogs. Take no chances on the new day." With that Edwards walked off into the darkness to check on the other gun teams.

"I'll take a turn," Harris offered to give Scott a break.

"Thanks." Scott backed off and took a drink of water. "You got any more of those coffee packs?"

"Yeah." Harris scanned. Some heat signatures had caught his attention, but it was nothing distinguishable. "Over—"

The scream of rockets cut him off. His mind immediately registered several rockets. Yells went up throughout the camp, but to no avail. Within one second Camp Michael Foxtrot had erupted. Harris kept his face buried in the night sight, so he didn't see the camp light up from the quick series of explosions, but he felt the earth shake. His ears rang. He could hear Scott's voice; he'd survived the explosions. Harris looked for targets; he saw nothing. He stuffed his fear and prepared his mind for more incoming.

"Scott, you see anything?"

"No. I lost my night vision. My eyes are adjusting."

Orders were shouted. Marines were manning their posts to prepare for the attack. Harris wondered if Reese and Sheridan were still alive to man their gun. Was Edwards still alive to give orders?

"Drones! Drones! Drones!" somebody called out. Shortly thereafter came more explosions. The center of the camp was getting pummeled hard. The Pricks seemed to have done their homework. They had their coordinates.

Edwards's Third and Caldwell's Fourth TOW squads were on the west side of the camp. Harris had liked that that side of the hill was somewhat steep, but the downside was that the bottom of the hill was thickly wooded and then descended farther west. This made it difficult to see much of anything between one to one and a half miles out. Anything about a half mile on the other side of the woods was a target. Harris strained now to see any kind of target between them, the woods, and beyond. Nothing. The incoming stopped.

"Come on, you Prick bastards! Get a move on it! We ain't sleeping tonight anyway. Right, Scott?"

"I was going to video chat with my girlfriend later. I suppose I can reschedule," Scott countered. Harris was glad to hear Scott's humor.

"Hell, man, go ahead. I'll hold the fort for you." Both Marines laughed more from nerves than from their joke. Sporadic bursts of machine-gun fire ended the laughing. Both Marines looked downrange, but still could not see anything.

More explosions. The cries for "arty" rang out. Once again the camp turned into hell on earth. Harris wanted to tell Scott this was the most ordnance he had ever experienced in one spot in the four years he'd been in China, but there was too much noise.

On an impulse, Harris lifted himself up from behind the sandbags to look through the night sight again. This time he saw hundreds of Pricks leapfrogging their way up the hill. Harris grabbed Scott by the shoulder.

"Fucking Pricks," he shouted and pointed straight ahead. Scott couldn't really hear him, but he understood the message. Part of Harris liked the balls on them to advance on the hill while under artillery fire, but he still wanted to kill the bastards. Scott got behind the SAW and began firing five- to six-round bursts. The advancing Prick infantry was about eight hundred meters out. They had a high-explosive round loaded in the TOW's snout. Harris saw no tanks or armored cars; he decided to fire into the tree line on the chance some kind of target was hidden in there.

The Marines of Charlie Company began to dish out their dose of hell to the advancing PLA. Fifty-caliber machine guns as well as forty-millimeter Mk 19 grenade launchers and mortars were fed into the advancing People's Army.

Harris felt the warm buzz from his adrenaline as the firing progressed. He fired another missile, reloaded, and went to his rifle. He had four missiles left and wanted to have something to shoot if a bigger target showed up. The closest Pricks were still about six hundred meters out and just beyond his rifle's range of point accuracy.

"Wounded?" Edwards, seemingly out of nowhere, shouted at him. Harris and Scott answered no. "Fire discipline. Let them get in range before you shoot. Keep an eye out for tanks, armored cars, or trucks beyond the tree line. If they're coming at us with grunts, they may be trucking them up." Edwards took a quick inventory of their ammo and was off again.

"I'll be glad to hear a gunship any fucking time now," Scott quipped.

"Won't be too much longer. Our arty will start in on them," Harris reassured him.

"Goddamn, it figures!" Lieutenant Colonel William "Bulldog" McGregor quietly cursed. He didn't want to seem rattled in front of his command and cause panic. He had just gotten word that Camp Michael Foxtrot was being attacked and appeared to be surrounded. They were requesting air and artillery support. He was in the process of requesting the same for Camp Charlie Foxtrot. The intel he was getting from Regimental was all of First Marines was under attack, perhaps the whole First Division. Every camp between Zhengzhou to Luoyang, maybe even Xianyang, was under attack. Any air or artillery support was going to be far and few between at this point.

Camp Michael Foxtrot was about twelve miles northwest of Camp Charlie Foxtrot. Both camps were under assault from all directions, with who knew how many Pricks between them. He hated this.

"Captain Hudson, radio back to Captain Shelby that the entire battalion is under assault and may even be surrounded." McGregor, having been in a similar situation years before as a young officer, hated to say what he was about to. "Do not expect help tonight. We will relieve as soon as possible, but for the time being Camp MF might as well be the Alamo."

As the sun was coming up, the PLA had failed to take the hill. Some began to retreat to the woods for cover. Chen had felt the temptation, but had stayed. He felt pride for having done so, though it might cost him his life. Sergeant Liu wasn't falling back. He was ordering his men to dig in. As some of the regulars ahead of them began to retreat, Sergeant Liu shot one in the face. When he ordered the others to dig in, they obeyed. Chen summoned the courage to look out of the foxhole; the American line was six hundred meters away. It might as well have been on the moon. Sergeant Liu told them to hang in there, not to give up. Help was on its way. In fact, a 12.7 mm machine gun had been set up. He'd seen soldiers crawling up with shoulder-held air-defense missiles and 80 mm rocket launchers.

As the sun rose, his pride felt a bit diminished and the happiness was gone. Assaulting a Marine base was different than ambushing civilian traitors or killing an unsuspecting soldier. In the light of the new day, Chen wanted to be somewhere, anywhere, else. Sergeant Liu preached that he was the master of death and that he controlled life. If they ran, he'd kill them himself. If they stayed together, they would win. As individuals they would lose; as the People they would win. As several rounds from Marine grenade launchers exploded forty meters in front of him, Chen gritted his teeth and screamed. At that moment in his mind he gave himself to the People's Republic of China. He was all in. He would not retreat. He would not quit. He would win with the People or die for the People.

"Remember the Alamo," Captain Shelby stated out of the blue, and laughed at his own dark humor.

"Sir?" Gunnery Sergeant Fletcher asked, not in on Shelby's private joke.

"Camp Michael Foxtrot just became the Alamo," Captain Shelby said somewhat absentmindedly. His thought process was moving rapidly. "For the foreseeable future we're cut off with no support." The commander pointed at the perimeter of the model of Camp Michael Foxtrot in the company headquarters. "We want to establish secondary defenses for each part of the camp, here, here, here, and here. Ultimately, if we are not reinforced, anyone who's alive falls back to here." Shelby pointed at his command bunker. "When I call…" Shelby thought for a moment. "When I call 'Alamo,' call in arty and airstrikes on this goddamn hill. Damn well pray we got some kind of goddamn air support by then. You read me, Gunny?"

"Aye, aye, sir," the gunny answered with a hard determination that could only be cultivated by twenty years in the United States Marine Corps.

Lieutenant Xi Tian rui felt lucky they had made it up to this point. He'd seen so many "first waves" of an attack destroyed by the US Marines, but six hours later he was still alive. Secretly he wondered how the US Marines managed to hold a line so much better than the PLA, but he would never dare ask that question out loud. He considered himself lucky this time to have a platoon of Gansiduì attached to his company, but what good was good luck if he ended up dead in the end? He was alive now and trying to stay that way. He had just been commended over the radio by Lieutenant Colonel Li for holding the line. He didn't tell the lieutenant colonel that he too might have turned and run if it had not been for Sergeant Liu. The man was a demon on the battlefield and exhibited a confidence that proclaimed he could not be killed. He was enough of an inspiration, or a terror, to keep his line from collapsing. Now, however, Xi didn't really know what to do. Political connections could get him promoted, but didn't give him a clue how to defeat US Marines.

Harris had it. He'd not slept in over twenty-four hours, and it didn't bother him a bit. He was feeling that lust, that buzz he got from battle. He'd been raised to believe all life was a gift from God and not to be taken lightly. Nor did he take it lightly, but the exhilaration he felt from battle had grown over the years. He'd spent many nights wondering if his father had felt it, and he thought that he had. His father had spent his entire adult life fighting evil and protecting the innocent. As a boy, his father had told him that many men were content to ignore evil; but if all good men turned a blind eye to evil actions, then evil won, and the precious lives of the innocent were destroyed. His father had died fighting evil. Before he'd been in battle, Harris had wondered why his father hadn't just stayed in Kansas and fought evil there. He thought now he understood. It was more than just going somewhere to fight evil; being among men who were willing to go to any extent to fight evil made the fight sacred. Harris felt it was an honor and a privilege to fight alongside such men, as he did now. Harris knew their situation was dire. He didn't want his fellow

Marines to die, and he didn't want to die himself. But at this moment he knew there was no other place he'd want to be; come what may, he wanted to fight evil, he wanted to fight that fight with his friends.

The only thing Major Thomas L. Henderson had ever wanted to do more than learn how to fly was to be a US Marine. As a boy he'd been fascinated by the stories of his great-grandfather, who'd served as an infantryman with the Fifth Marines during World War II. He grew up reading Marine Corps history and learning of its warrior culture. This had fed his desire, his ambition, to become a Marine. By the time he had turned eighteen, before the Sino-American War, he was on the verge of joining; but his father had talked him out of it. His father wanted him to go to college and study business so he could learn how to make money. At that age making money was not a motivating factor for the young Henderson. His father had played on his son's desire to learn how to fly to get him to college. He told his son if he got a degree, he could become a Marine officer and learn how to fly. The tactic worked. Young Tommy enrolled at Iowa State University, but he didn't study business as his father had wanted. He enrolled in NROTC and got his degree in history.

Henderson never had the privilege of meeting his great-grandfather, but the man was still an inspiration to him throughout his Marine Corps career. It was the memory of the elder Henderson's service that motivated him to volunteer for this mission. They were told from the outset that this would be a volunteer-only mission. As bad as it was at Camp Charlie Foxtrot, it was more dire at Michael Foxtrot. After an intense seventy-two hours, they needed to be resupplied and the wounded needed to be evacuated. Henderson barely needed more than a second to volunteer.

He flew one of three CH-53s that flew into the camp to deliver ammo and evacuate the wounded while attack helicopters strafed the PLA. The CH-53 helicopter was an obsolete aircraft. At the start of the Sino-American War the need for aircraft was high. What was left of the old machines was refurbished and brought back into service in the Mexico Campaign. Since then, they had just been used to transport supplies, but not for combat. The only reason they were being used in this desperate situation was that they were the most expendable.

They took some small-arms fire during the landing, but it seemed like a blessing after dodging the shoulder-launched rockets. The crew expertly unloaded the cargo under the direction of a steely-eyed gunnery sergeant and loaded up wounded Marines to be evacuated. Henderson said a quick prayer and took off to work his way out of the hell he had flown into. From the air he momentarily wondered how anyone could survive down there. All he could see was exploding earth, fire, and tracer rounds. The distraction of the combat below was interrupted by a massive thud on the port side. The helicopter no longer soared, but seemed to pull and want to spin. He could feel the heat and hear the screams of burning Marines in the back. Henderson fought for control of the helicopter, but it was a losing fight. The CH-53 spun and fell. In his last few seconds he thought of his great-grandfather, meeting Christ, and finally of his wife and three daughters.

"Cease fire, cease fire!" Sergeant Liu ordered. "Don't be fools! Surely they will take the wounded out when they leave. Shoot them as they leave; that way you will kill more Marines!"

Private Yuan held the crosshairs on the Marine CH-53 as it rose into the sky.

"Steady. Wait. Let it rise high enough to cause maximum damage when it explodes and falls," Sergeant Liu advised. "Fire! Fire now!"

Private Yuan depressed the trigger of the shoulder-fired antiair rocket. His aim was perfect. He nailed the Marine helicopter. He had hoped for a bigger explosion, but he could tell he damaged it. The CH-53 had lost control, spun, and crashed back into the Marine camp. Two seconds later there was a secondary explosion. Yuan savored the fireball.

"Yes!" the private cheered and pumped his fist into the air.

"Well done, Yuan!" Sergeant Liu slapped the soldier on the back. Private Yuan turned to smile at his comrades, who were cheering him.

The back blast had caught Corporal Gorton's attention. He'd seen it in the corner of his eye. He fought the temptation to look at the CH-53. He did not want to lose the spot where he'd seen the back blast. He trained the scope of his sniper rifle around the mound of dirt from where he'd seen it. There was movement and a hand thrown up in the air. He held his breath. Within one second he saw the smiling face of the fist-pumping Prick that had fired the rocket step out just a bit from the earthworks. He pulled the trigger.

The back of Private Yuan's head popped open. Sergeant Liu was standing less than a meter from Yuan when he was shot. Liu dropped. He didn't bother to check his comrade; he knew he was dead. Liu dragged the body back into the depths of their trench.

"Don't be stupid, comrades," Sergeant Liu chastised his platoon. "Celebrate with your head down. Chen."

"Yes, Sergeant Liu."

"Go through his pockets. Distribute his ammo."

President Harmon sat at her desk, with her face in her hands. Her heart ached. Three months earlier she had announced the Federal Agency of Public Safety. The mainstream media were leery of her motivations at first. When she soon afterwards revoked the charter of state militias to defend the US border and occupied northern Mexico, she acquired enthusiastic support from the media. Of course, the creation of a large federal bureaucracy that encompassed all aspects of national security, foreign and domestic, had caused dissension with the right wing of her party. However, this allowed her to look more moderate and play to the nonaffiliated and non-decided voters. She thought the dissension fit her image as a consensus builder. She had come to believe that her campaign manager, with the help of the mainstream media, had pulled off a masterful triumph.

Islamic communities in the Great Lakes region had welcomed the deactivation of militias and seemed to be embracing the concept of the new "FedAPS." In a brilliant gesture of goodwill and "building cultural bridges," Harmon gave the American Jihadists Council, AJC, major input in designing protocols for the new Federal Agency of Public Safety. Her campaign was able to present this as a sign that the Harmon administration was healing national wounds and bringing Americans together to stand against the People's Republic of China.

Zhang suddenly became more open to discussion at the peace talks. Partisan attacks had died down with the buildup of military camps north of the Yellow River. Harmon believed that she had found an agenda that would propel her into her own term as president of the United States.

The polls had her anywhere from five to ten points ahead nationally. She was even leading in many of the key battleground states. Harmon had become optimistic about her ability to bring Americans together. As president, she would end the wars that no longer had to be fought, and focus the energy and resources of the nation into evolving as a people and a culture.

It was hard for her to believe that was all just a week ago. The PRC offensive had caused her poll numbers to crash over the weekend. Her advisors had assured her that Zhang was not behind the eastern offensive, that he had nothing to gain by such an action. They confirmed Zhang's accusation of this renegade general, upset by the peace talks, launching his own offensive. General Mythers assured her that if they focused their military assets in the east, it would all be over by election time.

Now he was telling her that they had "misinterpreted the situation." Zhang had baited them into committing resources in the east so the PLA could launch a massive assault to the west. Instead of peace talks, the North China Plain was a cluster of battles. Allied forces were dispersed, misplaced, or otherwise occupied.

She sat in conference with General Mythers and his team of FedAPS advisors at Camp David. President Harmon had just been advised that not one, but perhaps two US Marine battalions might be lost. They had been completely surrounded. Air and artillery support was just spread too thin as it was.

"Does the press know about this yet?" Harmon lifted up her head and looked directly at Mythers.

"Yes, Madame President." Mythers cleared his throat and looked down.

281

"Goddamnit, General!" Harmon exploded. All this was too much.

"Madame President, we have to get ahead of this. You should call a press conference immediately," Porter advised.

President Harmon shifted her gaze from Mythers to Porter. "Do it. Now!" Harmon ordered. She turned her attention back to Mythers. "If you can't tell, General, I am pissed."

"Madame General, I understand, but this is not a time to dwell on what has gone wrong. Instead we need to focus on fixing it. My generals and I have been working on—"

"Fix it!" President Harmon interrupted her new commander of FedAPS. "How do 'we' fix this? The election is in two weeks! How do we possibly fix this by then?"

Harris watched the sun rise for the third time since the Prick assault. He started thinking Scott ought to be back any minute. As if on cue, Scott scurried into the earthen machine-gun pit with more ammo for the .50-caliber machine gun they were now manning.

"I got some chow with the ammo." He pulled an MRE from one of his cargo pockets.

"What'd you get?"

"Chicken à la king."

"Goddammit!" Harris hated chicken à la king. "You know I hate that shit!"

"Well, fuck." Scott was a bit indignant. "I'll eat it. You're fucking welcome, by the way."

"Give me the cheese and crackers." Harris didn't feel hungry, but it'd been about twenty-four hours since he'd eaten. He wanted to keep his strength up.

"This one's got peanut butter." Scott had torn into the packet.

"Same fucking difference." Harris took the food. He manned the gun while Scott ate. Then the two switched roles.

"I saw Hastings while I was getting food and ammo."

"Yeah? Glad the bastard's still alive."

"Says he's tired of pulling your weight for you. When this is over, you owe him a bourbon of 'his choice.'" Scott laughed as he talked, appreciating the joke.

"Ha! Typical Hastings. Tell you what, Scottie, next libo I'll buy you both a round."

"I'll fucking hold you to that."

"You do that," Harris managed to reply with a mouth full of crackers and peanut butter. He washed it down and lit up his first cigarette of the day.

Lieutenant Xi didn't mind getting his ass chewed out by the colonel; it was better than being on that damn ridge, getting shot at by Marines. What he didn't like was the message that they needed to be more aggressive.

"It's the fourth day; we've not advanced. Why?"

"Sir, my men are attacking uphill against a fortified position. We've made three attempts. My company is down to about two-thirds strength. The Marines are dug in well, sir, but we will take them." It was a bit of theater on Xi's part. He didn't care if they took the hill or not. In fact, nothing would make him happier than if the whole assault were called off, or the whole war for that matter. The notion of a communist North and a democratic South didn't bother him in the least. He thought for sure it was a whole lot better than dying.

"Yes, WE will, Lieutenant."

This statement caught Xi's attention. He wondered if the colonel was going to lead the charge himself. The thought almost made him laugh; but since doing so would likely get him executed, he did not.

"We are being reinforced this afternoon. High command, President Zhang himself has ordered this hill taken. We will not fail. Do you understand me?"

"Yes, sir!" Xi gave a well-practiced gung ho answer.

"Our timing couldn't be better, Lieutenant Xi. The Americans are unorganized right now. President Harmon is a fool and has left her forces unprepared. We have the element of surprise and superior numbers. Our victory here can change the course of the war and lead to vanquishing the American force."

Xi was surprised to hear the colonel admit to a "change of course" could lead to victory. The PRC line was that they were winning and always had been, even if they had lost a quarter of China.

"Sir, we will win or we will die. I will be the first up the hill." Even Xi Tian rui was impressed with the passion with which he delivered this lie.

"We will intensify our artillery at 0330. Then launch the attack at 0400 hours."

"Yes, sir." Xi saluted and left the tent to go back to his command. All but one of his junior officers had been killed trying to get up that damn hill. Xi had no intention of charging up that hill if he could help it. His mind began to plan how to get Sergeant Liu to do it.

"Sheridan caught some shrapnel in the calf, but he's patched up and fighting," the corpsman, Doc Hansen, filled Harris and Scott in.

"So not many more wounded, Doc?" Scott wanted to reconfirm.

"No. Knock on wood, boys. All things considered, the last couple of days ain't been too bad. Just as well, too. Word is we're too far out, and air support is too damn sparse. For the time being anyway."

"What the fuck's going on that we can't get any air?"

"What kinda talk is that, Harris? You ain't gonna up and quit on us, are you? Go join a Buddhist temple or some shit?" Sergeant Bohanan crawled into the machine-gun pit. He'd brought an ammo can and two packs of cigarettes with him. He tossed a pack each to his two section members.

"That'll be the day," Harris grumbled.

"Heads up tonight. Intel on Prick movement. They'll try another attack, so stay sharp. Stay awake. Remember, green flares, fall back to the secondary defense. Red flares mean 'Alamo,' you beat feet back to the command bunker 'cause all hell is going to rain in on this hill," Bohanan reminded his section members.

"Roger that," Harris confirmed.

Bohanan slapped him on the shoulder and turned to walk out. "Oh, by the way, Harris." Bohanan spoke like he'd just remembered something. "Hastings says you're buying a round of drinks when this is all over. Scott, you keep his dumb ass alive. You understand me?"

"Aye, aye, Sergeant," Scott confirmed with a grin.

Seven minutes after Sergeant Bohanan left, Prick artillery and rockets rained in. Harris figured another attack was coming; the Pricks had probably been reinforced and their confidence was up.

"Goddamn cocksuckers!" Harris cursed. He was angry. His war lust was up. He was ready for the fight. Harris gave Scott a disapproving look when he lit up a cigarette in the dark.

"You think they don't know we're here?" Scott replied.

"Fuck it." Harris thought he had a point. "Don't smoke behind the gun. I don't need a sniper taking your stupid ass out."

Harris sat behind the gun as shells fell all around him. He prayed for peace of mind. He prayed for courage. He prayed for strength. He prayed to kill as many of the enemy as he could until he took his last breath.

Private Chen lay in the early morning dark. He, along with the rest of his platoon, had spent the last few hours crawling several hundred meters towards the Marine base. The order to assault would soon be given. Of all things at that moment it was the memory of his grandfather that came to his mind. He recalled the first time his grandfather took him to look at newborn chicks in the barn. His grandfather selected those that were fit to live and those that were not. The latter had their necks wrenched. Their lives terminated before they ever lived. He'd not thought of that time in over a decade, and he found absolutely no comfort in it at this moment.

"Comrades, soon we attack the barbarians that have invaded our land and have sought to enforce their democracy over the will of the People," Sergeant Liu began to address the company. Over the last three days he had advanced from platoon sergeant to platoon leader, and many said he should be company commander.

"Many of our brothers have given their lives for the People, as many more will before this war is won. As individuals we are nothing, we are worthless. As the People we are immortal, we cannot die. As long as we have the State, we are eternal! Today whether you live or die, the People's Republic of China will survive, and you will be our nation's greatest heroes in our collective memory."

"Fucking hell," Private Lin mumbled next to Chen.

"Shut up!" Chen was not in the mood for blasphemy. He looked up at the stars. Sergeant Liu said their service would make them heroes; the State would make them eternal. "Like the stars," Chen finished his own thought out loud.

"Everyone is crazy," Lin mumbled more to himself, "but what difference does it make? Tomorrow we'll all be dead."

Green flares shot up into the sky, their signal to begin the assault. Sergeant Liu ordered the fire teams to advance.

"Green flares now?" Scott asked, confused.

"Got to be theirs. They're—" Harris was interrupted by Scott's machine-gun bursts. Through night vision, Harris could see Pricks popping up all over the hillside. They were leapfrogging their way up in fire team rushes. Harris heard the nearby buzz of an observation drone and blasted it with the twelve gauge. He slid another shell into the magazine. He wanted it fully loaded for what was about to come.

Between bursts, he could hear shouts from within the camp. He thought there had to be confusion over the green flares. Should he and Scott fall back? Pricks were as close as two hundred meters, a lot of them.

"Fuck it!" Harris shouted out loud to himself, his voice lost in the machine-gun fire. He picked up Scott's M5 and began shooting at individual targets. He'd rather die killing than running.

Lieutenant Xi began up the hill after he'd seen to it that all his platoons had begun to advance. As a consequence of survival, he was now the company commander. This would be a great career move for him. Xi could be promoted to captain if he could stay alive. He never did believe in taking risks, and he wasn't going to start now, by leading his company up the hill. He would command from behind the best he could. The trick was making it look like he led from the front.

The Marine fire was bad, but seemed less intense than it had been two days before when they had tried. Perhaps they really could take this hill, in which case he would want to make himself seen on the top. He dashed several steps and dropped down for cover with his radioman right behind him. They tripped over a prone soldier with an eighty-millimeter rocket launcher. Kneeling, he leaned over the man to see if he was injured or dead.

"Comrade, are you all right?" Xi asked, feeling for wounds.

The soldier whimpered.

"Courage!" Xi yelled at the man as he slapped him and began to pull him up. "Help your comrades! Fight like a man!"

"Sorry, sir." The soldier weakly pulled himself together.

"There." Xi pointed up the hill towards the flashing barrel of a Marine machine gun. "Shoot there!" Lieutenant Xi ordered. The small soldier struggled to control his trembling hands and prepared to shoot the rocket launcher.

Lance Corporal Scott was in excellent form behind the fifty-caliber machine gun. He was fast and accurate. Harris felt inspired. They could hold another day. Both were caught a bit by surprise when the weapon ran out of ammunition. With speed and precision, they loaded the last ammo belt into the gun, and Scott went back to killing. Harris turned around to reach for the M5.

The impact caught him by surprise. In an instant Harris thought of everything: his family, his home, the war, his death. His body slammed into the earth. His ears rang. His mind spun. His body was pounded by dirt and sandbags. He could move. He could breathe. He was still alive.

"Excellent!" Lieutenant Xi commended the small soldier, who looked surprised to have hit his target. "Now on to victory!" Xi slapped the soldier on the back.

"Yes, sir!" The soldier ran off. Lieutenant Xi sincerely hoped the soldier did not get killed. Xi wanted the man to live so he could tell others of how he was inspired to heroics by the "Great" Lieutenant Xi of the People's Liberation Army.

Harris thrust himself out of the mud and debris. He scrambled to find his weapon. He looked around, trying to figure out from which direction the enemy was coming. He saw a dark figure not twenty meters away, firing a weapon. It looked like a Prick, so he shot him. Without seeing another immediate threat, Harris began digging for Scott. He found him. Scott was dead.

"You hit?" Edwards asked as he ran up. "Harris." It wasn't a question, but an acknowledgement of fact. Edwards did not know who he was talking to until that moment. Harris stared back with a stunned look. Edwards grabbed him by the shoulder harness and shook him hard. "Are you hit?"

Harris went from stunned to angry. Without a word he knocked Edwards's hand away. Harris reached for his rifle and began to shoot at the barrel flashes in the dark. Edwards took cover and returned fire upon the advancing Chinese.

Reese and Sheridan manned the last TOW gun that had any missiles left. Sheridan covered Reese with the SAW. Reese sighted in through his night sight on a two-and-a-half-ton truck hauling an artillery gun.

"Good enough," Reese said to himself. "Fire in the hole!" Reese shouted for Sheridan's benefit. Sheridan didn't take time to respond. Pricks were charging up the hill and were way too close. Killing them had his complete attention. Reese hadn't noticed the advancing Pricks; he was too focused on the truck.

"I got you! You son of a bitch!" Reese rejoiced at the impact of his missile, only to be knocked down by a Prick bullet. His chest ached, and he could barely breathe, but his body armor had kept him alive. Reese forced himself back up and found the shotgun. He fired at Pricks not thirty yards away.

"Out of rounds!" Sheridan yelled after the SAW went silent. He began firing a ten-millimeter pistol he'd acquired the day before.

In the noise of the battle Reese could not hear, but he felt the click from the empty shotgun. He wanted to joke that there was never a good time to run out of rounds, but decided to save it for another time. He knelt down next to Sheridan to reload with speed and precision.

Both Marines fought with fury and grace. Neither of them noticed the Prick grenade that landed in their gun pit and took them out.

In the early light of dawn Captain Shelby cursed at another denied request for an airstrike. No sooner had he cursed than he quickly gave thanks for Marine artillery striking at the base of the hill. He started to think again that they might have a chance. Risking stray bullets and snipers, he stood on top of the command bunker to get a quick 360 of what was happening. Shelby would have cursed again had there been time. He ordered the green flares to go up while they could still be seen. The commander was nagged by the notion that he should call "Alamo." From the enemy numbers he saw, he doubted falling back would be enough.

Sergeant Liu was confused at first by the green flares. They had fired theirs off. He thought that they must be an American signal. Then he was struck with inspiration.

"Reinforcements! Reinforcements have arrived! Push harder! Push harder! See our green flares! Victory is ours!" Liu screamed at the top of his lungs. He turned and fired at a flash he'd seen in the left corner of his eye. He hit his target and ran to the foxhole, hoping he had only wounded the Marine.

When he jumped into the foxhole, he saw a Marine struggling to breathe. Liu's 5.8-millimeter round had hit the neck and pierced the young Marine's windpipe. Liu took cover so he could savor the gurgling death throes of the young Marine. Liu's only regret was that the Marine was already so close to death. He missed administering and extending the pain to his victims, but this was war. Sacrifices had to be made.

Edwards noticed the green flares. Harris had not. Harris was in a zone. Edwards had seen him like this before. After six years in combat, Edwards had seen no one better at killing than Harris when he was like this. It baffled him a bit. When bullets weren't flying, the kid spent his time reading his Bible and writing letters to his mother. In combat he was a demon.

"Perhaps an angel of death," Edwards mumbled. They had to fall back. Edwards hadn't had to fall back since Luzon. He knew Harris had never had to fall back; the man had only known victory. Edwards had to wonder, if Harris refused to fall back, would he leave him or fight to the death with him?

"Harris! Green flares! We got to go!" Edwards yelled.

Harris ignored him.

"Harris! Fucking fall back!"

Harris paid him no mind. His M5 ran out of bullets; he reached for another magazine, but was out of those too.

Edwards grabbed him by the shoulder harness and ran. "Fucking move, Harris! Move!"

Harris reached for his knife. In his fury he was tempted to slice Edwards's belly open. Just as quickly he composed his thoughts. It was Edwards, his friend, his mentor. It was surreal for Harris. He'd never fallen back in his life. They'd always charged ahead and won. He was angry over what was happening here. After all the victories, how could this happen? He followed Edwards.

They made it back behind the line of piled earth and sandbags. Edwards had no sooner landed over the wall than he was back up, firing his twelve gauge. He saw Sergeant Bohanan firing his grenade launcher. Harris realized he was weaponless. He felt like he was naked in public. This had never happened to him before. He spun around and saw piles of weapons behind him. He grabbed an .458 SOCOM, spare magazines, and dashed back to the line.

Private Lin could not believe his luck making it up the hill. US Marines were falling back. He'd never seen that before and hadn't thought it was possible. Could the PLA have told the truth for once? This didn't seem possible. He ran up on a foxhole and jumped in. He landed on a dead Marine. He looked up and saw Sergeant Liu. Lin did not like the man. Something about Liu gave him the creeps. The guy was always preaching about the supremacy of the People.

Lin had never cared much for the People. His mother and father had been factory workers. They were never paid enough. The People's Republic of China claimed they existed for the benefit of the people, but his family had never had enough. Ever. Never enough medicine. Never quite enough food. Never enough money for these things. His father paid extra taxes because Lin had been born; he was the only son with two older sisters. His father had always told him he was worth the cost. Lin had always wondered why a government that had nothing to do with the birth of a child could dictate the number of children in a family. Growing up never having enough to be comfortable, he went to school where teachers had watched over his sex life. He'd been expelled from school for showing too much attention to a girl. Lin's entire life, anything he needed, anything he wanted was not of importance to the People's Republic of China. Then the war came to their homeland. Suddenly Lin Lei was important to the State.

Sergeant Liu had his back to him, firing at the enemy line. Lin thought of shooting Liu in the back of the head. He wanted to just hide in the foxhole and ignore the whole battle. Instead he fell in beside Liu and shot at the Americans, since hiding was out of the question.

"Keep moving forward! We must keep moving forward," Sergeant Liu proclaimed. Lin instantly regretted not shooting Liu in the back of the head. Lin stared at the sergeant, afraid to move forward and afraid not to. Three more Red soldiers jumped into the foxhole.

"Forward, Comrades! We must keep moving forward!" Liu ordered. One of the soldiers let out a cry and sprang up; the other two followed. Lin found himself right behind them. He saw all three go down in front of him. Lin felt himself falling before he felt the pain in his left thigh.

The gun wound to his leg hurt more than anything he'd ever felt. He dug his fingers into the dirt. Lin wanted to scream, but he wanted to go unnoticed more. He lay facedown. Then he felt himself being pulled back into the foxhole. It was Liu. Suddenly Lin was glad he had not shot him.

"How are you?" Liu asked.

"My leg. I've been shot. My leg, it's broken." Lin's voice quivered from his pain.

"It's all right. Remember, you're a hero of the People. Your memory will live on forever." Lin took little comfort from Sergeant Liu's words, and even that disappeared when he noticed Liu's knife. He reached to block it, but it had already reached his throat by the time he'd grabbed Liu's hand. Lin struggled for a bit, but his strength was fleeting. Lin's last thought was why he did not shoot Liu in the back of the head when he'd had the chance.

Liu stayed in the foxhole. He looked around; the advance seemed to have stalled. American artillery was dropping in. He had as good a place as any to wait. Killing Lin had not restored his confidence as the master of death. It had not given him the sense of control he craved. Liu struggled to find empowerment in this chaos. He decided to hide and wait.

Private Chen was falling back when he came across two red soldiers trying to reassemble a Type 88, 12.7-millimeter machine gun. He assisted, and it relieved his guilt from having retreated from the Marine fire. American artillery was falling nearby, but not on them. It seemed as safe as any place on this battlefield to hole up a while.

Lieutenant Xi saw artillery coming down fifty meters in front of him. He decided to hole up and looked for his radioman, but didn't see him. He was irritated that the fool could not keep up. Then it occurred to him that he might be dead. Xi decided to work his way back down the hill until he could find his radio. After all, he had to be able to communicate with headquarters.

The exchange of gunfire was starting to die down. Harris kept looking for any Prick he could kill. It didn't matter to him if they were running forward or away.

"If they're dead, they ain't a problem!" he shouted to Edwards.

After several seconds, Harris could find no one else to shoot. He slid down behind the sandbags. They had survived the recent onslaught. He reached for a cigarette to find his hands shaking beyond his control. He laughed from exhaustion and the momentary relief.

"We ain't dead yet, so we ain't lost yet." Edwards smiled. He too found his hands unsteady as he reached for his smokes. "Fuck!" he cursed and handed Harris a lit cigarette before lighting one for himself.

"Second Section, Second Section." Sergeant Bohanan was trying to get a head count.

"Sergeant Bohanan," Edwards called out.

"Edwards, Harris, good to see you! Either of you wounded?"

"No," both Marines answered in unison.

"Good. Scott?" Bohanan looked at Edwards.

"Dead," Harris answered. Bohanan felt a chill from the tone in Harris's voice. It unnerved him a bit. He'd thought himself beyond that sort of thing.

"So's Reese and Sheridan. We've lost Washington, Caprese, Jefferson, Renoir, Jacobs, Caldwell, and Riccardi." Bohanan looked directly at Edwards. "Other than me, you're the last NCO in the section. Gordon's got First, with Rameriz, Martin, and Delany. You got Hastings, Jonker and Sokolov. I'll send them down here."

"What do you got Hart doing?" Edwards asked.

"He's dead." Bohanan paused. "Listen up. Stay hydrated, understand? If you're a heat casualty, you're as good as dead. Canteens, weapons, and ammo are stockpiled in our center. You see red flares, you hear 'Alamo,' you fucking get your ass back to that command bunker. Understand? You think it's hell now, hold on. It will get worse, Marines. Questions?"

"No," Edwards answered. Harris just shook his head.

Bohanan smiled. "Look alive, Devil Dogs! We'll earn our fucking pay this month!" The sergeant laughed with bravado and went back down the line.

"Edwards?"

"Yeah?" Edwards turned back to Harris.

"Why didn't we join the fucking Air Force?"

"Fuck if I know, brother. Fuck if I know." They both laughed at their situation.

By the time Harris had finished his smoke, he saw Hastings making his way over. Harris laughed again; it felt good. Even with all the mud and blood, Hastings's cheeks still looked ruddy like a little kid's.

"What are you laughing at?" Hastings squinted his dark brown eyes, but smiled in return.

"How'd your stupid ass stay alive in all this bullshit?" Harris regretted the question as soon as he'd asked it. It was meant to be funny, but it didn't sound that way to his ears.

"Hell, man! I heard you're buying drinks after work. Wouldn't miss it for the world, my friend!" Hastings slapped his best friend on the back and offered him a cigarette.

General Huang Jianguo looked over his intelligence reports with mixed emotions. He had hoped for better, but had not really expected it. The surprise of the eastern offensive had initially given them great momentum. That was now lost, and in fact, PLA forces were now being pushed back. The only good news was the American counterattack had left Marine battalions in the west isolated from reserves. The Marines' extreme left, 1/1 and 1/4, were the most vulnerable. Especially 1/1 that had been split between two camps. Huang debated with himself as to whether he wanted to go for the destruction of two battalions or concentrate his resources into the destruction of one.

Huang had been raised to keep his thoughts and feelings to himself. In the People's Republic of China, it could be dangerous to share what you thought and what you felt. Along with discipline, his parents had taught him caution and discretion. As a military and political officer, he'd had to learn to calculate and weigh risks and rewards. He did so now.

If he failed to achieve the political victory he had promised, Zhang would most likely have him shot. On the other hand, if he scored a huge military victory, he could very well gain enough political capital to overthrow Zhang. However, Zhang was very cautious and protective of his political power to the point of paranoia. If Huang scored a huge military victory, would Zhang see him as a threat and thus have him shot?

Huang stared at the battle map on the wall as he drank his tea and smoked a cigarette. He thought it logical that even a minor military victory would cause the political defeat of President Harmon. That was his primary objective, after all. Huang was convinced that a President Tang would be thoroughly detrimental to the American war effort. A less spectacular victory might make him less of a political threat.

If he committed the last of his reserves in the west to destroy the American left, he could, with Zhang's blessing, roll the American left flank. Thus still score a huge military victory, but not be as intimidating to Zhang, who could take credit for the success.

All the contingencies made his head hurt. He rubbed his eyes and scratched the top of his head. He needed to sleep. He couldn't worry too far ahead about things he could not control. He made up his mind. He would concentrate the last of his reserves on the American left, focusing on one battalion, to guarantee at least minimal success. Once victory was achieved, these forces could continue to move east if Zhang so desired. It was settled; General Huang's, and the PLA's, top priority was the destruction of First Battalion, First Marines.

Lieutenant Xi had been stuck on the hillside all afternoon. It would be dark within the hour. The momentum of the morning assault was lost. While the Marines had fallen back, they were condensed into a smaller perimeter and seemed twice as tough as they were before. He thought surely they had to be weakening. The Marines were surrounded; unless supplied by air drop, the PLA would throw more red soldiers at them than they had bullets. Being thrown at the Marines again was what worried Xi the most.

For as alone and isolated as Edgar Ragnarsson felt at that moment, he knew it was nothing compared to what the Marines under his command were going through. He'd barely eaten and hadn't slept in days. Seventh Marines, his reserve regiment, had been taken from First MarDiv and given to Fifth Marine Division in the east. First and Fifth Marines had been getting hammered for four days. Whatever other resources the PLA was lacking at this point in the war, population was not one of them. All reports were basically the same. Wave after wave of ChiCom soldiers. Assault after assault on his bases. Half of First Marines were surrounded, and it had been difficult at best, and impossible at worst, to get supplies to them.

It now appeared that his line was stabilizing. He could now look at getting reinforcements and supplies to First Marines. The question that hounded him was if he could do it in time to do them any good?

For the last ninety-six hours Colonel Liddell prayed he could live up to his nickname, Lucky. He'd always worked under the philosophy that a man created his own luck. However, it was the micromanaging of the Harmon administration that had created this bad luck that he now was trying to fix. Every single one of his battalions was engaged in combat. He was having to look at the real possibility that First Battalion could be lost. He knew Billy McGregor would fight to the death if it came to that. Liddell had to see that it didn't come to that.

"About fucking time!" Lieutenant Colonel William "Bulldog" McGregor exclaimed into the radio mic.

"Is that how you talk to a superior officer?" his cousin Colonel "Lucky" Liddell responded in the first lighthearted moment he'd had in four days.

"Sir, you can fire my ass if I'm still alive when this is all done," McGregor countered. "Arty, you know we'll hold out or die trying. But don't take too long. Charlie Company is cut off from us. Those boys may not even have twenty-four hours if they don't get help."

Harris was down to his last pack of cigarettes. He laughed when he realized that bothered him more than being surrounded and running out of ammo. He had all his magazines loaded up with .458 rounds. He'd always thought the large-caliber rifles were badass. He'd joked with Hastings that he could die a happy man now that he had one.

"I could take a nap." Hastings worked to shake off his drowsiness.

"Go ahead. I'll wake you up if anything exciting happens," Harris said with a grin.

"Yeah, go for it," Newton chimed in, not aware of the humor the other two saw in all this.

The three of them were manning the last .50-caliber machine gun left. The Pricks had backed off for the time being. Combat had dwindled down to a few odd shots here and there and an occasional grenade or artillery barrage.

"I miss autumn. I miss being back in Nebraska this time of year."

"Yeah. Spring and fall were always my favorite times of year." Harris joined in the nostalgia.

"Me too. Hell, I even miss all the freaks that come out at Halloween," Newton joined in.

"What the fuck's your deal?! Kids trick-or-treatin' are freaks?" Harris acted indignant about the issue.

"No, the fucking witches where I come from." Newton defended himself.

"You got witches at home?" Hastings took a turn at acting incredulous.

"Hey, I don't believe in that shit, but they do. They flock around town all dressed up in their bullshit. But you know they buy shit, so it was good for my dad's business."

"Where the fuck you from?" Hastings asked with his usual tactfulness.

"Salem, Massachusetts, you fucking pogue bastard."

"Hey, man," Harris chimed in on the good-natured hazing, "I thought you were from the United States."

"Blow it out your mouth, fucking cocksucker." Newton gave back as good as he got.

"Sun's going down, Devil Dogs." Harris became more serious. "They'll come for us by morning. Be stupid not to."

"You're a goddamn cheerleader." Newton was irritated the fun had ended.

"It'll be what it's going to be," Harris said, trying to detach from his emotions about what they faced. If he thought too much about Kansas, his brother and sister, too much about his mother, it would break his heart. He'd be a sobbing mess, with no chance, however slim, of survival.

"Well, hell, then I'm going to have another smoke before it gets too dark." Hastings pulled out his pack and lit up. The other two Marines joined him.

"You act tough now, Bulldog, but don't come running to me when you get lung cancer."

"Fucking blow me, Harris."

Lieutenant Xi was perplexed. He'd been ordered to place the reinforcements as fast as possible. The faster he fulfilled his orders, the sooner they'd renew the attack. High command wanted this company taken out as soon as possible. But if they accomplished the mission, they would only move southeast to join the forces attacking the rest of the battalion. Xi saw no point in winning one fight just to be killed in another. The flip side was, if he had to attack, he'd rather do it in the dark. It was easier to hide, but if he could put off the attack, perhaps luck would intervene and conditions would change to something more favorable. Xi hunkered down even more under his field jacket and smoked his cigarette. He thought it was ironic to be fighting the Americans. He'd always admired their freedom-based culture. He closed his eyes and thought of how fortunate to be born where people control the government. He thought the Americans must be the happiest people on earth. No wonder the Marines were such fierce warriors; they had so much to fight for, so much to lose if they lost. How could the People's Republic of China ever defeat such a people? What did they have to fight for when they really had nothing to live for?

301

Xi regretted not deserting and surrendering to the Americans earlier in the war. He would do so now, except the Marines were surrounded. PLA reinforcements were arriving. The Marines would be dead within the next twenty-four hours. He knew there was no way they would surrender. He'd learned enough to know they'd never surrender.

Xi lit another cigarette. He hated his life. He hated what he was doing. He hated stressing out over how he could stay alive and continue such a miserable life, but then what else was there?

Sergeant Liu looked at the stars. He couldn't sleep. It was too dangerous, for one thing. He was too hungry, for another. He never could sleep when he was hungry. He'd spent all day in this foxhole. Judging by the sounds of shots throughout the afternoon, he figured the PLA had not fallen back too far. Nor were they advancing. Liu didn't want to think he could die; he was the master of death, after all. However, he didn't want to be stuck in a foxhole to be captured by Marines if his army retreated. He feared that they'd know who he was and what he had done. What if they did to him what he had done to others? He didn't want that. No, he had to make his way back to his army. Whether they retreated or attacked again, he wanted to be with them. He wanted to stay alive.

Sergeant Liu slowly crawled out of the hole he'd been in for the last several hours and began to crawl his way back to the People's Liberation Army.

Hastings was asleep. Harris was wide awake. He was envious of Hastings's ability to sleep anywhere, anytime. Newton was starting to nod off despite his best efforts not to. They were all exhausted.

"Newt, catch some sleep. I'll work the gun," Harris volunteered.

"Thanks, man." Newton was happy to take him up on the offer.

Harris got behind the gun. He scanned the horizon through the night-vision optics, as he'd done for the last few years. He was feeling melancholic. He was feeling homesick. He missed his family. He missed the home of his childhood.

Through his father he had learned early that death is a part of war. He was a Christian; naturally he thought of Heaven. He looked forward to Heaven, but still he didn't want to die yet. It did not matter what he wanted, for now he was surrounded by death.

"Son, life is the leading cause of death." He heard his father's joke in his head, and it made him smile. He wrestled with the idea that he'd never see his family again in this life.

He decided those instant moments of fear and not knowing if you'd live or die were preferable to spending all night contemplating your own death. He wished they'd just get on with it and let it be what it was going to be.

"Fucking commie bastards! Come and take this fucking hill if you got the balls!" Harris shouted.

A few cheers sounded throughout the Marine Camp.

"What?!" Hastings sat up, sleepy eyed. "It's going down?" Newton was so worn out he didn't stir.

"Nothing," Harris answered. Two minutes later Edwards was there asking what was going on. Two minutes after that, Bohanan was there asking the same question.

"Goddamn, Harris, you trying to get them to drop a mortar round on your ass?" Bohanan complained. "Listen, the shit's going to go down soon enough. You just keep your head clear and mouth shut until then."

Colonel Fu Chen loved the power and privilege that his rank and authority had over so many of his comrades. Unfortunately, there were still many in the People's Liberation Army of the People's Republic of China that had more rank and authority than he. Throughout his career he'd always found those people were quick to give him objectives, realistic or not, that he was to accomplish. They were always quick to take credit for his success and to blame him for his failures. Colonel Fu had rarely failed.

Now he was looking at a potential failure that could end his career or his life. He was ordered to assault and take the hill before sunrise. He was ordered to assault once all his reinforcements arrived. Little more than half the reinforcements had shown up. Sunrise was within the hour. If he attacked now and failed, he would be blamed for going before all the reinforcements arrived. If he waited and the attack failed, he be blamed for waiting too long.

Taking the hill was his best chance to save his life and his career. He decided to attack now. The sooner the better. He issued the order to his junior officers.

Lieutenant Xi wasn't happy about the orders, but he wasn't surprised either.

"Sergeant Liu, prepare the men to attack," the lieutenant ordered.

"Yes, sir."

"Sergeant."

"Sir?"

"Tell the men our orders are no retreat, no surrender. Give no quarter. We take this hill today, or we die."

"Yes, sir!" Sergeant Liu smiled. The idea of massive death excited him.

304

Captain Shelby stood on top of the command bunker, scanning the surrounding territory through his thermal night scope. He could see two-and-a-half-ton trucks still driving into the woods. Lieutenant Colonel McGregor had told him to hold tight; there might be relief by the end of the day. If they could last that long.

"Gunny, what I would give for a few more TOW missiles right now."

"Sir, right now I'd be happy with just a few more rounds of 10 mm." Neither spoke of how they'd never had trouble getting air support, or anything else, when Clark was president.

"It won't be long. We ain't got much dark left. If I was them, I'd want to hit while it was dark. Maybe they'll wait. I don't know how many more men they're going to truck in, but they got absolutely no advantage to waiting at this point.

"Gunny, make sure everyone's awake. Have platoon sergeants remind everyone about the Alamo."

"Aye, aye, sir."

"Harris, wake up Newton," Edwards ordered. Hastings was already awake. "Stay sharp, Marines. Pricks are loaded up. It'll probably go down soon. Remember the Alamo: you see red flares, popped red smoke, whatever, you haul your ass back to the command bunker."

"If the CO can call in an air strike, why not just do it now?"

"Who knows, Hastings. Who cares at this point? It is what it is." Edwards looked them all individually in the eye. "Look, you all know the deal. This is where we earn the title US Marines, boys. It's our last stand, make it our best."

"Semper Fi, Corporal Edwards," Hastings said without a trace of his usual sarcasm.

"Semper Fi, Devil Dogs." Harris pulled out his smokes and handed one to Edwards. He took it and nodded his thanks. "Ain't like we were gonna live forever."

"Semper Fi, Harris, you optimistic son of a bitch," Newton chimed in as he took a cigarette.

PLA artillery had been resupplied and reloaded, with orders to hold nothing back. All units had gotten the word that Colonel Fu wanted the hill taken. This time there would be no retreat, no surrender, no prisoners. To drive the colonel's point home, machine-gun units were placed well behind the infantry units. No retreat.

The artillery barrage started later than anyone thought it would. It didn't last long enough for the Red Army. It lasted too long for the Marines.

Sergeant Liu's men thought he was a demon. He seemed to bring truth to the rumors that he couldn't die. He ran into enemy fire and came out alive when many others fell dead. Unlike Lieutenant Xi, he was an inspiration to his men. Many hoped his luck would rub off on them—had to be better than falling back into their own machine guns.

Liu got his platoon up to within one hundred meters of the Marines' defenses. Mortars were hammering the dug-in Marines. Liu ordered his men to advance in fire team rushes. There was no going back. This was where they would slaughter the Marines.

"That's it for the fifty," Harris shouted as Newton fired the last rounds of the M2. Edwards didn't say a word, but his look showed frustration. "We got a thousand rounds for the SAW." Harris handed out bandoliers of 5.56 mm for the rifles.

"Set it up," Edwards ordered, although Hastings had already started.

Newton had switched to a rifle. Pricks were advancing faster than they could kill them. Hastings was on the SAW.

"Fucking bastards are making their move." Bohanan seemed to have shown up from nowhere, but then everyone was focused on the Pricks. "I saw from the command bunker some hard-ass mother fucker leading them up here. I want to flank that cocksucker."

"Let's go." Edwards grabbed his M5.

"Edwards, you and Newton cover us. Harris, Hastings, we'll haul ass to the right then charge the sons of bitches."

"Sergeant, how are we going to remember that much detail? Keep it simple, will you?" Hastings hadn't lost his sense of humor or his smile. Bohanan took time to smile back and he was off. Hastings and Harris scrambled to keep up. They ran down about twenty-five yards.

"Remember, mortars kill you sitting still as much as running forward." Sergeant Bohanan jumped and ran into the exploding earth and flying bullets. Three seconds later he was on the ground, shooting. Harris jumped up and sprinted at an angle to the right of Bohanan. *"I'm up. He's sees me, I'm down,"* from boot camp went through his mind in a flash. He noticed the sharp pain of scraping his knuckles from landing on his right fist, but he didn't take time to deal with that. At fifty yards he felt close enough to spit on them; he'd never fought this close to the enemy.

A Prick popped up and went down from Harris's .458. Body armor or not, the big round took Pricks down. He'd shot three Pricks by the time he saw Hastings go down to his right and roll over shooting. Bohanan was up in a flash and landed about ten yards forward and left of Harris. No sooner had he gone down than Harris was up. He made a point to land on his right forearm and let the armor take the brunt of the impact. That was when he realized there were more Pricks on their right. Harris was concerned for Hastings on the right. Did he see them? Harris jumped up and went to the right, dove and shot. He hit two Pricks. Hastings opened up the SAW. Bohanan fired into the Pricks directly in his front. Their charge seemed to come to a halt. Hastings covered their right. Harris looked to their front and saw Newton and Edwards make devastating use of their rifles.

Harris gave a quick prayer for a gunship, but figured it just wasn't God's will today. Only thirty yards now separated them from the Pricks. Harris wished he had a hand grenade, then wondered if the Pricks had any. Bohanan jumped up and ran at the Pricks to their front. Harris was caught a bit off guard, but quickly compensated and laid covering fire. He saw Bohanan return fire and wondered how he was still alive. Harris jumped up, sprinted ten yards, and dove. Hastings covered their right. Harris saw a hand grenade fly into Bohanan's position. No sooner had it landed than he saw it fly back towards the Pricks.

"Fuck!" Harris exclaimed when he saw Bohanan jump up again to advance on the Pricks, only to go down again.

"Fuck!" Private Chen exclaimed. He'd always found Sergeant Liu to be courageous and daring. But who were these Marines? It was Chen's first pitched battle against the American force. He was learning why they were considered elite. When they were surrounded and should have lost all hope of victory, they were attacking. The machine gun to their front had laid down overwhelming fire. The Marine riflemen were deadly accurate. Some of his comrades had turned and run. Where was Sergeant Liu? He couldn't see him anywhere. He knew Liu wouldn't run. Everyone said he couldn't die. Where was he? Even with the threat of being shot by PLA machine guns, the temptation to run was strong. The PLA was throwing everything at these Marines and they weren't giving an inch.

Suddenly, caught a bit by surprise, he saw a Marine running right at him. He couldn't be more than twenty meters away. He could see the fierce expression on the Marine's face. Surely he was a demon from the otherworld. Chen's body flooded with fear. Chen's mind said, "Run! Fool, run!" but reflexively he raised his Type 95 assault rifle and fired. The Marine went down. He hit him! Did he? He'd been instructed about the effectiveness of the American body armor. He threw a hand grenade, as he'd been instructed, to make sure. Chen thought he had probably killed the Marine, but he was still concerned for Sergeant Liu. Where was he? Chen jumped up to run to the right of his line to look for Sergeant Liu. No sooner had he jumped up than he went down. The pain in his lower leg was greater than anything he had ever felt. With no medical education or x-ray, Chen could tell his leg was broken by the bullet that had struck it. He tied a tourniquet around the upper part of his leg and began to painfully crawl to whatever looked like a safe space, with the fear of death nagging his mind.

Harris had seen Bohanan go down, then the hand grenade go up. He saw a Prick, probably the same bastard who'd taken down Bohanan. He fired a little too quickly and thought he'd hit low.

"Hope you fucking suffer," Harris mumbled after he shot. He jumped up and dashed to Bohanan. His section leader was dead.

Sergeant Liu didn't know what to do. He had never froze in battle before, but this was like nothing he'd ever experienced. Death was all around, but Liu couldn't find his usual satisfaction. He didn't feel like the master of death. He felt helpless. He felt scared. He felt paralyzed. What could he do? He lay still. Perhaps everyone would think he was dead. Perhaps he could gain enough time to figure out what to do.

Hastings dove in next to Harris. He thought Hastings had made some smart-ass comment, but he could not make it out. He'd ask him what it was about later. A grenade went off nearby.

"Motherfucker!" Hastings screamed. He'd taken shrapnel in his right arm. He was on his own to work it out. Harris took over the SAW. "My right arm's broke," Hastings screamed. There was nothing Harris could do about it. He fired the SAW. He knew more grenades would come. They had to get out, but how? He wondered if Newton and Edwards were still alive. Could they cover them?

The SAW was empty. Hastings managed to throw another two-hundred-round drum at him.

"Run for it, Billy, I'll cover you," Harris yelled at the top of his lungs.

"Fuck no, I ain't leaving!"

"Shit!" Harris yelled as he fired. He couldn't hold the Pricks off forever. There was no time to argue. He saw what looked like a black ball drop in from the corner of his eye. "Grenade!" he called out, but didn't know if it would do any good.

Hastings picked it up with his left hand and threw it back.

"Ha! Bastards!" Hastings cried. Harris thought he even heard him laugh. "Keep killing! I got your six!" Hastings screamed into Harris's ear.

This is it, Harris thought. *This is where we die.*

"Grenade!" Hastings called out. Harris did nothing but keep firing. Hastings managed once again to pick up and throw back the hand grenade. How long could this last? Were they blessed? Perhaps, but no one was immortal in this life. Harris fired off the SAW ammo while Hastings fired a 10 mm pistol with his left hand. Pricks were just thirty feet away.

"Grenade!" Hastings called out again, although Harris had seen it coming in.

Harris heard and felt the thud from the grenade's explosion. It was too close. Hastings had not thrown this one back. He screamed and fired. The barrel glowed. The drum ran out of rounds. The SAW was empty. Harris glanced back at his best friend's blood-soaked body in the mud. There was nothing he could do for him. Their friendship had come to an end. Harris lost his fear. He felt the rage, the lust, to kill. He decided this was his place to kill. It was his place to die. With this acceptance, he found peace of mind.

He took the 10 mm pistol. He had one extra magazine for the .458. He jumped up and ran to the nearest crater. Three Pricks. He aimed and nailed one in the face. The other two fired. How could they miss? Harris didn't miss. He moved on to the next. One Prick threw down his rifle when he missed Harris at close range. He dropped to his knees and threw up his hands. Harris shot him in the head. One shot, one kill. He saw another Prick running away; he aimed and hit him in the middle of the back. Harris slammed in a new magazine and slammed the bolt forward.

Red flares exploded in the sky above him. He knew it meant something—Alamo. He was supposed to fall back to the command bunker.

Another Prick popped up; Harris shot him in the chest. The Prick's body armor had saved his life for a short time. Harris put another round between his eyes. While his pain was great, Harris felt an exhilaration of control in all the chaos. He felt a sense of control over life and death. Harris ran toward the enemy, to kill or be killed.

He saw another Prick running away and aimed for the back of the head and hit him. Harris kept moving forward. He jumped down into a Prick foxhole and shot a soldier hiding there. He looked up in time to see three more Pricks running at him. Harris killed two, but then was knocked down when a round hit his body armor. The Prick came jumping into the foxhole, screaming at the top of his lungs. Harris jumped up and reached over for his rifle, but grabbed a Prick entrenching tool instead. His years of playing baseball gave Harris a deadly accuracy in clubbing the Prick upside the head and knocking him down. Harris came down with all of his weight behind the blade of the shovel onto the Red soldier's throat. Harris continued to drive the e-tool down with all his might, severing the head from his enemy.

The hairs on the back of his neck stood; he felt the danger. Harris turned around with great speed and was immediately knocked back with what felt like the force of a Mack truck. He flew back and fell. The landing knocked the air from his lungs. He struggled for breath and kept his panic away. Harris thought his left collarbone was broken.

A screaming Prick came at him. Firing, but not accurately, almost panicked, he thought. The bastard had a nasty V-shaped scar on his face. His bolt stuck back, out of bullets. Harris reached for the 10 mm, but it had fallen from his belt. As Harris fumbled for a gun that wasn't there, the Prick smiled, pulled out a knife and dove onto Harris. He could only really use one arm to defend himself. His left arm was weak and almost useless. With his right, Harris was able to catch the arm with the knife. The momentum of the Prick's fall carried forward into the thrust of the knife. Harris felt the sharp, quick pain slice through his cheek to his ear, quickly followed by the burn and the blood. His bleeding blinded his right eye. Harris fought his pain. He held on to the Prick's arm with his right hand. He reached up with his weak left arm, grabbed a hold of the soldier's ear, and yanked down as hard as he could. The Prick screamed. He hooked the Prick's left leg with his own and arched with all his strength. It was not enough. The scarred-face Prick, with his right ear dangling from the side of his head, pulled the weapon free and smiled. Harris threw a right punch and then another. Before he could land a third, the Prick had caught Harris's right hand with his left. Dazed, the Prick smiled again. Harris arched his back again, not willing to quit, trying to throw the Prick off him.

In an instant the Prick's face was gone. Harris closed his eyes. Blood, skull, and brain matter had fallen onto his face. He rolled the Prick off him.

"Come on." Edwards grabbed him by his shoulder harness and pulled him up. The twelve gauge Edwards used had ended the struggle with the scarred-face Prick. With all hell breaking loose, there was no time for thanks. Harris let himself be led as he struggled to stay on his feet and stay conscious. His head spun and he felt sick to his stomach.

"Don't you fucking quit now!" Edwards kept yelling. His arm was wrapped around Harris to help him run to the extent that he was able to. Lost in all the explosions, Harris had no sense of direction. He completely gave in to Edwards's control. "Hang in there, Harris! We're going to make it!"

Harris didn't believe Edwards, but he appreciated the attempt. He thought that he could not possibly have much life left to live, but he wanted to give it everything he had. He fought to stay conscious. He fought to move his feet. He fought not to vomit.

To his amazement, Harris found himself in the bunker. He thought it wasn't possible. In his head, he asked God how. This didn't make sense. How did it happen?

I'm not done with you yet, rang through his head as loud and clear as the bombs exploding. It wasn't until then that Harris noticed the sound of jets. He thought perhaps he was becoming delusional, perhaps he was dying.

"Fucking hang in there…" were the last words Harris heard before his world turned black.

President Harmon could not believe this had happened. She wiped her eyes with a tissue and then blew her nose. She had to pull herself together. She would have to address the American people soon, and she did not want to look like a discombobulated mess. She straightened herself out in the privacy of her restroom.

"Oh, how could this have happened?" she said to her reflection in the mirror and started to cry all over again. She thought she had done everything right. She had listened to the opinions of the world's top experts. She had implemented all of Mythers's recommendations, for the sake of the American people. Now she wondered how it all could have gone so wrong.

She thought it had to have been the PLA's attack on American forces. One week was just not enough time for her poll numbers to recover. But still, the American troops had held. Some of the Marines had been surrounded and still persevered. How could she be blamed for what ultimately was an American victory?

She shook her head. The American voter could be so fickle and ungrateful. They just had no concept of the job. They could not comprehend all she had sacrificed for them.

314

"It's not fair. Clark started the damn war in the first place," she said as she dried her eyes again. She pulled herself together. She always did. "Somehow, someway, I will survive. I am strong." She again spoke to her reflection.

She left the restroom. She had to. She needed to give a concession speech and congratulate President-Elect Tang.

President Zhang waved to the few hundred people gathered in Tiananmen Square. He wanted to laugh at how small the crowd looked in such a large space. He did not want to risk a large assembly of people. Besides, his special effects people would make the crowd look huge on TV. He could not have been more pleased with how the ceremony went. General Huang, while honored, had shown such humility and compliance.

Colonel Fu's widow had been a very nice touch. She'd conducted herself well and had delivered her lines with perfection. However, Zhang thought the most brilliant part of the ceremony was to publicly commend and promote Captain Xi Tian rui for his leadership and courage. It would give good cover for the historians to "de-emphasize" General Huang's role in the operation. After all, General Huang had not really won the battle.

Zhang marveled at his own ability to lie to so many people so well.

They truly are inferior beings, he thought as he waved and smiled. *This is brilliant. Of course, General Huang will have to be dealt with before he becomes a threat. But save that for another day, for now YOU are the People's greatest hero. Enjoy your day. You've sacrificed so much for this moment.*

Xi stood straight, smiled, and waved. He hated the People's Republic of China more than ever. The irony of this was not lost on him. He had just been promoted and decorated for bravery before the whole Middle Kingdom on national television. Yet he hated the moment, he hated the People, and he hated himself.

He'd felt the temptation moments before to denounce the ceremony live before the people of China. To tell them the truth of what he had seen and what he had done throughout the war, but he did not. He was not that strong, nor that brave. He could see over the course of his life how communism crushes those that give, and builds those that take. He lacked the courage to fight the system. It was too late for him to change now. He would just go along with it, no matter how much he hated it.

Benedict Xavier Tang smiled and waved to the crowd. He thought his victory speech had been a success. Admittedly the crowd wasn't as large as he had dreamed of it being on this day, but he figured the media would make it look larger and sound louder than it really was. Just like they had done during his campaign, and that was what really mattered. He marveled at how easy it was to lie to so many people. He thought most of them truly were inferior beings. He had told so many lies over his career, yet the media always covered for him, and the people always supported him.

He laughed on the stage at the people's gullibility. Everyone thought he was just enjoying his election victory.

What fools! They celebrate me as their savior. They've given me the highest office of the land when it has more power than at any time in its history. Fools!

Tang relished the moment and the opportunity to remake America in his image.

Harris opened his eyes. He didn't know what was reality. He didn't know what had been a dream. All he could see was a beautiful, feminine face. He wondered if she was an angel. He wondered if he had died and gone to heaven.

"Well, hello there," the beautiful face said. "How do you feel?"

"I…I hurt…all…over," Harris struggled to get out.

"I bet. You've got a few broken bones and a nasty cut. Don't worry, you're safe and in a hospital.

"Excuse me," the nurse broke off. "Doctor, Doctor! He's awake. Hold on there, Marine, the doctor wanted to talk to you as soon as you awoke."

Harris lay there. Not knowing what to think. Wondering where he was.

"Hello, Corporal Sean Harris." The kind-sounding voice came from a man in a white coat.

Harris thought there was a mistake.

"I'm a lance corporal, sir," Harris corrected the kind-sounding man.

"Not now, Marine. You've been promoted. By the way, I think Divine Providence has led you here."

"How's that, sir?" Harris forced out. He really didn't feel like talking.

"Corporal Harris, I'm Doctor Abraham Levine. I knew your father, Dan Harris. We served together in Mexico."

***

"I've never been able to remember anything from that damned bunker to the hospital," Harris confessed. "I nearly bled to death, or so I was told."

Levine sat in stunned silence, staring at the old Marine.

"I don't suppose old Doc Levine would be any relation to you, would he?" Harris asked to fill the silence. He was not used to Levine's lack of words.

"Levine is a common name." Levine found himself wanting to deny what he had just heard.

"Naw, I figured. It would take an act of Divine Providence for that kind of coincidence."

"I...I'm sorry. Can we call it a day? I'm...I'm feeling beat...Mist—" Joel caught himself wanting to call him Mr. Harris "—Harris."

"Your call, Mr. Levine. Hell, I ain't going nowhere."

Joel Levine numbly collected his things.

This man is everything my grandfather said about Marines. This man knew my grandfather in the war. Could they be telling the truth, and everything else is the lie?

Levine tried to push the thought from his mind. If he went there, it would make everything too complicated. It could cause too many problems.

This is not how THIS was supposed to happen!

Joel wanted to run. He did not want to deal with the conflict of acknowledging the truth and doing as he had been ordered. However, he could not shake the feeling that his grandfather was speaking out to him again through this old, convicted Marine.

Act of Divine Providence?

Joel quickly walked away. In his flustered state he dropped his notepad and pen. He was relieved that at least it had not been his laptop. As he picked up his notepad, he saw some of the words he'd written.

This Marine knew my grandfather.

Officer Reed was beginning to take Harris back to his cell.

"Wait!" Levine called out, almost panicked.

Harris and Reed stopped and turned in surprise. Levine stood up and walked over to them.

"Mr. Harris, please"—Levine had regained his composure and a sense of courage—"tell me everything you know about my grandfather."

ABOUT THE AUTHOR

T.S. Ransdell was born and raised in Kansas. He served as an infantryman in the United States Marine Corps, and is a veteran of Operations Desert Shield and Desert Storm. After leaving the Marine Corps, Ransdell earned a B.A. in English Literature and an M.A. in History, as well as Secondary Education, and taught history for eleven years. Ransdell currently works as a full time writer and lives in Arizona with his family.

Please feel free to contact him at ts@tsransdell.com with any questions or comments.

www .tsransdell.com

www .facebook.com/tsransdell

Books by T.S. RANSDELL

LOOK FOR THE CONTINUATION
OF THE LAST MARINE

IN 2017

CPSIA information can be obtained
at www.ICGtesting.com
Printed in the USA
LVHW041525020423
743272LV00003B/456